KELD HEAD

THE KEEPER OF THE HOUSE

By

LINDSEY J CARDEN

KELDAS
CHRONICLES

Published by Keldas Chronicles 2014

This is a work of fiction. Names, characters, businesses,
places and events either are a product of the author's
imagination or are used fictitiously. Any resemblance to actual
persons, living or dead, events, or locales is entirely
coincidental.

ISBN 978-0-9569442-5-2

Printed and bound by CPI Group (UK) Ltd, Croydon, CR0 4YY

A catalogue record of this book is available
from the British Library

Acknowledgements

This being the last of the Cumbrian trilogy I wanted to write a special thankyou to the people who have helped me get my Keldas family saga up and running.

To Chris Harland, for the support and belief in tirelessly reading the loose pages of my manuscript into the early hours from her bed; without Chris the books would have remained on A4 paper in a folder on my desk. To Paul and Donna Middleditch @tenfathoms, who I believe, through their contemporary and impeccable art work, they have encouraged people to pick up the books in the first place and look inside. I know people say you can't judge a book by the cover so I hope my stories match Paul's excellent art work. And to my lovely husband, Teddy, whose patience and encouragement in letting me pursue this dream in the first place and not allowing me to get too preoccupied with delusions and my love for storytelling.

I was inspired to write this Keldas family saga after reading the Herries Chronicles written in the 30's by Hugh Walpole. I enjoyed reading them as they always took me back to Cumbria, the place I love. I decided to write a more contemporary series that would not only be a good read, but I imagined people browsing around a book shop in the Lake District on a rainy day and picking up and taking home a permanent reminder of this lovely part of the world.

And to David Keldas, whoever he may be.

With grateful thanks
Lindsey

CONTENTS

CHAPTER 1 DRAGONFLIES
CHAPTER 2 YOUNG BULLS
CHAPTER 3 WASDALE HEAD
CHAPTER 4 CHRYSALIS
CHAPTER 5 MOUNTAIN MAN
CHAPTER 6 A FUSION OF FRIENDS
CHAPTER 7 BACK TO BADNESS
CHAPTER 8 NORTHERN LIGHTS
CHAPTER 9 LIONS AND LAMBS
CHAPTER 10 GREEN WINTER
CHAPTER 11 COLD SNAP
CHAPTER 12 SNOW BLINDNESS
CHAPTER 13 GYPSIES, TRAMPS AND THIEVES
CHAPTER 14 LETTERS OF LOVE
CHAPTER 15 THE CUMMACATTA WOODS
CHAPTER 16 BIG TREES
CHAPTER 17 MUTATION
CHAPTER 18 THE GOOSE IS IN THE DOCK
CHAPTER 19 PARASITES
CHAPTER 20 SEA VIEW
CHAPTER 21 RED GERANIUMS
CHAPTER 22 SNOW PRISON
CHAPTER 23 SPRING AND THE THAWING SNOW
CHAPTER 24 RIVERS OF WATER AND IRON
CHAPTER 25 KELD HEAD
CHAPTER 26 ARABESQUE
CHAPTER 27 SWEET SUGAR HILLS
CHAPTER 28 BLUEBELLS AND FOXGLOVES
CHAPTER 29 HORSE THIEVES
CHAPTER 30 A DECISION OF CONSCIENCE
CHAPTER 31 WAR IS OVER –WAR BEGINS
CHAPTER 32 THE BIRTH OF OBSESSION

1

DRAGONFLIES

1903

The Duddon River danced a relentless path from its icy portals on the Seathwaite fells, twisting at pace, fifteen miles through land to the sea. A young man knelt almost prayerfully at the river's edge cupping the sweet liquid in his hand; it was the first fresh water he'd drunk in months. He carelessly spilled handfuls of it over his head and face and laughed; cleaning his body and his soul; anything to rid himself of the stain of Coldrigg Gaol and vowing he would never return.

On the other side of England, the River Swale twisted its way through the green cornfields of the North Riding of Yorkshire from its source on the slopes of Birkdale, nourishing the vegetation and the creatures of the land. A river of life and hope for those born and raised by it; for those whose genetic code was created and nurtured from its resources. Beth Richardson was one of those creatures; beautiful in form and personality.

She sat by the river sketching, humming, smiling. Then suddenly she was troubled, sniffing the air as an incoming breeze swept away the sweet aroma of newly cut grass and replaced it with one of musty smoke.

Beth lay back in the long grass which was dried to hay by the late spring sunshine, and tried to let her other senses overtake her. She heard a skylark and watched it overhead, held as if by an invisible cord, wondering how something so small could have such energy; it would have young somewhere. The noise of the river was rushing and babbling on fronds of weeds and rosebay-willow-herb that fell into the edge of the bank. There was the smell of sweet clover in the grass and Beth tried to let it mask the smell of the smoke.

She had learned various ways of not letting bad memories get the better of her, and had managed to push other things into her mind, which she had successfully done since she was ten years old. She began to say under her breath: A: Alchemilla, B: Begonia, C: Cornflower - today she listed flowers, another day it would be animals or countries or writers and artists; anything to forget the day her mother died, when the infected clothes and bedding from the sickroom were burned.

And today there was another bonfire. Her father had given them permission to clear the schoolroom: that was Beth, Christie her brother, and Irene the maid. Beth was soon to come of age and Christie was sixteen today and the schoolroom was no longer needed. So they had burned some of the moth ridden furnishings, the heavy drapes that no longer cascaded but hung with sadness in the huge windows of Sugar Hills. There were desks and chairs thrown on the fire, it wasn't wasteful as they all had wood worm. The Richardson family kept many books, and the most battered and useless were discarded.

Today Beth failed in her mind game and allowed temptation to lead her by the hand and take her to a place she didn't really want to go. She recalled sitting on a small chair in the schoolroom as her father uttered his grim news. He'd said: 'No tears, Bethy,' his grey eyes heavy with grief. 'We won't sorrow as the rest do. We have to show faith and belief.'

'But Daddy, I do believe, but I must sorrow, how can I not? I loved Mummy.' Her words of candour had cut him deeply; of course she was right; she spoke as she saw.

'Darling girl ... you should learn not to let your mouth overtake your mind ... you must cultivate the art of long-suffering.'

2

And so no tears were shed in public that day. But as she had sat on the hard chair, her tiny feet shod in brown polished boots, propped up on the spar of the chair, her slim legs covered in the thick lace and fabric of her petticoat, she could no longer hold herself as warm urine seeped down her legs, she had pulled the voluminous petticoat around her to absorb the wet, letting her dark shining hair cover the shame on her face, longing to run away and be changed.

So today the chair had gone and yet she knew the memories would always stay.

'D: Dog rose ... E: Eye bright.'

She failed again in the battle and stopped at E and thought of her brother; poor Christie, how was he coping? Beth never knew how her father had given him the news. But Christie was only five years old at the time. Yet maybe it was hearing the shock of his mother's death at such a tender age that had been the catalyst in making him the delicate young man he was.

Beth heard the metal kissing gate clink and squeak as it opened; she didn't need to look up. She knew it would be Irene, she had heard her humming a tune from the lane. Then quick footsteps came closer as the soft paws of a spaniel ran through the long grass with Irene.

'Bethy...? Bethy?'

'I'm over here, Irene.' And she sat up in the grass and straightened her plain grey cotton dress.

'There's some mail.'

'From Daddy?'

'Yes, I think so. And I've got a letter from Tommy,' Irene pulled two letters from her apron pocket.

Irene's plump and rosy body fell down beside Beth. The grey dress she wore was a close yet grubbier match to Beth's. She handed over a letter and then noticed the sketch pad in the grass and picked it up. 'Ah, you saw the dragonflies again.'

'I heard them first.' Beth smiled.

'It's a good one.'

3

'If you like it, you can have it. And when I'm a famous artist it may be worth a fortune. Look, I'll sign it.' And Beth picked up the pad and scrawled her name: *Elizabeth Richardson.* Then she took the letter from Irene and looked at the post mark. 'It says Westmorland, Irene. It feels thick. Must be a long one. Have you read yours?'

'Yes, Tommy's well.'

'Then tell me what he says, Irene, please - well, what you can, before I open mine.'

Irene moved her body closer to Beth and the two girls bonded in their emotions.

'Well, he says he's enjoying his new job. He has a lovely pebble-dashed cottage and he works along with a young gamekeeper.' Irene kept glancing back at the letter, in order to remind herself; there were some things in it she wouldn't tell. 'He says it's colder in Northumberland.'

'I'm really pleased that he's found work at last.... Maybe now he'll propose. Now you have a home to go to. Ah, but I'd miss you.'

'You're jumping to conclusions, Bethy.' Yet, inwardly, Irene hoped she was right.

Beth lay back in the grass and opened the letter from her father, and read. 'It says his business is nearly finished. He's happy; he's hoping to travel to the west coast to buy a shorthorn bull. He's been staying in Grasmere near where William Wordsworth lived. My aunt is well and he'll soon be home.' Beth silently read more as Irene took little notice, she was still dreaming of Tommy and an impending proposal. And Beth read on, "*and so my dear Bethy, as you are soon to come of age, I have arranged for you and Irene to stay with my sister in Kendal for one month during the summer. I never thought the day would come when I would let you out of my sight. I trust you completely my dear, and I feel it's time you came out from under my wing, so to speak. Aunt Charlotte will take you to lodge in Grasmere. I just have one more visit to make to Millom and a lecture to give in the village hall and then it's home. I have written to Christie and I hope you receive your letters simultaneously. I have plans for his future, but to start with a fishing trip to compensate him for you going away."*

The two young women wandered back to the farmhouse, linking arms. Irene had pushed her letter from Tommy into the top pocket of her dress. She carefully held the small sketch of the dragonflies, loving the gift like a treasure. She reflected on the holiday in Lakeland and felt a deep sense of foreboding. These girls had grown up together, and Irene was thrilled at the prospects of Tommy's future, yet if he did propose and she went to live in Northumberland, she would miss Beth dreadfully. Yes, they had grown up side by side, but with different destinies. And her fate didn't necessarily lie in Tommy's hands, but with Beth's father, Sir Franklyn Richardson.

Irene had tremendous respect for Sir Franklyn; but he was to be feared. She knew it was he who'd helped Tommy find the work in Northumberland. And country folk knew one another and helped one another, from poor tenant farmer to gentry. Franklyn Richardson had business links over the border and in Northumberland. He sold grain, bought sheep and cattle, and invested well, he preached to the staunch English and Scottish societies, and entertained their disciples. He was a local Justice of the Peace and regularly sat in court and saved or incarcerated the good and the bad. But Irene also knew his reasoning for "letting Tommy go" as Sir Franklyn had put it. Though Tommy was respected as a good and honest worker, skilled as a woodman and river bailiff, he also had an interest in game, but it was his interest in Irene that had sparked his move. Sir Franklyn would never have seen Tommy Bright without work, but encouraged his progress in the new placement in Morpeth. There would be no shenanigans on his property and he expected his children and staff to live by the same morals as he: sound and righteous, but at times, pious and unfeeling. His truth was just as Beth had felt, tempered with too much passion; his four-squareness hard to bear. Yet his respect and honesty came from every corner of his being. His strength and determination at bringing up a young family, the loss of his dear wife, the chasteness and fidelity he had shown in widowhood. No hypocrisy, but honest beliefs, with the freedom of speech and respect he had as he spoke as a layman in the pulpit. Everyone loved farmer, Sir Franklyn Richardson, but quaked at his words.

Irene's parents were the cook and stockman; a middle-aged couple. They had worked at Sugar Hills all their married life and arrived as such; no single woman apart from Irene was allowed to work in the estate. And Irene guessed the time was coming when she would be moved on, as Tommy had. She also suspected Sir Franklyn was pleased she was plain and plump and maybe that was the reason she had stayed as long as she had, coupled with her devotion to Beth and Christie. Maybe this holiday was a gesture on Franklyn's part for her also, one last farewell to them all.

Christopher Richardson was throwing a box of papers on the bonfire when the girls pushed open the wooden gate in to the paddock, his fawn work pants were smothered in soot and his cream shirt would slowly suffer the same fate. His corduroy cap already pulled low over his eyes. He grinned when he saw Beth.

'I'm to go on a fishing trip with Daddy, Beth.'

She came across and saw the joy on his mouth but not in his eyes, 'And I'm going to the Lake District with Irene.'

'No...?'

'Oh yes, Christie. Yes, he's letting me go out into the big wide world at last.' In fact Beth had been in the big wide world as she put it; even Europe, but never without her father's watchful care.

Christie's pale face was reddened and his cheeks glowed with the heat from the burning paper; he brushed a blonde curl from his pale blue eyes. 'Things are changing, Bethy,' and a great fear seized him. He'd never told anyone his worries because he felt no one would understand: his desire to please and be liked: his fear of his pending masculinity and lack of strength. He thought his angelic curls were wrong for a man and that his frame was slight and weak. How could he run his father's business, and yet as his father aged and his eyesight diminished it was clear Christie would be the one to manage Sugar Hills, and soon. Oh yes, he loved working with John Dowson, Irene's father, and John loved Christie too. Yet John had despaired because Christie couldn't hold a calf as he castrated it, or he couldn't grab the woolly fleece of a sheep to pick it up and toss it in the dip or shear it. He couldn't lift a heavy milk churn onto the wagon. And Christie had seen John's despair.

And then Christie worried over much about the animals: his barn owl with a broken wing, his black spaniel, Lottie. Then there was the field mouse that he'd rescued from the cat. Annie Dowson, Irene's mother and cook, had scolded him and said he was soft. Then he openly wept as she kicked the cat away, 'Christie Richardson ...! How can you ever shoot a rabbit or kill a pig!' he couldn't tell his father but, in his mind, Sugar Hills could become a place for every sick and straying cat or dog, or barren cow and lame horse.

But Beth had noticed the fear in her brother's eyes. 'It's alright, Christie.... I'll be home in a month – four weeks, that's all. You'll be away a week in Eden Valley with Daddy anyway.' But that didn't help, it just brought another anxiety as he hoped he would never catch a salmon or a trout and have to watch it struggle for breath as he often did with his asthma, or have to club it on the head to kill it.

Christie kicked the old wooden box firmly onto the fire and felt the heat touch the leather of his work boots and told himself if he didn't move his foot away and let it burn, he could learn not to feel the pain.

He wandered back to the house and Beth followed. The brightness of the paddock and the late spring sunshine in the fields contrasted to the coldness and darkness of the stone farmhouse at Sugar Hills. The coolness was welcome from the blazing heat of summer but gripping and angry in the depth of winter. Sugar Hills sat between two great landmasses, the North Riding Moorland and the Yorkshire Dales; temperate in warm dry summers, cool and frost-ridden with the snow in winter. The north winds blew down from Black Hambleton and the westerlies from the Pennines, wet with rain; the silvered winds blew in from Scarborough and dropped off Sutton Bank like a draught from a volcano and, in summer, warm breezes ambled up from the Vale of York. The little town of Thirsk was only a stone's throw away and the Great North Road was on their doorstep. Yes Sugar Hills had weathered it all. Its red pantile roof was textured from the winter's hail and snow. Its small turrets on the eaves made it seem like a small castle. This place was a folly, once a hunting lodge for some rich gentleman but now a sanctuary for one Sir Franklyn Richardson, J.P.

The young people walked indoors and peered into the old schoolroom and wondered at how big it looked without any furniture.

'John said he'd paint it as soon as he gets time.' Christie was back to his enthusiastic self.

'Maybe Daddy will make some shelves and bookcases for you, Christie – bespoke - for your new books; maybe find a grand designer.' Beth went under the window and swept her arms out in gestures. 'A comfortable chair here, so you can study properly for university. And when you're master of this house, all the servants will come and get their wages each week as you sit at this table with an accountant. Then as you hand them their pay, you will always say "thank you", just as Daddy does.'

But Beth's words made him shudder, and Christie used his books as a diversion and picked up his new insect manual from a box and started to look up the dragonfly that Beth had sketched. He looked for the translucent green body, its large eyes and paper- thin wings and started reading. 'It could be a Southern Hawker. But, if it is, it's early. They are usually found near boggy land and ponds.'

Beth left him with his anxiety as she had done a hundred times. She went to her room and washed her hands in the old basin and enjoyed the feel of the cold water under her fingers and palms, and thought how unfair it was that she had always to be the one to pacify Christie.

She had begun mothering him when she was ten, helped by the nanny who was now long redundant. She tried to recall the way her mother taught her and emulate it in Christie, but he didn't always respond to her love.

Christie's anxiety at her leaving for the Lake District had completely taken away her joy. She went to sit by the bedroom window and let the sun touch her face as her eyes rested on the soft pink embroidered roses on one of the cushions. She smiled again and began to re-read her father's letter. He'd said there were gentlemen and vagabonds in Westmorland; some lazy, some with no work. There were religious folk and atheists; commoners and gentry. He'd described the mountains – green or dark, some clad in heather, others in whinberry. There were guides that would take you on the high fells or to ramble around the lakes and hills. Some of the hotels were grand, others pokey; some were small and some damp and foisty, but the architecture of the blue slated houses in the villages was wonderful; some stone faced, others white washed. Beth couldn't imagine what she and Irene would do for a whole month – walking – drawing – socialising - reading. So cultivating in her mind, she decided to buy some new pencils and paper and hope that her father would buy her some new clothes. And then a feeling struck her, one that she'd never imagined before and that was the sudden desire for someone to love; a man. Could it be that this would happen? Was her father's decision to let her out from under his wing, a way of telling her she could soon marry? He'd never spoken of it, yet he'd never spoken against it. He'd spoken of chastity and honour but Beth figured he would find it difficult speaking to her. Irene had hinted many times about her love for Tommy, but was wise not to influence the young Beth Richardson. But Beth wasn't naive; she knew about nature, she'd lived at Sugar Hills all her life and seen birth and death, and the kindness and the savagery of it. She knew how new life started and how old life was butchered. And although the folks they associated with were gentle folk, she knew the farmers and the words they spoke. It didn't embarrass her, but she understood the way of life that her father intended for her was a modest one.

Pondering again on Irene and her love for Tommy, Beth hoped one day Irene could find happiness, and yet all the while wanting it for others: her dear father, Christie, and Irene, yet never allowing it for herself. If only Beth knew how her father had worried and tried to protect her. He had assumed she would be as plain as her mother, but she wasn't.

She knew Christie wished he could be as tall as she was, and of course Irene had envied her, she being short and stocky. Beth was tall and slim and dark: raven haired with clear blue eyes.

Pulling down William Wordsworth's journal from the book case, Beth started to glance. There would be no daffodils to find in august; they would be long gone; maybe a few lingering foxgloves. The ling and heather would be sprouting its mauve and purple carpet as they did here in Yorkshire in mid-august. She imagined hot balmy days, hopefully not much rain – then the thought of romance returned. She pondered over the young men she knew here in Thirsk, close friends of her father's who were honest men, church men, trustworthy, but she considered them dull. She thought of the farm lads she knew and considered them brash. She thought of Jane Austen and the Bronte sisters - marry for money, not love. No, surely, that had gone with the century; besides, she had no money to attract anyone – Christie would inherit all. And knowing her father as she did, her choice would have to be sound. What would he look like? Tall, short, fair, dark, would he have whiskers or be clean shaven as modern men? Short hair or long? She was tall and like her father straight- backed, her lover would have to be tall. She wouldn't want to dominate a man; she would want to be happily subject. Her father, despite his age was considered dignified and charismatic, yet never described as handsome. He was grey haired and grey bearded, sadly he had lost the clear vibrancy to his eyes.

As Beth flicked through the journal she thought William Wordsworth to be handsome, as he appeared so in his portrait, and she wondered if there was a man in Westmorland the same.

F: Feverfew.

2
YOUNG BULLS

Sir Franklyn Richardson's reputation always preceded his actual presence. By good folk he was admired and revered, by others he was to be bypassed and broadly. He travelled to Cumberland from Liverpool on a tour that mixed business with his greatest love, his faith. He'd lectured in Manchester at the Free Trade Hall, at Morecambe and then Keswick. He wasn't a ranter but a fluid and charismatic speaker. He could tell the parables and bring them to life. Folks were captivated but there was always a purpose: a sting in the tail; a "go away and sin no more". He reached the heart.

In his grey suit and waistcoat, white starched collar and shirt with a black silk cravat, Franklyn was pristine in cleanliness and composure; his beard and moustache trimmed daily. His tanned pigskin vanity case with its silver combs and bottles of lotions were a vital part of his luggage, along with a bible and note book. He travelled by train from Morecambe. The train seat cleaned first with his own brush and the antimacassars replaced. He travelled the coastal route across the Kent and Duddon estuary, then up to Millom. He'd already secured lodgings with a Christian family in Haverigg called Penruddock. They'd given the finest and Franklyn took none of it for granted. He encouraged the children, prayed with the parents and dressed ready for his last part of his tour: to buy cattle near Millom. The grey suit of layman Richardson had been replaced with the green tweeds of farmer Richardson. And as he stood under the shadow of Black Combe, wishing he had time and the good health to walk up it, he wandered around a tethered shorthorn bull and said: 'The bull is just what I'm looking for – a pink nose too; a grand animal. We'll shake hands on the deal then, Mr Kellet?'

Both men peered at the beautiful red roaned coat and clear eyes of the bull.

Franklyn held out his hand and as Samuel Kellet grasped it, he felt the crushing pain of Franklyn's fingers in his; the hand shake meant everything and it sent Samuel into a brutal fit of coughing. Franklyn patiently waited for the elderly man to compose himself.

Samuel Kellet leant against the barn door and breathed deeply. 'I'll see to the transport to Thirsk. I'm sorry my boys weren't here to meet you,' but he wasn't at all. And Samuel started to thumb through the wad of money that Franklyn had given him. 'You'll nay be disappointed in yonder bull ... he can do the job, like. He's not lazy ... he knows what it's arl aboot.'

'Well he'll be an asset to my herd, good straight back, strong loins.' Franklyn looked about him at the grand farm under Black Combe and said, 'So you're selling up, Mr Kellet?'

'Well, nay, not exactly... expanding!'

'This is a beautiful farm, sir. Is business good for you then?'

'Business is grand, Mr Richardson. I've sold this 'en, and bought two new farms ... one near Hawkshead and t'other close te Grasmere. They're good investments.' Samuel stuttered a little on his words as if to choose carefully what he told Sir Franklyn. 'I've begetten two lads.... Fine young men.... Both schooled at the best establishments and more learned than I.... The eldest getten medals for fighting the Boer and the young un's as dull as a barn door and I daren't think they can live together. They're as dissimilar as me and thee. It's best things are split now, afore I'm gone.' Samuel cleared his throat. 'I'm nigh on fifty-three and I won't see fifty-four. I've a tumour raging in me lungs and nought can be done te stop it.'

Franklyn understood what was behind the cough and was sorry. He thought Samuel Kellet typical of this Cumberland place – brown swarthy skin, dark receding hair, blue eyes that were now tinged with yellow.

'Well, it's been good to do business with you, Mr Kellet, and I wish you a peaceful end.'

'I've made my peace with God, Mr Richardson,' and Samuel moved away before Franklyn could put on the hat of a preacher.

Another handshake and Franklyn left. Samuel didn't watch as he walked away, he just wandered into the farmhouse and banged the door shut behind him, then fell into a hard chair as another fit of coughing overtook him. It was minutes before he could compose himself, drinking water poured erratically from an earthenware jug on the table, with a handkerchief muffling his face. And with tear ridden eyes, he pulled out of his pocket Franklyn's money and flung it on the table. He sat up and looked at the dishevelled pile of money and the desire so strong was to sweep it aside onto the floor with his arm; what was money without life?

He clenched his hand into a fist and banged it on the old pine table as cutlery and china jumped and clattered in response. Samuel was about to let his emotions release as more tears when he saw a shadow pass the window and heard the muted voices of his sons. Two young men burst into the house, clad in work clothes, corduroy caps and braces upon fine linen shirts, course tweed trousers, stained but respectable. One ignored Samuel and went to sit in a chair by the range, the other came close.

'Has Richardson gone, then?'

'Aye.'

'Did he buy the bull?'

'Aye, Freddie, he did.'

'Did you get the right price?'

'The right price for him, mebbe.'

'You look tired Father, why don't you go and lie down.' Fred rested his arm affectionately on his father's shoulder. 'We'll finish off, won't we Rob.' But Robbie Kellet was sat with his head back; long strands of dark hair from his fringe fell on his forehead, his blue eyes closed and feigning sleep, but his mouth, smiling.

Samuel was beyond chastising him. He'd long given up. His two sons so different that if he hadn't loved and trusted his dear departed wife he would have said one of them wasn't his; but which one, he didn't know. Fred was short and sturdy, brown eyed and sandy fair hair clinging to a receding brow. Robbie was taller, slimmer, handsome fellow, always cheerful – rarely unhappy – rarely sensible.

Samuel felt neither were like him and in his mind had disowned them often: one for his stupidity, the other for his sobriety.

'I daren't think I'll mek this move, Freddie.'

Fred Kellet stood up again and paced the room. 'You have to ... we're not leaving you here.'

'It'll kill me, son.'

Robbie opened one eye then quickly closed it again.

'There's a good room at Keld Head waiting for you, a sunny window that will look onto the fells. We've hired the nurse.'

'Stop it, Freddie... stop it.' And Samuel began to cough uncontrollably, spitting and trying to speak in broken words. 'Blast it Robbie – waken up boy.' And Samuel pushed his chair on the hard floor and it screeched as he intended it to. 'Waken up!'

Robbie sat up in the chair, bemused, and pushed his dark hair neatly back off his tanned brow, and his sham look of innocence softened his father's heart.

'Come hither, mi lads.' Samuel stood up and used the table as a support and started to hobble around it. 'I've done what I can,' his voice broken. 'I want a fresh start.' He pulled a document from out of the walnut cabinet and looked at the writing, but held it close to his chest so the boys couldn't see its contents. 'When I'm gone I want you to put this on my headstone.'

Robbie rolled his eyes and not looking at his father rested his head back on the chair.

'I want nay more of this, Robbie.'

And he threw the document down on the young man's lap. 'I want respect. We'll no longer be known as Kellet. I've been reading Mr Wordsworth's poetry. Trying te better mi education at this late state o' life. I want to be buried in a grand place and you will write this on my headstone: Samuel Keldas - K- E- L- D- A- S. And that is my dying wish as to how I will be remembered and from now on you'll both trade under that name, or yea'll ne'er get a penny.'

Robbie started to laugh, but stopped himself as he realised his father wasn't joking.

'There's no need to laugh, young Robbie. This is your doing. You've brought nothing but shame on this family. And now things will change.... Grant me this dying wish?'

Fred Kellet looked up at his older brother for reassurance.

'Leave us, Freddie.... Give me and Robbie a bit o' time together.' The older man gestured to his youngest son.

Fred walked outside knowing full well it was Robbie and him alone that had forced his father's decision. And he too had been saddled with his older brother's reputation.

Samuel waited until they were alone and Robbie now repentant came and sat by his father's side.

'I'm sorry, Father.... What can I say?'

And Samuel could sense the humility in his voice.

'I can't help myself.'

Then Samuel pushed a folded newspaper towards the young man. 'I thought you were still abroad, son. I didn't know you were in the clinker.'

'How could I tell you? I couldn't cope with the shame and I didn't think you could either?'

'Is any of this true?' And Samuel looked the young man into his clear blue eyes.

'I'm not a horse thief ... I stole nothing. The animal truly belonged to Edwin. I just helped get it back.'

'Edwin Wilding will be the death of us both, Rob.' Samuel didn't like the Wildings, not just because of their attachment to his son, but because they were poor farmers and cruel to horses.

Robbie's eyes fell towards the table. He could no longer endure the look of death in his father's complexion.

'Your mother always said the Wildings were bad meat. Bad for you Robbie ... and she were right.'

Robbie reached across for the newspaper; grateful that the column was tucked away with the cattle prices, thank goodness there had been a murder that week in Whitehaven and it had dominated the headlines. No one would be interested in the acquittal of a young man who'd bravely fought in the Boer War.

'Well, we'll soon be away from here, son. We should have done this years ago.'

'I know and again, I'm sorry.'

'You understand what I have to do? Why I canna let you inherit it all?'

Robbie shook his head and let it fall into his hands. 'You know money means nothing to me.'

That was the truth; all that was important to Robbie Kellet was life itself: vitality, energy, anything he could sink his body into: hard work, hard play; walking the hills, climbing the rockiest places in Cumberland, his horses, talking and singing, laughing and pretty girls. Robbie was generous and had the need to help any lost soul. And that's what he'd tried to do for Edwin Wilding in retrieving the stolen horse, but it had all backfired. The mare was rightly Edwin's; she was worth a hundred guineas, but now Robbie's name was implicated and had been dragged into court, no one could prove his innocence or his guilt so they were both released after spending a torrid three months in Coldrigg Gaol.

Samuel Kellet had lain awake many a night worrying over his two sons. As long as he stayed alive he could keep things afloat and it was only because of Fred's loyalty that the place kept running, more than Robbie's patches of hard labour. But if things were left as they were, Samuel feared Robbie would lose the lot. He should rightly have been heir to all, but to give Fred the new farm, Spickle Howe; at least he could have half the inheritance. It was a small farm with good land, a fine stone house and buildings, it was at the back of Hawkshead; inferior to the farm at Keld Head that Samuel was to bequeath Robbie.

Samuel had been tempted by the history of Keld Head; Grasmere being a village of poets; the farm had soft grassland that plunged down to tarns and rivers and up to the hills. It had an old Pele tower which was statuesque and brought dominance and that fed Samuel's love for the arts. He'd worried if he'd made a mistake in giving Robbie Keld Head but that was how his last Will and Testament would read: Fred Kellet - Spickle Howe and Robert Kellet - Keld Head. There was a romanticism of the close proximity to William Wordsworth's grave and the property was far enough away from Black Combe to have some anonymity, although Samuel knew the Lakeland farmers and they, in the main, knew him and his wayward son, Robbie.

It was Keld Head where Samuel wished to die, despite his ancestors being a Cumberland brood; his mother from Carlisle, his father, Whitehaven. His farm under Black Combe, White Banks, had yielded well and had sold for a good price. They had been weeks in packing and selling; some stock they would move; some were already installed at the two new farms. Robbie had managed that day to buy well; his eye for a good beast was better than Fred's.

Samuel had lost his dear wife last summer. She'd died of a bronchial sickness, but Samuel guessed that anxiety over Robbie had quickened her departure. His affiliation with the Wildings was a dangerous one. They were a family of travellers; it was once said that Edwin's ancestors lived wild in caves up at Honister. Their brood were now scattered but some settled in over the west coast of England.

Edwin Wilding was a horse dealer, and Samuel considered him a horse thief. He farmed in Wasdale; he was purely a tenant, and he had a wife and young family- children with black hair and black eyes, always grubby. Samuel had once pulled one out of a ditch, it was face downwards. The child was too young to get out alone, only being about two years old. Samuel had heard splashing and it was a lucky chance he was passing. He carried the wet and filthy child home, back to the Wilding's farmhouse. He had to bang on the door to get attention. When Nance Wilding finally arrived, scantily clad, she swore at Samuel for disturbing her. No "thank you"; she never said thank you. Samuel even considered she may have put the child there herself. And these were the type of folks that Robbie was associated with. Thank goodness they had no daughters. Yet Robbie bonded with them, he was as dark in skin, if not in nature to the Wildings, and he was the blue eyed boy.

When Robbie left his father you would have thought he would be sober in spirits. But as soon as he was outside and away from the stench of the old man, he breathed in a chestful of sweet sea-scented air, and could smell the damp sands of Silecroft beach and it immediately restored him. He heard a noise in the dairy and assuming it to be Fred, burst in. Fred was washing the churns amidst hot steamy water and the smell of ammonia. Robbie saw his brother and laughed.

Fred looked up and seeing Robbie's smile, it lightened his mood. 'Is he serious, Rob? About the name and all?'

But Robbie couldn't reply as he fell back against the wall laughing, and his laugh was infectious. And so Fred started. 'He's going crazy, Rob.... The pain must have got to him.' Fred poured cold water into the churn and Robbie went across to help, rolling up his shirt sleeves and dropping his braces from off his shoulders, he bent low.

'What did he say ... what was the name again?'

'I never heard such a name in all my life as that. I dunno.... Kellas or Keldas or summat.'

'It was Keldas wasn't it: Keldas: K.E.L.D.A.S!'

'Why in the deuce use that name?'

'He's doing it on purpose, Freddie ... he wants to humiliate us ... me especially.'

'Well he's doing a good job. We can't do it can we, Rob?'

'You know I'm not a man to be trusted, and this I certainly cannot do.' He threw a clean churn onto the floor.

'Lower your voice, Rob.'

Then Robbie stopped scrubbing, and looking deep into his brother's eyes said, 'Look, Freddie ... he'll not hear us from the grave.'

Fred continued to scrub and knew his brother was right but wished he was wrong.

Fred Kellet had lived in Robbie's shadow; six years younger in age, yet six years older in mind. He'd gasped for air when his father had told him he was to have Spickle Howe farm. He felt Robbie would hate him for it, taking a huge slice of the inheritance, but Robbie didn't and in some ways that concerned him the more, worrying over Robbie's disinterest. The farms were soon to be signed over, and the monies and transactions would be complete, and one evening over supper his father had told the boys his plan. Robbie should have Keld Head, at least being the eldest he should have the best farm - the cream. Fred was nearly twenty and Robbie twenty- six. Neither had been close to marriage; Fred didn't have the confidence and the attraction; Robbie had both but not the desire. He'd told Fred he would never marry because he would make someone unhappy; then he would change his mind and laugh and say a wife of his would be the luckiest woman in the world and have fine and healthy babies.

Yes, Fred truly lived in Robbie's shadow and, despite being a rogue, it was Robbie everyone loved. Fred was like a child at school, always overlooked as a scholar; a mediocre worker, usually coming second, honest, reliable, steadfast, but always runner-up. You would have thought Robbie's influence may have led Fred astray, but it didn't. Goodness ran through Fred's bones; kindness, too; sensible in everything. Fred didn't want to be like Robbie but he envied him. He wouldn't imitate his fractious nature, yet wished he could be more adventurous; travelling; walking; seeing other places. Fred had friends a plenty, but they were as sober and as dull as he was. Talkative, but slow and droning: he never stopped. Robbie's friends always made Fred laugh and he knew they shouldn't, sometimes they scared him and he was glad to get away and he wished Robbie would leave too. But Robbie nearly always got the upper hand, and if they were in any kind of trouble from a fight, a loss from gambling or horse racing, Robbie always talked his way out of it. Yet when their mother died it was Robbie that had wept and Fred helped his father all the more and got little praise.

The buckets and churns were washed, the shippon cleaned down, the cattle out grazing; late morning was a quiet part of the day. The two brothers had been up early and milked the shorthorn herd, and Robbie in that, had kept his promise this

20

week. They were both aware of Franklyn Richardson's visit today and their father had stressed beyond reason that the place be spotless and peaceful. Fred had worried over the work but he needn't have as it had all been done, and more. Their father had cooked them a hearty breakfast at 8 o'clock and then sent the young men away. There were still some cattle left to move to the new farms; it was a pity Robbie had asked the Wildings to help, but they rarely let him down. The cattle were to be split and some sent to Hawkshead and the rest to Keld Head; delivered at a good price. The young shorthorn bull was surplus and had been scrubbed and washed and now sold. Robbie had reared it and fed it.

Seeing his brother in good spirits had pleased Fred today, especially with the visit of Franklyn Richardson. Fred knew of his brother's short spell in prison and had expected him to be acquitted from the horse stealing charge. But Robbie had feared he may be found guilty and banged up in Coldrigg Gaol for years. Fred's secret of knowing that his brother was no longer abroad was hard to keep from their father, who, until that day, didn't realise his firstborn son was sleeping and working in a place only a few miles away and living in shame.

The churns were gleaming, the milk had gone, and Fred wandered up to his room. His father was asleep by the kitchen fire side; the money from the sale of the bull was still piled on the kitchen table. Robbie had gone for a walk in the meadow and had promised to be back by three.

Fred could see the sweeping curves of the Duddon Estuary along the coast line through a small window in his bedroom. The room had been a sanctuary as his father had argued with him and wept when he read in the local paper about Robbie. Today Fred didn't want a cat nap on his old bed, but had borrowed some of his father's books on dairy husbandry. He also found Mr Wordsworth's journals and looking and reading about Grasmere; Fred wished he was to have Keld Head. There was some passion today in that steady beating heart; he smiled again as he considered his father's plea to change their name and raised an eyebrow at Robbie's refusal to fulfil his father's wishes.

Fred eased slowly downstairs and in the parlour found some old encyclopaedias and looked up the word Keldas, and there it was. He quietly crept back up the stairs not wanting to disturb his sleeping father, and kept his finger in the page and fell down onto his bed.

Keldas: An old Nordic name that means a well or a spring. H*mmm that sounds good*. Kellet: - a green or stony slope. Then he began to repeat his name as it would sound: Frederick Greenbank Keldas. Yes, it sounded grand and had a gentleness about it and was becoming of Fred's placid nature - Kellet: harsher, blunt, yes, just like Robbie. And as Frederick Greenbank Keldas lay on his bed and daydreamed he knew in three weeks time he would hold a document that would say he was the legal and sole owner of a small farm.

To be a land owner, Fred knew the responsibility was enormous. He knew he would have to have a labourer to help him and had already spoken to a man in Sawrey about this. He would have his own home to run, he hoped he would have sufficient capital to hire a woman to come and cook and clean, a wife one day would be good, but that seemed farther away than ever.

Fred guessed he would have to help Robbie as he knew his brother had made no plans and would do everything on the last minute. The only plan made for Keld Head was for the services of a nurse to come and tend to their sick father, if he survived the move. Fred knew it would be an unspoken rule that he would always have to travel back and forth from Hawkshead to Grasmere to help.

And today Fred Keldas, in one sense, had come of age.

3

WASDALE HEAD

The last full day of Franklyn Richardson's tour of Lancashire, Westmorland, and Cumberland, was to end in Wasdale, then a journey to Lancaster and back home to Yorkshire. He was keen to see his family and his property.

He shaved a few stray hairs that morning with his razor sharpened; not a nick or graze. He padded his face dry with a pure white towel; his beard trimmed and moustache combed.

Squinting, with poor eyesight, he looked in the mirror, concerned as to how much longer he could shave cleanly. How much longer could he read or smile on his beautiful daughter and son and his cherished Sugar Hills? Clipping a few stray hairs from his nostrils he looked at his grey suit hanging on the wardrobe door; he had pressed it himself as he didn't think Mrs Penruddock could do a sufficient job, despite her insistence; Franklyn could insist the greater. He had a clean white shirt ready and he pulled out of his ever-growing trunk full of gifts and keepsakes a newly starched collar. He had three spare ones just in case.

There was no preaching planned today but he still wanted to dress formerly for his trip to Wasdale. He was to meet the warden at the chapel and wanted to make an impact on him as much as the warden would want to impress Sir Franklyn.

There was to be lunch at The Wasdale Head, a fine hotel; the only hotel. It had been highly recommended and although a walk on the high fells of Gable and Pillar had been suggested, Franklyn would only admire the beauty from afar. He was anticipating the view from the verges of the lake, which some had said were green and lush pasture and others, wild and wretched. Franklyn would write about it and preach about it and describe it in rich and verbose tones to his associates and laity back in North Yorkshire.

He'd ordered a trap from a local man who had impressed Franklyn with his knowledge and propriety. They were to drive the lakeshore.

The guide shook hands with Sir Franklyn and in a deep northern drawl, welcomed him. Franklyn was sufficiently impressed with this man's appearance: green tweed suit, red cravat and handkerchief; clean shaven. But there was an unclean smell about him that he hadn't noticed before. And neither had Franklyn's weak and tired eyes noticed the stains on the tie and the greasy blackened edges to his suit.

As they drove along the lake road Franklyn worried that he'd made an error of judgement as the landscape, screes, and mountains appeared to be falling into the lake. He was glad he hadn't brought the children. Stupefied by the grandeur of the mountains proximity to the lake, and the dark and turbulent waters of Wast Water; cold and black that spring morning, fear almost seized him, and he tried to tell his driver to turn back. But the man continued to drive the trap, regardless, almost recklessly, with the white pony trotting at pace along the narrow track by the lake. The guide was talking non-stop, gesturing, with pipe in mouth, carefree.

As the trap dipped and plunged into pot holes and puddles on the roughened ground, Franklyn held the seat, his hair becoming ruffled despite the layers of oil and preparations he'd used that morning. He wished he'd listened to Penruddock and missed Wasdale, he wished he'd let Penruddock drive him but Franklyn had felt the trap the best way to see the lake in the fresh Cumberland air. He wished he hadn't hired Edwin Wilding. He'd met the man only once at Millom Station when he'd taxied him to the Penruddock cottage.

'Shall I drop thi at the inn or do yer want to gan straight te chapel?'

'I think the chapel, sir. Drive steady man!' and as they plunged into yet another pothole, he thought this man to be careless.

24

Franklyn contemplated walking but feared this god forsaken place and thought it unsafe. Another pot hole and Franklyn noticed Wilding laugh.

'There'll nay be any body alive 'ere, sir, that thi can preach te.' Edwin shouted back. 'Heathens and all in Wasdel.'

Franklyn could believe it. 'So will you join me then, Wilding, in a little diversion and take time to reflect.'

'I've nowt te reflect aboot, Maister. That's my spot ovver yonder and it teks plenty of reflecting on itself.'

A low farmhouse grew out of the hill; single story at the front with a sloped roof that appeared to grow into the mountain. It was surrounded by a stack yard, a small barn and stables. Horses and ponies grazed with cattle and sheep.

Robbie didn't return that evening as he had promised Fred, and neither did he return that night, but chose to walk to Wasdale. He truly had intended going home to help Fred but an argument with a woman in a public house in Eskdale had niggled him.

He took the old drove road from Millom to Eskdale and followed the river. It had been a wonderful day; sharp and clear. The mountains would ease his mind as he contemplated the ensuing death of his father and becoming a landowner, but neither sat comfortable with him. He loved the mountains and they loved him; they always beckoned him. He knew the fells around Grasmere were gentler than here in Wasdale; wonderful, yet not as stunning as Mickledore. He thought of Fred back at White Banks Farm and was sorry he'd burdened him with the evening's milking, but he couldn't resist the walk; he would have to make it up to him. Robbie's incarceration in Coldrigg Gaol had made him more restless and wanting to be free; he anticipated walking under Scafell's grassy western slopes, and then his mind would ease as it always did. There was a long scramble up to Mickledore then over the top and down the valley below.

Robbie had spent the night in a shepherd's bothy in Eskdale. It stunk of sheep muck and daggings which now rested on him.

And as he walked down the steep scree, scuffing his boots and dusting his trousers; he remembered the woman.

Sally Mook was a barmaid; a pretty lass, he thought, but mouthy and unclean. Robbie was a man skilled in the art of banter; to him congeniality came natural. His presence at any inn would usually lighten the mood of the patrons and landlords. He could tease because he didn't mind being teased. Robbie would befriend anyone and had many such acquaintances but he couldn't always recall their first meeting; man and woman alike. He knew some women, local girls, would do anything to wed him, but Robbie never loved one of them, he'd never met a woman he could propose to and he'd been choosy with whom he kissed. But this woman on this particular night had irritated him. She was, ironically, a relative of Edwin Wilding's, and the sister of the man from whom they had recovered the horse. Robbie knew that she desperately wanted him, and her eyes told him that, but his mood that afternoon and his new found freedom said he wanted fun, so he teased her, stating: 'If you didn't have such a darned fooled name as Mook, I may court you. Have you ever considered changing it? I'm to be acquainted with the way it is done, it seems.'

'You could change my name in church, Robbie.'

What had he done; it was a stupid comment, one he wished he could retract. But as tea time came and Sally washed the glasses and the bar was cleaned, she came to him as he sat alone in the inn. She sidled up and rested on the seat beside him, stroking his dark hair, holding his hand and attempting to pull him towards her. He knew what she wanted and was in no mood to fool around. He must try and act with some sensibleness.

'So what would I change my name to, Robbie?'

'I spoke in jest, Sally.... That must be of your own bidding.'

'So you're not going to help me do it? You're a free man now, I hear... I guess time's made you long for some female company.'

'Aye, company alright, but not of your kind.'

26

'So your flirtatious words have no meaning, sir.' She spoke with false grandeur.

'My words come too loosely, you must know that.'

'Then you shouldn't speak and make proposals that are false. You lie about not being a horse thief and you lie to your women.... Aye, you know what they say: Rob Kellet, afore he robs you?' Sally laughed loudly, an ear piercing shriek. 'I can silence the talk if you want me to.' She ran her warm finger up his arm in one last attempt to lure him, and then pulled her body in close to his chest. But he pushed her aside and he resisted her once more. He didn't like her forwardness, and he didn't like her reputation and who she'd led astray. 'If I lie down with you, Sally, I lie down with every man you've ever lain with.'

The rebuff, Sally couldn't tolerate, so she cursed him and made Robbie's refusal all the more valid. 'Aye, gan back te yonder dreary household ... te yon dying father and miserable brother.' She spat words in her true manner.

That finished him. So he spent the night in the bothy, glad at his happy escape, but as he felt in his waistcoat pocket he noticed his pocket watch was missing and he knew who had stolen it. His immediate thought was to return to the inn and confront her, but didn't want the hassle. So as he stood at the door of the bothy he looked one way to home and the other to Wasdale and felt walking the hills would repress his anger.

On seeing Wast Water he started to run down the steep grassy slope, his knees jarring, minding not to fall. He stopped abruptly at the edge of the lake, and feeling warmer with the run, stripped off his clothes and shook each item in the cool air wanting to rid himself of the touch of a malodorous woman and the smell of a herd of sheep. He folded each item neatly into a small pile and then he noticed his wallet had gone. What did it matter, he was a free man: forget it.

Dipping his feet carelessly into the icy water, anger made him dive and splash and writhe as he rubbed himself clean; a mission of necessity and one of mind. As he plunged he gasped for air, once, twice, several times as the cold stupefied his lungs making him barely able to breathe. He would go no deeper as

27

he knew the folly of swimming in the cold could drown a grown man. Finally, chilled to the core he gingerly crept out of the water to dry himself, his bare feet slipping and aching on the rocks and pebbles below.

Franklyn Richardson had to check he wasn't seeing an apparition as he absorbed the sight of the pale flesh of a naked man against the cold and awesome lake. The rocks on the scree tumbled down beside him and made this god fearing man dread this barren and hostile scene the more.

'Stop the horse, Wilding! Turn back, turn back.'

But Edwin looked across and seeing Robbie bathing in a place he had often swam in, began to laugh. He pulled the pony's reins up sharp and the trap came to an abrupt halt.

'Daren't fear Mr Richardson... I knows the man.' He whistled loudly, the pony jostled in the trap and Franklyn grasped the sides once more. 'Yonder young man is insane ... crazy as a wasp in a jam jar, but I knows his father.' And Edwin laughed and shouted. 'He canna help 'isself. Come hither, young Robbie ... come and meet this gentle man who can cleanse thi soul.'

Franklyn raised himself upright, composing his spirit, and considered his situation. He thought this a fine opportunity to live as the Lord did and to speak consolingly to all, without prejudice. 'Then ask the young man if he needs assistance, Wilding.'

'Come and get thi sen on this trap, Robbie. Thy'll be the better forrit.'

And Robbie immediately recognising Edwin, stepped quickly into his trousers as they stuck to his damp legs; grinning as he saw his friend. He grabbed his shirt and his waistcoat, stumbled into his boots and ran to the waiting trap.

Franklyn tried not to let his terrors show as he saw the dark haired handsome young man before him, dishevelled, unshaven; he could have been the devil himself coming to entrap him. Then a deeper thought sprang through him as he considered that this could all be a ruse and he might get robbed.

'This young man will come te church with us, won't ye, Rob?' Edwin was still laughing.

'I would love to, my friend, but I'm not one for church. I need my belly filling first. I don't think I've eaten for three days, not since I left her majesty's service. But I would be happy to share your trap, sir, if you wouldn't mind giving a poor soul a ride.'

Franklyn, astounded at Robbie's manners and articulate speech, didn't reply but edged to the side of his seat to let the young man climb in.

'Then I'll take your silence as a yes, sir.' And as Robbie turned to get a closer look at the gentleman he was to befriend, he muttered to Edwin. 'Who is he?'

'This is Sir Franklyn Richardson.' Edwin proudly announced.

'Ah ... then maybe I will walk, thank you.'

'No, stop, wait.' Franklyn released himself from his seizure. 'Allow me please to do a charitable act and at least take you to the head of the valley, or wherever you choose. Maybe a visit to the church would be beneficial.'

Robbie knew whichever reply he made would be a mistake as he guessed this was the man who'd bought his father's bull. 'I'll be honest, sir. A ride with you would benefit me greatly, but I will skip church if that's alright.' And Robbie hauled himself up onto the trap beside Franklyn.

'Aye, the Kellets are a heathen brood.' Edwin spat as he drove the trap on to the chapel.

'Your name is Kellet, young man, are you from Millom?'

'I'm from over the hills and far away.'

'Then are you related to a farmer called Kellet?'

Edwin interrupted. 'Nay, this young uns insane, as I said, sir. He knows nowt aboot his father nor his mam.'

Robbie grinned. 'There's a lot of Kellets about these parts, sir. And saying I'm a lunatic, I'd never know anyway.' And arriving at the inn, Robbie jumped off the trap.

Franklyn was relieved to walk to Wasdale chapel alone as Edwin waited. Sorry he was unable to save his poor soul from iniquity.

Franklyn wondered how Wilding tolerated living here, this morning was a fine one, and yet the fells still looked merciless and he considered Wasdale would be inhospitable, especially in the rain and snow of winter. Yet Edwin Wilding was a fine man. Small and sturdy in stature; strong set body and clear eyes. The young Kellet man he had to admit was a healthy, handsome looking fellow, who had clear blue eyes, good teeth, a few fine lines around his eyes that showed he would laugh and smile a lot, but nevertheless a rogue and if Edwin was to be believed, a lunatic. To bathe in these cold, icy waters, to sleep in the fells, not to eat for days was barbaric. Franklyn had read that these Cumberland men folk were idle and lazy but he thought differently. He recalled Samuel Kellet and his pretty farm under Black Combe, the good living he had made, the fine cattle, and to expand to two separate farms. He had seen some of the miners, religious men, honest and hard working and some with no work, trawling the length of the country to find it; the deprivation of some of the cottages along the coast road to Egremont, Bootle and Millom.

An hour with the warden of Wasdale church told Franklyn there were many righteous and unrighteous folk in Wasdale and not unlike the poor Kellet boy he'd just met.

Lunch at Wasdale Head was satisfying. Robbie had enough loose change in his pocket to pay, along with some real ale: Cumberland sausage, bread to dip in gravy, and turnips. Men folk wandered in and out; some idle, some not.

Franklyn was approaching the front door of the inn, when he met Robbie again. A blonde woman just leaving the public bar had shouted his name.

Robbie appeared at the door and not seeing Franklyn, confronted the woman.

'You witch, Sally. Give me back my watch and my wallet.'

'Call me a witch,' she screamed. 'If I'm a witch, what are you Robbie Kellet? You didn't think I was a witch when you were philandering with me in Eskdale.'

Robbie grabbed her arm and began to shake her. 'Give me my watch!'

Franklyn couldn't tolerate this, as the scene was stealing his tranquillity. 'Leave the woman be, young Kellet.' Franklyn approached and shocked Robbie; 'This is no way to treat a woman.'

But Robbie wasn't to be turned and no longer cared who the man was; his bull was sold and paid for and the money probably still lying on the kitchen table. 'She's no woman, sir. She's a harlot and a thief.'

'You're the thief,' she screamed. 'Yes, sir, believe me, he's a horse thief – he stole from my brother.'

Robbie shook his head and the smile left him. 'She stole my watch, sir. I don't lie, Mr Richardson, and I will come back to that church with you and swear on the holy bible.' Robbie backed away.

'And is this true?' Franklyn looked at Sally and for the first time noticed her appearance; her hair dishevelled; a low cut revealing blouse; her skirt, short and tattered at the hem; bare ankles in grubby boots; unwashed.

Sally pulled out the watch from her cleavage and dangled it in front of Robbie. 'He gave me this, sir, as a gift. You see we were to be wed, and this was a token of his love for me. I should be Mrs Sally Kellet.'

'And is this so young man?'

Disbelief seized Robbie. 'I've never proposed to any woman ... no one.... She's lying,' and he grabbed her hands, but Sally was strong and she pushed Robbie away and, as he lost his balance, he fell and pushed Sir Franklyn Richardson, lay preacher, Justice of the Peace and gentleman farmer to the ground.

Robbie fell on top of him, happy his watch was safe in his hands and now laughing. He would get his money back another day.

Robbie attempted to help Franklyn to stand as the woman continued to scream abuse; saying words Franklyn had never heard and certainly would never understand. He stood and coughed, a little winded from his experience.

Sally stepped forward. 'I'm sorry sir, I'm sorry. My argument isn't with you,' and she started to brush with her grubby hands, Franklyn's jacket, and straighten his buttons and lapels. Then she slipped her hand into his inside pocket and stole his wallet.

*   *   *

Robbie left Wasdale and the Wilding's farm and borrowed Edwin's grey mare, Tilly. He always borrowed her to ride back to Black Combe. Glad she still belonged to Edwin as Tilly was the cause of his imprisonment. When the horse saw him coming with the bridle in his hand, she whinnied and with her head high, trotted across the paddock to meet him; despite knowing she had a long walk to make to Black Combe, she loved Robbie and knew she would have a quiet peaceful few days at the Kellet farm. Good grassland, clean hay and kindness.

Robbie talked and muttered to her as they wandered the hills and mountain passes together. He didn't expect her to break into a trot, he just let her have her head and she knew the way. He would often sleep in the saddle if he and Edwin had had a wild night somewhere. Tilly would always take him safely home.

'I'm a fool Tilly ... oh, I'm a fool.' The mare flicked her ears. 'Thank goodness I've got you.'

She shook her head as the reins and bridle rattled loosely. And Robbie continued to regret his actions, as he always did. At least he would be home before dark and help Fred with the milking and be there for the early morning. He knew his father would rant at him. He would have to take it; apologise, this was his fault; again. He wouldn't tell him he had met Richardson; he would let that one lie. He shuddered to think what Richardson would do when he discovered his wallet was missing. He had seen it happen and should have said something; he cursed Sally Mook. No doubt Edwin would have enlightened him. He hoped Edwin would have been paid. Then a deeper thought struck him that Richardson would call the police, believing he may have stolen the money. The thought of returning to Coldrigg Gaol gripped him, and he sat up straight, looking over his shoulder. He thought of Sally Mook and decided to forget his own money, he wanted no more dealings with her; yes, that would be his punishment. In a few weeks he would be a gentleman farmer in Grasmere with more barmaids to get to know and they him. Maybe this name change of his father's was a good idea after all. Maybe some folks would mock him for it, but he had few acquaintances in Westmorland and that would suit all of them. He knew the route back to Wasdale from Grasmere would be arduous, and to see Edwin would mean a trek over Sty Head and that could be dangerous. He hoped Tilly could make the walk. He might buy her off Wilding as he would need a good horse; give Tilly some peace; she deserved it and as more remorse set in he worried if Fred was actually out here looking for him.

He stopped as his eyes scanned the rocky scenery. Then wandered north to the green fields chequered with houses and cottages, this scenery enriched his heart once again and tempted him, and grateful of what this land did for him, Robbie wandered home with an easier mind. And he begged Tilly to walk on.

The problem being that Robbie wasn't the rogue that everyone thought. He just seemed to attract attention and trouble and maybe his associates didn't help.

His father had warned him, so had his dear late mother. She'd begged him not to frequent the inns and bars, and not to associate with the Wildings; she had warned him to be careful of women but he hadn't listened, and so he called himself a fool time and time again. But he kept on making the same mistakes; he was twenty-six and should be wiser. He blamed the war in South Africa for warping his mind to danger; he'd seen things a man wasn't made for. He'd been an unwilling accomplice in burning the farmhouses, and killing the livestock and making the children homeless. He wanted to forget that. And although he had volunteered, Robbie soon hated the way the Boers were treated, and after his first battle the volunteer spirit was knocked out of him and he wished he was back home, as he did now.

Franklyn Richardson left Wasdale a poorer man. He didn't notice his wallet was missing until he came to pay Edwin Wilding for the trip. He was relieved to be back at the Penruddock's house in Haverigg and relieved Penruddock was there to pay the bill. Franklyn felt a fool at his loss; he had been naive. The contents of his wallet were thankfully, small, as he had taken Penruddock's advice to travel light in the way of cash and valuables. So embarrassed at his naivety, he didn't contact the police. He couldn't be sure when his wallet had disappeared; he certainly had it when he dropped a large donation in the coffers at the church.

Penruddock tried to persuade him to press charges; he knew the infamy of the Wildings family and of Robbie Kellet. But Franklyn declined, quickly stopping the conversation so he could erase a humiliating experience from his mind, and as he sat on his train for York and he watched the moors pass before him, the arches on the viaducts and bridges; the little steam train rattling along, he silently prayed for the souls of the young people he had met in Wasdale and felt himself a richer man.

Then Franklyn worried over his dear Bethy. He had promised she could travel to Westmorland and felt he'd made an error of judgement, but he'd promised and wouldn't go back on that; he would certainly make sure that she was well looked after and his sister was a good and reliable guide. Surely the folk in Westmorland were softer and more like Mr Wordsworth than some of the families he had met nearer the coast. She would go nowhere near Millom and Wasdale. Surely the gentler slopes of Grasmere would be a safer place.

4

CHRYSALIS

Beth could see her father was tired and this journey had weakened him. His train had been delayed in Settle then York and although he was weary he also looked troubled. She thought she had an ability to read body language, but she wasn't always right. She had learned with Christie over and over again to talk to him when he appeared depressed, she knew when her father was worried because he was always uncharacteristically edgy and had a furrow on his brow. And as he walked into the house he dropped his bag on the cold tiled floor, a symbolic gesture that there would be no more travelling for him for some time.

'Will you tell us all about the Lake District, Daddy?' Beth tried to ease his unhappiness and came forward to kiss him. Christie was standing behind her, shy and pensive, waiting to step forward and shake his father's hand.

Franklyn evaded the question and said that he wanted to speak to the both of them, separately, the next morning, and on that next morning as Franklyn sat in his office with all his unopened mail he spoke to Beth first.

'My darling Bethy, I want to wrap you up in cotton wool, but I know that would be foolish.'

Beth was sitting on a chair covered with a grey, velvet like fabric embellished with mauve hydrangeas; she nervously rubbed the soft fibres with her fingers as she followed the shape of the petals around, seeing faces and animals in each one. 'Has something upset you, Daddy? Did things not go well in Cumberland? You sounded happy in your last letter.'

'I won't lie to you, Bethy. I had a very unpleasant experience with some young people in Wasdale that I do not wish to recall, unless the Lord wanted me to do so.' Franklyn couldn't rest; he wandered around the study, then threw his head back and

35

rubbed his forehead and pinched his nose. He stopped and straightened some books on the shelves, and not looking at her said, 'I fear I may have made a mistake in letting you go to the west; to the Lake District.'

She sat up and folded her arms, shocked and worried of what he would next say.

He turned and looked at his daughter, her rosy complexion, her innocence, her beauty, her dark shining hair. 'You're twenty- one soon, Bethy. Many around these parts are women when they are thirteen, but I'm not sure if that's what the Lord intended. I've heard scullery maids know more of the male sex than I do myself. One day you will fall in love.... I've never constrained my words when it comes to the facts of life and it's hard to speak to you as a woman would - as your mother would - but my dear, I want to protect you, yet, I want you to live as a woman should; marry, produce a family, everything that your mother and I had before she died.'

Beth coughed and cleared her throat. 'Daddy, I know you care and you love me.... I think I understand what you are trying to say. I want these things too, but properly and happily, but I doubt I would be chosen by anyone, anyway.'

Franklyn's heart was torn as he nervously saw in his daughter, as others would, her true beauty, and that was in her character.

'Bethy? Promise me ... promise me, you will remain chaste. That you'll not let the flights and fancies of this new era, when folks are more interested in this so called "new morality" influence you. When books like those of Mr Darwin are meant to turn good people away from the Lord and have no one to question their conduct, which can only bring disaster. I knew when the new century turned it would bring a release; gone are the Victorian days that I knew as a boy, and I have been troubled to think of what awaits us in the future.'

Beth stood and came across to him and let her arm slip around his shoulders and she rested her head on his chest. 'I'm excited, Daddy; I have all my life before me; things to paint, stories to write, things to learn. I'm longing to go to the Lake District. If it were fine enough for Mr Wordsworth, surely it would be fine enough for me. I won't have time for young men and their ways. I want to follow Mr Wordsworth's trails and go to Grasmere. I've poured over his books; I've looked at the maps and want to see the plants that grow there in those stony walls, the moss on the rocks, the bracken and the fir trees, the beautiful hills and mountains. Aunt Charlotte will be with me, and Irene. Aunt Charlotte knows the area well; her home in Kendal is close to where we will stay, isn't it?'

Franklyn held his daughter lightly and listened to her and envied her youth. 'Then go Bethy, go.' He moved away and sat at his desk, happy he had said the words he'd prayed hard about that night and, having accomplished that, turned to a more businesslike mode. 'Now Elizabeth, I have some more news for you. When you return from Westmorland I have an assignment that I think will excite you.... I hope you agree to this and once again this is not compulsory, I will let you decide. I won't force you or dissuade you.'

Beth straightened her shoulders and wondered.

'Mrs Armitage has a vacancy at the school and she feels that with your knowledge of art and botany you can help the children. It was she that asked me and I have mulled it over and consider it to be a good prospect for you. Just think of the influence you could have on those girls?'

'But Daddy, I don't know enough yet, I couldn't possibly teach.'

'You won't be alone. Mrs Armitage will help. I want you to consider this while you are away. Reflect long and hard on this. Mrs Armitage is in no hurry. But she was very insistent her choice of you was a good one.'

Beth wondered why he hadn't spoken of this before. It was as if something had made him change his mind over her future. She recalled his usual view of Mrs Armitage and that would be one of indiscretion. He had once considered her a busy body, a gossip, a righteous woman, yes, but at times, foolish. And as she tried to read her father's thoughts and intentions for her, whether rightly or wrongly, she considered this new position at the school was one her father would intend for her to accept, yet let her believe it was she who had made the choice, much like he had done with Irene's lover, Tommy Bright.

When Beth left her father's study she was wringing her hands, happy at his concern and obvious love for her, but disturbed at his goading. She'd seen huge beasts like shire horses, boars and bulls turned in their tracks by the twitch of a rod or a board, gently nudged into the right course, just as her father was doing with her.

Beth looked up and noticed Christie at the top of the stairs above her; there was a gallery window and a small rail. He had clearly not heard her, completely immersed in his own thoughts. If the window would have been open she would have gone to shut it, afraid of what he was thinking.

She stood for a few moments and watched him and wondered what her father had in store for Christie; poor Christie, sixteen and still childlike. Surely her father's conversation with him would be different.

'Christie?'

He wheeled around. 'Beth?'

'Father wants you to go in now.'

Lowering his head, he stepped down, straightened his waistcoat and tie, and pushed up the silver gaiters on his long sleeves to reveal his delicate effeminate hands and straightened his cuffs.

Beth smiled at his demeanour as he raised his spine straight, yet inside she knew he would be trembling with nerves.

The next time she saw Christie he was with John Dowson in the stables, seeing to one of the work horses. A bay gelding had picked up a sore on its neck from the chafing of a harness and collar. Its withers were blistered and sore. John Dowson was a good horseman and locals often called him in if any horse needed doctoring. Christie was supposed to be holding the animal's head as John applied vinegar to the sore, but the horse flinched and then threw its head upwards knocking Christie in the face. The boy fell to the floor.

'Hold tight boy, get up.' John yelled, but as Christie stood and grabbed the halter he failed again as the horse pulled away.

John lost patience. 'Thy'll be nay good young sir for yer father. Thy'll nivver be maister o' this house. Unless yer wekon yer'sen up a bit.'

Beth didn't blame John for what happened next, because she had often wanted to say the same herself. Christie dragged himself up and left at pace, pushing Beth sideways as he passed.

Beth was torn: to follow Christie or help with the horse, but John Dowson noticed her dilemma. 'Leave 'im be, Bethy.... The lad's got te larn. Come hither and tek this halter.'

Beth complied and struggled as much as Christie, but persevered.

'He'll be nay use te thi father, mi lass, weren't that un. He's nay cut oot. He's delicate, like. Too delicate. He's like a lass ... nay disrespect, mam. Woah, woah.' He smoothed the horse's head and put the lid back on the glass bottle wiping his hands on a brown apron he was wearing. 'I canna mek owt of him. It's nay his fault. He's meant fer other things; he's like yer mam, Bethy. She were delicate just thi same. God rest her soul.

'He knows nowt aboot farming. Nay use fancying aboot wi science an the like. He needs to larn man's work ... proper work.'

By lunchtime Christie hadn't returned. Franklyn had gone to Thirsk to settle his finances. The Dowson's sat silently with Beth and Irene at the dinner table. John was remorseful, worried even at his tone of voice with the boy. Annie Dowson was more worried over the wasted meal. Irene and Beth could bear the silence no more so decided to go and look for Christie. Beth checked his bedroom and Irene the study.

Beth tapped on Christie's door and getting no reply, eased the door open slowly. His room was tidy and his bed, although it had been made that morning, was crumpled. She looked at his desk and shelves but found no clues as to his whereabouts. She opened his wardrobe door but all appeared intact. She ran down to the back door and looked at the rack of shoes and boots neatly set out in rows on an oak stand. There was an empty space and Beth guessed that would be where Christie kept his boots.

Beth helped Annie and Irene clear the lunchtime dishes and then relieved of their duties the two young women decided to walk the fields and look for Christie. They checked every field, thinking where he might hide, they walked the river bank, watching the fast flowing River Swale, not daring to look in the water as both of them feared of what they might find; and they returned to Sugar Hills, disappointed.

When Franklyn returned, John Dowson was waiting.

'I'm sorry te say, maister, but the boy's missin'. He should a helped me with th' milking but nivver turned up.'

Franklyn threw down his papers and leather case on his desk. 'When did you last see him, John?'

'Oh, maister, I said summat awful te the lad, I'm a blathering idiot. I regret it now, sir, boy do I regret it. He were 'elping me wi Rossy. The gelding 'ad a bleb on its withers,' John wiped his brow, his voice broken. 'He could nay 'old its 'ead, so I barracked 'im aboot it. I'm sorry te say ... and Christie stormed off, sir. It's my fault.'

Franklyn stood bolt upright, his heart angered, 'It wasn't what you said, John, it was me.... I knew the boy had taken things badly. Don't punish yourself.'

'Well, I'm still vexed with miself, sir. And thank yi fer yer honesty, but in my own 'eart of 'earts, I'll tek the blame. I hope and pray nowt bad's befallen him, sir.' And again John took a crumpled handkerchief from his apron pocket and blew his nose.

'We'll send some of the men out, John. Don't worry. It's a fine evening. We'll find the boy. He hasn't got the stomach to go far.'

But that evening the men came back disappointed. Beth and Irene could barely work for their anxiety. Beth knew she wouldn't sleep that night as she heard her father put out the landing lamp. She noticed he had left the back door unlocked and left some lamps burning in the kitchen. It would be a short night and daylight would come early. Beth lay flat on her bed distraught. Christie had never spent a night away from their family and certainly never alone at night in the outside world.

She sat up on her bed listening for every sound that might be him returning, she had sat in the bedroom window until dusk, as the sun fell over the Hambleton Hills, leaving red and gold rays. She once lay awake worrying over a kitten that had strayed, and every hour she got out of bed to check if it had returned, and as the night hours ticked by, she was sensitive to every sound: Was that the back door? Was it just her father doing exactly the same as she, but still no Christie.

Worn out at daybreak, Beth heard John calling the cattle in for milking. She washed and dressed early and threw on some old clothes. She checked Christie's room as she passed his bedroom door, afraid to open it, but his bed lay empty.

For three nights and three mornings, Beth had the same routine. The whole household disjointed and exhausted by Christie's disappearance. Her father had called the constabulary and the men continued to search, but none found any clues as to Christie's whereabouts. On the fourth morning Beth could stand the strain no more and feared she had lost her brother forever. She left Sugar Hills for the abbey ruins, a place she always went for solitude. The high walls were riddled with weeds: valerian and wild clematis tumbled down the ruin. The small chambers housed a few stray sheep and lambs, resting and sheltering. Beth leant against the old stone gothic archway and wept. She fell to her knees, her tears burning her eyes more than the lack of sleep. She murmured gentle prayers, speaking like a woman drunk, wiping her eyes; her nose, sore; her lips, quivering; her head thick with the blood pressure rising; heartbroken. She fell into an involuntary sleep and woke for what seemed hours later, but was merely a moment and she saw Christie standing over her.

Beth rubbed her eyes wondering if she was dreaming.

'Don't cry, Bethy, I'm sorry.'

She looked at his body; his skin, grubby and his clothes damp and muddied; his blonde curls sodden and flattened to his scalp. He was shivering. She struggled to stand as she held onto the sturdy walls, nervous in case this was an apparition.

'Christie ... Christie,' she held out her hand to him and he took it and fell into her arms and wept; Beth felt the soft stubble of his beard as it touched her face, the deeper tones of his voice as he groaned in her arms. 'Christie ... Christie ... don't cry... stop it now. Everything will be well.'

But he couldn't speak any comprehensible words and continued to sob.

Beth brushed his brow with her hand and pushed him gently away and held his shoulders and looked into his tired blue eyes. 'Why, Christie ... why did you go?'

'I don't know what to do, Bethy.' He was shaking his head and he wept all the more.

'Stop it, Christie ... stop it now. Nothing can be worse than this, we're all worried sick. I haven't slept for three nights and I doubt Father has, either. He is beside himself and so is John. He thinks he drove you to this.'

'It wasn't John.' Christie managed a full sentence. 'No, not John ... oh Bethy, I can't take this ... I'm useless, and Daddy's going to send me away!'

'Don't be silly. He won't do that.'

'He will ... he will ... he is doing. I'm to go to Northumberland to work with Tommy Bright. He said I need to learn how to manage Sugar Hills. He says I need the experience and Tommy can help me ... but I don't - I don't want to go.... I won't go!'

Beth put her arm across his shoulder and tried to lead him out of the ruin. 'Come home Christie, for me ... come home. Daddy loves you ... we all love you.'

Beth fell on her bed, relieved her brother was safe. Her head ached with stress. Her father had bought her a small glass snowscene globe as a keepsake from the Lake District. It was of Mr Wordsworth's house at Dove Cottage, nestled under some mountain scenery. She took the little toy and shook the globe frantically. She watched the snowflakes fall to the ground and settle one by one on the tiny mountains and then it was all peaceful. Beautiful scenery, tranquil; she kept the globe still in her hand not daring to move it again and unsettle the snowflakes.

5

MOUNTAIN MAN

S amuel Kellet had mixed feelings about leaving White Banks Farm as it nestled lazily under the shadow of Black Combe. He'd been born there and so had his two fine sons. He wouldn't miss Black Combe but he would miss the sea. He loved the taste of the salty air when it rained, watching the westerly breezes blow in clouds shaped like mushrooms, cauliflowers, fat and fluffy, grey and white, then black with snow. Then the streaks of mare's tails pushing out to the Isle of Man or the sunsets on a fine evening; the sun reddened like it was a burning ember falling to the earth and into the sea, lost forever. It was too late for him now and he'd used every meaningful and purposeful breath to end his life in Grasmere, beneath the poet's hills that would elevate and comfort him.

Samuel had heard of Robbie's brush with Franklyn Richardson and had cringed. He'd hope that Richardson was no wiser of whom Robbie belonged to, and yet every visitor he saw on the lane he expected to be the police. But they never came. Edwin Wilding had let it be known, in a drunken frenzy, that Richardson had been robbed in Wasdale by a barmaid. Sally Mook added to the story, saying it was Robbie who'd taken the money and that she had spurned him for not letting him have his way with her. And that he had pushed the righteous preacher man to the ground and then robbed him. The news filtered back to Millom, Fred heard it first and argued that it wasn't his brother's fault. He hadn't told his father, fearing it would finish him, but the postman wasn't as kindly and told all the valley. But the following day when Samuel went to the barn to watch the boys packing he said: 'Is it true, Robbie, what they're a telling me.' A familiar question.

'It depends what they're telling you.' Robbie threw another box onto the cart and didn't look at his father.

Samuel was holding onto the door like it would shut and close Robbie away for good. 'Daren't mess with me, Rob. I'm old, but I'm nay fool.'

'No, but if you believe other fools instead of me, what chance do I have. Would I really philander with a filthy Mook?' he was indignant.

'Well, strike me dead, son ... if this *is* true, thy'll nay get a thing, mi lad. It all goes te Freddie. You've got two hours to make yer mind up afore we sign the documents. Two hours!'

Fred defended his brother. 'Please, Father, believe him. The Mooks are just trying to make trouble for Robbie because of the horse.' And Fred gently took his father by the arm and led him to a bench. 'Sit down, this stress is no good for you.' But Samuel wrenched his arm away and insisted. 'Is it true, Robbie? Did you beat up Richardson and rob him?'

Robbie lowered his head and wanted to laugh. He hated fighting, he hated any kind of violence, his time in Africa had taken away any desire for warring and hostility. He didn't care if his father stripped him of his inheritance, he didn't care if Fred took both farms, he didn't want the responsibility of Keld Head, anyway; he didn't want to be tied; he felt it would be worse than being bound to a woman. He needed his space and knew if he pushed this, he would get it, and a lifetime of it.

Robbie turned and looked at his father as they argued the familiar problems, and something inside him said this could be the last time, as he saw his father trembling, amazed he wasn't coughing.

Fred was sheepishly moving boxes and the silence embarrassed him.

'I'm waiting.' Samuel, sitting on the bench, held his walking stick in his two hands and rested his chin on it.

'I can't let you take this to the grave with you, Father. I am not lying. You know I've been stupid. You've seen it since I was a boy. But if I take Keld Head, I'll look after it, if not Fred will do a good job. I'll leave it up to you, what you decide. Yes, I met Richardson; a kindly sort of man. He invited me to go to church with him, but I wasn't quite dressed for it or I would have gone.' And he couldn't help but smile a crooked and mischievous smile.

'Since whenever have you been a church man, Robbie?'

'You don't really know what's in my heart.' He spoke truthfully. 'I went to the inn to get back some lost property and Sally Mook pushed me into him and we fell. It was she that robbed him, not I.'

Another long and embarrassing silence came.

'Haven't I heard all this a'fore? How do I know this is the truth? You said you never stole that horse, you were just getting it back for Wilding and now this is just the same ... aye, just the same.'

'If you don't believe me, there's nothing I can do or say to make you. I've never lied to you,' and that wasn't quite the truth either, but latterly Robbie hadn't lied; he was man enough to admit all and defend his name when necessary.

'You'll take Keld Head, Robbie, and let this be the last of it.'

Fred's shoulders dropped with relief as he had worried at the small age of nineteen how he could manage two farms. Robbie's shoulders never moved.

'But I tell yer one thing, son, ye daren't bring anymore shame on our name again while I'm alive. I'm going te Frazer Piercy today. We'll sign these papers and Keld Head will be yours, but from the day we get to Grasmere ye both have te become churchmen. Every Sunday and more if need be, and while I'm with ye, we'll be known as the Keldas family from then on and I will instruct the solicitor as such, and our name'll be changed forever, all good and proper.'

The lunchtime visit to Frazer Piercy and Son was to be in their Millom office. Fred had planned to wear his best suit because today he would become a landowner. He'd seen the horse was ready and the trap cleaned. He would take the reins; he usually did. Not that Robbie ever wanted to drive; this was just another thing he always left to Fred. Robbie would much prefer to be in the saddle. He would take Tilly if he had her, or prefer to walk. And today he chose to walk. When he told Fred he would meet them at Millom, Fred worried. 'Drive with us, please, just today. The old man wants you by his side.'

'No, Freddie, I'll walk. The air will do me good; give me time to reflect on my upcoming status.' And reflect he did. Robbie walked the lane down to the sea along the headland and watching a few birds; the eerie tones of a curlew calling ripped through the chilled air. He met a local man, a butcher, on the lane and was happy to pass the time of day; hands deep in pockets, in no hurry. He stopped and leant on a gate and watched some lambs gambolling about, always looking for new ways to hurt themselves, ferreting in hedges to escape. He didn't particularly have any affinity with sheep, they were hard work. Often lame: they had four legs because they always needed one to keep them upright. Horses and cattle were his love and the occasional woman.

As he walked to the headland he stopped and looked out to sea, there was a clear blue sky, yet the sea looked grey. In the distance the Isle of Man was visible today and the Solway coast. Breathing deeply the salty air, he threw his head back and shut his eyes. But Robbie wasn't a man of the sea, he was a mountain man, he much preferred the green close cropped hillsides, the ling and heather growing up the sides of the fells, these boggy and craggy hills were more of a pleasure to him. He checked his pocket watch; still time. He slid his gold watch back into his waistcoat pocket, looked right and saw the headland leading to Scotland. The large gateway of Coldrigg Gaol in the distance, which he knew as he always did, he would have to make a mile detour to avoid passing it, like it would drag him inside if he got too close.

Close to him on the lane was a cottage belonging to an elderly German woman, who was always pleased to see him and flirt; she would feed him cakes and home brewed beer. He turned his back to the sea and looked at Black Combe and saw the blue sky pushing its way eastward on top of Scafell and Bowfell and longed to be there. It would take more than today to enjoy them. His boots itching to walk, but his mind preventing him, and looking down at the shingle on the beach, he had no desire to walk on it and have to struggle, slipping on the uneven surface.

He was twenty six and some would say approaching the prime of his life, and if this was it, there was only disappointment, he had wanted a kind of ecstasy, utopia, nirvana, call it what you will and he strived to find it and just when he grabbed its hand and felt he could stay here and die happy it would slip away from him. Nothing brought him lasting satisfaction; he was disappointed with the world and the near death experience fighting the Boer had fuelled that. But he had no desire to travel further than these shores, he was at his happiest with the smallest of things: a ride on Tilly's back; him and the horse alone with the mountains; a swim in the lake; he sometimes slept on the warm grassy slopes if the sun was out and felt he would blend into the mountain like he belonged to it; like he was its offspring and not that of man. If he saw a deer or even a stoat or a weasel teasing a rabbit, a sun set, a sun rise, it raised his mood. Then a good meal and a good woman, but once he had finished he would push the woman and the plate aside, content for a few minutes; tired, or once the water was dry on his back or the mountain was conquered as his knees faltered back down the slippery slopes. Robbie's heart had a yearning for real contentment and he would search and search until he found it.

His responsibility to his father and brother today were his overriding powers. He contemplated how it would feel to have the keys to Keld Head in his hand and believed it would momentarily satisfy him, but how long before the responsibility would weigh on him and make him tied and bound and unhappy. He wondered how he would feel when his father died; would he grieve inconsolable, or would he be strong for Fred and glad his father's torment was over. This was to be his last night under Black Combe and unlike Fred hadn't dressed for the occasion. Most of the animals had been moved, what decent furniture they had was divided between them: a good bed, and the best walnut dresser for his father's last days. He wouldn't celebrate in the pub because there was nothing to celebrate. And he couldn't drown his sorrows because he wanted to be clear headed. The journey to Grasmere tomorrow would take up most of the day.

His father had insisted that he left Black Combe in the trap and not in a coffin and it appeared he would get his wish, regardless of the cough that tore at his lungs and the blood he spat. He would make his final journey to Keld Head sitting in the trap with his two sons by his side. The plot in Grasmere cemetery was bought and paid for with room for two more.

Robbie didn't relish the legal jargon that would be poured out by Frazer Piercy, he considered the man to be a drunkard yet he knew that Frazer considered him to be worse. He would shuffle papers and in a condescending manner, using superfluous words to show his superiority and impress, yet it impressed no one.

Samuel Kellet sat with his youngest son by his side in the grand office of Piercy and Piercy and Sons. He was pleased for once that Frazer was late, because Robbie hadn't turned up. Fred was fidgeting in the chair, nervous as if he was to give his very life away, never mind receive the grandest of an inheritance.

'He's not coming.' Samuel grunted and felt his heart jumping erratically, something he was getting used to.

'He'll come ... he has to come.' Fred choked on his words and rubbed his index finger under his collar and wondered why it felt so tight.

'He'll nay get a thing, Freddie. I'll see te that.... I'm nay kidding, son.... I'll do it ... I'll do it! It only teks me signature and the deed'll be done and it'll all be yours and that's it.' But inside Samuel was heartbroken.

The office door burst open and Frazer Piercy, a tall thin man in a black suit and white shirt emerged; his face drawn and wrinkled, his nose red and bony. Frazer looked at the two men waiting and paused before he spoke. He took Samuel's hand and with stinking alcohol fuelled breath, 'Where's Robbie?'

'Dang it, Frazer, he's not come.' And Samuel stood with a surge of adrenalin, shaking and sweating.

'This is awkward, Samuel, we can't sign the papers without Robbie.'

'We don't need Robbie for what I have in mind...!' Samuel's voice sharpened and young Fred, bemused, followed his father into the solicitor's office.

'Do you know where he is, Freddie?' Frazer quizzed, expecting the usual answers because nobody ever really knew where Robbie was.

'He promised, Mr Piercy ... he promised.... He said he would walk and meet us here.' Fred looked at the clock which seemed to be ticking louder and louder with each moment that time elapsed. It was already twenty minutes past their appointment.

'Let's give him ten more minutes before we start.'

'We'll give him nay more minutes, Frazer. That boy's had it wi' me.'

Frazer looked down at the papers on his desk that had been drawn up for the two farms; one, Spickle Howe the other Keld Head. He'd put little pencilled crosses where each signature should go. 'Samuel, you must act. You know your health is failing quickly. Fred cannot manage two farms.'

'I can't, Father, Mr Piercy's right.' Fred was glad to have an ally.

'Then I'll keep Keld Head and let Fred have Spickle Howe. I'll die there and then she will be sold and the money goes to Fred.'

Frazer Piercy moaned inwardly then spoke soft and condescendingly. 'Samuel ... Samuel ... we must settle this now; I don't want you to regret your actions, although heaven knows why I'm defending this boy.'

'It'll be young Robbie that regrets his actions, Frazer, not me. There's nay place for regrets where I'm oft te. Besides, I have another job for you and I want it doing all legal and proper.'

Frazer was now wishing he had taken more whisky.

'I want to change our family name. On reaching Grasmere I want to be known as Samuel Greenbank Keldas ... Keldas you get it. K E L D A S.... Kay, eeh, ell, dee, ay, ess. It's Nordic. It nigh on means the same as Kellet, and my boys are to be called the same, or they'll get nowt. And my property stays as it is.'

49

Frazer looked at Fred, but Fred nodded in acknowledgment.

In the passage way outside, a banging of some doors caused a small shudder to come over all those in Frazer's office. Someone knocked on the door and in walked Robbie. Brown suit, white shirt, hair neatly groomed, his moustache trimmed, he walked across to Frazer. 'I'm sorry I'm late, Frazer.' He winked at Fred. And a moment in time that would be the constant concern for future generations was now being staged; four men about to act in a drama with the curtains not closing for decades.

It was Samuel who broke the silence. 'Yes, Keldas will be our new name won't it, Robbie, Freddie. It sounds grand. Where do I sign?'

The journey to Grasmere was made in fine weather. They left Black Combe in sunshine; Samuel began to cry the moment he awoke that morning. Robbie was there at his side as a dutiful son. Fred didn't know how to respond. The nurse- come-housekeeper, Mrs Borsch, a broad woman from Carlisle, who had steely coloured hair pulled tight back with a centre parting, was to travel with them. Robbie observed her and guessed she could pick his father up singlehandedly in her arms if need be.

Frazer met them at early dawn with the keys to Keld Head and Spickle Howe. He would take the keys of White Banks Farm away for the new owners. He handed Robbie the keys and they stuck in his hand. He paused and hesitated. 'Robbie, if you lose this place you will have me to answer to.'

Robbie snatched the keys; he'd no intention of losing Keld Head and ever having to answer to anyone again, let alone Frazer Piercy.

The trap arrived with Fred as driver with the bay, Topper. Robbie would ride Edwin's horse, Tilly. She had been bought for a high price.

Samuel stopped sobbing as they reached Broughton and a meal was taken at the inn, then they rode on to Torver and Coniston. When Samuel got within sight of the mass of mountains above, the Coniston Old Man and Wetherlam, a great fear and trembling came over him. Today Robbie would play the dutiful son and, on Tilly's back, he never left the side of the trap to reassure his father. Robbie rode easily letting Tilly have her head, the reins falling loosely; he glanced left and saw Dow Crag when Samuel began to tremble.

'I'm a blathering fool I know, son, but these mountains make me feel like they're gan te bury me.'

'You'll not be buried today, Father.' Robbie was confident. 'I think the Lord will grant you a safe passage to resume your new life in Mr Wordsworth's shadow, under a new guise. It's best you tell him about our change of name, though, for the Lord will be confused as to who you are. Here, take some brandy.'

The journey was to take them to Elterwater then over to Grasmere. Robbie glanced up at the mines and the fells and wished he was on them. And although he knew hundreds of men were working that quarry, he envied the graft that they did instead of playing nursemaid with the formidable Mrs Borsch, but nothing stirred in the distance and the mountains were as still as a photograph. The sound of the two horses' hooves ringing on the gravel road and the wheels on the trap, the only noise apart from Samuel's fits of sobbing. Passing motorist trundled by but neither horse was unnerved by them. Robbie was glad his father had settled again and only hoped that when he reached Keld Head he would recuperate in the new farm. Robbie hadn't explored the place in any detail, but he had known Keld Head from history with its Pele tower, and there were many like it in Westmorland.

The arrival at Keld Head brought a surge of adrenalin to Samuel. He walked around the farmhouse, pleased with the newly installed stove in the kitchen. His walnut furniture put in the bedroom with a small window that overlooked the fells, with the lake in the distance. He wandered around the outbuildings, the dairy, and saw the new herd and the best of his old one mingling, grazing in the lush meadows. The land here was softer. The close clipped grass pasture bursting ready to bring a good milk yield and new spring lambs. But it was the tower that tempted Samuel the most, it would only ever be used as a store, but its hard earned survival had inspired him and gave him a deep sense of purpose; its romanticism and prominence as a house could be spotted easily by all who ventured here.

This farm had once belonged to a stately family and Samuel hoped one day that Robbie would settle here with a family of his own; find a wife to love and pacify him; one who would love and respect him, although it troubled him that he could never foresee how things would turn out. He had two fine sons; one would always help the other. He considered Robbie reckless and Fred, dull; one had the speech and patience of a diplomat, and the other the strength and stature of a king. Samuel's hope was held hanging boldly like an ensign on the tower, waving and flapping in the breeze. And as the weeks passed and Samuel's health stabilized, he was still a poorly man and not even the charms of Keld Head could alter that, but he would live out his last days under these soft fells, with Black Combe no longer looming over him and oppressing him.

Fred Kellet arrived at Spickle Howe two days later after seeing his father settled with the nurse, the capable Mrs Borsch. He left him; reluctantly, at the mercy of his wayward brother, but this was his father's choice. He took the bay gelding and an entourage of helpers and at the grand age of nineteen became master of a small farm. Again he dressed for the occasion, for he believed that his appearance would magnify his being master of this house.

Samuel had employed Frazer Piercy's brother, Magnus, who had an office in Kendal to begin the process of a legal name change and letter headings were made that bore the name Samuel Keldas and Sons.

Robbie worked hard and it appeared his father's wishes and hopes would continue to fly like the imaginary flag on the tower at Keld Head. Yet Robbie had often done this; for months he would settle and graft like nothing on earth; no balance in this; rejoicing in the vibrancy of his youth and health. He walked out regularly with his father, talking of the land and what plans he should make for each new piece of pasture and each beast. They had three small cottages close to Keld Head and a new housekeeper and cook was employed, a woman called Nora Given; her husband to be the dairyman. And on Sunday Robbie sat with his father in church, with Fred beside him. His head bent low in honest and meaningful prayer.

6

A FUSION OF FRIENDS

Robbie wasn't listening to the sermon; he was admiring the back of a young woman's neck.

She was sitting in the pew in front of him between an elderly steely haired woman and a chubby blonde. The girl's dark hair was pulled up on her head and neatly pinned under a straw bonnet; a few loose strands had fallen onto her soft tanned skin. How could he concentrate?

He wondered at her skin tone and thought she could be foreign; surely not a gypsy. Most women were pale and insipid but this woman had been used to the sun; maybe she loved to be outside. She was a tall girl with deep blue eyes. He'd noticed her walk in. He'd seen her blush as he sat up from his prayer and respectfully nodded. He wanted to wink at her but this wasn't the place.

Beth had seen Robbie as he sat praying; his shoulders bent, his hands together with his fingers entwined; his eyes closed; a clean man she thought; a Christian man. His forehead was deep and tanned, with a bluish vein that slipped down one side. It was a moving thing to see a young man pray; an intimate thing.

When he opened his eyes and saw her looking, she blushed. But he had just smiled; a crooked smile.

Freddie was sitting beside Robbie and was flicking the pages of his hymn book almost goading the minister to hurry and sing the last song. The day was hot; a scorcher. And as Fred felt his shirt under his jacket sticking to his chest and spine he longed to remove it along with his neck tie.

The two brothers were alone, Samuel had been overtaken by the heat and been advised by Mrs Borsch to stay in under the cool walls of Keld Head.

Beth fanned her face with her song sheet as they finally stood for the hymn and the prayer was said.

Robbie bowed his head respectfully, but his eyes were not completely closed; he was still watching the pretty young woman and wishing he was more loyal to his creator. It was then that he saw her sway to one side and as she began to fall, he caught her in his arms and inwardly praised his maker for his watchfulness. The elderly chaperone squealed, yet the clergyman continued to drone out his prayer and say it louder; regardless.

Robbie held Beth in his arms, her dead weight resting on him, her head nestling in his shoulders with nought but the back of the pew between them. She stirred and her sleepy eyelids fell onto his kindly face.

'I'm sorry, sir, forgive me. I am so sorry. I don't know what happened,' she whispered.

'Can you walk? Come with me ... and I'll find you some shade.' His first words spoken were soft and gentle; still holding her in his arms.

Beth complied like a lamb.

Charlotte Webb, the elderly aunt and chaperone followed.

'It was the clergyman ...'

'Yes, I could say it in much less time and not send the mice to sleep.'

His words like sweet medicine caused her to smile, as he led her outside to a small seat at the side of the church and beckoned her to sit down.

'Wait here and I'll get you a cool drink.'

Robbie removed a dark green silk handkerchief from his jacket and went to a well set deep in the stone wall. He saturated the cloth and swiftly returned to the women.

He gave Beth the handkerchief to put to her mouth; the discretion he showed was apparent.

Beth dabbed her face and forehead and managed to compose herself. Charlotte Webb muttered in a high pitched tone. 'We can't thank you enough, sir. We are so sorry to inconvenience you.'

But it was no inconvenience, it was most convenient.

Letting her eyes settle on Robbie's face, Beth recalled the closed eyelids of the praying man and flushed. It was a moment she had waited for in the depth of reverie; that the man she was to fall in love with was standing solidly, majestically and irresistibly close to her side.

'My name is Robert Keldas.' And he lowered his head again.

'My name is Webb, Charlotte Webb with two b's, sir.' The elderly woman replied, and this is my niece, Elizabeth.'

'Have you come far?' He politely addressed Charlotte.

'We are on vacation, sir. My home is near Kendal. But we are currently lodging at the Prince of Wales. Do you know it? It is situated close to the lake.'

'I know it, yes.' And as he spoke Irene Dowson emerged from the church with Fred by her side. Fred wondered at seeing his brother with this beautiful girl sitting on the bench and wished he was holding her. But Fred always shut his eyes properly when he prayed.

Robbie managed to remove his eyes from her. 'Freddie, could you get this young lady some water from the well. There may be a chalice in the church she can rightfully drink from. Do you have a motor car or carriage?'

'No sir. We walked up this morning. The air was cooler then.'

'Then permit me to see you safely back to the Prince of Wales. Yonder Prince's hospitality will be greater than anything that I can offer.'

'No sir, if I can have a cool drink, I will be fine.... And I believe the walk back is on the descent?'

'I'd rather take you, miss. I couldn't bear the responsibility if any misfortune happened on the way. Look, here comes Freddie with some water.'

The small group walked slowly through the little town. Robbie wanted to hold Beth but knew she was in safer hands with her aunt. Never-the-less he still walked dutifully at her other side. Fred and Irene followed.

'Are you a local man, Mr Keldas?' Charlotte was polite.

'Yes, I farm over yonder. A small hill farm, up at Keld Head.'

'Is that near the Pele tower?'

'Yes, mam ... that is my farm. I own the property ... the tower.'

'What a wonderful building. I have noticed it often, from afar.'

'Then you must visit one day, Mrs Webb, and take a closer inspection.'

'No sir, I cannot presume on your kindness any further.'

'My kindness is insensible to thought ... my heart is usually the master over me and it always tells me to show charity. So how much longer are you here?'

'Two more weeks. We have been travelling the area.'

The small group walked slowly down a wooded lane, clad with laurel and rhododendrons, fattened lambs chased each other, racing across small paddocks. Beth clung to her aunt, with Robbie to her left.

She could hear the soft tap - tap of the tacks on the soles of his polished shoes on the lane, as he walked straight backed, tall, dignified. She noticed his hands as he gestured and spoke enthusiastically of his farm. She listened to the soft, well spoken tones of his voice, an accent northern and not dissimilar to her own, yet it had a sharper pitch to the vowels.

'And do you have a family, Mr Keldas?' Charlotte asked.

'I live alone with my father. I'm afraid he's in poor health.'

'I'm sorry about that.' Beth couldn't account as to why she felt happy, and was cautious not to show it in her voice.

'He would normally have been with us today, but for this stifling heat.'

The party dissolved at the hotel; twenty minutes of sheer pleasure for Beth; her weakness no more, her spirit restored and vibrant. She was ushered indoors by Aunt Charlotte and found it hard to resist not looking back.

Climbing the grand staircase to her room, she said. 'Please leave me... I'll be fine.'

And on closing the door Beth realised she was still holding onto the handkerchief of Mr Robert Keldas.

'He's a true gentleman.' Charlotte said over lunch, 'and a churchman too.'

'His brother was a nervous, quiet sort.' Irene now spoke up.

'They were very dissimilar.' Beth tried to recall Robbie's complexion, dark skinned, dark hair; a little long but swept back and neatly combed. His body clean with a woody fragrance of lotion that she could still recall as she was held in his arms. The brother, fair haired and receding for a young man, a ruddy complexion.

'And to look after his ailing father.... Please pass me the potatoes, Irene.'

'It was a kind offer to let us look at the Pele tower but I feel we couldn't possibly assume on his kindness.'

'Ah, but neither do we want to offend his hospitality; he made that clear, in a humorous fashion. Besides, I still have his handkerchief to launder and return.'

Robbie and Fred took the long walk back to Keld Head side by side. Robbie strode out enthusiastically, righteous as to his good deed. Fred was beside him, struggling to keep pace.

'A fine girl,' Robbie said as he whistled.

'She's not your type, Rob.' Fred smiled.

'And what is my type, young Freddie?'

'Well, not your usual type.' And he laughed as he kicked at a stone.

'I'll tell you what, Freddie, you know nothing of me ... what I really like.'

And Fred silenced, sensed a serious tone to his brother's voice that he had never noticed before. Perhaps things were changing as well as their name, and maybe their father could be right. Fred had felt himself elevated in stature when Robbie introduced him to the ladies as Mr Frederick Keldas. It sounded regal.

Then he dared to be impertinent. 'Well, she wouldn't want you, Robbie, if she knew where you'd just been lodging. A fine woman like that.'

And then as if someone had touched Robbie's warm heart with a sharp knife, he felt a deep pain as he knew his brother was probably right.

Robbie looked up the valley and could see Keld Head's Pele tower, he was proud of this piece of England he now owned. He'd worked hard to settle and help his dying father, he'd tilled the land into shape; good grass meant good quality milk, his father always said. But then he realised something about Keld

Head that he'd never thought of before, that it was sitting tall, aloft, overlooking Wordsworth's country, almost spying on the land below and he guessed as much as Keld Head's prominence was apparent, so would all his deeds and misdeeds. And the dawning of a sense of exposure embarrassed him, that everything he did from now on would become visible to all.

Irene closed the bedroom door and the two girls started to undress. Irene helped Beth with the fasteners on her dress, and Beth sighed as she let the muscles in her stomach relax.

'You were too warm, today, Bethy, that's why you fainted.'

'It's a bad time of the month for me and all.'

'You must take more care.'

'I will be alright in a day or so.'

'Mind ... it had its benefits?'

Beth knew what she was alluding to, but resisted.

'Come on, Bethy ... you wouldn't have fallen into the arms of one Mr Robert Keldas, otherwise, would you?'

Beth smiled and let her dress fall to the ground then put it on a hanger and hung it on the wardrobe. She went to the dresser and looked in the mirror, and pulled some pins from her hair. 'Don't start jumping to conclusions, Irene.'

'I'm sorry Bethy, but your face tells it all.'

'Nonsense.'

Irene sidled up to her. 'You liked him, didn't you?'

'What is the point, there would be no attachment to me ... he was clearly just a Christian man, doing a young woman a kind deed.'

'No intention my foot!' Irene came and perched beside Beth and both women sat looking through the mirror. 'I can tell when a man's attracted to a woman and I can tell you, Robert Keldas was attracted to you.'

'Stop it, Irene.' Beth started to tousle her hair and in her underclothes went and sat on the side of the bed. 'I can't allow myself to be enthusiastic about Mr Keldas. He may be otherwise engaged, he may not be the marrying sort. He has his elderly father to see to.' But Beth did allow herself to day

59

dream about Robbie as she lay on her bed that night; recalling his features, his blue eyes, his teeth, clean and smiling, a little crooked and not straight. And she hoped all the more that her aunt would suggest they did go to Keld Head to see the Pele tower and return the green handkerchief.

Three days later Robbie was in the fields scything thistles. The tedium of the work and satisfaction of seeing a neat and tidy meadow satisfied him. Each thistle wilted in the warm sunshine with little chance of spreading their fluffy seeds any further. Robbie hoped in time, with hard work, he would get this land into better shape than it already was. He was stripped down just to his vest with his braces dropped off his shoulders. The sunlight touched his eyes and he squinted and pulled his straw hat down further over his face. With each regular trip up and down the field so he didn't miss any, he stopped by the wall and rubbed his brow, taking off his Panama hat. When he looked up he saw three women walking up the lane and by the shape and deportment he knew exactly who they were. He stopped and waited till they were close and, as he finally could confirm their person, he glanced at his shirt hanging on the gate and walked swiftly to retrieve it.

Charlotte Webb spotted Robbie in the field and considered him to be a labourer but on seeing him remove his hat and the dark hair that characterised him, she slowed the pace as she could see he was purposeful in making himself respectful. And for the first time in his life Robbie felt ashamed before a woman. He slipped his shirt over his shoulders and buttoned it quickly, then straightened his hat and some straying strands of hair.

'Good day, ladies ... I'm sorry, I wasn't expecting you today.' But that was a lie because since their first brief encounter he had hoped Beth would call and return his handkerchief; he had watched the lane from every aspect. He'd even stood atop of the Pele tower. He hadn't strayed any further than his own land; his father believing his son was settling and being attentive to him. But Robbie was dutiful to no other than himself, to gratify his own heart and see Beth again, for he knew that this young woman had been captured by him as many others had. Robbie was usually satisfied with the conquest and then afterwards had diminished feelings. But Beth was tantalisingly different, almost untouchable, and as Fred had rightly implied, not of his calibre. Yet that was untrue because they were of the same status, and if Robbie had remained as chaste as Fred, a good match. And now this desire for Beth was something he couldn't control; his thoughts were paralysed with the attraction he had for her and he would go along with this insatiable instinct that he could not suppress.

'I'm sorry, Mr Keldas. I hope we haven't disturbed you at your labour. We purely wanted to return your property.' Charlotte said, as Beth held out the green silky handkerchief.

Robbie wanted to take her hand and kiss it. 'I hope you will stay a while and allow me to show you the Pele tower and my small farm ... perhaps offer you some refreshment?' The eye contact was a pleasing mix as he sensed he could now enrapture each of the three women. 'I wouldn't want Miss Elizabeth to swoon again.'

'Thank you, sir, but as I said, we had no intention of disturbing you.'

Robbie then grasped the full capacity of his enchantment and knew by his charismatic manner he could pursue this, as he had done often, not just with a young woman, but with his parents, his brother, and his friends. 'You must have walked a long way from the hotel and although I may not be as regal as yonder Prince of Wales, I feel I can match, if not better, his landscape.'

And the three women easily capitulated as he led them up the hill to Keld Head.

'I'm afraid my father is in his sick bed and will be unable to meet you, but my housekeeper would be more than happy to provide some light refreshment.'

'Keld Head is a beautiful place, Mr Keldas. We can see the tower from the hotel.'

Then unnoticed, he lowered his head, almost shamefully, 'I don't know if that's a good thing, Mrs Webb.' He gave a wry smile.

'Oh, it is ... it is.'

'These cottages belong to my farm,' and he pointed. He approached the yard and the gate was wide open and, as he led the women in, he felt a compulsion to firmly close and latch the gate. It was noted by Beth and it disturbed her.

He pushed open the door to the tower with his boot.

'There are four storeys,' he held the door open for the women, but looking into the dark and gloom they hesitated. 'Yes, I'm sorry it's dark.' And he went for a lantern and lit it and held it high.

Charlotte and Irene were intrigued by the place but, as for Beth, it held a deep sense of foreboding as if something evil had happened here, and she had no desire to enter despite Robbie's enthusiasm.

'It was built in the fourteenth century.' Robbie shouted outside to the women. 'There are several towers like this in these parts, on account of the border reivers.'

Charlotte edged inside. 'Is your family name Celtic, Mr Keldas?'

Robbie wanted to laugh at his father's whimsical ideas which now gave him an edge. 'No... It's Nordic. It means a well or a spring. I can see you are uncomfortable, Elizabeth.' He looked deeply into her eyes and his concern softened her as it would always do. 'The staircase is difficult to climb,' and he faltered. 'This is where they used to keep the animals.' And he pointed and then looked above. 'The folks would live up here, warmed and perfumed by the cattle.'

Beth was reassured by his wit. 'Do you ever keep animals in here, Mr Keldas?'

'I would prefer it if you called me Robert ... my father calls me Robbie.'

'As the noble Mr Burns?' Charlotte asked.

'Nay, I'm not so noble, mam. It is purely a name of, shall we say, affection, and it would please me if you called me as such.'

'Then thank you for showing us your property, Robbie.'

'But no, we don't keep animals in here anymore. I have a new shippon but I'm sure you're not interested in cattle.'

'Oh but I am, Robbie.' Beth dared to say his name for the first time. 'My father has a dairy farm over in Yorkshire.'

Robbie looked once more at her tanned skin and understood the origin.

'Would you like to see my cattle?' He led them back outside.

Beth glanced around, seeing the cattle grazing in the meadows under these beautiful hills. 'How far does your land go?'

'To the top of the ridge ... where the bracken starts. Do you like to walk, Elizabeth?'

And she looked up at the mountains: Fairfield, Heron Pike, Tarn Crag, Silver Howe. 'I walk out most days, if the weather is fine. It's good for the soul.... You can call me Beth.'

And conception began at that moment in time of a relationship that would give birth to a new and everlasting alliance, and all four stood quietly as if to recognize the moment and give it some dignity.

Then Robbie manoeuvred the strategy as he would always do throughout their lives. 'It wouldn't be wise for novices to walk these high fells.'

'And I have little knowledge, I'm afraid.' Charlotte said.

'Maybe you would like to walk higher, sometime, with a trusted guide?' Robbie addressed this as a question to Charlotte.

'I certainly wouldn't have the stamina and we couldn't presume on your time, anymore.'

'You will be delighted to know I am also master of my time and I bid it to be hospitable and benevolent. I hope you could trust my judgement.'

Beth looked at Charlotte, her eyes pleading with her to agree.

'That would be wonderful.'

'Maybe you would like some tea now. I always have time for tea and some crack.' Robbie opened the kitchen door and as they entered Beth caught her coat on a small potted geranium that was on a bench set into the doorway. The clay pot smashed and the geranium snapped. 'Oh dear me, oh no!' She bent to pick it up.

'Never worry of such trivialities, Beth.' He lifted the broken stems from out of her hand. 'Life is full of them.'

Three days later Beth and Irene arrived back at Keld Head; Charlotte Webb had allowed the girls the opportunity to show their maturity and had stayed at the hotel with a head cold.

'Thank you for the gift.' Robbie set a replacement geranium down on the window ledge. 'It was unnecessary.'

'I saw it in the town and it seemed fitting that I brought it ... a gift and a replacement for your kindness.'

'I wish all things could be replaced as easily.'

Robbie took Beth and Irene to Easdale. They walked up to the waterfall and on to the tarn. Beth walked well and easily, Irene not so enthusiastic. Then they made a steady climb up to the crags behind the tarn. Its height not so difficult as it framed the tranquil waters, but a sufficient climb to satisfy Beth's need.

Irene was soon tired, her short legs struggled up each slope as her skirt tightened around her legs and impeded her, but she would do anything so that Beth could spend more time with Robert Keldas. But close to the summit, in view of the crags, she rested her small and chubby body on a rock and insisted that they continued the next few paces without her.

Robbie walked slightly in front of Beth, his pace steady, but Beth kept up, walking easily, comfortably. She felt embarrassed at first to be left alone with him and remained silent, but satisfied she was safely in Irene's view. 'Tell me about your farm, Beth.' Robbie helped her.

'We have two hundred acres that runs down to the banks of the River Swale, near Thirsk, if you know it. It's called Sugar Hills. There is heather on the moor above us making the sweetest of honey for the bees.'

'And do you have brothers and sisters?'

'I only have a brother. My mother died when I was much younger. Christopher is sixteen ... my father has brought us up well, singlehanded.'

'I'm sorry to say but I know how that feels. My own mother died some years ago. Is Christopher interested in Sugar Hills?'

Beth laughed. 'Yes, he is, but Christie is a delicate boy. Don't misunderstand me, he loves the countryside and the animals, but he's more interested in the law and science. Father is sending him to Northumberland soon to get some experience, but Christie doesn't want to go.'

They struggled to the summit, Robbie glanced back and reassured that Irene was still in eyeshot, and safe, and glad of her presence as he couldn't trust himself alone with Beth. He allowed her to sit and rest for awhile on a flat rock as he stood tall above her. 'He could gladly come and work for me, if he needs the experience. I'd happily train up the boy.' He lowered his head, his eyebrows fell.

She nodded. 'I think my father has everything in hand, but thank you for your offer....This landscape is unusual.' Beth said, embarrassed a little. Grassy outcrops and moraines stubbled with reeds and bracken all around; the views were stunning. She dared to look at his face and he was looking at her now; wantonly; his blue eyes, his tanned skin, the elegance of his stature, all beckoning her.

He said it quickly. 'You must leave me your address. If I find I need an apprentice or if your father needs another placement for Christopher, he would be most welcome.'

7

BACK TO BADNESS

He leant on the polished oak bar of the local inn, a clock was ticking loudly. Some men were talking, some were laughing. The ale was good. Robbie was smug and satisfied. A few locals were at the bar, also a few visitors; strangers. He was tired and he appeared to have finally burnt himself out of every drop of energy in moving house; caring for his cattle; caring for his father; weary of composing his self restraint and emotions, and he felt the latter the hardest. Fred was beside him talking at length about his own problems; how to run his own farm at Hawkshead, but as Fred droned on, Robbie was happy just to listen and say the occasional yes or no, and during one of Fred's long and drawling sentences Robbie took out of his pocket and looked for the first time at the slip of paper Beth had given him. It read:

Elizabeth Richardson

Sugar Hills

Thirsk.

And the name jumped out at him and he stopped Fred in mid sentence. 'What was her name, Freddie?'

'Whose name?' and he sipped his beer.

'Beth ... Elizabeth. What was her surname?'

'Aye, I don't know, you're not usually interested in surnames, Rob.'

'Man alive, Freddie ... remember? What did she say her name was, please?'

Fred searched his mind to consider their first meeting at the church. 'The older woman ... the aunt, said she was called Webb with two B's. I remember that much as she purposely spelt it: W- E- B- B.'

Robbie handed Fred the slip of paper. 'I'm a fool, Freddie, an idiot.'

Fred looked at the hand written note. 'I suppose you assumed Beth's name was Webb, too.'

'At that moment in time I didn't care what her last name was. But now this Richardson,' he lowered his voice.

'What's worrying you?'

'Come on man, Richardson!'

'Ah, I see. Why worry ... there must be hundreds of Richardsons up and down the country.'

Robbie wanted to believe he was right. 'Didn't we send the bull to Yorkshire, though? The one that Franklyn Richardson bought?'

'Father dealt with all that. But it was Yorkshire, I knows that much.'

And Robbie groaned inwardly. 'It's too much of a coincidence, but if that preacher man, Franklyn Richardson is her father, then I'm for the gallows!'

'Sally stole from him, not you ... right? So, forget her Rob, you usually do.'

But that was the problem, Robbie couldn't forget Beth, he had never met a woman like her.

'I've told you before, Freddie. You know nothing of me. I know I attract the wrong sort. I can't help that.' He could really. 'I've never seen a woman like her: her grace and demeanour. I'm attracted to her chastity and her honesty. That young woman doesn't know what she has, Freddie. She is a temptress for me.'

'Then she wouldn't be interested in you.'

Fred left him alone at the bar to take his trip back to Hawkshead. He'd only called to visit his father.

Robbie wondered what was happening to him, he was usually the optimist, and he knew some times he should be more sober in thought and outlook and look at life more seriously, but he rarely did. He'd escaped too many skirmishes, apparently unharmed, and his latest threat of the gates of Coldrigg Gaol and three months under its walls, he could still hear the keys clinking in the locks and pitied the poor souls still incarcerated. He shuddered.

'Can I put you a whisky in there, Robbie?'

Robbie glanced across and saw the greasy black hair and pock marked face of Jimmy Mook, the brother of Sally. He was a sickly looking man with a hooked nose and the skin on his face like a jigsaw.

Robbie put his hand over his glass. He knew what this was about. 'You'll not make a fool of me in here, Jimmy Mook.'

'Nay, ye can do that for thi sen, young Robbie.'

Jimmy came to shake Robbie's hand and Robbie reluctantly took his. 'What are you doing over here in these parts, Jim?'

'Surprised to see me, eh?'

Robbie wasn't surprised, this family appeared to follow him around the more he tried to distance himself from them; he knew they did it on purpose; they were embittered about Tilly.

'I've been hearing stories about you, Robbie.' Jimmy spoke loudly for all in the bar to hear and he began to sing. 'Ride a cocked horse to Banbury Cross, to see a fine lady on a fine horse.'

Robbie didn't think it funny.

'Is that why you took my mare, Kellet, to impress fine ladies up at Keld Head?'

The thought that Jimmy Mook had been watching him, all the while he charmed his visitors from Yorkshire, sickened Robbie. 'You know she isn't your horse. Anyway, she's mine now, all good and paid for which is something you never did.'

'That's mebbee so,' Jimmy grinned, 'and then they tell me yer old man's gan crazy - demented - and changed thi name to summat fancy. What a joke?' And he fell on the bar laughing as he ordered a whisky.

Robbie, baited by the trap, knew he should leave but pride prevented him. 'It's always galled you hasn't it, Jimmy? A name like yours ... Mook, eh? What does that mean, oh yes, let me see, a back side ... a sheep's back side!'

Jimmy grabbed Robbie by the shirt collar. 'You see this man, this fine young man,' he spat. 'Don't let 'im fool ye gentle folk here in Grasmere. His name's nay Keldas but Kellet and he's a horse thief and a womanising crook and goodness knows what else.'

Robbie felt ashamed and was glad Fred had left. He was consoled that his father lay dying in bed under the stone walls of Keld Head, keeping his mind clean and safe from anymore abuse.

Robbie didn't finish his beer but left and wondered if he would ever be able to remove himself from his impropriety.

Sunday morning and Charlotte was packing, just another day and they would be gone. The head cold she'd had all week had now completely overtaken her and weakened her. She insisted the girls went to church alone.

Charlotte had been satisfied that she had looked after Beth and Irene well. The girls were rested and refreshed. It would be months before she saw them again. Beth would start working at the school in September and begin her training. She was pleased the holiday had been a success; even the chance meeting of Mr Robert Keldas. Beth had told Charlotte of his request to employ Christie if he didn't settle in Northumberland. Charlotte insisted she told her father, and was certain Franklyn would approve with Robbie being a gentleman and a churchman.

Beth and Irene sat quietly in the church, only two of a small congregation of maybe a dozen. Fred was sitting alone at the rear and Beth dearly wanted eyes in the back of her head to see if Robbie had arrived.

The sermon droned on and Beth discreetly slid the sleeve of her coat to check her wrislet. She guessed that in five more minutes it would be over, and she was right. They stood, and turned to leave and Fred was waiting by the door.

'Good day, Beth. Good day, Irene.' And he held his cap and he rolled it nervously.

'Good morning, Freddie.' Beth spoke and looked deeply into his brown eyes as to a clue of Robbie's whereabouts.

'Is your aunt unwell?' Fred was polite.

'Yes, she is, I'm afraid. She has suffered a head cold these last few days.'

'Are you both well?' Fred continued.

69

'Yes, we're fine. And your father?'

'I'm sorry to say his condition has deteriorated. The doctor isn't very optimistic.' And the girls noticed a quaking in Fred's voice.

'And is Robbie with him today?'

'I'm afraid not. I've left my father with the nurse. I must get back.'

'Oh, I'm sorry.' She had a look of dismay.

Fred didn't want to lie. 'I'm afraid he had to go away, miss.'

And Beth's intuition told her Fred was being cautious with his words.

Beth threw her clothes in the trunk, not caring if she folded them or not. That wasn't like her. She'd glanced across to Keld Head every daylight hour watching the tower, hoping Robbie had returned. She could see his cattle and sheep roaming the lush green pasture, spots of white, black and brown. The last two days had been spent in Ambleside buying gifts, but around every corner and at the sound of a male voice she looked for him.

She held a pain of disappointment but couldn't let Irene or her aunt know how foolish she felt to be so smitten by this man who'd caught her in his alluring arms. And as much as she tried to fool herself all was well, she guessed it wasn't and Fred had clearly hesitated over his brother. But if Beth could have seen further, she would have seen an outline of a man on a grey mare, sleeping rough in the hills beyond Keld Head, then Greenup Edge, High Raise, the track to Rosthwaite, Stonethwaite; Robbie was heading slowly westward, slumped in the saddle.

He stayed the night with a family in Rosthwaite who he knew well. They fed him but were disturbed because for the first time in his life they noticed that he was melancholy. He rode through Seathwaite and usually stopped to say a welcome greeting to farmers and labourers but today he didn't.

Robbie slept one night under Great Gable up at Sty Head; a landscape of untroubled sanctuary, with only Tilly as his companion. Eating dry bread as he sat by the small tarn and wishing he was in it; chewing the crust and ripping it with his teeth as a pastime rather than a pleasure. Dried grasses and wild mountain thyme acted as a pillow, their tiny flowers only visible to those eager enough to peer. He rubbed some of the purple flowers in his hand and the sweet scent reminded him of Beth; he couldn't rid himself of this woman. Robbie had nearly made the biggest mistake of his life if she was Franklyn Richardson's daughter. He wished he could mutate and lose this skin he was in and be another, then he could love her, unbiased and unafraid.

Tilly slowed in her pace as she reached the familiar land under Sty Head. She had a reluctance to drop into the valley below, into her former cruel and meagre home in Wasdale. Robbie gave her part of a small bag of provender that he had in a saddle bag, knowing there would be little for her the other side of this mountain other than grass.

He'd once considered at death he would want his remains taken to this mountain pass. He lay back on a flat rock to watch the sun drop behind Gable. Some had branded these lands as savage, yet the people below, some of them good, some of them not so much were hospitable sorts. They had to fight nature to farm this land; but if they befriended you, you were closer than a brother, but if they scorned you, you were worse than an animal.

As Robbie left Keld Head he knew his father was dying and he would never see him breathe again. And in this he was cowardly. He didn't want the memory of a corpse in his head; he had enough of that in South Africa. He knew it was wrong to leave Fred with more worry and to work and grieve alone, but he couldn't help himself. He'd left his father sleeping; the nurse knitting socks frantically at his bed side; and Robbie could no longer stand the constant clicking of needles. He'd kissed his father and in a waking dream Samuel had seen his fine boy, touched his face and his fine skin with his hands and slept again, satisfied the son of his youth had made a handsome man and was now settled at Keld Head.

Robbie turned Tilly forwards and dropped down the rocky path under Great Gable. Her hooves digging into the shaley path, her teeth munching on the snaffle bit; her only consolation was that Robbie was walking with her, holding the reins, allowing her head, and talking softly.

He tethered Tilly under the low roof of Raike's Farm; he could hear children playing in the yard; there was some washing on the line that still looked grubby and had probably hung there for weeks. He loosened Tilly's girth on the saddle, watered her and rubbed her neck before heading for the farmhouse. As he stooped under the lintel of the back door, a chicken flung itself at him, scratching and squawking, brushing passed him leaving a black sooty air in its wake and covering Robbie in soot and filth.

'What in heaven's name's going on?'

A youth of about twelve slid down the grey slates on the roof like he was skiing, and landed at the door behind Robbie, laughing, 'Has it worked, Mam?'

Nance Wilding emerged holding the latest Wilding offspring in her arms, 'Well, it's nivver our Robbie? I'm sorry aboot yer shirt.'

'Nay, matter about my shirt, Nance. Don't treat God's creatures like this.'

'Well, yonder awd hen's near useless when it comes to gitting eggs, but she's a fine bird to chuck down yonder chimly. We 'ad a blockage and Edwin's nay bothered aboot it.'

Robbie moaned inwardly. The kitchen smelt foul.

'Edwin's not 'ere, Robbie,' and she swayed aggressively from side to side to rock the baby. 'Ye can stay if yer like but there's nay food ... the best I can offer is a warm bed.' But that was no consolation as that would be filthy too.

'Where is he?'

'Ye'll know better than me where he teks 'issell off te. He's nay worked in yonks and the bairns are starving.'

Robbie took from his jacket a roll of money, unfurled some notes and pushed them in Nance's hand. He wouldn't sleep here or she would steal the rest.

'Feed the bairns, Nance, don't give a thing to Edwin ... if the man won't work he shouldn't eat.'

'You're too good for these parts Robbie Kellet.'

'Some would say otherwise.'

'You look sickly?' Nance said.

'No, I'm not ill.' He leant back against the stove, it was stone cold. 'I'll stay at the inn, Nance. When Edwin comes home, tell him where I am, please.'

'How's yer father?'

Robbie didn't reply because he didn't believe she was really interested.

As he left the farmhouse he could hear the child crying louder. He walked slowly back to Tilly. 'You're not staying here tonight my girl, so don't worry.' He tightened her girth on the saddle, mounted onto the mare's back as she spun around in a hurry to be away from Raike's Farm.

Robbie slept long and hard in the back bedroom at the Wasdale Inn with his roll of money under his pillow. In the morning he heard the little Herdwick sheep droning and bleating on the fell side. And as a maid crept into his room, he turned over in bed and told her to clear off. He slept for close to three days, his only worry was that Tilly was safe. He'd paid the landlord well to feed her and keep her under lock and key, but Tilly would be restless and wanting to be grazing free. And she became the only reason he eventually emerged. He washed and shaved and put on a clean shirt from his bag and walked under the great mountain of Pillar's shadow. Tilly heard him whistling and called out. He leant on the stable door and spoke softly to her, thinking she would be the only female he would ever flirt with again.

'Dang it young, Robbie! I've bin backards and forards fer close to two days, ye lazy lummack.'

Robbie wheeled around. 'Edwin!'

'What's the matter, son. Tis Grasmere nay grand enough fer thi?'

'Oh, Grasmere's fine alright and so is Keld Head.'

'You then is it...? Itchy feet?'

'Aye, something like that.'

'Did ye want me, like?'

'Not really, Edwin, the day I want you will be the day my mind becomes deranged, but saying you're here.'

Edwin was clean and he was smiling and Robbie guessed he'd been home and eaten some of the forbidden food.

'Come on and I'll buy thi some grub.' Edwin said.

'What, with my money, Edwin. Have you any left of what I paid for Tilly?'

'Aye, well, yonder bookmaker in Millom 'as most on it ... greedy so and so.'

'Then buy me a meal with what you have left, Edwin, because there'll be no more.'

The two men ate outside, Robbie was crunching the end of a chicken bone in his teeth, and Edwin could no longer chew with his sparse toothless mouth.

'Mook found me in Grasmere.'

'Aye, thowt he might.' Edwin watched Robbie eating. 'I did nay tell him.'

'No, I hope not, but there's many around here who would.'

'He'll leave you be, now.'

'He'll never leave me be, Edwin, and you know it. Not now that I have Tilly.'

'I daren't like to see thi in sore straits, young Robbie. You never let the likes o' Jimmy Mook get te thi.' Edwin did care for his young friend. 'Can we do owt te help, thi lad? Nance's baking bread today.'

'If only a crust of bread would take away my problem, I'd eat a whole loaf.'

'Ye father, then...? 'as he passed?'

'Probably, and I guess Freddie's on his horse right now looking for me.'

'Ye should nay let young Freddie chase aboot after yer, Robbie.'

'A wise thing to say for such a feckless idiot,' Robbie smirked.

'Well, if it's Jimmy Mook that's bothering thi. I'll lather him cold when I set upon his gowky fizzog. He'll be in yonder watter. Drownded ... a gonner.'

74

How many times had Robbie heard Edwin say that; Robbie didn't want Jimmy Mook dead and in the bottom of the lake for he knew he too had a young family to feed, as much as he despised the man.

'Tilly's in grand fettle.' Robbie said.

'Aye, she's in better fettle wi you. So if thi's nay ferreting over Jimmy and yonder grey mare, it must be thi father yers grievin' aboot or a lass, but I've nivver seen thi brood as much.'

Robbie didn't reply and thought of Beth and Charlotte Webb with two b's and their righteousness made him despise his friends even the more.

Robbie lay back on the seat in the August sunshine. Dark clouds gathered out at sea and in an hour it would be raining in Wasdale. He wondered if he set off back now he could reach Sty Head before the worst of the rain fell, then an hour maybe and a dry lodge at Seathwaite.

He left Edwin in the garden sleeping and dreaming of home baked bread.

Then rain came in drifts as suspected. He found his cape and put on his broad brimmed hat, a gift from his father, and he trudged on to Stockley Bridge.

In driving rain, Tilly's ears pinned back but she still walked swiftly, breaking into a trot on flatter parts of the path. Rain ran down Robbie's cheeks and back. He didn't care if he was sodden, he somehow felt he deserved it, but was sorry he had made it hard for Tilly.

He looked up through the gloom as fine mist blew over Seathwaite Fell, and he saw coming up the path from the ghyll a man on a horse. It was someone on a bay and he knew it was Fred. They met on the path beside the beck facing each other. Robbie moved Tilly in closer beside Fred's horse, and the two brothers were united as their legs touched, as the horses jostled. 'He's gone, Robbie.' Fred was saturated, his brown eyes reddened with grief. Water dripped from Robbie's hat onto his lap; he didn't speak but just looked compassionately at the younger man. But Fred at the sight of his older brother was overtaken by grief and yielded to the tears, as his chest heaved and he moaned. Robbie reached across as the two horses fidgeted, anxious to keep moving. He laid his hand on Fred's arm and gripped it tight and waited. Finally Fred composed himself and turned his horse. The gelding responded, its back now to the rain.

'I don't want you to ever come looking for me again, Freddie. You're too fine a man for this.'

And although Fred knew it was a tough request to comply with, he also knew it was a tough quest doing this search, looking for his wayward brother and he knew he could never stop.

In silence they walked to Stockley Bridge. Fred couldn't see the tears in Robbie's eyes as they mingled with the raindrops. As they reached Seathwaite, Robbie slid off Tilly's back and left Fred sheltering under a hay barn. He banged on a cottage door and pleaded with the woman to let them stay the night.

8
NORTHERN LIGHTS

Beth had just posted a letter to Christie. They had parted tearfully as he had headed north for Morpeth. She was sorry that the only man she could write to was her brother. Beth knew of other friends, Irene especially, who had found suitors and Beth's trip to Lakeland and her father's wish to one day marry had put a desire in her heart, which was now strongly rooted and nurtured by the attention of one Robert Keldas.

Beth had foolishly watched the postman for three weeks in a vain hope that Robbie would send a request for Christie to work at Keld Head. She felt foolish that she had allowed herself to be so smitten by a man she hardly knew, so disappointed she hadn't seen him in church on that last Sunday. She often tried to recall him asking for her address and wondered if she had imagined it. She had spoken to her father of the offer and how Robbie had invited them to look around the tower at Keld Head and had guided them to Tarn Crags and the waterfalls. She had also told Christie of Robbie's kindness and behaviour in church and the offer of some dairy experience if he ever needed it.

She had begun her new work at the school, helping the children paint and draw; walking them out on nature study classes, picking up from the ground sweet chestnuts and hazelnuts and sketching the intricacies of their seed casings. She decided not to allow her heart any more grief over Robert Keldas and let it be focused on teaching.

Christie's life in Northumberland was never going to succeed as long as he told himself he would hate it. He felt it cold, despite only being late September as cold winds chilled by the North Sea mercilessly attacked his fragile body. He found the locals to be friendly enough but the farm labourers were hardened men. He lived close to a colony of miners; hard working but uncouth. And although many were friendly sorts, some of the younger farm labourers regularly taunted Christie over his delicate stature.

He worked most days with Irene's suitor, Tommy Bright. Tommy was the only good thing there. Christie was sure his father could never have seen his lodgings, as unlike Tommy's cottage, Christie's lodgings were pitiable; a small room in the top of an old farmhouse with a crack in the window pane, taped over, that allowed an eerie wind to whistle through it and mingle with the noise of mice scratching under his bed. There was porridge for breakfast most days, wholesome enough but sticky and dry as it had been put onto boil at four in the morning ready for the men. The land owner was a self - righteous man called Peter Ridgley, a friend of his father's, who didn't let his righteousness touch the farm. Tommy Bright had tolerated working as gamekeeper and river bailiff because he didn't want to let Franklyn Richardson down; the pay was good, and if he could work hard maybe he could propose to Irene and someday bring her here to live.

Tommy believed Peter Ridgley treated Christie well, apart from the lodgings, but he could see Christie was struggling. He had heard the name calling, lads whistling at him and saying he was like a woman. Tommy sheltered Christie as often as he could, but then he too would get an earful. Christie was supposed to be there six months; this would have to be his career.

One evening Christie burst into Tommy's lodge. 'I can't bear this anymore. Someone has taken money from my room.'

'You should na leave thi ackers lying aboot, Christie.'

'I thought I could trust them. I know I'm naive.'

Tommy looked at Christie and wanted to tell him to shape up a bit. Be a man. And looking at this angel faced youth, the blonde stubbly chin was a poor attempt to grow a beard like his father's. And Christie's curls were anything but manly and his soft voice, once beautiful in song in the Sand Hutton church choir, but now was breaking in its tone.

'If you kick back at em, Christie, they'll do it all the more. Just have a laugh on em, and get on wi it.'

Christie sat in front of Tommy's fire, wringing the soft white flesh of his hands. 'They'll never stop, Tommy, they hate me.'

'They daren't hate you boy, that's just as it is in life, you've been sheltered ovver much at Sugar Hills.' Tommy pushed the kettle on the fire grate. 'Look, sleep here tonight. In the morning you'll be warmer and better fer it.'

When Tommy awoke next morning Christie had gone. He folded up the discarded blanket and looked at the clock.

Tommy followed his usual routine and went to check the game; check the guns; feed the dogs; walk the woodland and the river bank. He was just on one of those walks around bait time when he heard some men working in the field and was relieved to see Christie among them, as the October sunshine managed to push through a dreek day. The land was being ploughed and harrowed, corn was being drilled and, as the men threw off their jackets, they stopped to take their bait and let the work horses rest, Tommy saw Christie leaning on a tree trunk, alone, reading. The other men in a group were laughing. Tommy walked away.

As Christie leant against a tree he relaxed, he was sleepy. He put his book down and shut his eyes. Suddenly an arm enveloped him around the neck as someone put their hand over his mouth. Christie grappled and wriggled attempting to be free, but had no strength.

'Quiet, boy, if ye know what's good fer thee.'

He could hear laughing as another arm enveloped him at his waist and the more Christie struggled the more hands were upon him, tearing at his clothes and stripping him. Pulling at the buttons on his shirt and trousers and ripping them. Bare-chested, Christie struggled to free himself as the white skin on his upper body and torso was coated in green paint.

Tommy heard the muffled screams and ran back along the river bank. Jumping and struggling through reeds and bushes; he knew it would be Christie. On reaching the style he saw him struggling beneath five young men, as they painted his partially clad body.

Tommy cocked his rifle and screamed at them and the laughter stopped.

He jumped the style and cautiously approached, 'I don't care if I'm sacked fer this. But ye'll lay no more hands on that youth.'

'Just 'avin a bit of a lark, Tommy.'

'Well, there'll be nay more at that boy's bidding.'

Christie now free, set about a useless task of cleaning himself of the paint as he pulled his clothes back on. He didn't cry, he was livid. He went back to the farmhouse, to his room, and grabbed the few personal possessions he had.

Christie wasn't seen again.

Tommy told Mr Ridgley what had happened and the men were sent out looking for the boy. Reluctantly Peter Ridgley wrote to Sir Franklyn.

Franklyn Richardson took the letter from Peter Ridgley in his hand and slapped it down on his desk. 'Bethy, I have some bad news for you ... please sit down.'

Beth's face flushed but she wouldn't sit.

'It's Christie.'

'What's happened, Father?' Her heart melted.

'The boy's missing again. Ridgley's men have searched the land for three days and can't find him. Tommy Bright said he was having trouble with some of the farm boys.'

'What can we do?'

'I don't know ... I don't know. I always believed Christie to be weak, but now I think differently. If he gets something into his head nothing will avert him. If he wants to leave Ridgley's place then that's his decision.'

'But Father, he's only sixteen!'

'And sixteen is enough these days. There are lads of seven working in the mills and mines. Christie will have to make his own choices in life, if he doesn't want me to do it for him.'

'Please don't abandon him, he couldn't bear it ... I couldn't bear it.'

Franklyn came to Beth and put his hand on her shoulder. 'Bethy ... Bethy. I'll not leave him. If he returns like the prodigal, there'll be a fattened calf waiting; you should know me better than that. But how can we search the length and breadth of the country for a boy who is weak in form but with the mind of an ox?'

Beth looked for Christie every day; she went to the abbey ruins early each morning thinking he might be there. She left a note under a stone, begging him to contact them, pleading with him to come home. She didn't understand why nobody seemed to do anything. She couldn't understand her father's decisions. She feared for Christie's safety as no other and believed he wasn't strong enough to find his way through life.

   As she sat in her bedroom window watching the lane for any signs of the boy she noticed the little glass snowscene that her father had bought her in Westmorland. She picked up the globe and saw the pretty cottage of Mr Wordsworth. She shook it and held it close to her eyes and let the little flakes of tinsel entrance her. As they settled to the floor she noticed how calm and tranquil it looked and hoped that one day her life would be as settled.

Robbie was alone in a field of stubble, they didn't harvest much corn but what had been left by the former owners had been sold. Robbie had re-sown with grass to have extra grazing for the herd he wished to expand. He'd had a hard morning ploughing with one of the horses and now his back ached. He doubted he could ever afford any of the new machinery that was speeding up and improving farming; Robbie loved his horses and he was a man of tradition and he would become set in time. He finished the furrow close to the wall and went to find his lunch that he'd wrapped in a white cloth. He untied the horse and took it to the stream for a drink, then left it eating grass by the river bank. He looked for his pack and it was missing. He pushed his corduroy cap back on his head, bemused. He looked around but was completely alone. He wondered if on his early morning stroll to the meadow he had left it on the kitchen table. But no, he clearly remembered leaving it by the wall.

As he wandered close to the wall, still searching, he found an empty stoneware jar of beer, discarded and smashed as if it had been dropped in a hurry. He looked in the near distance and couldn't decide whether to walk back to the farmhouse. He glanced at the horse and the field and thought another hour would finish it. He left the horse grazing and went to the stream and cupped his hands and drank the clear water. Then he splashed some on his face and rubbed the long dark strands of hair back off his forehead and sat in the grass watching the horse eating.

Robbie had worked through grief as he suspected he might, weeks had passed since the death of his father, and although expected, it had been hard to grasp. He had never known his life without his father's influence. He'd loved Robbie as any father would, too much sometimes when discipline was needed. Samuel had filled a space in Robbie's life and now it was empty. There was also a vacuum at Keld Head; the only relief from his father's death was that the infernal Mrs Borsch had left, handsomely compensated, and the clicking knitting needles gone with her.

He waited a half an hour to rest the horse, then he tackled her up again.

The field was done in the hour as Robbie had expected, he was famished and now his back ached the more, his legs weakened so he wandered back up the lane to the farm. As he took the horse past Tilly's stable door, out of the corner of his eye he noticed it slowly closing. He stood motionless and watched and listened; not a sound. It would be Mook.

Robbie quietly dropped the long reins on the plough horse's neck, and let it walk alone to the stone water trough. He edged quietly to the stable door and kicked it suddenly open with the flat of his boot. It ripped open.

'I'll kill you Mook if you come here again!' Robbie shouted and burst in.

He heard a gasp and saw in the corner a youth, blue eyed and muddied in face with straggly blonde hair holding the cloth with Robbie's bait in his hand. Tilly was beside him, eating hay.

'Don't kill me, mister.'

'Who in heaven's name are you boy?'

'Please don't hurt me.' And the boy pulled his knees in close to his chest, clinging to a rough coat over his body.

'Did you steal my bait?'

'I'm sorry, sir, but I was starving.'

Robbie eyed the boy then mercifully stepped back as he saw his terror. 'There's a gaol over yonder fell for the likes of you.'

'Is there, sir; I'm sorry, please don't crack on me.'

'Where are you from?'

'I'm from Northumberland. I've walked for three weeks, I think. I don't even know what day it is.'

'You should have stayed there lad, why come here?'

'I was looking for a gentleman. A Mr Robert Keldas.' Christie eased a little.

'Was you now, and why's that?'

'My sister said he may have work for me.'

Robbie, momentarily stunned, gripped the stable door with his hand but Christie didn't notice his shock.

'What's your name, boy?'

'Christopher Richardson.'

'And what's your sister's name?'

'Elizabeth. My father is ...'and Robbie held up his hand to stop him. 'Don't tell me anymore.'

'I'm sorry, sir.'

'Wait here. I don't want you to leave this building until I come and get you no matter how long that takes, you hear me? Keep an eye on that grey mare, don't let her out.' But Christie wasn't planning on going anywhere.

Robbie closed the stable door and bolted it. He tethered his work horse up to the fence and went indoors to find his housekeeper.

'Nora. Could you prepare a good meal please, enough for two...? I'm famished. Someone stole my bait; a fox, no doubt. Be quick about it please, I'm in a hurry. Do we have any beef left?'

'Yes, but it'll be cold.'

'Cold will do. Once you've done it leave it on the table and go home.... I'll see you tomorrow.'

He went to the store and filled two brass pans with water. He pulled a tin bath from the closet and slid it onto the kitchen floor. He ran upstairs to his father's room and raked through the few clothes that were left. He held a white shirt up to the light to examine it: spotless. He found some underwear, socks, trousers, and neatly folded them in a pile, the boy was small, his own clothes wouldn't fit.

He pulled the counterpane off the bed and checked the mattress. Found clean sheets, pillows, blankets, re-checked the room, and left.

Robbie went back to Christie. He was still sitting in the same place, holding his arms around his knees.

'Watch the kitchen door.' Robbie pointed to the farmhouse. 'When you see a woman leave, come indoors and I will see to you.'

'I'm sorry, sir. But will you be able to put me in contact with Mr Robert Keldas?'

'You can see him soon enough, but I think you should wash and change first.'

Nora Given left and Robbie waited by the stove watching the pans boiling. He lifted one carefully, his hand wrapped in a towel, and tipped the hot water into the tin bath. The door knocked and Robbie shouted, 'Come in, Christopher.'

The boy edged for the first time into the sturdy walls of Keld Head and thus began a friendship that would bind these two families indelibly.

'We have no luxuries here. You're welcome to some good food, cold though it is. But you can have a hot bath and I have found you some clean things.'

Christie humbled himself by bowing slightly. 'When can I meet Mr Robert Keldas, sir? It concerns me that I am putting you to trouble.'

'How did you know Robert Keldas lived here?'

'My sister told me that there was a chance of employment.'

'There is a chance of employment, boy. But this is a respectable household, I don't hold with thieves.' Robbie's teasing was imperceptible to the boy.

'I'm woefully sorry, sir. I have never stolen a thing in my life accept for these three weeks I have walked from Northumberland.'

'You are well spoken, Christopher. You use refined language.'

'Thank you sir.'

'How did you know this farm?'

'My sister told me there was a farmhouse in Grasmere with a tower and saying this is the only one, I hoped Mr Keldas might be here.'

'Then I am he.'

Christie rubbed his hand to his face; relief. 'Would it be possible to apply for the position then, sir?'

'You clean yourself up first then I will see you clearer....Take off those filthy rags. Do you mind wearing a dead man's clothes?'

'As long as he's not still in them.'

The crooked smile emerged; this boy would get on well with Robbie.

Robbie was about to leave him discreetly when he noticed green paint on Christie's body. He wandered up to the boy and pulled his sodden shirt to one side. 'What happened to you, Christopher?'

'This is why I left Northumberland; because of the paint!'

He ripped his shirt off and Robbie stepped backwards. The boy smelt rancid. 'Who did this to you?'

'Farm lads, sir.... Working with me.'

'So why did they do this?'

'They said I was green.'

'And are you green, Christopher?'

'Yes, sir. I guess I am.'

'Then they did right.' Robbie threw the boy a towel. 'Never run from trouble. A coward dies many times but a brave man dies only once, remember that. Get in the bath and I will scrub you clean.'

Robbie sat across the table from Christie and watched him eat the first good meal he had had in weeks that he hadn't stolen or begged for.

'So what am I to do with you?'

'If I could stay here, sir. My sister said you could train me up.'

'Shouldn't you be training in Northumberland?'

'I can't go back. If you have no work, then I will leave.'

'And where would you go?'

'I'd just travel. Until I found work.'

'Aye and you'd be dead before the winter's out, Christopher.'

Christie lowered his head and stopped eating. 'I'll work for nothing, sir. I'll sleep in the stable.'

'Yes, I have no money and I need a guard for the horse.' Robbie eyed him and awaited the boy's reaction, but there was none. 'Nay ... you'll sleep in my father's room. It's ready for you. Did you tell anyone you were coming here?'

'No, sir. No one knows where I am.'

Robbie shook his head and wandered around the kitchen then stood with hands in pockets looking out the window across to the old Pele tower. He picked up and watered the red geranium that Beth had bought him, now permanently situated on the window sill. 'Then we must put that right straight away.' Robbie was ashamed; he knew his hypocrisy would be apparent to God alone; him a rogue and wanderer counselling a young man about the rights and wrongs of life.

'I don't think I dare go back, sir.'

'Then you must write and tell them you're here and safe. Your family will be beside themselves with worry.'

'I can't write to my father, you see he will send me back to Morpeth.'

'Then you must write to your sister.'

'I'll not write to her, sir. I wouldn't know what to say. I am ashamed of what I have become. Would you write for me, please? I know she respects you and speaks well of you. She said you were a good man.'

'You have a lot of demands young Christopher for a lad that I should let sleep in my stable and look after my grey mare. Your sister knows very little of me.'

Robbie stayed awake until the early hours. He sat by the hearth until the fire died down. He'd sent Christie to bed and told him to rest for three days and not worry about work. He went to the bureau and opened a small wooden box and found Beth's hand written address. He had a dilemma, and yet maybe someone was holding him in his mighty hand, urging him and coaxing him to act; giving him a second chance to right all his wrongs. Or maybe it was temptation sent by the devil himself wanting to drag him further into the mire he was trying to get out of. Who did this boy really belong to, who was sleeping safe and reassured upstairs? The innocence of this knowledge was truly blissful but the reality, fearsome. Yet why did it feel so good to help this boy? and why did it hurt so bad? As reckless as it was, Robbie wanted to remain in innocence and would go to great lengths to do so and decided, as Beth's young brother slept long and hard in his father's old room to put pen to paper.

Keld Head Farm
Grasmere
Westmorland

Dear Elizabeth

In the first instance I hope you don't feel it improper for me to write to you as I worried I may have imposed myself upon you when you visited Westmorland, but an event has occurred that I could not prevent it.

I believe I have some good news for you and your father and it is under this circumstance alone that I write. It is my pleasure to say that I have in my possession the precious life of your young brother, who has travelled long miles to find me and to seek employment.

Christopher is safe here with me at Keld Head. He told me you had mentioned the possibility of work here and I am happy that you felt you could do that.

He has hassled me to write as he feels incapable due to remorse. But he wanted to put you at ease. I know I should have written to your father but Christopher insisted I confide in you and you alone. I do not know if this was a sensible decision to make as I fear neither of us appear to be endowed with wisdom, and I suspect your brother maybe the victor if it was challenged.

So I beg that you pass on to your father that Christopher can stay here as long as he wishes and come into my employment. He will have free board and lodgings and a small allowance. He told me of your farm at Sugar Hills and that humbles me and although Keld Head may be inferior, I can honestly say I can teach him to be a good stockman. The only request I make on Christopher's behalf is that no one attempt to return him to Northumberland or back home and he is adamant if that happened, he'll leave.

But I must add that if you and you alone wish to write to him or visit him that would be agreeable.

I am sorry I know nothing of your family and your circumstances but I genuinely want to help the boy.

Incidentally, while I am writing, I must tell you the sorry news that my father passed away. He was peaceful to the end. I'm afraid I made a poor nurse and am now in low spirits. Christopher will be a good companion for me. My brother, Freddie, would send his regards if he knew I was writing and so I send them in his behalf.

And finally, although I should have done this foremost, I ask after your good health. I am certain you would have been anxious and I hope as the bearer of good news it makes me happy to know I may bring you some comfort.

Your friend

Robert Keldas

The pen scratched away at the rough manuscript, the nib was gently laden with ink as not to spoil the precious document; the hand writing, neat and masculine.

9
LIONS AND LAMBS

Irene saw Robbie's letter, sitting with others on a silver plate on the polished oak hall stand. She dusted around it, peering, looking over her shoulder, and looking again. Yes, the post mark definitely said Westmorland. She didn't recognise the hand writing; and it certainly wasn't Charlotte Webb's as hers was as precise in nature as she was. No this was a man's hand, neat and articulate.

She glanced at the clock and in twenty minutes she could stop for lunch.

Once she had finished helping her mother serve up, there was only her father and the bailiff to feed as Franklyn Richardson was away. She could run to the school with the letter for Beth, if her mother agreed.

She finished cleaning, her mind fully absorbed in the letter. What a wonderful time to come when they were all still reeling over Christie's flight.

The meal was served and Irene begged her mother to take the letter. Franklyn wouldn't be home until late evening.

Irene pulled on her bonnet and jacket and hurried the two miles to the school, flustered and breathing heavily, she walked to the back of the small playground and hoped Beth was outside, but she could see her through the window in the classroom teaching as the children had obviously finished their lunch.

Beth had her head lowered, painting a scene. The children were doing the same. Irene tapped on the window and Beth looked up; fourteen young heads turned around.

Wondering at Irene's sanity, Beth composed herself and went to the window. She opened it and Irene whispered. 'It's from him ... it's from Westmorland.... It must be Robbie.' And she handed the letter to Beth.

'Hurry away, Irene ... bless you,' and she shut the window.

Beth returned to the desk at the front of the class, checked her wristlet and waited. She could do no more. She couldn't leave the children and she couldn't risk being caught opening her mail, she would have to wait another hour while they painted.

She lifted her sketchbook and glanced at the drawing. It was a small Pele tower, set in a hillside of rocks and crags. This was the fifth one she had sketched. She stared at the sketch but was unable to re-start. Putting her hand in her pocket she caressed the soft paper envelope and longed to read its contents.

Beth stared long and hard at the unopened envelope; if Irene had been there she would have chastised her. Then she looked at the post mark, the type of paper, the black ink and the well written letters of her name. She took a small palette knife from her desk, and carefully sliced open the envelope, not daring to damage it because this was a letter she would keep for the rest of her life.

Taking a deep breath, not daring to look in case Irene had been mistaken, she carefully unfolded the letter and saw the words on an embossed letter heading that said Keld Head. She let her breath go and read.

The wonderful news that Christie was safe with Robbie momentarily overwhelmed her more than the import of the letter. She stopped reading and let her head fall onto the desk; relief. Tears of joy filled her eyes. She muttered a brief and silent prayer of gratitude to some almighty force that had heard her petition. She read on and re-read, repeating over in her head his humble words. *"I worried I may have imposed myself upon you when you visited Westmorland," "If you and you alone wish to write or visit him that would be agreeable." "He told me of your farm at Sugar Hills and that humbles me."*

Despite the good news Beth found words of disappointment as she later read them to Irene, but Irene was more positive.

'He says it makes him happy to bring you comfort, Beth, he's a keeper is that one.'

'A keeper, yes maybe, but for whom?'

Beth reluctantly showed the letter to her father and she hoped he wouldn't insist that Christie came home, but Franklyn was overcome with thankfulness and could do no more than instantly pray for the soul of his dear boy and kindness of the one that had befriended him.

'And is this the Mr Keldas who helped you in church, Bethy?'

'It is Father, yes. His brother is a gentle sort, too.'

'Then I owe this gentleman a great deal. And, despite his humility, I believe he used much wisdom in writing to you in the first instance, as not to disturb Christie. I feel it should be you that replies and with much gratitude. And will you thank him on my behalf and insist that if Christie ever becomes a burden he must send him home at once.'

But Franklyn didn't tell Beth his underlying feeling that this may be a permanent attachment for her. He remembered the farm in Grasmere with the Pele tower and thought it a grand place; he recalled the mischievous flicker in Beth's eyes as she spoke of the young Mr Keldas; who was he to deter the hand of God.

Christie couldn't hold a ewe still, but Robbie didn't mind because at least someone was holding it. Nora's husband, Albert, was employed for daily milking and that was all. Robbie also had a shepherd come labourer, Jackie Bainbridge, a kindly, hard working man. Christie would only count as a half.

Robbie didn't criticise him, nor flatter him, but just laughed. Christie had brought a lighter side to life at Keld Head since the death of Robbie's father and even his angelic appearance brought a kind of dignity to the place. Robbie told the other men to go easy on him; no one knew who he was or where he had come from, only Fred was privy to that, and he implored Robbie to find out the truth about Christie's father, but Robbie always declined.

The Keldas brothers enjoyed teaching the boy and he was a willing student helping at Spickle Howe as well as Keld Head. He no longer jibbed at the tasks he was given and as the weeks turned into months his physical shape altered, his height progressed with good cooking from Nora; Christie felt he would never want to leave.

The boy soon learned of Robbie's personality, and began to love him as a brother. He didn't like it if Robbie disappeared, as he still did for days at a time, but Christie didn't complain like the other men; he just got on with things. Letters passed between Beth and Christie frequently, and after a polite and welcome reply from Beth to Robbie, he became wary of any further contact and learned all he wanted from Christie; questions were asked and carefully worded.

The nights drew in and the sheep were brought to lower pastures to flush them on good grass ready for mating, their tails cleaned and dagged of muck, ready for spring and the oncoming lambing time. But Christie's love became Tilly and he found a true friend in the grey mare. One day Robbie found him in the stable grooming the horse, rubbing her coat energetically, keeping her hocks clean of mud. Robbie examined Tilly, then looked over his shoulder to see they were alone, 'Keep a watchful eye on Tilly.'

'I really love her.' The boy replied.

'I can see you do, but others feel the same way, she's valuable. If you ever see any strangers about the place … let me know… always lock the stable door when you finish with her.'

'Is it Mook you're worried about?' Christie looked into Robbie's eyes and awaited a reaction.

'What do you know of Mook?'

'Nothing, sir, nothing at all.' Christie was embarrassed at the urgent tone to Robbie's voice. 'It's just that the day when you found me in the stable, you thought I was Mook. You said, *"Come out Mook or I'll kill you!"* '

'Yes, and I had a better surprise that day,' and Robbie threw the saddle on the mare, flattened the girth then pulled it tight. 'I used to think I was a young man, Christie, and when my father was alive, I was. But now you're here, I feel older in years, but maybe someday you can help me be older in mind. I'm going away… I don't know when I'll be back, maybe an hour, maybe a week.'

'Do you have business?'

'Yes, I have an appointment with my mind, and until I meet it and manage it, it will never be satisfied.'

Christie pulled off the horse's halter and slid the bit of the bridle into Tilly's mouth, then stretching upwards to reach the top of her head he slid the bridle over her ears. He would say no more; sorry Robbie was leaving him in what seemed to be sore spirits.

'If you're worried about anything, tell the men or Freddie. But don't ... and I repeat, don't ever come looking for me will you.'

'No sir.'

Robbie had been away three days, the late autumn sunshine and the unseasonal warmth kept him away. He rode over Dunmail to St John's in the Vale, stayed a night at an inn close to Threlkeld, then on under Mungrisdale Beck and topped Souther Fell. He saw no signs of the cavalier army supposed to haunt the fell, and wondered if he did see them he might join them, his mood was sombre. Robbie was still grieving.

Back on the road home he stayed with a woman in St John's who had a guest house and a stable; he avoided the road as much as he could. The woman at the guest house had a daughter called Clarissa Hutchinson, she was only sixteen, and she reminded Robbie of Beth. He was attracted to her and she him. Robbie liked her sense of fun; she was a passive, kindly sort of lass. Loved animals and children and she managed to tempt him out of his gloom. She walked the high fells with him and as they rounded the ridge to Clough Head and on to the high ridges he kissed her and wished she was another.

'I might return when you're a bit older and bring you home with me,' he said.

Clarissa thought with his roguish charm, he would say this to all the women he met, and she would be right.

He lingered in St John's longer than he should, as a day's riding would have seen him home. It would only be Christie's good humour that would tempt him back.

* * *

93

Christie was digging out a water rail in the paddock when he saw a man in the yard looking in and out of each building, then banging on the farmhouse door. At first fear seized him but his love for Robbie took control and he walked up behind the man and purposely startled him. Christie stood tall with a pole staff in his hand. 'Are you Mook?'

Edwin Wilding spun around. 'Bye the lads! What 'ave we getten here?' and laughed.

Christie eyed the man, small, tanned skin, greasy, greying black hair. 'Well, are you Mook?'

'Nay, I'm not Mook, boy, and thi insults me te think yer implications are otherwise. Where's Robbie?'

'I'm sorry, sir, but he's away.'

'Away? Aye, that figures.... How long's 'e bin gone?'

'Two or three days.'

'Did he state where?'

'No sir, he just told me not to go looking for him.'

Edwin grinned a wry smile, 'He allus says that. But when yer find him, young feller's glad yer come. Aye, I'm nay Mook lad. My name's Edwin Wilding and daren't ask me te spell it cos I daren't know how, but that's mi name awright. So why did ye think I were Mook?'

'Because Robbie said if he found Mook, he'd kill him.'

'Why, young Robbie could nay kill a pig let alone a man ... any road, I've come te give 'im some advice, like. So what do the call thi, boy?'

'Christopher Richardson.'

'And where thi be from?'

'Sugar Hills ... Thirsk, sir.... That's in Yorkshire.'

'I knows where that is. I sent a bull there on'y this year. Is thi father a preacher man?'

'He is sir.'

'Well I'll be blowed and strike me pink.' And Edwin sat on the mounting block and blew his nose on a filthy red handkerchief. 'By jings, me lad.... This is a yarn. 'as Robbie told thi te say that?'

'No sir.... It's true.... That's who I am.'

'Then why the deuce are you 'ere? And what does Robbie think on yer being Sir Franklyn Richardson's boy?'

'I don't think he knows. He never asks after my father, it's as if he's not interested.'

Edwin swung his short legs and tapped them against the stone and pulled out his pipe.

'My sister found me this place, sir. Robbie's helping me learn farming. My father has 200 acres in Thirsk and one day it will be mine and I have to learn, and quick.'

'Is yer sister beautiful, Christopher?'

'Yes, I believe so, sir.'

'I knew there'd be a lass involved.... I knew summat were mothering 'im.' Edwin laughed. 'And 'as young Robbie getten designs on her, like?'

'I don't think so.'

'Well, mark my words young feller me lad, that sister o' yours 'as broken 'is 'eart, and Robbie's a blasted tapper ... aye, gone in the 'ead, 'e is.'

'Why, sir?'

'He's playin' wi fire, awreet, if he's getten designs on ye sister.... Does yer father approve?'

'I'm sorry, but I don't think Robbie has designs on my sister and besides, my father doesn't know Robbie.'

'Young feller's a blatherin' idiot, Christopher.... I think this tale of yonder father should stay settled wi you an meself, an no other, you 'ear me.... Nivver and I say, nivver, tell Robbie aboot this chat we're 'avin. Let's keep this atween us lad, it's fer the best, believe me.'

Christie lay in his bed that night pondering. He sat up and rested his head against the mahogany board, the springs in the mattress creaked in the silence. This house was desolate without Robbie. He listened for the dogs barking, but he was still alone, his only consolation was that the Givens and Jackie Bainbridge were only a stone's throw away in the cottages on the lane.

95

He didn't like Edwin's secrecy and the implications that Robbie had designs on his sister, but thought he must know better.

He longed for Robbie's return and every noise in the yard, as the gate clicked as Jackie Bainbridge checked the animals; he listened for Tilly's hooves on the cobbles, but nothing. It would be two more nights before Robbie returned.

Christie contemplated going looking for him, hoping as Edwin had implied, Robbie would value his concern. But he knew nothing of these hills and all his days fleeing from Northumberland and being lost over Sticks Pass, sleeping in hedge bottoms or under the shadow of a crag, Christie knew it wouldn't be wise. No, he must stay put. He mused over Edwin's assumptions and he worried that it was the only reason he had been hired. He loved Beth and he could see with his youthful eyes she was beautiful and never considered one day she might wish to marry. The thought niggled him; he would ask Robbie when he returned. Christie didn't know where Edwin Wilding had gone; he disappeared as quickly as he came. Christie told Albert Given, the dairyman, about his visitor, but Albert said Edwin was a friend of Robbie's and despite his manner, a decent sort and not to worry, but Christie wasn't sure.

Robbie stared up in the twilight to the distant tower at Keld Head, eerily shaped amidst the bedarkened hills. He pulled Tilly to a halt and stopped and peered on the horizon as the clear blue sky of a fine day was now darkened by deep blues. Slithers of smoke rose from the chimney pots and a soft meagre lamplight twinkled through the windows, the gaslight was burning as Robbie saw his home and the usual sense of remorse overtook him. He considered Christie living inside Keld Head's walls alone and wondering – hoping he was still there. He shouldn't have left the boy alone, yet, he was no guardian and purely a tutor, and consoled himself with that thought; if not for him Christie would still be sleeping under a hedge, yet his sense of responsibility over-shadowed his sense of reason and he remained guilt ridden.

He clicked Tilly onwards with a slight touch of his heels to her belly; he crossed the beck, through the woods, stealthily moving to his property as he often did, so no one could see him.

He slid off Tilly's back and unlatched the gates and the dogs announced to everyone he was home.

Robbie felt a shock from behind as a man grabbed him by the neck, thrusting his arm under his chin. 'I've bin waiting three days fer thee, Robbie.'

'Man alive, Edwin,' Robbie gasped and tried to turn. 'That had better be the smell of your grimy hands around my neck, and no other.'

Edwin laughed and released him as Robbie wheeled around and grinned.

'Sweet mother of mine, Edwin ... you're a sight for sore eyes.'

'Aye and yer eyes would be the better, lad, if thi let them rest a little. Why ye should o' come and live in this tender valley with this waffey tower . . . gloomy as a prisoner's netty, it is, bye 'eck.'

'It was to get away from the likes of you, Edwin. Are you staying?'

'I've slept, if that's what ye call it, in yonder tower fer three neats. And if thi 'asn't a warm bed I'm gannin back te mi wifey and childer.'

Robbie led Tilly to the stable and Edwin followed. 'If yer can giv us a bit a tatty an' a hot meal . . . mebees a glass o' two o' good strang brew, I'll be gan bi morning.'

Robbie noticed Christie peep through the unlatched farmhouse door. 'Come on boy, do your job and see to Tilly.'

Christie had almost had a seizure when he heard the men wrestling; he liked Edwin's humour but he didn't like to see him with Robbie. And it soon became apparent that in Edwin's presence, Robbie was a different man, cheerful yes, but coarse in language and speech, saying words he didn't understand. And later in the evening as they sat around the table with empty beer bottles and gravy stained plates, Edwin's bad manners were confirmed as he sipped the last of the gravy by tipping the plate to his mouth, then dabbed it clean with Nora's home cooked bread.

'Waint ye have a drop o' tonic, young feller mi lad?' Edwin was fascinated by the boy.

'No sir, I don't drink.'

'You're not of the Temperance Society, are you, Christie?' Robbie asked.

'Lips that touch liquor shall not touch mine.' Christie replied.

'Well, I'll not kiss you boy, but some would want to.' Robbie said as Edwin almost fell off his seat as he laughed.

Then remorse fell as Robbie looked into Christie's bright eyes and clean skin and couldn't help but think of his beautiful sister that he'd tried to forget, wondering if she would have said the same. And afraid Christie would hear worse things as the night drew on, he said. 'Leave us be now, Christie . . . get yourself up the dancers.'

Christie reluctantly slid off his chair; he didn't want to leave Robbie with Edwin. He didn't like Robbie being with Edwin. In his young mind he felt his presence acted as a restraint, but Robbie persisted. 'I don't want Edwin corrupting your young mind like he did mine.'

The door to the stairway closed and Robbie put the beer away. Edwin grinned. 'Since when 'ave I corrupted thee, Robbie? I thinks yer did that thi sen. Becoming sorry now at mi company ... there were a time when thi were glad on it.'

'And I'm sure there will be many more occasions, Edwin. I couldn't forsake that toothless smile of yours, now could I?'

'Well, it's all to yer benefit I've come, travelling long lonely roads, te save thi neck.'

Robbie wandered to the range and threw two logs in the grate and slammed the door shut with his boot.

'I can look after myself.'

'Aye, that's where yer wrang . . . yer canna look after thiself . . . yer father knew it and I believe that young un, Christie, already knows it.'

Robbie mused at his words and pulling a hard chair up to the hearth fell back, letting his head rest on the red tapestry fabric.

'I can't bear to be alone, Edwin. And then I can't bear it to be hemmed in. I can't control that - never could.'

'Well daren't stay alone . . . get thisen a wife! Folks'll talk seeing that youth here and not living in servant's quarters.'

'I thinks if folks knew me well enough they would only see that I'm helping the lad.'

'Nay body round these parts knows that, Robbie.'

'Huh, that's maybe true. But Mook has already dragged my name through the mire in this village. When my father died, we paid that greedy and corrupt solicitor for that fancy name to be put on his headstone, all legal and proper, and when I look at his grave now and see "Samuel Keldas" carved in that beautiful stone, it makes me happy to know he died believing that was true, but I don't know if I can keep temperate as young Christie implied. Blimey, I've seen them women of the Temperance Society and only a blind fool would want to kiss them, anyway.'

'Bye, I'm made up today, lad. You're in better fettle than last time I saw thi.'

'My father used to say that a good name was the first gift you were given, so to treat it with respect, and I didn't. I don't know if I can turn my life around, but I'm trying.'

'There, ye gannin all melancholy again, young Robbie. I daren't like te see thi broodin', I like to see that crooked smile o' yon.'

Robbie sat forward. 'So, tell me why you've really come. It's a long walk over Sty Head just to see my crooked teeth.'

Edwin struggled to stand and pushed the chair back and it screeched on the hard stone floor, his back ached and his legs bowed as he struggled up to the other fireside chair. 'It's Mook and his sister, Sally, they're after thi. They're spoutin' off everywhere. If he can't have Tilly, he'll have you, and thi shirt off thi back, so watch it.'

'Why does he do this to me, Edwin? What have I ever done to him?'

'It's jealousy, that's all.... Who wouldn't be green-eyed o' you. Good looks ... property ... mebee he wants a taste o' it, like. Tilly's a fine mare and he didn't have the ackers to buy 'er, but you did. Any road, it's as well we getten her back.... She'd a done nowt at Mook's sorry spot.'

Robbie thought she was doing "nowt" at Edwin's sorry spot either.

'Any way, it's as well your 'ere now and outta the way, so te speak.'

'Aye, but he soon found me.... I can still smell his stinking breath.' Robbie stood and paced around the kitchen, then looked out under the gaslight to check that the gate in the yard was shut. 'I should mend that gate really,' he shoved his hands deep down into his pockets. 'But while it's difficult to open, it's safer. The dogs always hear it scratching on the cobbles.'

Edwin left as he had said after breakfast and Christie was glad to see the back of him. He noticed Robbie seemed pensive and quiet today, but had thrown his arms around Edwin as they parted. When Robbie came back indoors Christie pulled a letter from his pocket.

Robbie noticed and waited.

'I have news from my sister. It came while you were away.'

Robbie held his breath a moment before he spoke ... 'How is she?'

'Very well, she says.'

'Good, good, I'm glad,' and once again Beth's pretty face came back to his mind.

'Er, she has a question for us, sir.'

'Us, Christie?'

'Yes, sir, us.'

'What's the question?'

'She wants to know if she can come and visit me.'

'Where is the "us", Christie?'

'Well sir, I'll read it if you don't mind.' Christie opened the paper as his hands shook, hoping he could read it properly: "*Father says I can come to Westmorland over the winter while the children are off school for a short break and stay at the Prince of Wales.*" '

Robbie was frustrated with the boy and stood forward, impatient to see her words. Christie noticed his urgency and stepped back.

'It doesn't say "us," Christie, you lied.'

'I never lie sir, never ... let me finish ... please be patient.'

Robbie knew he'd acted rudely and walked away to the door and grabbed his jacket. 'Work needs to be done young man ... no more larking about.'

'But please, please let me finish.' Christie rattled the letter in his hand and held it to Robbie. 'You read it, please.'

'Nay, I won't touch your letter.'

'Well let me finish.' And Christie stood taller, straightened the page and said: ' "*would it be possible to visit you and Robert?*" There you are, "us"!'

Robbie grinned. 'Robert, my Sunday name, eh, from a Sunday girl....Will she come with your aunt with two b's, or pretty Irene?'

'No sir, she'll come alone.'

Cheered greatly by the news, Robbie grabbed the shepherd's stick but the word "alone" struck him as dangerous.

'Can I ask you one question, sir?'

'Be quick with your moidering lad, there's work to be done.'

'I know sir, but could I be indiscreet and ask if you have designs on my sister?'

'You are honest with me, Christie, so I will be honest with you.... Yes, at one time I did. Your sister is a beautiful young woman. What man wouldn't have designs on her, they would be a fool or blind not to.' He lowered his head and put on his hat. 'So why would your father let her travel alone?'

'She is to travel by train and he deemed it to be safe.'

'Why would he feel she could visit here alone?'

'Because my father believes you to be a gentleman, and he knows I would be here.'

'And do you think I'm a gentleman, Christie? Your father can know nothing of me, can he son?'

Christie was stunned as he felt Robbie was hedging around a question that neither knew how to answer. The silence became long and uncomfortable. Christie coughed. 'Most times I believe you to be a gentleman.'

'Then most times you are wrong, Christie.'

'Well, I know you are as kind to the animals as I am. And I believe you do the best for me. But I don't think your friends are very gentlemanly, and they bring out the worst in you ... bad company ... bad habits.'

'You look like an angel and speak words of wrath, but I love your honesty ... so what shall I do. Shall I allow your sister to visit "us"?'

'Well, sir. I would love to see my sister, and she will be happy to see me here and settled with you; it may be good for her.'

'Maybe, maybe not.... Haven't you some cleaning up to do in the dairy?'

'Yes, sir.'

'Then go and do it and when you've finished come back and write a letter to your sister and tell her she can come and visit "us".'

10
GREEN WINTER

It was what they called a green winter; the fields and fells translucent, warm and damp. Droplets of water glistened on the laurels and rhododendron leaves making a shiny glow. Everything sparkled. The birds and wild fowl were happy, preening and bathing in cool water, the visitors arrived and walked. But then the fog came and a dank cold as winter set in. Keld Head's tower became invisible to watchful eyes and Robbie found he loved the fog as it kept him secure, wrapped in its filigree blanket.

He awaited Beth's arrival like a man who knew his future would soon change as quickly as the winter would.

Robbie was no novice when it came to women but a beginner when it came to love. And that thought worried him. Things he would usually say, words of seduction came easily; flattery, impudence and guile. He was a past master but he would have to change.

He allowed himself to think of Beth often, and decided if he still felt the same way about her when his eyes next fell on her innocent countenance, he would have to confess his true feelings and his true personality. But when the day came for her arrival he coerced Fred and Christie to go to Windermere for her.

Robbie feared rejection, something he wasn't accustomed to. He also worried about his impulsive nature if he were alone with her. He showed a wilful naivety and was reckless, and if Franklyn Richardson was Beth and Christie's father he would take that risk. He couldn't bear the truth. He was to hide it under a rock and let it remain there as long as he could. Only Fred knew of his fears but Fred said no more than the usual, that he was being a fool.

103

And so Fred and Christie left for Windermere Station in the trap with Fred's horse, Topper, trotting the twisty road on another dreek and foggy morning.

The train was slow and Beth was excited. She clung to a leather travelling bag containing her purse and tickets. She watched through the rain speckled windows as the motion of the train tired her. The green fields of the dales would soon turn to grey slate as they approached Westmorland. She had left Sugar Hills at seven in the morning with the farm manager for the eight o'clock train to York. Change at York then on to Leeds, then to Settle. She had left her father still in a quandary of whether he should have let her go, but he trusted Beth's judgement and knew if he was to win back his son, she could help by playing mediator.

Beth was excited to see Christie, all his letters had said how happy he was with Robbie, he had hinted at times at Robbie's see-saw life style, but most of all the kindness of the two Keldas brothers.

Beth really believed Robbie to be the man she was in love with the day she fell into his arms, and was a worthy suitor, but she doubted he would show any further interest in her. She had tried not to let herself dream too deeply about him; but her heart always won over her head and as the train pulled into Windermere Station she straightened her brown coat and put her hat carefully on her head, her beautiful hair was falling loosely over her shoulders. She spotted Christie sitting with Fred Keldas on the platform bench in the winter's gloom, eyeing the train carriages and looking for her. Her first reaction was one of elation as she could see in a few months that Christie had grown in stature and looked very well. His complexion clear, his blonde hair curling and washed in the soft Lakeland rain. And it wasn't until she had Christie in her arms did the thought strike her that Robbie wasn't there.

The trip to Grasmere was pleasant. Fred drove the small trap with Christie sitting with Beth in the carriage. Fred talked at length, turning to her as he did so. 'I'm sorry my brother isn't here to meet you, Beth.'

'I ... er ... didn't expect that, Freddie. He must be very busy.' Yet she had hoped beyond reason.

'He has business to attend to,' Fred shouted. 'I hope you don't mind me being your driver.'

Beth didn't mind at all and thought what an agreeable and honest face Fred had, nothing like Robbie, yet smiling eyes and a pleasant gentle disposition. Christie had spoken well of him in his letters and it appeared Fred Keldas helped Robbie more than expected up at Keld Head.

A fresh wind was blowing off the lake. Beth was frozen after sitting for hours on the warm train and she wrapped her hands together tightly in a fur muffler. They took the Ambleside road and stopped for afternoon tea at an inn near the Low Wood.

Freddie swelled with pride at his assignment of helping Beth and to be in the company of a fine woman, one to be admired. He installed Beth and Christie in a small room overlooking Lake Windermere as the waiter served the tea.

The views across the water sharpened as the fog finally diminished. Clear sky exposed the lake as icy blue, with the fells and frost above them almost making a perfect reflection, Beth was overwhelmed.

'It's a pity the train didn't go any further.' Beth started the conversation.

'Yes, Mr Wordsworth is responsible. He didn't want the unwashed masses descending on Grasmere.'

'But they still do,' and Beth smiled at Fred and dared to glance into his deep brown eyes and saw the likability and attraction of the younger of the Keldas brothers. Then the thought struck her had she fallen into Fred's arms instead of Robbie's that day, would she have been as smitten with him? The question was raised but the answer wasn't there and she pushed the thought to the back of her mind. 'I would like to visit my Aunt Charlotte while I'm here, Freddie. Would that be possible do you think?'

'Yes, if you didn't mind travelling by train again. Either me or Robbie will help you to the station. Or you could catch one of the new tour buses but they don't run as often in winter.'

Beth picked up the hot tea that had just been delivered. The cake and sandwiches were arranged on a china cake stand which was painted with horses and carriages and hunting scenes.

Fred was the next to speak and that wasn't unusual. 'Christie helps me quite a bit a Spickle Howe. Don't you?'

Christie sat forward on his chair wanting to tell Beth of the smaller of the two farms and how he loved working for Fred, it was a pleasant escape from the anxieties he sometimes had for Robbie.

'Aye, that's when Robbie lets him go.' Fred said.

'Is Robbie well?' She finally asked, looking at Fred.

'Err ... yes, Robbie's always well ... he has the constitution of an ox.'

'Does he have farm business to attend to today?'

Fred noticed Christie looking concerned, awaiting a sensible and honest reply, because, as usual, neither of them knew where he was.

Darkness crept in as they arrived in Grasmere. The bright lights of The Prince of Wales' Hotel were welcoming; Beth was exhausted with travel.

Fred and Christie left her to unpack once they had seen the luggage carefully hauled to the bedroom. Christie promised he would visit in the morning after milking and said that was what Robbie had intended.

Beth's hotel room wasn't as grand as her last visit. The small attic room was cold and cheerless, but as she would see in the light of day, it still had a good aspect of Keld Head. Beth washed and changed out of her winter suit, then lay on her bed in her lace petticoat and bodice. She let her head fall back into the soft downy pillows and drifted into a pleasant sleep.

Hunger caused her to eventually stir and sliding her long pale legs off the bed, she idled around the room. Her turquoise satin evening dress was already hanging on the wardrobe door to let any creases drop out. Irene had helped her pack and had folded it neatly in brown paper. Her father had insisted she always dressed well for dinner but in his absence she was nervous at dining alone, yet knew he would be proud of her modest yet appealing dress sense.

She brushed her hair and curled her fringe and decided to wear her hair loose, letting the soft dark curls fall over her shoulder. She powdered her cheeks and her chest and dressed. She had brought her mother's gold chain with jade droplets that dripped into the curve of her chest, with earrings to match.

As she entered the busy dining room there was much talking and clinking of glasses, a quartet of musicians were playing badly in the corner, a slow and dreary song, possibly a Lakeland hunting song. There was a pleasant smell of roasting beef and venison, and the mass of glasses and silverware glistened beside deep blue napkins.

The waiter took her lacy stole and helped her to a small table in the corner of the room which suited Beth's mood.

She straightened her dress and glanced at the menu but before she could order the waiter returned. 'There's a gentleman on table five who requests your company, Miss Richardson.'

Dismayed at the invitation, Beth strongly declined and didn't want to glance any further around the busy dining room.

She fidgeted with the silver napkin ring and held her head low when the waiter returned.

'I'm sorry, Miss, but the gentleman has insisted you would want to dine with him, and asked me to tell you he is Mr Robert Keldas and he reassured me that you and he are well acquainted.'

Beth was uncomfortable. She knew she should be calm, wondering if Christie was with him. Her eyes searched the room and saw Robbie walking towards her; she barely recognised him.

'Hello, Beth,' he stood tall over her table. 'I'm sorry... that was an insensitive request... maybe you wish to dine alone.'

'How lovely to see you, Robert. I was feeling nervous in this large crowd and was lacking confidence.'

'If you wish to dine alone so be it, but if you wish to remain seated here in this cosy corner I could relinquish my table and join you?'

How could she refuse him?

'And if you are concerned over a chaperone, I believe there are chaperones enough in the room.'

Robbie wore a black suit with a black silk cravat. His white shirt was pristine. She noticed a gold watch chain on his waistcoat, his skin was tanned and clean shaven; his milky white teeth shone as he smiled.

He pulled up the chair, 'Waiter, please, can we have more cutlery?' And he gently eased into the chair opposite. 'I was afraid I may have overdressed this evening but on seeing you, Elizabeth, I know I made the correct choice, but heaven knows if I can stomach this hunting dirge the band are singing.' And his quip relaxed her.

'It's a lovely surprise to see you, Freddie hinted you were away.'

'I was away, but now I'm here and all the better for seeing you. But now my conscience is already telling me that I have imposed myself upon you again.'

'It is no imposition, it is a pleasure.'

He straightened the starched napkin and slid it on his lap. 'You look very well.'

'Yes, I have kept well.'

'Was your journey good?'

'Satisfactory.'

'And did my brother and yours take good care of you?'

'Oh, Robbie,' then she stopped, 'I'm sorry,' she held her hand to her mouth and understanding her dilemma, he helped her. 'Call me by whatever you like, Beth, if you and I are to be friends.... You choose a term of endearment and that makes me happy.'

She was embarrassed to let her feelings show, but he was so captivating that he drew words out of her as she was intoxicated by his charm. Her cheeks flushed with a rosy glow and only added fuel to Robbie's love for this young woman.

'Christie looks wonderful. I cannot thank you enough for the way you've helped him. And that is why I feel I have imposed myself upon you.'

'Ah, well, that too is no annoyance. The boy amuses me with his golden curls and angelic eyes, yet sometimes he has the mouth of a viper with his counsel. My only disappointment is that he has no sister the same.'

'He does, but she would need peroxide.'

'May no peroxide ever touch her hair,' and he lifted his hand then managed to stop himself from touching the soft tresses.

Beth saw the gesture and the realisation and implications of her flirting with this dinner guest, she felt ashamed. Her father had warned her and she had been foolish to be tempted by Robbie's flattery and good looks. She wanted to leave, embarrassed and he noted her discomfort.

'I'm sorry, Beth, I spoke out of turn.... I always do this. If Christie were here he would scold me.'

'No, it's me that should apologise. I owe you so much in helping Christie.'

'Well, I must say that my attention to you is an honest one, Beth. My father taught me well. When I was a boy I used to try to catch butterflies in my hand. I can recall running through the meadows on hot sunny days, but when I caught them I used to damage their tiny wings with my clumsy fingers.' He leant back in his chair, very much at ease with his little tale. 'Father said that young women were delicate things - like those butterflies. He told me I had to learn how to treat others. Not to damage their tiny wings.' Then a serious tone came to his voice, and she admired him the more for it. 'I'd like to get to know you better, Beth, if you and your father would allow it. I have great affection for your brother and I feel that his sister has touched my heart the same.'

There; the question was asked. The thing he had tried to suppress was now loose and careering out of control, as he set out on a course that he hoped could bring them both lasting happiness.

The silence was expected with the ecstasy of the moment and Beth showed greater courage. 'In some ways I'm very much like Christie.' His words of love cautioned her. 'But when you speak of affection, I fear that if you begin to feel the same of me as you do Christie, you would be disappointed.'

'I'm sorry, Beth ... I misuse the word. It was a foolish statement, because the affection I could have for you would be greater, and very different.'

They paused, yet eye contact was minimal. What was he saying? Why was she listening? Were these words of a man who used his tongue recklessly or were they the expressions of a kind and honest gentleman? She would know the answer to that in the coming months.

She replied coyishly. 'I think in many ways you'll see Christie and I differ greatly, and I think that is the same as you and Freddie.'

'Nay, I'm afraid the gap is wider in our case. Freddie is far the greater man than I.'

The waiter interrupted them to order but no menu had as yet been looked at. Beth hurriedly and clumsily tried to order. Everything on the menu was irrelevant now; she would eat nothing that could be relished and savoured as much as this conversation with him.

She clumsily ordered the trout but Robbie was eloquent and ordered the braised beef. And as he sat and drank water, the wine list being refused, she observed him intently.

He ate like a true gentleman; the way he held his cutlery, the way he lifted his glass to his mouth. He didn't speak when eating and he never interrupted her. She noticed his finger nails, clean and neatly trimmed for a farmer, his hands slim and tanned. Occasionally the twisted smile came that she would grow to love and long to see; deliciously impudent but warm. He had everything. Yes, Irene had said this one was a keeper and surely she was right.

'What plans do you have, Beth?' He dabbed his lips with the white napkin.

'It depends on Christie. How long will he be at work?'

'The boy won't be missed for the work load. But I guess you know that.' She understood well. 'But I never tell him that.'

110

'Then I will do just as you planned for him. Maybe I could be of some use. My father said I should help.'

At the mention of her father, Robbie quickly and purposely interrupted. 'The boy needs no help!'

She was perceptive and noticed a sharpness and anxiety in the tone of his voice. 'I think that's where we have gone wrong with him. Always stepping in, mollycoddling him. He was just a child when my mother died.' She nervously fiddled with the cutlery.

'I'm sorry you have no mother.' Robbie was remorseful at his sharpness. He wanted to ask of her mother but couldn't bring himself to do it.

He noticed her appearance; the satin dress, tasteful and modest. Was this the clothing of a preacher man's daughter? The gold and jade jewellery; he could see her chest moving as she breathed and he wondered if she was feeling as he was. Her skin was clear; no make-up, except a touch of rouge on her cheeks, or was it just a healthy glow.

'I came to see Christie but I won't keep him from his work.'

'You can help all you like. But I hope during your stay I can take you on some short tours of this beautiful county. Do you ride?'

'I do.'

'Then maybe when Freddie is over with his bay, we can borrow the horse and ride out together. That's if you have riding clothes with you.'

'Thank you, I would like that. I hope to visit my Aunt Charlotte in Kendal?'

'Then take Christie with you that day. Let your aunt see how much he has altered.'

Robbie glanced at his pocket watch and stood to leave. Beth would be tired from travelling although she no longer felt it. He left her at the table agreeing to call for her tomorrow and walk up to Keld Head with her. As he left the hotel and closed the doors he felt the cold of the night. His breath hit the back of his throat, hurting his lungs, but he didn't care. He pulled the silk tie loose from his collar and unbuttoned the stud. He walked the long lane to Keld Head alone, happy, satisfied with the woman he had fallen in love with as other Keldas men would do in the future. The lane was black with darkness but he still knew the way as the soft leather soles on his shoes, scuffed the gravel on the track. Robbie thought he would sleep well tonight and longed for the morning.

They met as agreed. Robbie took pleasure in walking her to Keld Head. He was in a spirited mood, enthusiastic, chatty, and pointing out the fells. Beth was wearing a long brown winter coat but underneath she wore her working clothes.

'I'm sorry, Beth, but I cannot have you working. I cannot pay you.'

'I expect no payment. You're in our debt enough in helping Christie.'

'But you are dressed for work,' and he allowed his eyes to wander about her person as he noticed she was wearing plain clothes under her long winter coat, and in her bag were work boots along with a sketch book.

'That's Silver Howe we are looking at. The juniper bushes on the fellside are hundreds of years old.'

'I may paint them before I leave. The dark colours look wonderful against the rock.'

'The children will be missing you.'

'I don't think so, they have a holiday.'

'You will teach them well, I think.'

'It is they that teach me, sometimes.'

'Do you draw well?'

'Christie may have told you so, but I disagree.'

He reluctantly left her working with Christie. There was some calves to see to, gentle and ideal work for a woman. Robbie stayed close to the farm and was busy doctoring one of the dairy cows that was lame. He worked hard all morning and Beth could hear him, shouting and laughing along with Jackie Bainbridge.

After lunch Robbie insisted she did no more. He watched her as she washed her hands in the enamel bowl, splashing water on her work dress. Her hair was tied back this morning and there was no trace of the finery she wore last night. She could have been a milkmaid, but she still looked beautiful.

The men left and Beth helped Nora clear the tables.

'No, miss, this is my work,' Nora insisted.

'But, Nora, I don't want to leave it to you. Let's do it together. And then I'll go and find my sketch book.'

Beth took a cloth and started to wipe clean the dinner table. 'How long have you worked for Mr Keldas, Nora?'

'Just five months, when he first took the farm.'

'Oh, have they not lived here long?'

'Oh no miss, they came from the coast, over Millom way.'

'I didn't know.' Beth continued. 'And do you enjoy your work here?'

'Well, it's not ideal, but it's good salary. My husband is the dairyman and village blacksmith.'

'Yes, I've met him.'

'Mr Keldas is good to work for, though. He treats us well.'

'Yes, I can see that in how he's helped my brother.'

'Yes, Christie's an angel. So he's your brother, miss, I didn't know.'

'Has he not told you?'

'No miss, we know very little of Christie.'

Beth stopped wiping the table but Nora continued clinking the pans in the hot water to scrub them clean. 'He was in a sorry state when he first came ... he had been seen sleeping rough up at Wood Close.'

'He must have walked from Northumberland.'

'Is that where you come from, miss?'

'No, Nora, I'm from Thirsk in North Yorkshire. You didn't know where Christie came from then?'

'No, Mr Keldas got us together one day and said we hadn't to ask any questions about the boy because he'd had a difficult time. He would have no gossip.

'So have you known Mr Keldas long?' Nora asked.

'No, only since the summer. We came up here on holiday. You may recall making tea for me and my aunt, and a friend.'

Nora waited for more, but daren't question Beth any further.

'He's well liked, is Robbie, miss.'

'I'm sure he is.'

'And I can speak no wrong of him, though others might.'

'Are you trying to tell me something, Nora?'

'I only know miss, that young Christie seems to make him happy. Robbie was an unhappy man when his father died.'

Beth helped clear the rest of the dishes then took her pencils and sketch book and walked away from Keld Head along the footpath up the hill. Christie had told her the best place to sketch. She saw the Lion and the Lamb across the valley and wanted to paint it.

She saw the shape of the rocks behind Keld Head. She could see Robbie's cattle in the fields, those wintering out, their coats black and woolly. Some in the fold yard were eating hay, with steam rising from their bodies, occasionally disturbed as someone passed by on the lane. She saw the stable and noticed a white horse, nodding its head over the stable door, bobbing up and down.

She watched Robbie for awhile talking to the dairyman, then he walked away and leant on the gate and bowed his head looking at the ground; maybe he was praying or meditating. The fellside sheltered her from the cool breeze as winter sunshine touched her face. She wouldn't sit long it would be too cold. Then she spotted Christie struggling to open the farm gate, the dogs barked and he appeared to be heading her way.

Beth continued sketching the rugged rocks, hoping the weather would stay dry so on another day she could move in closer and sketch them in finer detail.

Christie emerged up the hill, his face flushed, his slender limbs gangling at the side of him as he walked. He fell down by her side, gasping, and threw his arms around her neck.

'He's given me an hour or two off, Bethy, so I can come and sit with you. He said he wants you to be safe.'

'That was kind, but I'm fine here alone. I'm not lost or uncomfortable.'

'I know, I know... but Robbie said it was for the best. He said I hadn't to leave you alone. There's a rock shaped like a canon on the ridge, I'll take you up to see it if you like,' and he pointed and hurriedly said. 'I'll hate it when you leave, Bethy.'

'I know, but you are happy here, I can tell.'

'Yes, I am.... Does Father ever ask of me?'

'Of course he does.' And she slapped her hand on his knee.

'How is he?'

'Well, really, for his age. He complains of the headaches a lot more. The doctor is looking into it for him but doesn't come up with any solutions.'

'No ... I see.'

'How long do you think Robbie will let you stay?'

'He assured me I could stay as long as I like.'

'He does know about Sugar Hills, doesn't he ... that you will have to manage it one day?'

'Yes, I told him once about the farm.'

'Only once.'

'Yes, he says not to talk about it.... I think it humbles him.'

Beth mused over this. 'It needn't do, Christie. I know what he has here is on a smaller scale, but it is grander in aspect. Do you think he's really interested in us Christie? Nora told me he didn't let any of them enquire of you or our family.'

'I know, Beth ... he said the same to me once. But he IS interested.' They stopped fidgeting with words to watch two ravens cawing overhead and circling in the sky.

'He's always asking after you, Beth. I told him about the school and that child that was poorly that couldn't learn to read. He likes to know what you're painting. I think he has designs on you. That's the only reason he lets me stay.' Christie huddled in closer to his sister to let his blue eyes observe her countenance. She was flushed from the cold and the statement she had dared not to believe.

'I don't know what to do, Christie. Did he tell you we had dinner together last night?'

Christie sat up, shocked. 'He came home happy, I know that; singing he was. If I'd have known he was seeing you, I would have said more. Robbie is a good man, Beth, but he's not perfect.'

'I didn't expect he was. Do you think Father would approve?'

115

'You should be chaperoned.'

'Hmm. Yes, Christie, but we were never alone together. Robbie did mention that. We just dined in the restaurant and then he came home.'

Beth let the sketch book fall onto the stony ground as she moved her thighs to a more comfortable position.

'Do you like Robbie, Beth?'

She pulled her knees into her chest and gripped her arms around them. 'I love him, Christie ... I love him. Is that being stupid?'

'No, Beth, because I guess I do too, but maybe in a different way. Don't rush things though. Stay awhile and you will see what he really is. The good side and the bad side. He doesn't pretend. He's no hypocrite. And then if he does really care for you, you can make your decision.'

'Ah, Christie ... my little counsellor. You sound just like Daddy.'

'Oh heavens, no....'

They only spent an hour on the fellside, it was too cold to sit any longer; Christie didn't really look after Beth as he was supposed to, but lay back on the slope and shut his eyes while his cap fell on his face while she sketched.

Beth listened to all around her: Christie's soft breath as she realised he had fallen asleep; she would let him rest, he needed it. The farm was quiet, the cattle were standing motionless, the white horse had gone back into its stable and no doubt sleeping too.

It was the herdsman calling the dogs that made Christie sit up. 'I must get back. I must help.'

'Come on then, I'm getting cold any way.'

She linked his arm as they walked back to Keld Head and Robbie met them at the gate.

'Take your sister back to the hotel, Christie, before darkness draws in. I'll do your work this afternoon.'

'Thank you, sir, I'll get my jacket.'

Beth stood alone with Robbie at the gate as twilight crept in, and he saw the sketch book in her hand. 'May I see what you have drawn, please?'

She was uncomfortable. 'I ... I'm sorry .... I'm a poor artist.'

'And I'm a poorer critic.'

She laughed and held out the book to him.

'There's not much work done for the time you've been up there.'

'No, I think not.'

'If you ever finish it, could I have it, please? I would like it.' He dared to gaze deeply into her eyes. 'Can you smell the snow in the air today, Beth?'

She looked bemused. 'Smell the snow?'

'Yes, take in a deep breath.'

She did so as she sniffed the air and the cool breeze.

'The wind has turned to the north. It may snow tonight. If it does, stay at the hotel. Don't come to Keld Head tomorrow.'

She was disappointed. 'We have snow in Yorkshire, Robbie.'

'I'm sorry, I'm sorry.'

'If there's no one to collect me, I will find my own way.'

'Well, go carefully. We usually get a cold snap this time of year.'

11
COLD SNAP

The green winter ended and the cold snap began just as Robbie had said. It usually happened this way; the damp and rainy December turned into a frosty and cold January. Christmas passed unnoticed and the new year brought in the cold.

The view of Keld Head was the first thing Beth looked for each morning from her bedroom window. Where was Robbie? What was he doing? The man she believed she loved, in her eyes, could do no wrong.

Most mornings it was Christie that came to meet her, Robbie had insisted she never came alone but it seemed unwarranted.

Beth soon became to love the walk up the hill, the noise of the beck spluttering cold and refreshing water from off the fells; the little Herdwicks pulling at the grass and filling their bellies ready for the grip of winter; the mossy smell lingering in the moist air of pine needles and ferns; the lonely rocks on Helm Crag, begging for company. The change in the weather meant Beth's plan to visit her aunt in Kendal was difficult, so a meeting in Windermere over lunch was arranged to avoid travelling in the unpredictable weather. Robbie had said Christie could have the day off to travel to Windermere, but on the chosen morning of the trip it was Fred Keldas who once again took them. Fred was re-introduced to Charlotte, then left them to dine alone, but Fred's responsibility to spend the day in Beth's company was by no means a hardship. He knew well his brother's feelings for her but doubted his sincerity.

Charlotte, pleased to see her niece and nephew in good health and happy, relaxed in front of the log fire at the inn. 'Are you comfortable at the Prince of Wales, Beth?'

'Yes, I am. My room isn't as fine as last time. But it has a good view from the window.'

'And you, Christie? Is Mr Keldas treating you well?' Charlotte was delighted with the countenance of her nephew, seeing in his eyes the disposition and image of her late sister-in-law.

'Yes, Mam.'

'Freddie is a fine man, Beth, and very kind to bring you all this way to Windermere.'

'Yes, Freddie is wonderful. Both the Keldas brothers are.'

But the last few mornings there had been no signs of Robbie. Beth had asked the men discreet questions as to his whereabouts, but they gave no clues. For three days Beth never saw him, she spent most of the time helping Nora in the kitchen and she could tell the men were restless. Christie was completely lost and over lunch she caught the dairyman talking about Robbie, but then he stopped as she entered the kitchen. And later that afternoon when Christie walked back to the hotel, she tackled him about Robbie.

'Is Robbie ill, Christie?'

He dismissed a reply, hands in pockets.

'Is he away?'

'Must be.... Tilly's gone.'

'He must have business elsewhere then.'

'Look, Bethy, this is what he's like. He'll be back, don't you fret, as large as life and everyone will be relieved he's home. Sometimes he comes home filthy, unshaven like he has slept in a barn. Then other times he's laughing, joking, teasing Nora, spending money, giving money away. I wondered with you being here that he might settle; but well, no. Robbie's like what I said; he is what he is. What you get is what you see.'

Beth didn't answer as she put her arm in his and led him forward.

Robbie had stayed away for three days. His love for Beth was like a fire burning inside him, inconsolable. He hoped the days in the cold and the mountains would smother his emotions and extinguish the fire, but it hadn't. The problem was, it was easy to see her attraction to him. He knew women like he knew horses. He could taste the adoration. Robbie hoped the few days away would relieve them both of their obvious attachment to each other, but it had the opposite effect.

Beth had missed him so dreadfully, that she had pined. She wondered if Robbie wasn't as smitten with her as she and Christie had presumed, but Beth was wrong. She watched Tilly's stable, longing to see the grey mare return. She listened for Robbie's whistling, his teasing, but nothing.

Her time left was running out and she was beginning to wonder if she would even see him again, thinking her visit to see Christie had been the only salvation and her love for Robbie would be a disappointment. But Beth couldn't rid herself of him and she doubted she ever would.

The morning was fine and Beth dressed for warmth, the snow Robbie promised lasted only a few days and was merely a scattering. He told her when it lay still, it was waiting for more to take it away. Checking the clock Beth thought either Fred or Christie would be here to collect her. Maybe today Robbie would come home.

Robbie unlatched the gate and let Tilly walk to the stable. He had three days of a stubbled beard on his face and his cheeks were reddened with the cold wind. He saw Fred's bay stabled next to Tilly and remorse fell on him as he knew his brother would have helped the other men look after the farm.

He had decided not to allow Beth to love him anymore. He was no use to her. He would break her heart somewhere along the line. She should be with another; an honest man, loyal, sensible. He would flatter her no more and neither would he encourage her, but when Christie came out of the house, delighted to see him, ready to walk out for Beth, Robbie said, 'Are you going for your sister, boy?'

'I am sir, are you well? It's good to have you back.'

'Is it really, Christie, is it?'

'Yes sir, really.'

'I'm not in good fettle, you should know that, but don't worrit your pretty little head about me.'

'Do you want me to help with Tilly before I leave?'

'No, your sister will be waiting.' He looked at the boy, his stature and bearing so different to the one of former times and in that Robbie took some pleasure. He rested his hand on Tilly's bridle and looked at the ground. 'Do I look a rogue, Christie?'

'Yes, sir, you do.'

'Hah.... I knew you'd be honest. Then I will do. Saddle up Fred's bay for me please and water Tilly and give her some hay. I will go and get your sister today.'

'But you're tired, I can see.'

'Aye, I am and that will do very well. Tired and a rogue to boot.'

Beth could see someone walking down the hill, leading two horses, one a bay, one a grey. The person was too tall for Christie or Fred, but their face was obscured from view by a wide brimmed hat and a riding cape, and as she peered and watched as they drew in closer she could tell by the man's gait that it was Robbie.

Grabbing her winter coat and bag, Beth paused, wondering where he was taking the horses. Where was Christie? Could Robbie be really coming this way?

There was belief that if Beth could see Robbie as he really was, then maybe she would change her opinion of him, yet he knew he would be a fool to let a woman like her go. But if she did love him as much as he her, his appearance wouldn't change her mind a jot, and if she went along with this foolery, she would be as much to blame as him; he could rue this day, but he couldn't win.

He walked the horses down the hill, slowly; he hadn't pushed Tilly and they hadn't been far. He had stayed at an inn close to Ambleside and had spent the time walking under Wetherlam and up at the mine, laughing with the miners, doing business with the landlord. He walked with his head and shoulders bent low at his task. Longing to see Beth again but wondering if his scheme to disassociate himself from her would work; anxious of the stories he was about to tell. He had nothing planned in his mind, and he wouldn't rehearse anything, but come clean about his true name and personality.

It was a crisp winter's morning, he'd been up since five and was desperately tired, but couldn't let another day pass. He knew she was leaving soon.

The horses' hooves echoed noisily among the moss clad stone walls on the lane to Grasmere, the metal on the bridles, jingling. Tilly tossed her head up and down blowing fresh air into her nostrils; Fred's bay, Topper, was playful, and Robbie had to restrain him.

Robbie had little desire to walk much further, in fact a warm fire and a glass of brandy would be welcome.

Slipping on her coat, Beth ran down the stairs, greeted the valet and went to stand on the stone steps at the front of the Prince of Wales' hotel. She stood quietly in the still winter's air, her warm breath evaporating in the cold as she looked out across the lake. She had her hands wrapped in mittens and a scarf around her neck, her fur hat smothering her hair. She could hear the horses' hooves getting closer and hoped beyond reason that they would stop at the hotel and they did, she checked her watch and knew if Christie was coming he would have been here by now.

As the horses stopped she couldn't see the road but heard someone talking, men laughing, some man greeting another. It was definitely him.

He walked up to the hotel. Beth stood anxious, waiting, glowing, and her heart racing. He stood before her and she was shocked at his appearance. Tilly stood dead still and Topper continued to jostle his head. The horse swung around and Robbie shouted: 'Be still, won't you ... be still, Topper.'

Gasping as he held the two horses by the reins he said, 'Have you brought any riding clothes?' No "Good morning" or "How are you?"

'Er yes, I have something I can wear.'

'Then would you like to ride out today.' And realising his abrupt manner, he relented. 'I need to talk to you.' His voice was low and gravelly. 'Are you able to ride astride? I have no ladies' saddles.'

'Yes, of course. Shall I change then?'

She hurried up the stairs back to her room, raked through her clothes and found her riding breeches and some heavy boots. Her coat was broad at the skirt and she knew it would be suitable and she found some gloves. Wondering all the time what he wanted to say to her. Worrying where they would go and why he had come alone. Should she go with him? She should have listened to her conscience; the decision she would make would have a bearing on her whole life. *What was wrong with him?*

He helped her mount Tilly and reassured her that the horse was sound and docile. Fred's bay would be too much of a handful.

'Can you smell the snow today, Beth?'

'Yes, I can. I was just thinking it seemed warmer today, though.'

'Yes, it's been too cold for snow these last few days, but it might snow again later.'

They took the lane up the hill to Elterwater. Beth was comfortable on Tilly, glad the mare was more placid. Robbie was having problems with Topper, and irritated by the horse's playfulness continued to complain at the horse and this wasn't like him. When they left the village, away from intruders and on the quiet lane he was impatient to get the conversation started.

'I have to tell you something.... Don't answer me yet, just listen to what I have to say, please.'

His determination surprised her as he glanced sideways and looked her in the eye. Both horses were walking closely together; only inches apart; he would have moved in even closer if Topper would have settled.

She looked at his face and saw how grubby he was. She didn't like the stubble of his beard; it made him look darker; almost sinister. This was a different man she was riding with, without escort, and uncertainty took over her, and she had the same tremors that her father had months earlier when he let Robbie into his carriage after he'd spotted him swimming naked in Wasdale.

Her inclination was to stop and go no further, but he noticed her fear and he pulled Topper to a halt and the horse spun around as Robbie continued to jostle with it.

'I must apologise for my appearance. Do not fear me, please. I wanted you to see me today, and to be my companion; we must let these beautiful hills and God in heaven be our judge. Are you still willing to continue with this short journey?'

'I'm sorry, Robbie ... I do feel uneasy. Does Christie know I'm with you today? I may have made an error of judgement.'

'No, your little brother is oblivious to our journey, but if he were to know, he would counsel us both and our conversation would never take place.'

'You are unhappy today, I can see that. And I cannot understand what you want to discuss with me, unless it is about my brother.'

'No, Beth. You're brother is the furthest thing on my mind, but in his absence he has a greater presence for I know, although he would trust me implicitly, he would not permit this conversation.' He stopped and looked down and shut his eyes; it was as if he was praying, like when she first set eyes on him; maybe he was.

'May we continue, Beth, please? The movement of the horse consoles me and will help me with what I have to say.'

'I trust Christie's perception of you. But I still wish he were here.'

'What I have to say will not take long.' And so he started. 'I'm afraid I misled you.... My family have only lived here in Grasmere for several months. We come from Millom, over by the west coast. We farmed under Black Combe. My father was a good man, my mother, the better of the two. They brought me and Freddie up well, the problem was I always took advantage of their kindness. I'm afraid I am not the man you think I am.'

She interrupted. 'Excuse me, Robbie, but what gives you the insight into what I really know of you?'

'Ah yes, you are a wiser person than I. Then maybe you do know my true self, but I somehow doubt it.'

'Will you let me be the judge of that, please?'

He nudged Topper forward and Tilly also responded.

'And that is how I see you, humble, honest, and willing to accept your mistakes.'

The horses walked slowly now, Tilly not happy to be walking any further away from Keld Head.

'And mistakes I have surely made, for six months ago I was languishing in Coldrigg Gaol. Banged up for stealing the very horse you are riding.'

He saw the astonishment in her eyes and had empathy for her, 'I know this is shocking for a gentle woman like you.' There was a pleading for mercy on his face.

Beth felt she had been mortally wounded; and the blows from a lover hurt her more. She looked into his eyes, saddened with remorse and waited, but he didn't speak but just held her gaze. Did Christie know this, was her foremost thought? What would her father say? She momentarily felt cheated, and then something gripped her as a lifeline to hold on to.

Robbie watched her; had he succeeded or failed in his plan? He would soon know.

'I don't know what to say. You have said nothing to put my mind at ease.' She felt like she was in a trap. 'So am I to be imprisoned too, for riding this stolen horse.'

'The only prison you may be in, dear Bethy, is inside my heart, should I capture yours.'

She wavered at his declaration and swallowed hard. 'So is Tilly not your horse?'

'Aye, she's mine alright. A great injustice was done. But I bought her and extortionately paid for her, fair and square. This is a sorry tale I have, but Tilly was to be bought by a cruel man from a friend of mine, and although he took her away the payment never arrived. And so I helped my friend return the horse. We couldn't let her stable with such an uncouth and cruel man. We made a mistake in not letting the police take care of this and in that we were foolish. Thankfully the justice system was kind and my friend and I were released without charge after spending several weeks in the filthy hole of Coldrigg Gaol. But unfortunately for my poor father and brother I was wrongly labelled a horse thief. This week I have spent three nights in no man's land worrying about this. Christie knows nothing of my history. I needed to tell you so you could begin to see my true character, and probably any affection you may have for me, may turn to disgust. Do you now hate me, Beth?'

'You said a great miscarriage of justice occurred?'

'Yes, the claims were false.'

Neither spoke for some time. Beth felt as if this lane would swallow her up; the glistening water on the green laurels, the noise of the horses' hooves on the stone track; the bird song; then it was as if it all went quiet and she heard nothing. How could she, her heart was winning the battle over her mind.

'I'm not guilty of horse-thievery, but guilty of everything else. I brought shame on my family, so much so that my father felt we should move away. He was an astute man in his finances and had shares in shipping that served him well. We were able to sell the farm in Millom and buy two over here: Freddie's and mine. But my father was dying and he had one last wish and that was to change our name.'

He stopped, this was hurting. But she was still here, listening.

'My name is really Robert Kellet. Father changed it to Keldas legally. I wouldn't have inherited Keld Head if I'd have disagreed. He wanted respect and this name change gave him that and he died happy in the knowing.

'I've silenced you now, Beth.' And he pulled Topper to a halt and looked upwards to the horizon and saw the snow clouds hovering. He knew they should turn back, but he couldn't. He didn't tell her his fears.

The horses steadily descended the steep hill to Elterwater where stone cottages dozed in the warmth of the valley, welcoming lights glowed in the windows, wood smoke drifted upwards filling the air with sweet scent. Beth was mulling over in her mind his sorry tale; yet feeling safer with the cottages in sight. Her heart churned through his confession; the sorrow on his face. Then she noticed his hands holding the reins; they were spotless, as were his fingernails, so different to the rest of him and it became a source of comfort to think this man was really clean. She recalled his black suit and silk cravat; his gold pocket watch. His clean teeth and clear blue eyes and they all became a testimony for Robbie's character.

Christie had told Beth he loved Robbie; words he had never said of his father. "What you see is what you get," and that was true. He was hiding nothing from her. His leg was close to hers as the horses jostled down the lane and he caught her looking at his hands.

'I'm a God fearing man, Beth, but do I repulse you now?'

'Repulse is the wrong word.'

'So what is the word?'

She thought carefully before she spoke, clinging to Tilly's reins, her legs and heels squeezing the horse's belly to steady herself in the saddle. And as they descended the mare slipped and almost stumbled.

'Steady, Tilly. Be careful, darn you.'

'I won't fall, Robbie. I have known worse than this.'

'So tell me, Beth, what is your word? I'm in dire straits to know.'

She couldn't tell him her heart was in uncompromising control and he struggled to cope with her silence. 'Please talk to me. Please tell me you don't hate me.'

She spoke up quickly and suddenly. 'How can I say I hate you when you speak so candidly and with all you have done for Christie.'

'And is the boy the only reason?' almost pleading for mercy.

'I don't know what you want me to say ... you bring me out here in this beautiful valley - a winter wonderland. And I don't know where I am. I'm riding a horse that's an object of mischief, with no chaperone. And I don't know if I'm in a dream.'

'You're not asleep, Beth, but I wish I was. And I would waken and none of this would have happened and I would be a guilt free man. I've washed in a beck for three nights and two mornings. I'm only clean by Lakeland water. You may have witnessed me today close to my worst.'

She was feeling angry now with his self-pity and pulled Tilly up sharp. Robbie swung around and slid off Topper and led him to a small clearing tucked into the fellside beside spruce trees and rocks. Flakes of snow fell from the sky like pure white tears as their gentle sound hit his coat. He had never known the snow like this; a sound he would recall all his life. Tap - tap - tap, the snowflakes fell.

Beth raised her head; she was no longer afraid. She was exactly where she wanted to be. The snowflakes touched her face and she tasted their coolness on her lips. Robbie pressed on, away from the track into a small woodland. Beth slid off Tilly's back and jumped to the floor, and followed him, her long coat rustling as she dismounted. She let Tilly have her head and the horse plunged forward to find grass which would soon be smothered in the snow. Robbie came to Beth and looking deeply into her eyes, held her gently by the shoulders. 'I'm telling you this now, because I love you like I've loved no other. And I want you to feel the same, but I needed to let you see me at my worst; to tell you my true life and give you a choice, yet I hope beyond reason that you won't be turned by this news.'

She gazed at him, his face grubby, his hands clean, his crooked smile as his mouth parted. She breathed in heavily, still clinging to Tilly's bridle for reassurance at what she was about to say. She pulled off her gloves and rubbed together her cold hands to restore some circulation, trembling with the cold. 'I don't think it matters anymore what you tell me. I can see what you are like. I have sensed for some time you were troubled but I didn't comprehend its magnitude. I respect you Robbie for your honesty, your kindness. I don't like to see you gloomy like this. I want to see you happy, laughing.'

'I won't say anymore, Beth, if you don't want me as I really am.'

She was now shaking. 'But I do love you, Robbie, from the first day I fell into your arms, until now and more so for your honesty.'

'Bethy ... Bethy.... I shouldn't be alone with you here. This is wrong. I'll take you back home, but it makes me happy to know how you feel.' He took her hands and held them in his, warming them. He lifted them to his mouth and kissed her fingers.

'What does this mean, Robbie?'

'It means I'm an imbecile, but please reflect on what I have said. I'll take you back now and we will dine together this evening. Get warm and try to think clearly and if you will be my wife I would try to be an honest and unwavering man.'

'And if I don't?' she teased him, smiling.

'Then I will become more of a reprobate than before.'

'Then what choice do I have. Your demise would be of my doing and mine alone.'

He stepped closer and restrained himself. He wiped his face dry of the snowflakes. 'I have underestimated this weather. We should go back but I fear Topper will be more of a danger to himself if he keeps thrashing about in the snow.'

It fell thickly now, drifts of flakes covering them, her hat and coat bedecked in the beautiful snow.

'There's an inn in the village where we could shelter. It is a homely sort of place, but we will be safe and the horses will be looked after. I wish to maintain your integrity but at this moment in time your personal safety and mine is the most vital. Are you cold?'

'I am a little.' Yet she was glowing inside; she didn't care.

'Then I will take the wise course and we will shelter at the inn and hope this blizzard subsides and we can be home before dark.'

Robbie led the horses as he walked, holding Topper tightly by the reins. Tilly was passive and carried Beth safely down the steep gradient to Elterwater. The horses' ears were flattened back with the ferocity of the snow on their faces. Beth felt she was inside the little snowscene globe that her father had bought her. A proposal: she would remember his words forever.

12
SNOW BLINDNESS

The inn was crowded with stranded travellers. They dined before a log fire, squashed in amongst the clamour of men, women and children. The landlord, a kindly man, knew neither Robbie nor his escort. But as the afternoon passed quickly it was soon apparent there would be no safe return to Grasmere that day and Robbie quickly booked the last available room for Beth, so he could distance her from the other travellers. He would be happy to sleep in the chair in front of the fire in the bar.

'I suggest once we've eaten you go straight to your room. I don't know what clientele will invade this place tonight.'

'I will be quite safe, Robbie. Please don't fret for me.'

'Aye, well, maybe I know such places as these more than you.'

'Well, let's just be grateful the landlord had a room, as meagre as it maybe.'

'All the same, please leave me for the evening and I will call for you at first light. Providing there is a thaw we can travel back in the morning.'

'Would you knock the door before we settle for the night, I will worry, otherwise.'

'If you insist.... I will be discreet.'

The meal arrived and they sat quietly, Robbie's eyes flickered each time the bar door opened.

'You appear anxious?'

'Nay... I'm only minding the precious life in my care.' And his smile was contagious.

'I feel quite safe with you, though our plans have somewhat changed.'

'I have already compromised your integrity. It was a mistake to travel today when I knew it would snow. I don't know what I was thinking.' But he did know; he was a man in love.

'Yonder waitress is already wondering why a fine woman as you is having any kind of truck with a vagabond as me.'

The meal was tasty, and it was hot. Beth discreetly pulled chicken bones or maybe they were rabbit bones from the stew. The fatty pieces were left in the bottom.

The door swung open and a draught of cold and snowy air drifted violently into the bar. Men disguised in warm clothing; people just happy to be safe indoors.

'I think it best you withdraw to your room now. I will do as you ask, and knock on your door before you retire. Please give me a time?'

'I am tired ... maybe seven would be a good hour.'

'Seven it is.'

Fred kicked the snow off his boots and banged the front door shut. Christie was standing at the window, the curtains undrawn, looking out into the darkness.

'Where's my horse, Christie?'

Christie cleared his throat. 'Robbie took him.' And the boy walked towards the fire to warm his hands, purposely turning his back on Fred.

'I should have known.... Don't fret, boy, it's not your fault.'

'Well, maybe I could have dissuaded him. I didn't know it would snow.' He joined Fred at the table, as Fred leant back in the chair. 'Is there any food, Christie?'

'Yes, Nora left some pie and I think there's some broth.... Can I get you some?'

'No, I'll get it myself ... you're not here to be a waiter.' Fred's kindness touched Christie as it always would.

'Will they be safe?'

'They?'

'Yes, I think he took Beth. I saw him stop at the hotel. I think he intended her to ride Tilly.'

'Oh, my word.... He's a darn idiot at times, Christie.... He must have known it would snow. Topper doesn't do well in the snow... it spooks him. Beth will be safe if she's on Tilly, but he's

131

taken a big risk.... They'll not get back tonight, if they're still out in this.'

'I was hoping they were at the Prince of Wales.'

Fred mused at Christie's naivety, but all the while hoping he was right. 'Shall we batten down for the night, Christie? Do you have to check the animals?'

'No.... It's Jackie's shift tonight.'

'Aye, that's maybe as well.'

The clock ticked, the lamps were lit; the parlour was warm. Fred chatted none stop to Christie about the animals and Robbie. All things he had heard before. Every yap of the dogs outside made him glance at the door and he longed for Robbie to burst in as large as life as he usually did.

'Don't be anxious for them, Christie. And never ... never be anxious over Robbie ... there's no point. He'll do as he likes.'

'I can't help it, Freddie ... I'm a worrit, I know.'

'Well, I tell you what ... I'll have a wander to the hotel and check. But I'm not going larkin' about on the fells tonight. If he's been fool enough to go to Easdale, he'll have to answer for the consequences.'

'But he may have Beth with him!'

'I doubt he'll a been that touched to have teken her to the high fells. I've spent hours and hours searching for him.... My father worried like you did. My poor mother died of worry for him and as much as he drives me thrang at times, we all love him and that's no word on a lie.... He has sumatt, does our Robbie, and I daren't know what it is.'

Fred put on his top coat and hat; re-tied his boots and left Christie to worry. The lane to the village was carpeted in gentle cotton-like snow; pleasant to walk on, and thankfully the wind was dropping. The merest glimmer of a thaw was apparent. Fred cursed Robbie under his breath for taking his horse. It was no thievery, but just plain crazy.

The lamps of the Prince of Wales glowed in the night sky. Little droplets of water fell off the trees onto Fred's cap. Alone as always with his thoughts, Fred was glad his father wasn't here to see this night trek in search of a wayward brother, worsened by the fact that Beth may be with him.

He pushed the large brass fittings on the heavy door, and stamped his boots clean on the mat. The hallway was plush and sparkled with light. Fred stood in his work clothes and immediately caused a stir. The valet recognised him.

'Hello, Freddie. Can we help?'

Fred nervously rolled his wet cap in his hand. 'It's Robbie.... He may have left this morning with Miss Richardson on horseback ... have they returned, please?'

The man looked at the room keys hanging on small hooks behind the desk. 'Her key is still out. Yes, she rode out with him.'

'Could you check if she's in her room, please?'

The man left but returned apologetic. 'No, sorry, Freddie, there's no one about.'

'Aye... it'll be right.... I'll see you in the morning. Good night.'

What was he going to tell Christie?

Robbie took a brandy and managed to find a hard chair by the fire, most of the men were smoking. He didn't want to associate and join in their conversation; he was so very tired. What had he done? His talk of love and a proposal wasn't totally unplanned but he was lying to himself in thinking she would have snubbed him. And now he had led her away from safety to be holed up in this small inn, a place she would probably never have frequented.

Two men standing beside the bar close to Robbie were pushed and sworn at by a drunk; one of the men began to lecture the drunk. The man was dressed in black and had a sombre face, the other, his cohort, was slimy looking.

'If ye didn't drink so much you would be sweeter in disposition.' The slimy man said.

'I'll drink what I likes.' The drunk said.

'It is the curse of mankind ... the ruin of fathers and families.'

'I've nivver ruined owt.' The drunk slurred, 'cos I've nivver getten owt!'

Laughter was spontaneous, and with his eyes shut, Robbie was smiling.

'All of you here are living under the devil's guise ... you should all repent.'

'I'll repent o' nowt.... I daren't give a monkey's uncle fer thee, ranter.' And the man pushed forward, but Robbie was there first. He stood tall over the drunk. 'Leave the preacher be, he's only giving advice.'

'He'll nay advise me unless it's on me death bed, and then I'll mebee listen.'

'Well, with the way you're drinking that day may come sooner than you anticipate.' Robbie said.

'Thank you for your kindness.' The ranter shook Robbie's hand.

'Well sir, I do believe King Solomon said there was a time to speak and a time to keep quiet and I think you should learn when that's to be.'

'Your words of counsel have stung me. Praise be the Lord and bless you.'

'I've been blessed enough.' And Robbie returned to his seat and shut his eyes.

Beth lay on the bed, warm and cosy, the eiderdown was thankfully clean. The floorboards creaked below her and she could hear the hubbub from the bar below, voices droning; she worried where Robbie was. He said he would see to the horses. And that he did, but he couldn't settle. Beth hadn't wanted to leave him but she longed for the free time to allow her mind to finally ponder on his proposal. Was this real? Was this happening?

Sliding off the bed, she looked through the window as the snow fell in steady drifts, like cotton flowers falling as filigree below. Little lanterns bobbed outside in the darkness.

She could hear the door banging down in the inn as people came and went.

Lying back on the bed Beth said her prayers with forgiveness. She knew she was acting discreetly but it was a mistake to have gone alone with him. But the adoration she had for him outweighed any fear of dishonour. He had protected her as he always would.

The door tapped gently and she woke with a start, straightened her clothes and went to lean on the door. 'Robbie ... is it you?'

'Aye, it's me.... Don't open the door, Beth. But are you safe?'

'Yes, I am. Are you comfortable?'

'Of a fashion.' Robbie was leaning, his ear close to the door, whispering, when the two preacher men walked up the passage.

He stepped away from her door but the men waited. 'Please pass, sir.'

'Do you require any assistance?' The preacher said.

'No sir.... I'm just checking my charge.'

'Good night then and thank you once again for your kindness in the bar.'

Robbie didn't want to speak again. He had said enough.

The sleazy assistant out of earshot in their room threw off his coat and said: 'That young man isn't as righteous as you think, John.... That was a woman he was beckoning behind that door, I just know it.'

Sleep wasn't pleasurable, but it was sleep. The milkman arriving at four woke Robbie and he went to the stables to check the horses. The cold damp air was dripping with thawing snow, and he shivered. Tilly was pleased to see him and he threw into the stable some wads of clean hay he had bought from the landlord. Topper was settled and Robbie hoped he could get all his precious family back to Keld Head, safely.

He breakfasted in the kitchen and had some brief but amusing banter with the cook. The ham and eggs were hot, and the tea sweet and milky. He was still filthy and he feared he smelt all the more now of the smoke and stale beer.

He took Beth a tray of food up to her room at seven and gently tapped the door.

'Beth.... It's Robbie. I'll set the tray outside and meet you down stairs in half an hour.'

She waited a few minutes to rouse herself then brushed her hair. She had slept in her underwear, so quickly pulled on her clothes. She splashed her face with cold water from a large blue jug and found some cologne in the bathroom next door. When she met him her face shone; she looked beautiful beside him.

He waited at the bottom of the stairs, the horses already tacked up outside and ready to walk home.

'Good morning,' he said

'I'm so relieved you're safe. Did you sleep?'

'I slept alright. But my back aches like no other. I will have to walk with Topper. The snow is thawing but not enough to pacify him. You can ride Tilly. She won't be spooked.'

They stepped aside as the preacher and his mate emerged from the staircase.

'Good morning, sir.... Good morning, madam, he said, looking at the other man and thinking he was right with his assumptions last night. Then he looked at the young woman a second time and said: 'Elizabeth.... This cannot be you, is it?'

'Hello, Mr Penruddock.'

'My dear, I knew you were in Westmorland, but I didn't expect to see you here.'

'No sir, Robert and I were stranded last night in the blizzard. We had to stay at the inn.'

John Penruddock looked Robbie clearly in the eye for the first time.

'This is Robert Keldas, Christie's employer.' She said boldly.

On seeing Robbie with Beth, Penruddock's opinion of him changed, and he was reluctant to shake his hand, but did so with contempt. He knew the man from last night but he hadn't discerned his appearance. The name he didn't recall; but where had he seen this face before? John Penruddock searched his mind and would ask his friend later.

The walk home was silent apart from an occasional glance and reassuring smile. Beth sat high on Tilly as Robbie walked beside, leading Topper. The bay was settled but Robbie daren't risk riding him; if Topper spooked in any way the horse could slip and break a limb.

Beth had a heavy heart. To see John Penruddock was a surprise and a shock. Her worry of being with Robbie alone was well founded. But reflecting on his betrothal, it would justify their being together. She hoped she could consult her father before Penruddock had the opportunity to speak to him. She also hoped Robbie hadn't changed his mind.

He reassured her that they should dine together that evening; his heart heavy, too. Beth thankfully was unaware of his encounter with Penruddock last night. The knowledge that their life before them was to change had a sobering effect on their young hearts. Beth would remember this day for the rest of her life. For Robbie it meant safety and a new path and the realisation that he could keep his father's wishes and his good name; this young woman would help him do that. For Beth it meant comfort because she had found a humble and honest man. Words didn't need to be said for they were united in their destiny.

The birds were busy today; noisy in the bushes. As the horses walked uphill they struggled the long slushy lane to Grasmere. Robbie felt his shoulders ache with cold as he slowly walked beside Beth. His head was dipped in his customary fashion, hiding his face and his shame beneath his broad rimmed hat; longing to clean himself up.

They dined alone that evening in the hotel restaurant. The snow mostly gone but their promises remained. Robbie sat in his black suit and silk tie, this time a deep blue one. Beth wore her turquoise dress. He held her hand across the table.

'Do you have an answer for me?'

'You must be patient,' she glowered; of course she had an answer. 'You will hear my reply soon enough.'

He could tell by her disposition what that would be, he was delighted. 'The snow and the cold have brought a healthy glow to your skin.'

She was pleased to see him clean again; immaculate even.

'Robbie, you insisted you told me of your background but you know little of mine.'

He had feared she might insist this, but he would avoid her plea. Yet he could answer his question there and then and have his fears silenced or confirmed of who her father was, but

Robbie elected, unwisely, to remain in innocence because of the bliss it brought him. The question was too deeply buried to want to drag it out of his existence like a fish caught on a hook. He wouldn't take her bait.

'I know of Christie, and that is sufficient. I can see you are a lady and have been reared as such.'

'I have no money, Robbie. Sugar Hills will be Christie's farm.'

'Never speak of money. It holds no meaning to me.'

'No, you speak honestly again. I can see capital has no association with you and that pleases me. I will accept your proposal, Robbie. I cannot refuse, for you have captured my heart in a way that I doubt it will ever escape.'

'Then I will hear no more of your family, but of your father, whoever the man is, I can only praise him for the way he reared two fine children. I will declare my love for you Beth and I feel great affection for your brother. Do you believe your father will let me take your hand?'

'Yes, I know he will, when I tell him of your character. I am of age, Robbie. I can make the choice. My Aunt Charlotte speaks well of you and Freddie.'

'Yes, and maybe Freddie is the better man for you?'

'Maybe in your eyes ... he is a fine man, but he's not the man you are.'

'Well, Charlotte Webb with her two b's knows nothing of Freddie and me.' He fiddled nervously into his waistcoat pocket. 'Will you accept this token?' And he pulled out a small velvet box holding a shiny gold ring. He unfolded her hand and placed the ring in her palm, then closed her hand over it.

She slowly unfurled her fingers and noticed on the ring a tiny inscription on the inside of the bar and it read: "For my sweet heart."

'May I place it on your finger as a token of my love for you?'

Her hand wavered and she let him.

'I'll go home tomorrow, Robbie, yet I don't want to leave here. I will speak to my father, but I know what his answer will be.'

'Would you still marry me if he forbade it?'

She looked quizzically into his eyes and saw the depth of his love and felt a slight jab in the midst of her heart.

'That's hard to answer.... I love my father, but my love for you is different.'

13

GYPSIES, TRAMPS AND THIEVES

Robbie walked the long lane to Keld Head in the darkness, his hands in his trouser pockets, which were lighter from the ring that was in Beth's possession. He couldn't take the smile off his face. When he saw Christie he would tease him and rag him and say he was to be his brother. The blue silk neck tie was loosened, and he was whistling. He thought of Beth and wondered what she would be doing. In fact she was lying on her bed, with tears of happiness overpowering her. The love she felt for this man was overwhelming and the prospect of future life at Keld Head. She had longed that he kissed her as they parted, but he hadn't and in that he was the wiser of the two. He had only kissed her hand. She rolled the ring around and around on her finger. It was slightly too big. She would conceal its content to everyone.

The lane steepened and Robbie lingered in the cold, not wanting his day to end. He thought Christie may already be in his room sleeping but he would waken him.

Robbie wouldn't see Beth anymore this visit, as Fred and Christie would take her back to Windermere Station. He would have to work quickly and plan the wedding. He would insist they marry in Grasmere and Beth would have to agree. She may have to stay at the hotel or with Charlotte Webb for some days to account for the legal banns to be read here in Grasmere Church. The cords of love were securely in place, not stifling him but protecting him, and he was happy at that. He wished his father was alive as he would love Beth. At least one thing in his life was right.

A hand grabbed his throat and pulled him backwards. Robbie struggled to keep his balance. He grappled with someone who he hoped was Edwin, but then he heard a woman's piercing laughter ringing in his ears and knew it was Sally Mook, and she wasn't alone.

Robbie was pulled to the ground and as he fell his head hit the rocky wall on the lane, twisting his neck. A body dropped on top of him and tried to force his face into the ground, his neck was bent against the wall. He grasped a stone with his hand, his fingers and nails were ripped jagged as he raked through the muck and gravel that had accumulated.

He felt his jacket being ripped off, then his shirt. There was little speech with the exertion of the maul, just gasps of throaty air as Robbie moaned. Jimmy Mook was muttering obscene threats in Robbie's ears, his stinking breath in his face. It was like Robbie was eating the earth. Grabbing a stone Robbie thrust it backwards as far as his arm would bend, but he missed. Flashbacks came to him of Beth, sweet Bethy, sitting cosy in her bedroom; Christie up at Keld Head, already sleeping awaiting his early morning call. Robbie thought he would die here in this muddy lane with these despicable people, with more infamy and shame not just for his dear father, but also his brother and his intended. What would she think?

He had to rid himself of this vermin as he felt his clothes being pulled from his body.

'I'll tek everything off yer back, young Robbie.' Jimmy Mook spat. 'I'll do fer thee and that 'oss'll be next.'

'Get his watch... Get his neck tie. Get his wallet.' Sally screamed.

Another dull blow came to the back of Robbie's head and he capitulated; he could do no more.

Christie heard a commotion from the safety of the house; he was terrified. The dogs were barking and going crazy. He leaped from his bed and ran to the window. Grabbing his jacket, he pulled on his trousers, tucking in his night shirt. He found his boots; there was no time for socks.

The dogs continued to yelp and just under their tone he heard a woman shrieking and shouting; swearing even. It was pitch black.

A gunshot cracked through the woodland and Christie stopped, mortified. He ran downstairs, shouting: 'Robbie...! Robbie, are you there?' But there was no one else in the house. He grabbed a long stick from the hall stand, the one that Robbie used for the sheep. His hands were shaking as he lit a lantern and ran outside into the cold dreek night. He released the two dogs and they ran to the head of the lane towards the noise. Just the strange noise now of a man wailing and shouting. Christie's little heart was racing as he moved cautiously and bravely forward. The dogs stopped barking as if someone was pacifying them; someone they knew. 'Robbie...? Robbie...?'

Then someone shouted. 'Christie, mi lad...? Is that you? Hurry boy.'

Christie ran down the lane just in time to see two people in the darkness careering up the lane away from Keld Head; they looked like ragamuffins. Then he watched someone stealthily move after them holding the shaft of a gun. Christie stopped and shouted. 'Who's there?' Then he saw a bundle of mud stained clothes on the ground, or was it a man. The man was covered in blood.

'Christie ... Christie.... He's dead. He's dead. They've gan an killed 'im!'

The two spaniels were running through the woods searching for the enemy. Christie was terrified. What was happening? Who have they killed?

'Who are you? What's happened?'

'Come closer boy, and they'll see. It's Robbie, it's Robbie, he's done fer. He's a gonner!'

Christie recognised Edwin Wilding by his familiar red necktie, as Edwin moved backwards and knelt on the floor at Robbie's side amidst this macabre scene. And in the haze of the night and with the soft glow of the lamp Christie could see Edwin with a shot gun in his hand bending over a corpse, bloodied, filthy and battered.

'Have you shot him, sir?' Christie bravely shouted as he ran to Robbie, kneeling beside him on the sodden earth. Robbie was motionless, his head and neck bent against the wall; blood pouring from a wound. Christie screamed to Edwin again, 'You've shot him, Edwin...! You've killed him!'

Edwin continued to sob on Robbie's bare chest. 'I've nay killed 'im boy. I can shoot accurately ... my gun were aimed at another. Nay, someone else 'as done this at 'im and I thinks I knows who they be, and I've winded em alright with mi gun.'

Christie's little heart took control. 'Hold the lamp, Edwin, sit up man, and let me see to him.' And Christie wiped Robbie's hair from his eyes. What's happened to him? Whatever's happened? What have they done at him?'

'I daren't know lad, but if I aint a bin 'ere, goodness knows what they'd a done and he'd a bin laid here fer you te find.'

'He can't be dead, Edwin ... he can't.' Christie bordered on panic and the realisation of the master he loved so badly injured. 'Sit him up.' And Christie gently patted Robbie's face. They struggled between them to raise the limp body away from the wall that was half tumbled on top of Robbie. Christie ripped the bloodied shirt further off his chest and pressed his hand against Robbie's heart.

'He's alive, Edwin. I can feel his heart beat ... he's alive.' The boy frantically shook Robbie to try and rouse him, but he remained almost lifeless. 'Get Tilly, Edwin.... Get the horse and we'll manhandle him back to the farmhouse. Send for the police and a doctor, we must get Freddie. We must do something.'

'We canna lift 'im on the horse, boy, he's too big fer us.' Edwin shouted and sobbed the more.

'Then we'll drag him by the shoulders. Here, you take this side.'

'I love this man. Christie. He's like mi own flesh. Pray nowt'll befall 'im. Christie, pray lad.'

Christie slipped his arm under Robbie's shoulder and pulled him. Edwin did the same. The movement brought a shudder of pain into Robbie's head and he moaned as he fell sideways.

'Don't die on us, Robbie ... don't die.' Christie whispered under his breath. 'Keep strong.'

'If we get him home we'll send for my sister and get Freddie, he'll know what to do.'

'No boy, naybody must know o' this. She canna see a fine man the likes of 'im wi no dignity... he'll be humiliated. We'll get Nora, she'll 'elp.'

Beth barely slept that night. Robbie's words, the touch of his lips on her hands, her beautiful ring; everything was perfect but she was filled with sorrow to know she was leaving. This trip had brought her close to marriage and if her father approved they could be married in weeks. Robbie was all and more she could have hoped for. His honesty, his love for Christie had strengthened her love for him. As they parted she sensed she wouldn't see him again as he was uncertain who would drive her to the station. It was then that she noticed something about him and that was in all the months she had known him, he had never said goodbye, and he never would.

Beth had a deep sense of unease at the thought of telling her father. Yet she was certain he would approve; Robbie was the man he had told her to look for. There was no doubt in her mind, even his brush with the law wouldn't stop her; he had surely been an innocent victim who had made a bad judgement in retrieving a horse so it could be rescued from cruelty, and to have it as his own.

She had a last look at Keld Head's tower that following morning and in the crisp air it showed an eerie stillness. The cattle would be munching on hay in the byre. Christie would be relieved of milking possibly to keep Fred company as they drove to Windermere Station. Robbie may be up working and his fine clothes hanging in the wardrobe, waiting for their wedding day.

Robbie was washed and bandaged as he lay in a bed of clean white cotton sheets. His head and face bruised, his shoulders, scratched and torn. He drifted in and out of consciousness, dreaming of Beth with the gleam of the golden ring dazzling his eyes. He remembered her saying she would marry him. Then he saw Christie always there with him; his little face grave and solemn, bereft. He remembered thanking Nora for something but he didn't know what. He remembered swearing at Edwin for manhandling him. Night drifted into day. Then terror returned and a sickening memory of being beaten and stripped by the Mooks. Then Fred was there; dear Fred. The warmth and comfort of his family and friends intoxicated and helped to pacify him.

Christie was the main nurse and would dab Robbie's brow when he turned feverish. He slept on the bedroom floor most nights. Fred was roped in again; a desperate dash to help his ailing brother, hoping and praying he would survive; wondering at the consequences. In his youthful wisdom he, like Edwin, didn't want to involve the police and cause more infamy in this quiet sedate village of Grasmere. There was a slight chance Edwin may have shot and injured the perpetrators and they had a good idea who they were. Only if Robbie died would they call the police. And the following morning as soon as early light, Edwin and Fred searched the silver birch plantation hoping to find a wounded body, but there was nothing, only the blood stained ground where Robbie had lain.

Fred and Christie arrived at the hotel on time; Nora was left to be nurse, tired from being waken at an ungodly hour to help. It was a fine morning.

Beth's luggage was lifted onto the trap as Christie helped her up onto the seat. Beth noticed some scratches and blood stains on Christie's hands and wondered what he had been doing; maybe wrestling with an unruly animal? But when she looked into his eyes, she saw the tiredness and the fear.

'You have been working too hard, Christie.' Beth muttered as she sat beside him. Fred handed her a woollen blanket and then clicked the horse to walk on.

'Are you well this morning?' Christie said as they drove along the pretty lanes to Ambleside. 'I'm very much well, Christie. Sorry to be leaving though.'

Christie felt it was fortuitous she was going.

'Is Robbie well this morning?' A little disappointed he hadn't come to say good bye.

'He's still sleeping.'

'Sleeping, at this hour? Have you spoken to him since we dined last night?' her face was animated and alive with happiness.

Yes, Christie had spoken to him, long and hard but got little response. 'Er, yes, briefly.'

'Did he tell you our news?'

'No, Beth, what news?'

'Oh Christie, Christie, I'm so happy.' She twisted in her seat to face him and pulled a glove off her hand to expose a gold and diamond ring on her finger.

'Has Robbie given you that!'

'Don't sound angry, Christie.... Are you not pleased?'

'I'm sorry... I'm sorry,' he softened. 'Has Robbie proposed?'

'He has, yes, and I will accept, if father approves. He gave me this as a token of his love.'

Christie said no more. Uncertainty crept in and he was swimming in fear and wished he could say something courageous to pacify his sister.

The carriage wheels sped along the busy road, Topper trotting at a great pace, and Beth sensed Fred was driving the horse too fast. Through Ambleside there was no let up. Christie was looking at the lake, the hills, and wondering and hoping if Beth's wish would ever be granted. Would Robbie survive? What would she tell their father?

Beth could discern Christie was shocked at her news and hoped it wasn't disappointment; surely he should be thrilled at their engagement.

They arrived far too early at Windermere and as Fred watered the horse, Christie led Beth to a small waiting room with a log fire glowing. They bought mugs of tea.

'Does Fred know my news, Christie?'

'I don't know Beth.'

Fred hesitated as he opened the door into the small room then came across and sat beside them.

'Have you spoken to Robbie this morning, Freddie?'

He couldn't tell her that his words were only those of despair and prayers said at his bedside. 'I left him sleeping.'

'Then you mustn't know our news, either. We are to be married, Freddie.'

Fred shook his head, he couldn't help it. He took off his hat and set it on the table.

'You too are shocked.'

Fred discerned her distress and must pacify her. 'I'm sorry Beth. I was thinking that I wished it was me!'

She looked into his warm brown eyes; his fresh complexion from the cool Lakeland air. 'If I'd have fallen into your arms that day in church, Freddie, it may well have been you.'

Fred flushed with the sincere compliment. He lifted her hand as he noticed the ring that his brother had bought. 'It's a fine ring, Beth; he does love you.'

It was Christie who first got any sense out of Robbie.

'Does she know what state I'm in, Christie?'

'No sir.'

'Has she gone home now?'

'Yes, sir. Yes, she's back at Sugar Hills.'

'Will you tell her what happened?'

'No sir, we thought it best to wait.'

Robbie felt his voice break as he let his head fall back onto the pillow. 'I can't do this, Christie ... I can't live up to this ... I can't cope.'

The boy got up and sat on the bed beside him. 'Stop it ... stop it, Robbie. You're safe, you're alive. Tilly's safe, you'll be alright.'

Robbie twisted his head to one side but pain prevented him. 'What do you know about life, Christie?'

'You'll live, Robbie, that's what I know.... You're strong.'

'I'm not strong. I'm weak. How can I live with a fine woman like your sister? We were to wed, you know that?'

'Yes, she told me.'

'If she ever came to live here I would always be afraid of Mook tormenting her. It wouldn't be safe. If Mook doesn't kill me one day, he will kill her. How can I bring her here?'

'You'll break her heart, Robbie, if you let her down, she may already have asked my father's permission. She's tokened....

You gave her a ring, didn't you? You're betrothed. She showed me the ring and she's probably wearing it now.'

Robbie lowered his eye lids and quietly sobbed. Christie could do no more to console him. He'd never seen Robbie like this and didn't know what to do, so he reached for the flask of brandy, put it to Robbie's mouth and Robbie sipped, then fell back again.

'Tell her to have done with me ... tell her.'

'No, I won't. I never will.' Christie's young heart was bursting. A tear rolled down his cheek and he smudged it away. 'You once told me a brave man dies only once. You're not dead yet, you're alive. Please fight this. Mook must be stopped, for all our sakes.'

The doctor was sworn to silence. If anything leaked out they would know who had spoken. Edwin became venomous. He paced the kitchen, cursing Jimmy and Sally Mook, cursing himself for letting it happen, cursing Robbie for not listening and being too carefree about life. He'd warned Robbie and he hadn't listened. The Mooks had robbed him of his money and his dignity. Edwin had heard through village gossip that the Mooks were in Grasmere but couldn't find Robbie anywhere to warn him; little did he know he was proposing in the grand Prince of Wales' hotel. Edwin argued with Fred over reprisals. Christie could hear them from upstairs; Edwin shouting threats against the Mooks; he would kill Jimmy Mook if he found him. Fred calming him and begging him not to leave the house, or more harm would come.

Robbie's suit and fine clothes were ruined and Fred threw them on a bonfire. If Robbie lived he mustn't see them.

Beth didn't tell her father straight away about the proposal when she arrived home. She could see he was tired. It was John Dowson and Irene that had met her at the railway station. Irene as usual thrilled she was back, and desperate for any news on Christie's good health and of one, Mr Robert Keldas, gentleman farmer of Grasmere. But Irene also had news for Beth that she was longing to pass on.

When Beth saw her father dressed in a maroon quilted bed jacket, sitting alone by the granite fireplace with his two spaniels, he was in sober spirits and Beth noticed something was wrong. The room was dark and stuffy, dusty even. He hadn't let Irene clean for being in poor straights. He was clearly unwell and thoughts of her own happiness momentarily fled.

'You look tired, Daddy?'

He didn't speak at first, but lowered his eyes, then finally. 'I want to hear about your trip, Bethy, but foremost I want to know about my son.' He put his hand to his brow to relieve what must have been a raging headache. Squinting, and frowning at the lamp light he awaited her reply as if she was to tell him bad news. 'Is there anything you can cheer my sorry heart with, before I retire for the evening. But if you only have sorrow to speak of, it had better wait until the morning.'

She came close to him and knelt at his side in the semi-darkness. 'I have much to tell you, Daddy, and I hope you can see from my countenance it is all good news. Please sleep well tonight with the satisfaction of knowing both of your children are very, very happy.' and she came across, kissing him on the forehead. 'Please go to bed and I will tell you about Christie and some other things in the morning.'

She left him happy, but his manner and appearance had taken the glow off her face. She had purposely put the ring away in its little box, thinking she must at least ask for his approval.

The following morning Franklyn was revitalised, but not the same man he was. Beth knew he would be in his office. He used to walk out early with the dogs, a mile up the lane, say his morning prayers out freely in the open air, unhindered. He would greet the men as he passed, but today none of that happened. The dogs were itching to be out and restless and wandering about in the kitchen under Irene's feet.

'Where's my father?' Beth was neatly dressed in clean work clothes. Irene was washing the kitchen floor.

'He's still in his office. He had breakfast, if that's what you call it.' She pointed to a breakfast tray, still holding a bowl of untouched porridge and fruit; the tea-cup only half drunk. 'I'm so relieved you're home, Bethy.'

Beth straightened her skirt and walked with an air of gaiety. She tapped on his office door, and the voice that responded was fractured and weak, it didn't sound like her father.

'Come.'

Beth sidled in. Franklyn was sitting by the desk, writing, and appeared to have more colour this morning. He scratched another sentence on the thick paper and put down his pen, but didn't stand as he once would have to greet her. She kissed him.

'Your cheery news has brought a recovery for my soul, Bethy. I slept much better last night and my headache seems to have diminished.'

'I'm so pleased. Rest assured everything I have to tell you is good news.'

'So, tell me how my Christie is shaping up? Will he one day make a fine farmer?'

Beth stood over him, feeling like a schoolgirl and him the teacher. 'He is doing very well, Father. He's grown so much.'

'Is Mr Keldas treating him well?'

'He is, and more.... He has taught Christie so much. He's a different boy. A young man now. Confident, assertive, he's come right out of his shell.'

'Good, good. Oh, when can I see him? When will he come home?'

'I don't know that, Daddy. But he's very settled at Keld Head. You must ask him that.'

Franklyn had a tinge of disappointment, then punished himself as he realised it wasn't disappointment but jealousy of Mr Robert Keldas.

'So are this family as righteous as I have hoped?'

'Yes, it would appear so. Mr Keldas only has Christie's welfare at heart. Christie is working hard for his keep, I no doubt that. As I know his allowance is small.'

She stood and wandered over to the window and pulled back the heavy drapes a bit further. 'You must get some air. It's so stuffy in here. No wonder you get headaches.'

'I'm much restored today, Bethy, now as you are home and to know both of you are safe.'

She raised a little in stature as she breathed in the stagnant air. 'I have something to ask you, Daddy, if I may. Something I think you will be very pleased about.'

She quickly moved closer to him and took his cold hand. Her cheeks flushed with happiness. She took her hand from behind her back and showed him the ring; laying it flat on her palm.

Franklyn took her hand. He couldn't speak. He was shaking.

'Is this Mr Keldas's ring, Bethy?'

'It is, he has asked me to be his wife and I have accepted on your approval.'

Franklyn sat forward in his chair and cleared his throat. 'But you have his ring already, Beth.' Shocked at her intent.

'Yes, Daddy. I intend to wear it.'

'You show a headstrong attitude. Your heart appears to be already captured. Beg me please, first, before I grant your wish, to meet this gentleman that has bewitched my daughter as well as my son.'

'I hope you are not upset, but yes, I would like for you to meet him.'

'I wished you would have consulted me before you took his ring.'

She held her head low. How could she have been so insensitive? But she was naive. 'He has given me this ring as a token of his love for me. He's a good man - an honest man. The family are well thought of in the area. The farm, Keld Head, is beautiful. It yields well. It is close to Grasmere and Mr Wordsworth's house. The area is well known for its pleasantness but Mr Keldas isn't a material man; he has no interest in money, except to run his business honestly.

'And Aunt Charlotte has spoken well of the family.'

'So if I give my consent, when will you marry?'

'Soon, very soon. But I would have liked for you to come to Keld Head and see what a fine place it is. You must meet Robert and Freddie, then I know you will approve.'

'I am unwell, Bethy. Would Mr Keldas come here to Sugar Hills?'

151

'I doubt it, he is a very busy man. He insisted he couldn't travel to Thirsk.' There was a hint if disappointment, for she too couldn't comprehend why Robbie had shunned her as she tried to speak of her father.

Franklyn was torn, he wanted to ask about honour but didn't wish to insult her integrity. 'Then maybe my prayers have been answered and I didn't recognise it. I will go to Keld Head. Your news has restored me already. I want to see my son and where my daughter will spend the rest of her life, God willing. My health is failing Beth, but to be told my son is well, maybe someday very soon he will have my lovely Sugar Hills. And I hope with Mr Keldas's tuition, Christie can take care of this place as well as I have. I am pleased to know you have found a good man. You must always be honest with him Beth, and he you. You seem to be engaged and that is a vow before God. You must look to keep that vow. It makes me happy to know that. I must prepare myself to travel to Westmorland soon.'

'What is ailing you, Daddy?'

'My heart is failing. My eyesight is poor. I must make provisions for the future and it seems the Lord is helping me.'

Beth didn't go straight to see Irene, her heart was saddened at her father's news. Yet for him to say that her marriage would be an answer to a prayer cheered her.

When Beth composed herself and went to the kitchen, Irene's mother was already baking. The kitchen smelt of apple pies.

'How is your father today?'

'He looks better this morning. I hope I have brought him good news.'

'And Christie ... is he learning fast with Mr Keldas?'

'Oh he is, Annie, he is. You will see a great change in him.'

'I hope to see his pretty little face soon.' Annie smeared more flour on the baking board and rolled the pastry. 'Our Irene has news for you, Beth.'

Irene came over from stoking the stove and took a letter from her apron pocket. 'It's from Tommy ... he's finally proposed.'

'Oh, Irene.' Beth came close to her friend, the good news restoring her colour, and she hugged the girl.

But as Irene saw Beth's hand she noticed the ring. 'You have a ring?' She gently lifted her delicate finger. 'What is this?'

Beth stood back. 'I'm to marry Robbie, Irene. And we have my father's blessing.'

Franklyn heard the conversation in the kitchen; the women folk laughing and squealing, and he wondered how things were changing at Sugar Hills. He had prayed for his son night and day. And to hear he was progressing well was a good tonic. But the feelings of jealousy he had for the Keldas family, he hadn't anticipated; it crushed him and it was bringing something out of him he had tried to suppress: That another man, much younger than he, had succeeded in winning the hearts not only of his son, but now his daughter.

He picked up a photograph in a silver frame of his dear late wife. Beth and Christie certainly had some of her characteristics. He hoped he had taught them well and given them a sense of morality. Surely he could pride himself on that. He knew at times he had been heavy handed on them both with his desire to see them grow up unspoiled and righteous. He knew he'd made mistakes; some he had regretted. But had he been too hard on Christie? And now Beth so quick to fly the nest; had he repressed them both? And with his own health failing, his beating heart erratic, his vision poor. If he died soon, before he saw Beth marry, Christie would have to come home, but at sixteen it was still no age to run Sugar Hills. Franklyn had considered another manager, he knew it would cut the profits but this place couldn't run without one. Beth would be well provided for with some capital and a good life in the Lake District. He could do no more and would have to leave things be and in a secure and mightier hand than his. He muttered soft words at the photograph. 'I've done all I can.... I've done all I can.'

14
LETTERS OF LOVE

T o *my sweetheart.*
Dearest Robert, my heart is fairly bursting with the good news I have. Yes, at last I can write to you freely and unrestrained as the woman soon to be your wife."

'I can't read this!' Christie sat at Robbie's bedside with Beth's letter in his hand.

'If you don't read it, you will be out of this room ... nay, out of this house.' Robbie spat back at the boy.

'Hghmm.' Christie cleared his throat and continued. ' "*Yes, I spoke to my father today and he would be happy to give his blessing, but wishes to meet you first. In fact he went as far as to say our union would be an answer to a prayer.*

I also write with sadness that on my return I found him to be unwell. His health has declined so rapidly but I felt my good news helped to restore him somewhat, so it appears that our marriage would be of benefit to all the men in my life.

He was also delighted to hear Christie was doing well under his new tutor. And he made the request that he meet you and Christie at some point, at a place that suits your convenience. On reflection, I think if Christie would be agreeable that he should return to Sugar Hills briefly to see my father on the condition that he is free to return to your service. As for your good self, I will leave that to you when you meet my father, but he did express the wish that it be sooner as later. Despite his failing health, he would be happy to make the trip to Westmorland to meet you at Keld Head so he can see with his own weakened eyes what kind of farm Christie works at and the place where I will live, as he fears that soon he will be incapacitated. . . . . . . "'

Christie folded back the letter and put it in the envelope. He looked at Robbie lying on the bed and despite his remonstration wondered how much of it he had taken in.

154

'Do you want me to read it again, sir?'

Robbie opened his eyes and propped himself up on the bed. He raised one eyebrow and looked quizzically at the boy. 'Who is this woman that wants to marry me...? Is it the woman at St John's?'

'No sir. It is my sister.'

'Did I propose to your sister as well as the woman at St John's?'

'I don't know sir, I hope not.'

Robbie started to laugh.

'Stop it ... stop it.' Christie was crushed at his insensitivity.

'I will try and control myself for you, boy.... Do you consider this a good match, then, me and your sister?'

Christie couldn't reply. He hated the deception to see his friend near death and his sister oblivious. But bravery took over his young soul as he choked on his words. 'You must get better for Bethy.... You mustn't let her down.'

'I've let plenty of women down before, and some are now glad of it.'

'Not in my sister's case, sir.'

'So what of you, Christie ... if I decide to take a wife, will you return to your cosy farm under the Hambleton Hills?'

'I won't be going anywhere until you are well.'

'Or lying in the grave....' And Robbie twisted his head to hide his face from the young man. 'Leave me alone now, go.'

Christie took his jacket and rose from the chair. He looked towards Robbie's bedroom window, pulling the faded and heavy curtains to one side. The earth outside was frozen. He stoked up the fire in the bedroom by shovelling on piles of coal. In another hour it would be dark. 'I think it will be milder tomorrow,' and as he looked back, Robbie was asleep.

Christie wandered downstairs to the kitchen; he felt distraught; he loved this man but hated what he was saying. This wasn't like Robbie, or was it?

Edwin Wilding was slumped at the kitchen table, his head in his hands. Fred was standing beside him, hovering nervously around the table. Both men looked up as Christie came in the room. They noticed the letter was missing from his hand.

'Was it from her?' Fred's face was ashen.

'Yes, sir.... I read it to him.... He asked me to.' Christie stood as upright as he could before the two men. 'She will have my father's blessing to marry him. It was an answer to a prayer, he said.' Christie bit his lip.

Edwin then sat bolt upright. 'Then pray the Lord answers my prayers, and let me finish Mook fer good!'

Fred rested his hand firmly on Edwin's shoulders. 'You'll not leave this house, Edwin, until we know how Robbie mends.... Is he making any more sense, Christie?'

'Well, yes and no, but he was troubled over the proposal.'

Fred put on his jacket to do some work, to ease his mind from this turmoil and fear he was in. 'So what else did he say?'

'I don't know if I should tell you. I don't think he knew what he was talking about.'

'That bang on the 'ead as turned 'im into an imbecile ... a divvy. He'll nay be the same.' Edwin fell back on the table. 'I'll do fer Mook! I'll do fer him, alright.'

'He's not an imbecile, Edwin. Don't say that. The doctor said it was the laudanum.... He said it would confuse him. But at least the pain has gone.'

Christie went to sit at the table. 'He spoke of a woman at St John's and wondered if it was her he had proposed to. Can it be true?'

This statement was all Fred could take and he left the house, banging the door shut. The draught from the cold made Christie shudder, smoke belched out of the fireplace.

'He'll a wedded ev'ry lass this side o' Penrith, in is 'ead.' Edwin stuck his pipe in his mouth, chewing on it like a child would a dummy.

'No, he can't have ... not Robbie.'

'Nay ... yer daren't know 'im lad. He's nobbut a womaniser, that un.... Bye the lads ... that's summat any road ... he's coming te his senses mebee, if he's jibberin' aboot womenfolk. '

Christie hated what he was saying and wished Fred would return.

'He were like this when he getten back from South Africa. That did 'is 'ead in.... Aye it did. Messed up he were, until I took 'im under mi wing.' Edwin started to stuff his pipe with tobacco and Christie moved away.

'So will ye tell yer sister aboot it then young, Christie?'

'I don't know, Edwin, I don't know... I will ask Freddie what he thinks. My father wants to meet him ... that's the problem ... he wants to come to Keld Head.'

'Dang it, Christie, I'd fergetten aboot yer father.' Edwin lowered his voice and came close to the boy with smoky breath.

Fred Keldas was in control of a situation that he'd always feared, but never dared to think about. His father had told him so. He feared for Robbie's life and he feared for Beth. That poor woman ... that lovely young woman.... Christie must tell her, he knew that. He must encourage her to visit; she must be the one to choose what she did, not him, Edwin, or anyone.

Fred had a steady heart and a steady hand and although many had considered him dull and emotionless, he was racked with grief for his brother. The times he had wandered the hills looking for Robbie at his father's request; the tearful meeting at Sty Head. The drunken brawls when he was younger, gambling debts now paid, visiting him in Coldrigg Gaol, covering his head in shame as he entered the prison hoping no one would see him and tell their father. This was a lot for a young man to bear but Fred did it, and well.

Fred gave Christie some money to buy new clothes and get a haircut, also the price of his rail journey back to Thirsk. He almost ordered him to leave, to get to Beth quickly so she could decide what to do about the proposal but encouraged him more than anything else to return and not forsake his brother, for he knew Christie was the only one who could get any sense out of Robbie. He believed the news must be given to Beth by mouth and not by pen.

Fred had spent restless hours sleeping in his father's old chair at Robbie's bedside, much like he had done with his dying father. He was now managing two farms, ordering feed, moving cattle and sheep around. Glad he had good hands he could rely on, both here at Keld Head and at Spickle Howe. And as a young man just turned twenty, he ably filled his role.

He had seen how his father had been too easy with Robbie and that would happen no more; his brother must account for his actions. Robbie's foolish associates may yet cost him his life and could put his livelihood at risk. This would all have to stop and if Robbie married Elizabeth Richardson she could be the one to finally pacify him.

*   *   *

The Chimes
Haverigg
Cumberland

My loyal Franklyn

It is with sadness and fear that I write to you today and I also enquire after the health of your good self. But I have a concern that I must express to you forthwith, and hope that you do not consider my apprehension to be ignoble, but out of love and kindness for your family.

My concern is regarding your daughter Elizabeth and the news that she is betrothed to a Mr Keldas from Grasmere. I had occasion to travel close to the said village recently and was caught in a dreadful storm that meant I had to spend the night at a small inn near Langdale. The inn was awash with stranded travellers and I discovered the following morning that your daughter had also been stranded, but I am afraid to say she wasn't travelling alone but was in the care of Mr Keldas. Truly my fears could be unfounded but your good name and Elizabeth's chastity and honour, I suspect, may be at stake.

The news of her betrothal pleased me, but being witness to her un- chaperoned association with the said gentleman saddened me. I have witnessed firsthand Mr Keldas's charity and courage but am also concerned of his reputation. I know the young man's face from somewhere but I cannot recall ever meeting such a man named Keldas. I would advise you that their betrothal occur the sooner rather than later, for fear there would be gossip.

Your friend and brother in the Lord.
John Penruddock.

With trembling hands, Franklyn screwed the letter up into a crumpled ball and threw it on the fire.

Christie arrived back at Sugar Hills in the twilight of the early evening. He had planned to speak to his father tonight and Beth afterwards. He would return to Westmorland first thing in the morning. And as he walked the long lane to Sugar Hills he was nervous. He gripped a small leather bag that Fred had given him, his new boots, with flight of foot, barely touching the lane. He saw the turrets of Sugar Hills standing up in the darkness and it reminded him of the Pele tower at Keld Head. Fog loomed in and coated the cobwebs with dew on a tall and neatly clipped yew hedge. Everything was as pristine as he remembered. He saw the lights on in the Dowson's cottage and guessed they would have had their evening meal and John would have finished milking. Irene would be with her mother washing up the dishes. He stealthily crept past the cottage and went to the front door of Sugar Hills, straightened his jacket smooth over his waist and tucked his tie in neatly and tapped on the heavy oak door. The dogs barked as he pushed the door open and stepped into the hallway and waited; a stranger in his own home and becoming uncomfortable at the circumstances he found himself in.

Annie Dowson hurried from the kitchen and stopped, stunned, putting her hands to her cheeks in disbelief. 'Oh my ... it never is you, young Christopher Richardson?' and she stepped close to him. 'Let me look at you, honey? You are a happy sight for these sore eyes of mine. Oh, wait till your father sees you. You're just the tonic for him.'

Christie's young face flushed with the attention and he choked on his words. 'I'm glad to be back, Annie. But I have just come for the night. I have to return to Westmorland tomorrow.'

'Let me tell your father you are here, Christie.'

'Where is Bethy?' he coughed.

'She's with our Irene, talking weddings. Isn't it wonderful, Christie, two weddings?'

'Why are you still here, Annie, it's late?'

'I made your father some supper, he's unwell. Beth needed some time with Irene, he's been a strain on her and she has to have some relief.'

And Christie worried that he was going to put more strain on Beth's troubled mind. 'Is he in the study?'

'Yes, honey, go in quietly, he may be sleeping.'

Christie stood tall, took in a long and pensive breath and tapped on the door of the study and pushed it open. He heard his father's voice, quiet and restrained.

Franklyn was standing by a marble fireplace, his hand resting on the mantelpiece to steady himself; a grey shadow of his former self.

Both eyed the other, but Christie was the first to speak, and he spoke as a man. 'I'm sorry to find you unwell, Father ... I hope my disappearance didn't contribute to your illness.'

Franklyn couldn't let go of the mantelpiece. 'Yes, son, it may have, but your appearance tonight may also contribute to my recovery.' The words were choked. 'Is it really you, Christie, my son?'

'It is me, Father,' and Christie moved closer to him. 'Let me help you sit down, sir.'

And the young man took his father's elbow and felt the slender bones hidden under his quilted bed jacket.

'No.... Let me stand and look properly at my fine son.' Through glassy eyes, Franklyn gazed. Then thrust his arms around Christie's shoulders and embraced him.

As far as Christie was concerned that was the first time his father had ever touched him; but he wanted to keep control. 'I cannot stay. I must leave in the morning.... I must, foremost, apologise for my actions, and if you have the fattened calf ready, I am not worth it. I couldn't be a fool any longer and not visit, as you are so ill. I also needed to see Bethy.'

Franklyn rested heavy on Christie's arm and went to the sofa and fell onto it, then straightened his jacket.

'Then my prayers have been answered and this is all true, as I can see with my dismal eyesight that Mr Keldas has looked after you very well. I always intended for you to learn agriculture, Christie, and knew it would take years to do so, but this gentleman has made a handsome start, I think. As long as you never forget your future is here at Sugar Hills?'

Christie knew that was a question rather than a statement. 'I know that, sir, and I plan to fulfil that role when I'm ready, if that's what you still intend for me. Father, please remember I am only sixteen, I have much to learn, but the Keldas family are treating me well.'

'I can see by those fine clothes.'

'Yes, but I must return tomorrow. I have much work to attend to.'

'Then go. This family have turned you into a man, I can see that.... They have helped you more than I have.'

'No, it is not so.' Christie finally sat on the sofa beside his father; there was an earnest tone to his voice. 'I still have the principles that you gave me. And I hope I will always live by them. Mr Keldas has taught me many things,' and Christie knew there were many he could never speak about. 'I'm pleased you think I have grown.... I know I have.'

Then the noise of the dogs scampering in the hallway stilled their conversation, and outside Beth's voice, shrill and happy as she greeted them.

'Is that Beth, Christie?'

'I think so, sir.'

'Then bring her in here and let her see you.'

Beth and Christie spent an hour with their father. Christie spoke persistently, nervously, of life at Keld Head, all the time keeping an eye on the old long case clock ticking slowly across the room; a match for their father's failing heart; wondering how much longer they must talk before he was allowed to speak to Beth alone and unburden himself of his grim news.

Beth was speaking of a trip to Darlington with Irene. They had visited a dressmaker and Irene had been fitted for a wedding dress. Beth had eyed the products and the fabrics, the beautiful silks and lace, and knew if she were to marry Robbie it would be she who next chooses the fabrics. She anticipated that the quality would be grander for she knew her father's purse was much greater than the Dowsons'.

An hour passed and Christie was hungry, but daren't say so, and it wasn't until Franklyn became visibly tired did Beth become Christie's saviour. 'You are tired now, Daddy, and Christie must be hungry. Let me help you upstairs.'

Christie went to the kitchen where Irene and Annie Dowson were pretending to work. On seeing Christie, Irene shrieked, delighted.

Christie managed a thin smile for the first time that day and went to them.

'I told you, Irene, look, what a fine young man he has made in a few months.'

'I'm a hungry man if that's what you intend calling me.'

'There's plenty of food, Christie. I made it for your father but he has neither the intention nor the inclination of eating.'

And Christie could say the same of his patient back at Keld Head.

Christie sat in the old pine chair and looked longingly at the hot soup Annie passed to him. He dipped his head in silent prayer.

'How is Robbie?' Irene asked, sitting on the table, swinging her legs carefree, showing the lace on her petticoat.

But Christie could only nod gently as he ate. The mouthful of food helping him retain his secret.

'What a handsome pair they will make in their wedding finery, with Mr Keldas being so tall and dark and Bethy so elegant.'

Christie continued to let Irene talk and dream, and he knew the more she spoke the less he would have to.

'And is Freddie well? If I didn't have my Tommy I may have fallen for him myself,' giggling now.

'Yes, Freddie is very well.' In body, yes, but troubled in mind, he thought.

Annie slapped her hands together. 'Right, Irene, home now before you say any more things you might regret.'

Christie looked up from his plate. 'Annie, please tell John I will call and see him in the morning before I leave.'

'Yes, you will be a rare treat for his eyes my boy.'

Christie was finally alone in the kitchen, he heard Beth whistling as she came down the hollow stairway. Their father would scold Beth if he heard her and say that a whistling woman made a contentious wife. When Christie was a child he loved to whistle and sing on this tall and echoing staircase and today he knew Beth's little tune and it was one of Robbie's.

When she came in the kitchen she once again flung her arms around Christie's shoulders. 'Christie, this is wonderful.... Daddy is so happy tonight.' And with the warmth and comfort of her arms around him he let his head fall on her shoulder and wept.

The tears fell as they had never fallen in his life. He would recall until his dying day the look of shock on his sister's face, as her mouth dropped open. 'Whatever's the matter? Why are you crying?'

He moved away, looking out of the kitchen window into the bedarkened farmyard, embarrassed at his display of emotion. He wiped his face with the back of his hand. Took a clean handkerchief from his pocket and blew his nose. Beth came close, standing behind him, holding his arm to turn him.

'Christie, speak to me. What's wrong? What's happened?'

'I wanted to be a man, Bethy, oh how I have tried and tried these last few days.'

'And you are a fine young man.'

'I have held this in, but now I must speak. Please sit down for I have sad news which will concern you.' He pulled away from her and went to lock the back door and leant back on it.

'I don't sit down for bad news, not any more. I stand.' Her heart was heavy and she thought she knew what he was going to say. The lack of self belief had told her for some time that Robbie may change his mind.

'It's Robbie.... It's Robbie.'

'What do you mean? Heavens, Christie, tell me please, I beg you? Has he changed his mind?'

'Why no, oh dear Bethy. I know he loves you intensely, but he is ... ill.'

'My goodness. What ails him?'

163

'He may not make it. He may not last.'

He noticed her waver and she held onto the kitchen table. 'What is the matter? Has he some disease?'

'No, it's not that. He has been attacked.' Christie saw Beth put her hand to her mouth and the man in him was moved to step forward and console her and he took her trembling hand in his. 'There is a man who hates Robbie and he has attacked him brutally, and Robbie was left for dead. If not for Edwin Wilding, a friend, if that's what you call him, Robbie may have - may still perish. It was all about the horse, Tilly. The one ...' and he coughed not knowing of Beth's awareness, 'the one he claimed Robbie had stolen.'

'Oh my dear Robbie. What can we do? Why did you leave him?'

'Freddie said I must come and tell you his condition, so you can make a choice whether to continue with your engagement.'

'How can I not continue? Robert and I are betrothed. We as much have father's blessing.' She paced like a woman intoxicated around the kitchen, holding each piece of furniture as she passed. 'We have to be married, Christie ... we just have to.' She stopped and the rosy glow on her face turned to milky white. 'Robbie didn't steal the horse, Christie!'

'I know, I know, Beth. The night he left you, they found him strolling home and they struck him, robbed him, and beat him senseless.'

'So where is he?'

Christie gazed at her complexion, as Beth rung her hands through her dark hair.

'He's still at Keld Head. The doctor was called and we have nursed him several days, with Nora's help. This must remain private, Beth. Freddie doesn't want anyone to know and bring more shame on their family.'

'More shame, there is no shame, Christie, if the man was innocent.'

'No, but we must trust Freddie's judgement, it's his name at stake, too.'

'And mine, Christie. I will not forsake the man. Tell me, what is the extent of his injuries?'

The common sense in Beth and the fortitude she had took possession of her young soul, as it would always do. Her mother's untimely death had contributed to training her heart to be strong under duress.

'We cannot call the constabulary and the doctor is under oath not to speak. I'm afraid to say Robbie has head injuries that have confused his thinking. He talks nonsense and if he lives, the doctor fears he will remain so. He understands what's happened to him and I read him your last letter. Freddie fears you would never be safe at Keld Head if you marry Robbie. These Mooks will continue to take revenge. They could finish Robbie if Edwin doesn't get to them first and Freddie is doing his best to restrain the man.'

'Christie, I must come back with you.'

'No you mustn't. I fear your presence could confuse him the more. You must not leave father or tell him this news but I feel it best if you forget Robbie and decline his offer.'

'No.... No Christie, never! If his intention is still to marry, then it must be so and I will look after him and nurse him as a dutiful wife. How could I abandon him?'

'Then please write and give him happy news and maybe your intentions to wed may cure him. I will reply regularly to tell you of his progress.'

'Oh Christie, you are a brave young man. I am so proud of you. My heart is torn.'

He put his hand on her shoulder and they embraced, long and meaningful; their young hearts beating together in unison at their dreadful dilemma.

She pulled away and raised herself. 'Tell me, Christie, tell me truthfully before we part, does he still want me?'

'His words are confused, yet he feared you would not want him as he is; he said you should not love him anymore.'

'How can I not love him,' she moaned, and folded her arms as if to comfort herself. 'I will marry him, Christie, I must, whatever condition he remains in. Surely he would be happier and safer with me than any other. I will care for him and nurse him. And as for this man, Mook, I won't fear him. If Robbie intended me to be at Keld Head as his life-long companion then that will remain. What would my life be without him? I would have no life.

'Besides, Father has already told everyone our news. He struggled to stand in the pulpit but he preached of our prayers being answered. He's spoken of the Keldas family and their connections in Grasmere. I'm already as good as married in his eyes.'

'That surprises me. I thought he would want to meet Robbie first.'

'Yes, but there is something I must tell you, for Father and I have had a disagreement over Robbie.' She stopped and breathed heavily. 'I'm afraid while we were caught up in the snow storm, un-chaperoned, and had to spend the night at the Elterwater Inn. I'm afraid our visit was misconstrued by a friend of father's who found us there alone and he has discredited our name. Father was incensed with me, but more so with himself for giving me little guidance. I assured him of our integrity and Robbie's respect for me, as he has shown nothing but honour in my case. So I must remain a tokened woman. I already wear this ring,' she held out her finger to show him, 'not just because of the man I love but because of a man who challenged my reputation.'

Beth went to her room and immediately began to write. She poured out her heart in letter to Robbie, pleading with him to get well; stating over and over that she still wanted him. Stressing their vows; words poured faster than the pen would write. Ink blotted on soft paper, she didn't care that her brother would have to read this with his angelic voice; she loved Christie and she loved Robbie. She folded the letter, the first of what would be many and left it on the table for Christie to deliver by hand tomorrow.

'I can't read anymore, sir.' Christie dropped his hands.

'Heaven help me, Christie, read it!'

'It's too personal. Let's save it for when you're feeling better.'

'I am better. If you don't read it, I'll be off this bed and kick your back side like I would a mangy sheep dog.' Robbie was sitting on the edge of his bed, unshaven, his stripy night shirt draped over his knees.

The relief Robbie was still alive and survived the crucial three days had been overwhelming, but now something had overtaken him and his desperation to get out of bed was another trial.

Christie coughed. " *'How can you tell me not to love you, when I love you more than any man.*" Excuse me,' and he coughed. ' *"My heart bleeds for you Robert. I cannot bear to be so far away from you. I long for the day when I can come to Keld Head and never leave. But I cannot leave my father at the moment. He is hoping to stir himself sufficiently so he can make the trip to Westmorland.* " And that's it, sir.' Christie was glad it was over.

'Now get a pen and write something for me.'

'No sir, I cannot.'

'Do you want a whipping, Christie, because I will summon strength to do that.'

'I can see you could, and it cheers me ... whip me if you must, if it makes you feel better than the mood you are in today.'

'You still have the tongue of a scrupulous man.'

'Aye, and you one of a serpent,' Christie mouthed.

Robbie began to laugh. Vibrancy glistened in his eyes, and despite the yellowed bruising on his face and body, his skin tone was reddening and losing its deathly pallor.

'Then get me a pen, please, and yonder writing box.'

Christie lifted the oak box from Robbie's desk and found some ink and set the box on his knees.

'You will have to hold the ink or I'll spill it.'

Reluctantly, Christie sat beside Robbie on his bed, holding the inkwell tight in the writing box. 'I won't look at what you're writing,' he spoke, disconsolate.

'I have no secrets from you any more, Christie.'

Robbie sat up and tried to dip the pen in the ink, his hand shaking. It was just a simple letter D, but he couldn't do it.

'My hand shakes.'

'It will, you have been very sick.'

'Hold the paper steady.'

'I'm trying ... I'm trying.'

167

'You're in my light.... Get out of my light.'

Christie moved slightly.

'I can't do it, Christie.... I don't remember how to write.' The pen fell from his hand spilling ink onto the bed sheets and nightshirt. Robbie cursed with words Christie didn't understand. Black ink spread through the fabric of his clothes, and Robbie tried to wipe it with his hands, but the ink smeared onto his skin. Christie leant over and gently put the cork in the ink well and slid the box back on the dressing table. 'Tell me what to write, sir, and I will do it later. Get back into bed, you're cold.' And the young man covered him.

'You're a good nurse, Christie. But how is it that every time I try and think of my intended, it's always your pretty face I see. Are you like your father?'

Christie hesitated. 'You'll meet my father soon enough and can judge for yourself.'

'Do I know your father?'

'I don't think so, sir.'

'Then tell me what your farm looks like.'

'Sugar Hills, yes. It has a turret all the way around, like a castle. It's a folly.'

'Did your father build it?'

'No, he bought it.'

'And one day will you own it?'

'If my father dies, yes, one day I will own it.'

'Your father will die, boy. Mark my words, they all dies, as mine did. Do you deserve to inherit that fine property?'

'Maybe one day, if you can teach me how to manage it, but yes, I will inherit, not my sister.'

'You have a sister?'

Christie held back silent cries of anguish.

'Is she pretty?'

'Yes sir.'

'Does she have a voice that rises to a beautiful tone as she gets excited?'

'I believe she does. She laughs a great deal.'

'I remember her now. I wish I could hear her voice again.'

'She is to be your wife, sir.'

'No, I don't think so. I can't remember proposing. Have I met your father?'

Christie was getting used to this repetition now. 'I don't think so, sir.'

'Then if I am to marry your sister, I must meet your father....Write now, boy. Tell him to come, and soon, for I am too busy to travel.'

'You are too sick to travel!'

'Will you ask Freddie to send out a tailor.... It appears I need a new suit if I am to marry your sister.'

'I will. You are tired now. We'll write this letter later.'

'Who are we writing to?'

15

THE CUMMACATTA WOODS

Some had said that Edwin Wilding loved Robbie Keldas more than his wife; that wasn't in a romantic way but a filial one, as a son or a younger brother. But the bond that existed between them wasn't healthy for either because, despite his age, Edwin was a fool and Robbie was a sentimentalist.

Edwin hadn't seen his wife or children for weeks but Nance Wilding knew where he would be. Rumours had quickly spread to Wasdale from hill folk, shepherds and travellers, that Robbie Kellet, as was, had been robbed, left beaten and half naked and was close to death. The rumours must have come from the Mooks.

Edwin had taken his share of the nursing but not as ably as Christie, and now as Robbie was showing signs of recovery he planned to leave. In the mid-night hours Edwin took some bread from Robbie's larder, a steak pudding that Nora had made, listened earnestly that Fred Keldas and Christie were sleeping and crept away, just as slyly as he had arrived, with his shot gun and on foot.

Edwin wasn't a man of violence, in fact he was cowardly, and the scrapes he and Robbie got into were usually resolved by Robbie's money or fist or flight of foot.

Edwin hated his cousin's Jimmy and Sally Mook; the hate was nurtured from birth from his parents and theirs; two families scrapping over land, horses and chickens, but now the stakes were higher and Edwin would fight for Robbie's life. He didn't care what the consequences would be. He had no plan or idea concocted as to what his intentions might be, his overriding thought was to avenge what they had done to his friend. And he would finish this dreadful feud once and for all.

He decided to walk up over Greenup then down to Borrowdale; the route Robbie always took when he was travelling back to Wasdale. The rumours stated that the Mooks were staying at Grange and Edwin knew he could be there before daylight, get information then decide on his strategy.

The Mooks had bragged that they had harmed Robbie but couldn't retrieve their horse. They had stayed at Grange so they could have easy access to travel back and forth to harass him further and to get Tilly back. But since the attack the farmhouse at Keld Head had been well guarded by Fred Keldas, the Givens and Jackie Bainbridge the stockman, and Tilly was under pad lock and key. The Mooks hadn't intended on murdering Robbie, they just wanted to humiliate him. Sally could never accept his refusal of her; but she didn't want him dead; she didn't want to stop looking at him. The bang on the head was unexpected, they hadn't realised with the dark they were so close to the wall. But Jimmy had been scared senseless for he knew if that young man died, they would be implicated. But now he wanted more fun at Robbie's expense and lodging at Grange would give him that.

Edwin left Keld Head in fog. The weather was coming from the west and that meant a thaw. He'd underestimated the wet as he shrugged up Easdale, thawing water on the path saturating his shoddy boots, snow still lingering in the crevices on the fell tops. He had made another bad decision and should have waited. But he knew Fred would soon be up and awake and would have prevented him from leaving and he couldn't promise he was going home to Wasdale. The darkness was intensified by the fog that gripped his face like an icy mask and he didn't know if he was walking forwards or backwards. But Edwin like Robbie was a mountain man, born under the stars in Wasdale, and he had an inbuilt instinct that told him the correct navigation.

The only person who heard Edwin leaving was Robbie. He knew the click of the gate, he would always know that. The dogs hadn't barked because it was no stranger passing their kennel.

Robbie staggered from his bed. He looked into Christie's room and he was sleeping soundly; his baby face tucked cosily on his pillow. Robbie momentarily watched the boy, noticing his delicate features, then eased the door closed. He went to Fred's room and didn't need to open the door because he could hear familiar snoring, so loud that if they ever slept rough, Robbie would always hurl a boot at his head to waken him. But today there was no boot. He stood on the landing, pondering, worrying of the implications, but the decision he made was easily done.

He didn't wash; he would do that later in a stream. He staggered silently to dress in warm clothing, wrapping a woollen scarf around his neck and found his broad rimmed hat. His riding cape was downstairs on the hallstand. Robbie left Keld Head less than an hour after Edwin, on Tilly's back. He rode her through the paddock so no sound of clinking hooves would resound on the gravel lane. An hour into his journey in the fog and Robbie also knew this was a mistake. But he had to stop Edwin.

Tilly's hooves sunk into the wet on the Easdale pass; the horse nervous at this ungodly hour. Robbie thought of Christie and knew he would be the first to rise to feed up the cattle: he would surely alert Fred of his departure. He had time in front of him to do as he needed. A glimmer of Beth came to him and he thought of her handwritten letter declaring her love for him and her resolve to marry. Her soft features and beguiling voice swam through his troubled heart and nourished it. *"I love you more than any man." "When can I come to see you?" "My father wishes to meet you."* Robbie shivered and he pulled his coat collar up around his neck; Tilly seemed to know the way.

Every morning when Christie got up the first thing he did was to check Robbie's bedroom. He would quietly push the door open and listen for any stirring or breathing, then leave for work. Edwin would be the next to check. Edwin usually slept on the floor in the kitchen on the hearth rug. Once Christie left for work Edwin would steal into his warm bed; Christie never knew that.

Christie felt his heart jump as sparks of panic shot through him. He saw the dis-guarded night shirt, the empty bed; he lit an oil lamp and glanced into every corner. The bedroom was in disarray. Christie ran downstairs, his heels slipping on the wooden treads and saw Edwin's empty abode. Nothing left but a bottle of beer. He hurried back upstairs to Fred's room, and pushed open the latch. 'Freddie ... Freddie ... waken up.... Wake up!' Fred groaned and turned and seeing the anguish on Christie's face sat up. 'What in heaven's name's the matter?'

'They've gone, Freddie...! Edwin ... Robbie, they're missing.'

'Mother of thunder,' Fred pushed the bed sheet and blankets off. 'Check if Tilly's there; run boy, hurry.' He pulled on his clothes, hopping and jumping into his trousers and boots. He found a jug of cold water and splashed his face. He heard the back door rip open and Christie shouted up stairs.

'She's gone, Freddie, she's gone. But Topper's still there.'

Fred was the next to fall down the stairs, clumsily. 'What time is it?'

'Er ... it's five thirty.'

'How long have they been gone, do you think?'

'I don't know, but Robbie's bed is cold. I touched the sheets to check.'

'Right, Christie, we must act, and quickly. Saddle up Topper ... I will knock up the Givens and see if we can take Albert's fell pony. We'll be quicker on horseback.'

The thawing snow had left a carpet of snowdrops in its wake, pushing slowly through the January earth. The horses fidgeted in the yard, Topper as fractious as usual. The Givens' pony, Josser, was sure footed and steady. 'We'll travel over Greenup together. I can be sure he's gone that way. We'll head for Stonethwaite and if we don't find them, we will have to separate.'

'I don't know my way, Freddie. I've been to Greenup and no further.'

'You must ride to Grange and I'll ride to Wasdale. We will meet up at dusk if we don't catch them in Stonethwaite. It's Robbie we need to find, foremost. I can't worry what Edwin does; he will have to answer for that himself. We'll let the dogs lead the way. I'll take one you take the other; those little dogs love the man, so they will find him ... just follow the spaniels. When daylight comes we might even spot Tilly on the fells, surely her grey coat will stand out, unless there's still snow on the higher ridges.'

It all seemed a good plan in Christie's head. Fred sounded calm, rational; he'd done this before.

'But Robbie once told me never to go after him.'

'He doesn't mean it, son.... How can we leave him to his own devices when he can't think straight?'

Christie knew he had little choice; he hated the dark and he hated the fog; he wished he was milking, with his hands warm, clutching the cow's teats, and his head resting on their flanks, like a cosy pillow; listening as Albert Given whistled and teased the milk off some of the friskier animals.

It would soon be light; that was one consolation.

Edwin arrived at Stonethwaite, sat in a hay barn and finished eating the steak pudding. He wanted to sleep and thought if he rested his head for an hour he would be more alert as to his strategy; at the moment his plan was: no plan. The hay barn would provide him with warmth and rest.

He took off his boots and poured out drops of icy water. He rubbed his cold bare feet to dry them and restore some circulation. Peeling off his damp coat and neck scarf, he put his hat over his eyes and lay back in the hay. The sleep was welcoming. He would bang on cottage doors when he awoke.

Robbie wouldn't rush Tilly; he was baffled and blinded by the fog. The path was tricky for the horse and he didn't know his right from his left. Yet he knew Tilly's stride would catch Edwin's skinny legs and be quicker than he could walk, only if he could find his way; surely he knew that fell more than Edwin. He slid his hand in his coat and checked his pocket watch tucked in his waistcoat and squinted into the darkness. Telling time for a troubled mind was difficult; was it five thirty or was it twenty past six? This wasn't just a problem of poor eyesight. Did he have his watch upside down in his hand? So he twisted it to find the winder, he dropped it and it fell loose on his lap, held in place by the chain. He moaned at his disability with shaking hands. He pulled at Tilly's reins and she wheeled around as she stopped. Robbie slipped off the horse's saddle, clinging to her body for protection. He groaned in frustration, he stamped his feet on the rocky path below to circulate the freezing blood. Then he heard a blackbird, shrill and complaining and he knew it must be close to dawn.

Edwin splashed his face with water from the swollen river. He'd had an hour and the sleep had done him good. He walked to Grange and banged on every cottage door. Finally someone emerged, a sullied woman, smoking.

'The Mooks 'ave gan just this mornin'. I spotted 'em at the bridge up yonder, ont way te Greenup.'

'Dang it ... I've missed em!'

'Nay, man, they've only bin gone minutes. They won't be sharp.... Jimmy 'ad a skinful last neet ... 'e med enemies ... the beer med 'im talk ovver much.'

Edwin grinned, his few brown teeth bulging under his tar stained lips. 'Are they on foot?'

'Aye, and Sally's gibberin' like a fish wife ... you'll 'ear her afore ye see her.'

Edwin turned back to Stonethwaite.

Robbie sensed Tilly's hooves began to drop with a decline, the breeze hit him and he knew he was over the ridge. He slid off her back again and began to lead her down what he hoped was the track. A few cairns carefully placed by some shepherd guided him. They walked swiftly now, almost at a trot. The fog persisted and continued to wrap man and horse in an eerie cold blanket. Yet he was safe in the fog. Half an hour passed and he could smell wood smoke in the air and Stonethwaite beckoned; the village was coming to life. There was a farmhouse in the distance speckled in glowing lamplight. He stood at the lane end, Tilly pulling on the reins to eat the lush grass left by the thawing snow under the wall. He idled; he too was hungry and unlike Edwin hadn't had the presence of mind to eat.

Then he heard a woman's voice and knew it was Sally Mook. He heard the screeching, and Jimmy Mook cursing.

Robbie pulled Tilly in quickly and quietly on the soft grass behind a wall; there was a cluster of trees, a dense wooded area of silver birch and oak. He waited. Where was Edwin?

Sally Mook's voice rattled around this quiet valley and Robbie heard his name mentioned over and over again. They were clearly on their way to Grasmere. He thought of Christie; he would be milking now and wondering where he was. He hoped Fred was still at Keld Head and not on some mission of martyrdom to find him and make himself more righteous than he already was.

Then he heard a scuffing of boots on the lane and wheezing breath. It was surely Edwin.

Robbie clung to Tilly's reins and pushed her silently into the woodland and tethered her. She wouldn't give him away. From his secret hide he could see them all.

He heard Edwin cock his rifle. 'Daren't think the fog'll hide yer pox ridden fizzog, Jimmy.' Edwin spat. 'Come hither and let me ponder on thi yellow bellied eyes.'

The Mooks stood motionless. They turned, disorientated, not knowing where Edwin was.

'Are thi alone, Wilding?' Jimmy shouted and pulled a knife.

'Aye.... Ye'd like that, munt ya. Do fer me as yer did fer that young feller.'

'Nay, Edwin.... I won't touch thi clarty skin.'

Robbie edged to the wall and hearing the banter, breathed heavily.

Fred left Christie at the junction.

'Meet me at dusk, here at Stonethwaite, in that barn. No one hardly goes there. Well, no one except our Robbie.'

The mist so thick that Christie was soaked in it like someone trapped in a spider's web. One spaniel stayed with Christie and Josser as Fred left for Seathwaite with the other dog. He had told him to keep right on the lane and head for Grange. There was a family there who Robbie often stayed with; they were good allies. He was to find them and ask after Edwin and Robbie and wait. Christie was glad to know it was daylight and although that comforted him, the fog didn't.

He heard raised voices and an argument in the air. He pulled Josser to a halt; the spaniel stood its ground beside them. Christie slipped off the pony and listened; his young ears could hear the beck flowing and the voices tumbling with it, as if singing on the stones and rocks. A woman's voice then a man's then one he knew to be Edwin. Where was Robbie?

Robbie spotted Christie and Josser on the lane. 'Oh Christie, no boy, no!' his heart begging him not to act.

Then Robbie saw Edwin pull the gun from his jacket.

'I'll use it Jimmy, if thi uses that knife!'

Everything happened quickly. Jimmy Mook lunged at Edwin and Sally ran forward. Christie grabbed Sally from behind and restrained her by putting his hand on her mouth and another under her neck. The spaniel started yapping, then Edwin raised the butt of the rifle and hit Jimmy on the side of the head and the man fell to the ground. Not a mark on him.

Sally screamed and wrestled with Christie, unaware who it was restraining her, but she was no match for his youthful strength and he held her longer and harder than he had held any heifer. Robbie lunged forward from behind the wall and grabbed Sally from his clutches and pushed the boy away. 'Be off now,' was all he said. Christie understood and backed away. 'And take that yapping dog with you.' Robbie yelled as Christie bent low and took the spaniel's collar and left without being recognised.

Edwin watching on was mortified. He put his finger to his lips and beckoned Christie to keep quiet.

'Edwin, put that blasted gun down before you harm someone.' Robbie was still holding Sally and struggling to restrain her as Edwin bent low over Jimmy, 'Oh my word, Robbie, the man's a gonner!' Edwin shook Jimmy, but no life came. 'Waken Jimmy, waken, thi canna be dead.'

Hoping Christie was safely out of sight, Robbie let Sally loose and went over and bending low said, 'The man's dead, Edwin.... I've seen plenty to know what they look like.'

'Nay, Robbie, nay. He canna be.' Edwin's eyes danced around the corpse.

'Well, he is.'

'I'll hang ... bye, I'll hang fer this!'

Sally started to scream and Edwin raised the rifle, but Robbie snatched it from him. 'Sweet mother, Edwin.... If you live by the thing, you'll die by it, man. You know that.'

Then reality hit Sally hard, and fear caused her to run back towards Stonethwaite.

Sensing the seclusion Christie emerged from a gateway and ran forward.

'Did she see you?' Robbie whispered.

'No, no, I don't think so.'

'No one must know you were here.... Man alive, Christie, where's Freddie?'

'He's gone to Wasdale.... He said I had to meet him at dusk at the hay barn.'

Robbie growled. 'Argghhh. Then go now ... keep away from that woman ... go inside the hay barn and pull the pony in and keep that dog quiet. Wait until I come, you hear me.... do exactly as I say. Let me think ... blasted head of mine. Why can't I think straight? What shall we do with Jimmy, Edwin?'

'Chuck im int' river ovver yonder bridge. Watters swollen ... he'll sink afore anyone spots him.'

'No, not here, Edwin ... folks'll soon spot him if he surfaces. Too many people pass over here in daylight.' Robbie went for Tilly. 'Right.... Here, help me lift him. This feller can have his last wish and ride on this hoss's back. Give him that pleasure.'

They lifted Jimmy Mook's dead weight across Tilly's saddle and walked her slowly to a forest of trees and through the dampened woodland; rabbits were the only living things to see them. There was no path, so they twisted slowly in and out of trees; Edwin was now sobbing.

'Shut up, Edwin! Shut it. We'll be caught soon enough when Sally tells the constabulary.'

'It's dang awful, Robbie. I nivver meant to kill 'im, just frighten 'im, like.'

The woodland opened and some of the fog cleared but Robbie wished it would stay. Everywhere was silent. They walked for a few miles away from Stonethwaite, onwards towards Grange. They waited close to a clearing near the river and watched. They tethered Tilly and lifted Jimmy Mook's body and hauled it across the floor of the woodland and listened. There was some scrubland at the edge of the river which was in full flood from the thawing snow.

'Get rocks, Edwin.... let's fill his pockets and his kecks.' They re-buttoned Jimmy's clothes, and flung the corpse into the river.

'If this carcass floats underwater slowly to Derwentwater, we may have a few days of freedom left.'

'Do ya think it'll stay down?'

But Robbie didn't answer because he knew there was no choice.

Both men eyed each other. Edwin flung his arms around Robbie's neck, but Robbie pulled away. 'Go to your wife and bairns, say goodbye to them. Go now. Because when this is discovered they'll have us both.'

Edwin disappeared into the fog, back through the woodland, limping, stumbling. Robbie soon lost sight of him, but he could still hear the sobbing and staggering of feet as they slid carelessly on rocks and exposed tree roots.

When all was silent Robbie led Tilly high up the woodland away from the wall, towards the crags. He had no idea which direction to walk.

When he felt he was safe and far from sight he fell to the floor on a bed of wet leaves and snowdrops, kneeling in the mire. He looked skyward but saw nothing. Tilly beside him nuzzled the leaves, looking for grass. He let go of the reins and looked at his hands and wondered what they had done; what more mistakes had these careless hands cost him. Then he frantically rubbed them in the leaves and the earth to remove the badness and the filth of Jimmy Mook's body. He twisted and lay flat on his back on the snowdrops and rested his hands on his chest as if he was dead; all was now lost. Then feelings of worthlessness overtook him and he grabbed a handful of leaf mould, quietly groaning. Tilly stood by his side like a protective shield to hide his remorse; she nuzzled his coat looking for treats. His trousers, thighs and back were saturated, his pocket watch was hanging loose on its chain. And as he picked it up and twisted it, he could see for the first time that day that it was eleven thirty. He must have slept. He was shivering, more with fear than the cold.

Robbie lifted himself and listened, but there was only birdsong. He struggled to stand and wiped his eyes and forehead with the sleeve of his coat and mounted Tilly.

With a sense of natural direction Robbie left the woodland, onto the lane, a tall cliff loomed above covered in rocks and trees, sunshine was trying to push through the fog. He rode Tilly slowly, quietly, he wouldn't hurry in case he caused any commotion; he felt dreadful; his legs were trembling in the stirrups; his head was light; with each step he listened; where had Sally gone? His fears now for Christie were overwhelming him, hoping he was safe at Stonethwaite. He could be there himself in an hour at this steady pace.

As they walked, twisting through trees, keeping to the bridleway, he saw little traffic on the lane below and hoped their sin hadn't been discovered. He continued on, riding up and down stony paths on the fellside. He mused over his deeds and knew he had made a choice that would put his whole future at risk. His thinking still not clear, irrational thoughts took over, excusing himself, concocting ideas to cover his tracks. His fear of returning to Coldrigg Gaol, and hang was the worst.

He recalled Christie's hands on Sally's neck; had she known who he was? Did she see him through the fog? Then clearer thoughts came to him; deep remorse and sorrow that a man was dead; his foolish relationship with Edwin Wilding and poor Fred searching for him again. There was no more he could do, but find Christie and hope he was safe and undiscovered.

*   *   *

Stonethwaite cottages were visible across the field. Cattle were lowing and sheep were bleating. Robbie could see little movement in the village and on the lane as he kept the upper path. People knew him here. He mustn't be spotted. These paths were well known by Tilly as she walked sure-footed. He spotted the stone barn across a meadow. He stopped but saw no one, hoping Christie had done as he had said and was inside sitting, and quietly waiting. Robbie's head was aching as he climbed the rise in the field, keeping close to some holly bushes under the wall. He peered into the barn as he slid quietly off Tilly's back and took two steps forward, looking into darkened corners. He made out the image of a black pony and dropped Tilly's reins and walked inside; his boots silent on the soft hay. The little spaniel tethered to a beam wriggled and wagged its tail happy to see its master. The pony looked around and seeing him nodded its head.

Robbie could just see Christie kneeling on the hay, his head and shoulders forward, leaning on a small barrel.

'Christie,' Robbie whispered. No response.

'Christie!' a little louder.

The boy looked around, startled.

Robbie came to him and dropped to his knees by his side. 'What's the matter? What are you doing?'

Christie rubbed his eyes and turned. 'I was praying.... I must have fallen asleep. Are you alright?'

'The Lord won't be pleased with you for falling asleep in prayer, Christie.'

'I doubt the Lord will be pleased with me for laying my hands on that woman as I did!'

'No, son.' Robbie twisted and lay back against the barrel. 'It's all futile, Christie.... Hopeless, now. What can I do?'

'What have you done?' The boy looked terrified. 'Where's Tilly?' Christie stood up and wandered towards the door.

'Bring her inside, please.'

'What time is it?' Christie led Tilly to the hay.

Robbie checked his watch. 'It's about thirty minutes past twelve. We can't move from here until Freddie gets back, he may not be as long as you said. The fog is clearing. It may have cleared quicker from the west.

'What did you do with Mook?'

'You don't want to know, and it's best I never tell you. But hopefully it gives us time before anyone finds him to think things out. Oh, man alive, I wish you weren't here. Why did you come?' he shook his head.

'You're ill, Robbie – sick – I couldn't leave you. Freddie said we had to find you.'

'Huh yes, you're right. I am sick, Christie, sick in the head. Will your God forgive you for your hand in this?'

'I know he will sir, and you too, but that doesn't make me feel any better right now. I've never laid a hand on anything or anyone like that before, not even a bird. I hate violence. I hate killing, but I had to keep the woman quiet. I saw the man had a knife. He could have used it.'

'And did you see Edwin had a gun?'

The boy didn't answer.

'You must promise to keep quiet and not tell a soul, other than the Lord. You had no serious part in this tragedy. I would have grabbed Sally sooner or later if you hadn't have. I don't think she saw you. I don't think she knew who you were. I saw it all from the trees, but they'll come for me, Christie ... and Edwin, so they will. But you need not be implicated. When Freddie returns you and him go back to Keld Head together. I will return alone.'

Two young men on horseback with two spaniels galloped down Far Easdale faster than they should; their coats flapping carelessly in the breeze; neither speaking to the other. The horses' breath drifting upwards, panting, sweat saturating their necks. Josser struggled to keep up with Topper as their hooves clattered down the walled lane. Dusk was breaking and in the foggy distance Keld Head was waiting to defend them. The circumstances were just right for this living stone to protect them, it had done it all before and it would do it again and again. Ingrained in the stone and running through it like a fossil was the word "tragedy". It revelled in it because it was all it knew.

On the other side of England a pretty girl was sitting writing a love letter from the bedroom, high in the turrets of Sugar Hills. It said:

My dearest Robert ... my sweetheart.

I trust this letter finds you much improved and in good spirits. Your last letter was readable - just. Christie will be happy to be relieved of his secretarial duties. I'm so happy to think that in a few weeks time we will be man and wife; how wonderful. My dress is almost complete; the dressmaker is delighted with the results but complaining that I have lost weight due to fatigue and worry. Yes, The Prince of Wales is a fitting setting for our wedding breakfast and I am pleased that only close family and friends will attend. Christie wrote and told me of your new suit; how handsome you will look, my love.

My father has insisted as he is feeling much better, all down to the hand of your good self, that he would rather meet you sooner than later and wishes to see you before the wedding day. And he hopes to come to Keld Head. I am happy in a way as I fear your convalescence is slower than his. He wants to meet you and personally thank you and shake your hand. We will wait for fine weather, but if it comes next week we will travel by train. I will be relieved of my duties from the school and will remain in Westmorland so I can fulfil our legal banns.

I cannot convey to you in words my happiness. My dear friend Irene marries this week then leaves for Morpeth and I will not see her till our wedding day. Oh Robbie everything is so wonderful. . . . .

16
BIG TREES

Robbie thought it a ridiculous thing to do, to wear his new suit; his wedding suit. Nora had starched a white collar and he had a new deep red coloured necktie. He had shaved this morning in cold water; he may have to get used to that. His dark hair was combed, just a little over his forehead to cover the remnants of a head wound. His black boots polished; if he wanted to, he could see his face in them; but what he would see would be the countenance of a guilty and broken man.

Robbie had decided if nothing else there would be a sense of dignity today in what he had to do. He tried to breathe deeply and easily but couldn't. And he cheated his heart and lungs with short snappy breaths. Lastly, he put his gold hunter in the pocket of his waistcoat and walked downstairs.

Fred was alone in the kitchen, standing close to the oven, wearing the brown tweed suit that he'd bought for his father's funeral; his sandy hair neat and trimmed; he had nothing to hide except the scars on his heart for his brother and his father.

Both men eyed each other.

'Are you okay?' Fred asked.

Robbie didn't reply.

'Are you sure you want to do this?'

'What choice do I have?' The voice was bitter with little emotion. 'Has Christie gone?'

'Yes, he left half an hour ago.'

'Does he know what to do?'

Fred just nodded and walked closer to his brother. 'Yes, he knows, but he says he doesn't know why ... I didn't enlighten him.' Fred lowered his head. 'Are you hungry?'

'No, but thank you,' and Robbie went to the table, sitting half on the chair and put his hand on his face. 'Oh, Freddie ... how can I break her heart?'

Fred came to him and touched his shoulders. 'Is there any other way, Rob...? It will break her heart more if you don't tell her and bring shame on her family if you are incarcerated.'

'I know, I know.' His head was perspiring. 'If you weren't so slow, Freddie ... and you were the one to catch her that day in church we wouldn't be having this conversation, and it would be you waiting and under much better circumstances.'

Fred blew breath through his nostrils.

'Do you really believe Christie has no idea of what I am about to do?' Robbie looked at the lane out of the window for any traffic.

'He's troubled, Rob ... we all are ... he's no fool.'

'It's best I hang, Freddie, and then I'll ease your pain and bring you no more shame.'

'Stop it, stop it. Dang it Robbie, sometimes ... just sometimes?'

'Sometimes what...?' and he raised an eyebrow, quickly, quirky. He was skilled at this.

'Well, if you weren't my brother I would up and leave you to your sins.'

'You speak frankly at last ... you have become a man, Freddie.' And there came the crooked smile. 'Do you know what the hardest thing will be? To think that some other man's lips will eventually touch hers.'

Both men looked afraid as the sound of a motor car came down the lane. 'If it was to be you, I could cope with that.'

Fred looked out of the window and saw Beth step out of a vehicle, alone.

'Christie has succeeded. Do you want me to leave?'

'No Freddie, please stay.'

Behind the walls of Keld Head, Robbie had made himself a prisoner. For seven days he had watched the lane. He'd barely slept and when he had, it was fitful. Every bark of the dog or click of the gate; yes the click of the gate was the worst thing, as each time it sent a shock of adrenalin through his veins and into his heart. The men became suspicious of his request to

185

keep the gate shut; they were happy at Robbie's recovery but wondered at his sanity.

Robbie stood and lowered his head.

Christie sat on the bench at the back of the church. He could still hear his father's voice as he spoke to the verger; not loud, as it once would have shaken the timbers in the roof, but now it held a weak and sickly hollow; almost macabre. Occasionally he heard him mention Beth's name and then Mr Keldas. Christie counted the arches, five on one level, four on the other. He glanced at the new windows, colourful with the light. The rafters in the church weirdly constructed as a rib cage, and then on the windowsills pots of blue hyacinths. He counted the rows of seats, enough for a small congregation.

It hadn't been difficult to keep his father separate from Beth, as she was anxious to see Robbie for she discerned something was amiss. Fred had told him to give at least thirty minutes and, as his father questioned the verger, Christie was edgy.

In Christie's young mind there was devastation ahead. He too had listened for the police, or the Mooks. But they hadn't come. At one point Robbie had become disconsolate. Willing them to come and take him away, hoping that they may save him from this meeting and the conversation he was going to have today; he feared the police the less. He didn't want to betray Edwin and he wondered if Jimmy Mook's body had remained at the bottom of Derwentwater.

Christie was supposed to be learning agriculture, but the things he was learning, were things a young man shouldn't know as Robbie expressed openly his thoughts. The witnessing of the death of a man; the abuse of Sally Mook; it all had a scarring and desensitising effect on Christie's young heart. Things that had been sheltered from him by his father were unwittingly exposed by his tutor. He knew his father would strongly refuse Beth's marriage to Robbie, if he knew the truth, and Christie wasn't going to be the one to tell him, but the truth would soon be out. Christie hadn't preached to Robbie; he knew it wasn't his fault; they hadn't heard a thing of Edwin and all assumed he was laying low in Wasdale with his wife and children.

Wisdom had told Christie it was time to leave Keld Head for good; Robbie had insisted he returned to Sugar Hills, but loyalty and love made him stay; and he knew he was party to a crime.

He had an idea of what Robbie was going to say to Beth; and he knew it meant his sister would be torn.

Christie checked his watch; it was time to leave. 'Father ... Father....' Christie rose from the pew and walked slowly up the aisle of the church. 'It's time we left.'

'Come on, son, lead the way; I need to meet your mentor.' Franklyn held the young man's steady arm. 'How far have we to travel?'

Christie led his father to the seat of a waiting motorcar. 'Can you see the tower in the distance?' He pointed. 'That is Keld Head ... that is where I work.'

'I see nothing of any consequence these days. But I do recall a tower....Tell me of its aspect?'

'It sits under the fells. It's a fine building in amongst a small hamlet of cottages called Keld Head.... The tower is in excellent condition. Mr Keldas has kept it well.' Christie looked ahead and thought the gloom of the day made the place appear grim; it would always seem that way to him from now on.

Beth stepped from the motor car and rushed to the door of Keld Head; no one saw her silently pray as she walked. She braced herself because she had detected Christie wasn't stalling her father for nothing. He had been anxious since she saw him with the news of Robbie's attack; and yet despite his recovery, Christie was still as restless.

When Fred met her at the door; sombre in mood, she knew a trial awaited.

She smoothed the purple fabric of her long winter coat and removed the fur muffler and hat. She shook her head, letting her long hair tumble to her shoulders.

Fred took Beth's hand as he greeted her and fear for this young woman overtook him. He wanted to tell her to go home and forget his wayward brother but he must see this through; he believed at this moment in time he loved Beth more than Robbie.

On the kitchen table were cups and saucers, tea plates of red and gold with silver cutlery. A cake stand laden with fresh drop scones; home made bread and cheese was displayed on a wooden board. Nora had left the premises.

Beth dropped her hat on the table not noticing the food; she smoothed her hand across the polished table. 'Where is he?'

'In the parlour ... please come through. I will leave you in peace.' Fred spoke softly; empathetic.

Robbie appeared at the door, tall, elegant, his head raised. He didn't address Beth but Fred, and just repeated. 'Again, I ask if you will stay, Freddie.'

Beth moved a step closer, wondering why this coldness, but the barrier he had set in place was purposeful. Oh how she wished that crooked smile would appear. Robbie turned his back on her and walked into the parlour and stood close to an open fire.

'Sit down, Elizabeth, please.'

She took another step closer but he stepped back. 'I won't sit if you don't mind. Are you still unwell?'

'Nay, I'm not sick, Bethy,' the first words of compassion.

Fred was standing nervously at the door close to her, ready to catch her if she fell. Looking at the deep blue patterns on the carpet; he felt his feet were stuck to it.

He heard Robbie clear his throat.

'You must decline my offer of marriage, Elizabeth.... It must end now.'

Beth's mouth parted. 'I'm sorry, what do you mean?'

He straightened his neck tie. 'I mean, I'm not worthy of you, my dear Bethy. And if that man soon to arrive - your father - is who I think he is, he will forbid this attachment any way.' He spoke clearly; coldly.

Fred didn't look up, just raised his eyes, he didn't realise he had momentarily held his hand close to Beth's elbow.

'No, no, he would love you Robbie, as I do.'

'No Bethy, not now, not any more. I have done something that will bring shame on your family... your name and your father's name.... Our marriage would soon be over even if it got to be legalised. I may hang for what I've done. So despite your proclamations otherwise and despite being betrothed, it is best I do this now than later, believe me.'

Beth stepped backwards for something to hold and it was Fred.

She moved to the wall and faced it, then laid her palms flat, clinging to the wall for comfort. 'Oh dear life, what have you done, Robbie?'

He stepped up to her, his heart ripping. 'A man has been killed, Bethy ... Jimmy Mook, the man who attacked me. I never laid a finger on him not until he was dead but I helped throw him in the river.' There was no easy way to say this. 'The police will come and I will probably hang.'

'You killed a man, Robert!'

'No, Edwin Wilding did. Christie was with us.'

Beth bent almost double as she moaned, she put her hands to her ribs, Robbie came to her but she pushed him away. She had been cheated of love, declined a happy future, the cords of love had been pulled tight and constricted her.

'I'm sorry ... I'm sorry,' was all Robbie could say, he looked at her, his face only inches away from hers. 'I saw the end of this at the beginning, Beth.... You were too good for me - you were naive to want me. I will confess to your father my mistake and he will take you home.'

'No, you were beguilingly deceptive.' She had the courage to speak.

Her words of despair were rash and they shocked him; there were no tears. Then their young ears sensitive to noise heard a car come down the lane. Robbie rushed to the window and saw clearly Sir Franklyn Richardson lay preacher, Justice of the Peace and gentleman farmer, stepping out of a motor vehicle with Christie holding his arm.

That was it. It was all over, his last hope that this man was another, and that Beth would still say that she wanted him, had gone.

Three young people, shocked at Franklyn's arrival were stupefied by fear, and he was soon with them in the room as large as life with Christie beside him. No time for any more words.

'And which of you two fine young men is hoping to marry my daughter?'

Franklyn gazed through hazy eyes about the room, he didn't notice the tears on his daughter's cheek, as his eyes were drawn to Robbie's superiority; his height and stature, and noticed on his forehead the remains of a healing wound as he stood tall, dignified; handsome. Franklyn got eye contact and peered, Robbie equally as interested, looked back at Franklyn. Then he saw Robbie's clean skin and fine eyes, his exquisitely fitted clothes and he had the resemblance of someone, but Franklyn couldn't remember who. He never looked at Fred, smaller in stature, younger, with a ruddy complexion.

Fred stepped forward and said. 'It is me sir, if she'll have me!' Words were spoken, frozen in time.

Franklyn was disappointed. He looked around at Beth who was now standing equally as high in stature beside Fred and said: 'Yes, I will marry you, Freddie, if my father permits it.' Reluctantly, Franklyn came forward to shake Fred's hand. 'Thank you sir, thank you for the way you have treated my family.'

Fred just nodded. 'This is my brother, Robert,' and as Franklyn held his hand out he said: 'Young man, do I know you?'

'Yes, sir. It appears we have met before. We had a quarrel in Wasdale and it's as well your daughter is to wed my brother,' with a bitter tone. 'He is far more righteous than I. And I can only ask for repentance as I was a victim that day as much as you were.'

'Then I'm sorry, Robert, but your repentance isn't necessary.'

Robbie started to shake. He had underestimated Franklyn's kindness and mercy; this was not expected. Forgiveness, he hadn't anticipated. And suddenly everything was futile. He'd been a presumptuous fool, and that was the mistake he had made. 'Christie, I suggest you show your father around the dairy and the tower, and maybe later my brother will take you to Spickle Howe, our other farm, as it appears that is where your sister will live. Beth, Freddie and I have much to discuss.'

All three wanted them to leave. Robbie went to the door and watched them go, then shut it fast and turned. He saw Beth bite her lip as she waited his response. 'So my brother has become an opportunist and my betrothed a capricious woman!'

'What could I do, Rob. You said you could cope if she was with me. Beth's father looked so poorly and I didn't want to quicken his finish. I'll swear I've no intentions of touching her while you are alive on this earth.'

'And does that suit you, Elizabeth, or did you hope for more?'

'Don't be coarse, Robbie, you know what I hoped for and you have denied me of that.' Then Beth moved forwards and fell on his chest. 'You said I'm a tokened woman and so I am. He has told everyone back home of this farm in Westmorland ... preached about it in the pulpit.... It would break his heart to know that the man I love is about to hang! Freddie has saved him from that.'

'And what has he saved you from, Bethy?' he held her tight, as she wept. He looked up at Fred. 'You must either hate me or love me very much, Freddie.'

Fred spoke softly. 'It is the latter.'

'And you would sacrifice any future prospects of your own to comfort me as you said, in my last days.'

'I will.' Fred gasped and a triangle of love emerged bonded like steel.

'Leave us alone please, Beth.' Robbie asked. 'Go and see to your father.'

As soon as she left Fred seized his brother by the arm. 'I didn't know what to do. I couldn't let her suffer.'

'I can see the apprehension in your eyes, Freddie.' Robbie pushed him aside.

'The man looked as good as dead, he could die soon . . . then this could end.' Fred said.

'Oh, could die ... could die? What about *will* die, or what do you hope for? Are you afraid your engagement will be shorter than mine?' Robbie watched as Beth helped Franklyn walk across to the tower, her loving care of this genteel man apparent; he moved away from the window.

'You said if it was me, you could endure it. You said it Robbie, not I.'

'Yes, that was an overstatement, but since when have you ever listened to what I say.' He put his coat on.

Fred pleaded. 'I dreamt about her last night. I saw the horror in her eyes. I dreamt that we were being hounded by the Mooks and they said if we didn't cross the swollen river they would kill us all. But she couldn't do it, she was afraid, so I said to them, if I cross it twice, would that save her? And I did it.'

Robbie looked at his brother but the words failed; *and so he too dreams of her*? He was tired, he was grieving; he would say no more.

Beth sat on a small seat beside the tower and Christie took Franklyn inside, he rambled words incoherent, talking of border reivers and lakeland stone, mumbling about cattle and sheep.

As Franklyn eyed the tower, amazed at its presence and appearance, he said: 'Fred Keldas is quite young, Christie, younger than I expected.'

'He's a fine man, Father.'

'Yes, you always speak well of this family. What about his brother?'

'Robbie has helped me more than Freddie.'

'I'll be honest, Christie, I have never met two brothers so dissimilar. One a nervous chatterer and the other possessed of charm and wit. I may have preferred the charmer, despite his fracas with me; he appears an honest young man.'

'He is more honest than you will ever understand, Father. But remember you always taught me never to judge on appearances.'

'My son counsels me; he has cheered me today with his wisdom. "*Look not on his countenance, or on the height of his stature; because I have refused him: for the Lord see'th not as man see'th; for man looketh on the outward appearance, but the Lord looketh on the heart*".'

'If Beth wants to marry Freddie, she has chosen well. Her future will be happier.' Christie said embittered words.

Dinner at the Prince of Wales was a quiet affair. Beth could barely eat. Waiters were bowing as they served, and Fred felt uncomfortable at his manners, without the eloquence that Robbie had, he felt a poor reflection. Beth stood, excused herself and went to her room, claiming of a headache and that the day's challenges had been all too great, she had been a good actress in front of her father, but she could act no more.

Robbie had been invited to share the meal but strongly resisted claiming he had much business to do at Keld Head, stating he was soon to travel.

Franklyn spoke passionately to Fred of his farm at Sugar Hills, and the more he spoke he became enchanted with Fred's acumen and knowledge of farm management and soon understood that although this man was young in years he was mature in his thinking.

Beth stood at the bedroom window staring into the darkness, the lamplights of Grasmere flickering in the night sky; it would be the way she would always see life from now on; Keld Head was buried in the darkness, as was Robbie; there, but not present.

She had replied to his decline of marriage in anger, and rashly, her acceptance of Robbie in the first place, done with more thought than that of Fred. But she consoled herself in what choices she had. She would willingly have a marriage of convenience to keep her dear father's wishes intact and her own good name and reputation. She doubted she would ever love anyone as she had Robbie.

Robbie's dreadful feud with the Mooks brought out his weaknesses and his strengths to the fore; but to have Christie involved was unforgiving. Loyalty was important and if Robbie couldn't fulfil his promise of marriage, she knew with certainty that as noble and as loyal Fred Keldas was, he would care for her.

Thoughts of Robbie dying at the hand of a hangman made her shudder. She would have wanted to be with him to the end, but the cruelty of his refusal of marriage, denied her.

Robbie's words came back to Beth; he had called her capricious; how could he say that? Is that how he really saw her? To have given him up so easily without a struggle, because of one sentence he'd made in desperation to save her integrity. Then the thought struck her if he was taken tonight she may never see him again and that panicked her. Her head thumped with guilt. Her brain hurt with thoughts of how they could change matters, but while her father was alive she knew there would never be any other answers. She considered dressing and going to Keld Head; no one would miss her; they could elope together. Her father was in deep and meaningful talk with Fred and Christie; he would leave tomorrow and as for her, many anxious days remained here in Westmorland as she stayed with her Aunt Charlotte.

A gentle tapping on the door aroused Beth and stopped her from an imprudent course.

'Who is it?' she was uncharacteristically sharp.

'It's Christie.... I'll die if I don't speak to someone.' He said in muffled tones.

She hurried to the door and unlocked it. 'Are you alone?'

'Yes, please let me in!'

She stepped aside behind the door as Christie gazed at her dishevelled hair, her tears leaving traces on her skin. They embraced, united in their fears. It was sometime before either could speak and it was Christie who spoke up first. He straightened his spine and walked to the centre of the room near the light.

'I know you consider me weak, Beth, but I have strength you can depend on if you need to get out of this reckless situation.'

'Reckless ... is that how you see it?' She came to him and slid lazily onto the bed, her legs weakened with worry.

'You cannot go through with this, Bethy.'

But she ignored him, her voice inarticulate. 'Did you know that Robert had met Father before?'

'No.... No, I didn't. That was news to me too. I understand now why he never wanted to speak of him.'

'Well, don't worry now Christie, for that is the least of my problems, it explains many things. How involved are you in this dreadful murder?' Words she never expected to say in her life.

Christie sat beside her on the bed and took her hand. 'Don't hate him. Bethy ...'

'Hate him! Hate him ... how can I hate him so quickly. I love him still, but I must know the truth.'

'He's an honourable man, I told you. He went to find Edwin because he was afraid he would do something stupid like this. Edwin was breathing threats of revenge against the Mooks for what they had done to Robbie.' Christie sniffled a little as he spoke. 'Fred and I had to find Robbie, he was still - *is* still poorly. So I rode to Stonethwaite with Fred, but before we found Robbie we separated. When I found them I just saw Edwin and Jimmy Mook, the man had a knife and a woman was with them. I restrained the woman from behind. She didn't see me. She wouldn't know who I was, and then Robbie arrived and took her from me, but Edwin foolishly attacked the man with the butt of the gun; he had no ammunition. And the man was dead.'

'And what about Robbie.... What did he do?'

'I don't know what they did with the body, but no one saw me, Beth. The woman ran away, scared. And I met up with Freddie and came home with him.'

'And does anyone else know of this?'

'Only the woman.'

'And will she tell the police you restrained her?'

'I have no idea, but Robbie and I are both innocent.'

'I was going to go to him tonight, Christie ... is he safe?'

'I beg you to keep chaste, please don't go. Father will leave tomorrow.'

'And then what?'

'Then we wait.... We've waited seven long days and nights.'

Beth curled her legs beneath her and looked at the fibres on the counterpane and ran ridges with her fingers up and down the weave. 'Tell me straight away when they come for him, Christie, tell me.'

Christie just nodded. Then he stood up to leave and said, 'If you still want to go through with this marriage, maybe we could stall things. Make excuses. Then see what happens.'

'No, Christie. I know what you are thinking. Yes, Father is very poorly, but he wants to see me wed. He believes ...' She checked her words, 'he believes he may die soon. His heart is failing, we didn't tell you because we wanted you to stay at Keld Head and learn.'

'Aye, well, I'm learning alright.' He took in a sharp intake of breath. 'But not just about farming. Anyway, Fred wants you to come and see him at Keld Head tomorrow.'

17

MUTATION

Keld Head became a prison rather than a fortress, alone that night, apart from two spaniels. Robbie was back in his work clothes, it was all over. He tried not to think of Beth but Franklyn Richardson. He kept the lamps low and the fire in the hearth pathetic; the horses were safe under lock and key. There was no needless leaning on alcohol as nothing could bring him any comfort. He'd been a fool, even in repentance. Trying to unravel his past was impossible. He hadn't started the feud that existed between the Mooks and the Wildings but he had become a catalyst. He didn't believe some deity was punishing him for his actions for he would reap what he sowed, made of his own doing. He understood the God that Christie spoke about was more loving than that. He hoped dear Beth would be absolved of any wrong doing, but how rashly she had spoken. He had underestimated how easily a man could forgive; and as things had turned out, if not for the dreadful manslaughter of Jimmy Mook, Robbie could have taken Beth as his wife with a clear conscience of his mistakes in Wasdale which now appeared as nothing.

A noise outside made the little spaniels run to the door and bark: 'Hush, Jessie ... hush, Mollie.'

It was far too early for Fred and Christie; with ears pressed against the back door Robbie listened. His heart thumping, he opened the door quickly and the little dogs ran outside; it was only a deer, jumping in the mist. The cold night air was deliciously fresh and welcome as it touched his face; but he couldn't enjoy it. Glancing across the valley into the distance he saw the flickering lamps of Grasmere and the Prince of Wales. He wandered across the yard and took the opportunity to check the latch on the gate; of course it was closed.

He whistled for the dogs and they complied, wagging their short stubby tails, then one was side tracked and ran back to the stable door. Robbie shouted strongly, cursing now. And the little dog skulked towards him, and he lightly kicked it and pushed it back inside the farmhouse.

In his mind Robbie had considered what Sally Mook's strategy would be. But she was a drunkard and no rational thinking could possibly come from her. If she had gone to the police he would already be in custody, but then would she want to incriminate herself as it would surely be said that she and Jimmy had attacked him in the first place.

When he heard Fred and Christie chattering, purposely clattering the gate as they opened it, he went upstairs to bed. He didn't want to speak to either of them. What the morning would bring he had no idea; new terrors, perhaps. Would this be his last night at Keld Head and he would spend the rest of his days in Coldrigg's impoverished prison.

There was only one thing certain and that was Franklyn Richardson would be on his way home tomorrow, and the worries over the man that had stolen his peace for the last few months would leave with him.

The night passed as all nights would from now on with terror; up and checking through the window several times; more than necessary. But when daylight arrived it brought new tortures, to see his beautiful Beth again.

Four young people sat around a table conspiring. Their solid group had widened with Christie now in the saddle.

'Did your father get away alright?' Fred asked, more verbal and in control. 'You should have gone back with him, Christie. You're not safe here, and not just from the Mooks. If the police know you were involved....'

The boy looked woefully at Fred and knew he was right. But loyalty was the overriding quality and it won the battle over the fear. 'I want to stay with Robbie as long as I can.'

'So you want to witness my demise.' A wry smile appeared on Robbie's face.

'No, it is the opposite. I want to help you. If I'm implicated, then I am also a witness.'

'Aye, and what might that do to your father?'

'I'll do as I like.... I think my father has been deceived enough. I know he is weak in body but you underestimate his fortitude of mind.'

The boy's words cut at Beth but healed Robbie as he stood to leave. He had helped with the milking that morning and had a few accounts to settle on paper. If he was to be hanged or incarcerated he wanted his affairs to be intact. He pushed himself up from his seat and Beth was quick to follow, Fred watched them leave.

Robbie walked into the fresh February air, and breathed deeply as he spoke, 'Shouldn't you stay with your intended.'

'Don't punish me, Robert,' and she ran forward, caught him by the arm and pulled him round. 'Why did you call me capricious?'

'Beth, we won't have this conversation, not here in view of the whole of Grasmere.' He spoke without any emotion, and without removing his eyes from her face.

'Yes, we will speak, Robert, we will.'

'You have a fire, Bethy, that I hadn't discerned afore. What blithe spirit you have to flee from this union; I never saw one stronger? How quickly you changed.'

'Did you want me to refuse Freddie and marry you whatever! A man sentenced to a life in prison or worse.'

And for the first time he saw a woman of great character. He lowered his head. 'Does it pain you to know that's exactly what I wanted. Just to say ... just to say...' and he breathed heavily. 'Just so I would have known you still wanted me, no matter what. But I still wouldn't have let you marry me.'

'How could I have said that in front of my father ... but yes, I do want you.' She moved close to him and embraced him and her head fell on his chest. He put his arms around her and led her to the tower.

'Is this really what you want, Beth?'

'I want to turn back time and be with you in the snow, looking at the hills.'

'That will never be....' He said.

'I will love you all my life.... I will never be rid of you. You will be in my dreams, my waking hours, my happiness and my grief. Nothing will ever take you away.'

'Then it comforts me to know that, and if I die a guilty man I will take that with me to Sheol.'

She sat on a small wooden stairway and watched him as he lifted a sack of corn onto a barrow. Then he stepped to the door and quickly stepped backwards; he didn't want her to hear him say. 'Oh no ... not now.'

But Beth did hear and she stood up quickly and wondered what horrific sights awaited her.

In the valley about a mile in the distance she saw a vehicle. Men in dark suits were spilling from it, cascading across the fields, some hiding behind walls.

Beth caught his shoulders and clung to him. Neither spoke. Robbie looked at the stairs but there was no hiding place; he didn't want to run from this, but he couldn't let her see his arrest.

'Go, Beth. Go now. Take Christie, but for heaven's sake go!'

'No, Robbie, no, I will stay with you till the last.'

'They could shoot ... it could be dangerous.'

'They won't shoot with me here with you.'

She stood close to him, her hand on his rapid beating heart.

He looked at her face. 'I should have kissed you when I had the right ... but I believed you didn't want it.'

'Then kiss me now, Robbie. Before they come - give me that pleasure.'

He looked at her innocent face and thought of the other women he'd kissed; how could he refuse her.

On the day that Robbie met Franklyn Richardson, and lost his dear love to his brother, an elderly couple walking by the lakeshore of Derwentwater with their small Pekinese dog had their day ruined by what appeared to be a bundle of rags floating in the lake. Along with swathes of drift wood, the bundle was wedged under a tree on the banks of the swollen lake.

The man wouldn't have considered it of any consequence until the smell of rotting flesh caught his breath. He pulled his wife to one side and went to investigate; cautiously poking at the bundle with a heavy stick. He stepped backwards quickly when he saw truly that the bundle was in fact a dead man.

Christie heard footsteps running and stopping on the lane. The spaniels and sheepdog were barking crazily. Fred jumped up from the table and ran to the window. 'This is your last chance to leave, Christie.'

'No, I stay... where did Robbie and Beth go?'

'Never worry. He won't run. He wants this over and done with otherwise the guilt would kill him.'

Fred opened the door and stepped outside and shouted to the police. 'You needn't hide, you are quite safe....Why have you come?'

Someone shouted back. 'Stay where you are. Don't move.... We have firearms!'

Fred held up his hands as policemen ran from all corners, closer than he had anticipated.

'Are you Robert Keldas?'

'No sir ... I am his brother.' Fred shouted.

'Step away from the house. Keep your hands held high.'

The police grabbed Fred and pinned his back against the wall of the house then spun him around and checked his body for weapons.

'Where is your brother?'

Inside the tower, Beth clung to Robbie's arm and pulled at his jacket, preventing him from leaving, but he was too strong for her.

'Leave my brother be.... It is I who you're looking for.'

Then screams of, 'No, no,' as Beth clung to him, still trying to pull him backwards.

Ten men surrounded them with rifles pointed at their heads. 'Have mercy on this woman, I beg you,' Robbie shouted.

Someone pulled Beth away. 'Don't treat him like an animal,' she screamed, sobbing.

Robbie held his hands high. 'You don't need your weaponry....
I'm not a violent man.... I will come with you.' But no one was
listening and caring as they overwhelmed him, and purposely
pushed him to the ground pulling his arms up on his back, then
wrapping handcuffs around him; thrusting their knees into his
back to hold him down, and pushing his face into the cobbled
yard.

It all became bizarre; the humiliation, the shame, and Beth
still screaming; like still life; an age; everyone watching this
indignity.

Helpless, Robbie lay on the earth, his head throbbing, until
another vehicle pulled up close to them and someone dragged
him upright. He turned to find Beth, searching for her amongst
the throng of people, but she was still tugging frantically to
release herself from the clutches of a policeman. Their eyes
met and Robbie feared that would be the last time he would set
eyes on her in reality. He turned and lowered his head and
stepped into the van; the relief was immense.

Christie ran to Beth to console her.

Fred asked. 'Can I go with my brother?'

'No sir, you must let your brother answer for himself.'

It wasn't Sally Mook that had alerted the police that Robbie
had been in Grange, it was the good people of Stonethwaite. No
one had seen the siege in the fog, but someone had seen
Robbie; the man on the grey mare was easily recognisable.
Many had spoken of Edwin Wilding banging on cottage doors
but no one had seen them throw Jimmy Mook's body in
Derwentwater. Edwin hadn't left Wasdale; he had remained
with his wife and children in the deep valley, watching from
doors and windows. His motive was that if he was caught he
would exonerate Robbie's actions and not let them hang an
innocent man; he wouldn't take Robbie with him to the grave.
And if the judges were merciful his willing plea of
manslaughter and self defence could hold true in his case.

The Mooks' few weeks in Grange had sealed their own fate;
idle talk at the local hotels and inns in Rosthwaite. They had
revealed their rift with Edwin and Robbie, and people had

spoken frankly and innocently to the police. Those who knew Robbie spoke affectionately.

This wasn't a man of violence and had only denounced him for being foolhardy. Edwin had claimed to have thrown the dead man in the river himself yet Sally had said that he wasn't alone, and that Robbie was there with an unknown woman.

Edwin was the first to be locked up in Coldrigg Gaol, with no news of his friend. The barristers and solicitors gave no hint of Robbie's arrest.

The prison was a grim place; the food, poor. Men found the time passed quicker if they could work; many gambling for tokens of cigarettes. Edwin was kept in isolation as a prime suspect in a murder case.

Edwin heard each door banging as new inmates arrived. A strike in Workington and a riot had put the prison and the police force at full stretch. He knew Robbie had been interred when cat calling and whistling rattled around the prison. Edwin feared for Robbie's safety. Robbie had heard all this before and dreaded it; he would rather be dead than suffer the abuse and indignity. There was no association but both men quickly heard of the others arrest.

* * *

February 1904

My dear Irene.

Please be prepared for a dreadful shock. Please keep this letter safe and let no one else see it, not even your parents or Tommy.

I hope my father arrived safe and well after his short trip, happy after his visit, which is more than I can say for me. There is still to be a wedding, but I am afraid to say I am to marry Freddie instead. I cannot as yet tell you why, or how, for the circumstances are, and will remain a secret and this will be a marriage of convenience, because my dear Robert will not be in a position to marry me. But I could not shame my father and tell him the truth. I insist that these details be kept secret. My father's memory was in ignorance of which Keldas brother I was to wed and Aunt Charlotte is confused, but not overly so, as we always travelled with Freddie and she did have a preference for him. All I can say is that the dear man has helped my family out of a grievous trial. I will write again soon with more details. I humbly write this with tears, but I know I will be loved and cared for in Westmorland. I gave this note to father's nurse so it would be delivered quickly by hand.

I trust your wedding plans are going well......

* * *

The exposure of Keld Head's tower to the world was always a source of frustration for Robbie. When he first set eyes on the farm his father had bought for him, he felt uneasy. Samuel Kellet was starting a new life for his family, a new name, and believed no more impropriety would come. Surely Robbie had learned his lesson with the horse stealing incident. But Samuel hadn't considered that the consequences of this sin would last for generations. And now Keld Head stood proudly for all to see, not caring for the infamy of its present owner but wallowing in the drama.

Many locals had come to view the tower with its close proximity to Grasmere; thankfully the hill walkers kept a short distance away, as the bridleways and footpaths beside it were of no consequence as they didn't directly reach the high fells. The folks of Keld Head had taken Robert Keldas to their hearts in the few months he had lived there; fun loving, hard working; tidy; the tenants in his cottages considered him a good landlord; though sometimes when they saw him chattering with their daughters as he rode by on his grey mare they hoped he wouldn't linger. And although no one other than the Mooks had any grudge against Robbie, to see the police swarm around this small valley was a surprise. His seizure was done with such ferocity it was gossiped about and considered to be for a grave and scandalous crime.

Fred hoped beyond reason that their name would be kept out of the newspapers, but the massive police presence had added intrigue. And it was soon smeared amongst the Cumberland and Westmorland farmers that young Robert Keldas had been arrested on a murder charge.

* * *

MUTATION

March 1904

My dear Irene

I am longing to see you in your wedding dress and glad your day will be happier than mine. I don't want what happened to me, to overshadow your day. Please do not fear for my happiness; I may walk the aisle silently kicking and screaming but my heart will marry Fred Keldas in dutiful subjection.

Please do not be disturbed at Christie's demeanour; he remains an angry young man. He has promised to take the responsibilities and work hard for my father, and has now resolved to leave Keld Head. There is nothing there for him now. I'm afraid my dear Robert has fallen into misfortune and can no longer accommodate him. I also have news of my wedding. Father's health is declining so I have persuaded Freddie to come to Thirsk so we can marry here. He is a good soul and only wants my happiness. I just have a little business to complete with preparation of my home which will now be at Spickle Howe, Freddie's farm near Hawkshead, where we will return after our wedding day.

Please do not be concerned about my marriage to Freddie. He is a loyal man; Robert said I should have married him in the first place. When I next see you, you will be Mrs Bright and I soon to be Mrs Keldas. I am more than happy to bear that name and live my life in Westmorland.

Please try and be happy for me Irene.
You're beloved Elizabeth.

*   *   *

The small chapel was full, but Fred saw nothing only his beautiful bride dressed in white lace, the veil over her eyes concealed tears. Fred gripped her hand tight as he always would, two young people bound in a unity of consolation. Beth felt strength as she said her vows because she really believed she could honour and obey him. It wouldn't be difficult because she was already doing that. The love, well, that was there too, but perhaps not quite the same depths and strength as she had for Fred's brother.

Fred had had his judicious proposal fulfilled as Franklyn lived on, revitalised at his daughter's union.

Ladies in large coloured hats dressed in fur and feathers with ridiculous splendour. Many whispered of Fred's youthfulness, but could see no wrong in his character. To see Elizabeth Richardson clinging to his arm as a sign that she was, and always would, depend on him; a young man now of just twenty. Some wondered at the whereabouts of the older brother, and the lack of relatives on the Keldas side; just a few elderly aunts had travelled, too old and too senile to gossip about their wayward nephew, and would, for their own self respect, not speak of Robbie.

Christie was in complete harmony with the arrangements and would travel with Beth and Fred to a secret location in Northumberland to share a false honeymoon.

The journey to Northumberland was made in silence. Fred had nervously walked the walls of Sugar Hills with Franklyn and Christie; yes it was a beautiful house and good land, but Fred was eager to leave. Franklyn was suffering too much himself to notice his daughter's demeanour and her husband's fear; his heart was crushing in on him. There was a brief thought that if Franklyn perished before the wedding day, Fred would willingly give up his bride and save her for another; but that wasn't to be and Franklyn managed to keep himself alive just long enough to unwittingly punish them all for their deception.

John Penruddock's family were purposely omitted from the guest list, but he was made aware of Beth's marriage to Fred Keldas months later, bemused and dismayed and suspicious. He knew of Robbie's arrest and had a brief consideration of a prison visit to help the young man who had once helped him, but Penruddock's spirit soon dissuaded him and declared that the prison chaplain be the best one to help.

18
THE GOOSE IS IN THE DOCK

A silver hairbrush was carefully set down on the polished mahogany dresser, as the early summer sunlight reflected on the glass in the mirror. Somewhere a clock was ticking loudly, just like a heartbeat; but it wasn't Beth's. The pace of each beat was quickened by fear and encased behind a concrete wall.

She recalled Robbie's last words to her: "*You were naive,*" and she had said, "*yes, your beguiling manner deceived me,*" but it hadn't. In fact in her mind Robbie was probably the more open and honest of them all.

It wouldn't be long now.

She stretched as she slowly stood; it was tension that controlled her rather than contentment. Her suit was hanging on the wardrobe door, ready; brand new. She looked at her engagement ring; Robbie's ring, and set it back in its box where it had remained since her wedding day; she now wore Fred's ring; not so brilliant; plain and austere; but given with love and accepted with gratitude.

She could hear Christie talking to Fred downstairs, so glad he was here. She wanted to look beautiful and that wouldn't be difficult and, as she contemplated, she realised more care was taken of her appearance today than she had done on her wedding day.

She hadn't seen Robbie in four months, and it mattered how she looked; neither men had allowed her to visit the prison.

Life at Spickle Howe was good. Fred was a loyal husband, a kind husband, and she had some happiness, despite the loss of her lover and now also her father. But her bedroom, a room of solace, wouldn't be entered by her husband. In it she kept many personal possessions: the mahogany dresser was one of them. It came with her from Sugar Hills as had other items of furniture, all strong reminders of her father. Franklyn had died suddenly and dramatically in the pulpit, when a seizure took hold of him. It seemed right somehow that he should go that way; with his boots on and leaving a mark on everyone present; his final sermon speaking of hope and repentance and forgiveness.

Spickle Howe was nestled in a wooded area behind Hawkshead and it gave Beth too much solitude; which wasn't a good thing for her. She found comfort in painting and sketching, the deer, robins, much wildlife; she always had Robbie's two spaniels for company. Fred left her for days on end working hard to run two farms, not knowing for how long. She wrote many letters to Irene and Christie, who was still learning as the benefactor of Sugar Hills with the help of the manager.

Fred was a good husband; a good provider in seeing to Beth's needs. But to stay at home with a wife that didn't love him in the true sense was a sacrifice. There were times when he struggled, and he would stay at Keld Head. Beth was never allowed to visit Keld Head as it was deemed unsafe. Tilly was secretly despatched to Thirsk where at Sugar Hills Christie could console himself that he was helping Robbie, whatever his outcome. Christie regularly travelled back and forth to be close to Beth and Fred.

When Beth and Fred sat together at meal times or with business to do, Fred kept her aware of his dealings with the two farms; not just to pacify her, but because he needed the reassurance. Beth was level headed in most things and astute, extra men had been hired to help at Keld Head but the farmhouse remained, in the main, empty. Fred couldn't risk having tenants there in case any of Jimmy Mook's relatives and cohorts returned for revenge. He couldn't afford the luxury of a manager. So the house became a temporary shelter for Fred when he needed it and the land farmed as best as he could. Nora was asked to keep it clean and dry, but every time that Fred slept there, the coldness of the house and the damp night air ate right through him. He despaired at the waste, always hoping that Robbie would soon be free, but he knew whatever the consequences, this place would never be a happy home.

What Coldrigg Gaol could do to Robbie could shape the rest of his life.

Fred's love for Beth grew, but he silently despaired at their wasted lives. It was an irony that he had won the woman he loved but the knowledge that her true attachments lay at Coldrigg Gaol, stifled him.

Beth had a lovely demeanour, smiling, genuinely pleased when he returned. She made extra care that the home was pleasing for him, doing much of the work herself. Occasionally when they walked out together, looking at the fields and the woodland, checking the cattle and sheep, he wanted to take her hand, but knew he must keep his promise. Their conversation always flowed easily as was usual for Fred. And he sensed she felt safe with him. But how long he could live like this, he didn't know, maybe time would help him, and if the courthouse freed his brother, the relief would be tremendous that a life had been saved, yet harder knowing that his brother could return and reclaim the wife that was truly his.

He and Christie spent any spare time visiting Robbie at Coldrigg and today was the start of the trial, and not just for Robbie and Edwin.

Fred had warned Beth to be prepared, for Robbie was much changed. The crown court was in Dalton-in-Furness and would be a cold and austere meeting place; they may not even get the chance to speak.

Robbie fastened his tie and slipped on his jacket, the sleeves a little long now, trousers a little slack, but they fit better than the prison garb which was purposely made too big, with no belt so a man couldn't hang himself or escape in a hurry. Frazer Piercy had suggested his best suit, and in it Robbie was still an impressive man, but the judge would be no fool. There would be no arrogance on Robbie's part today; the months in solitary confinement had humiliated him enough. So at least today he could have some peace and fresh air; if only briefly.

The prison chaplain had been paid by someone to pray with him that morning, but somehow the indignity of Coldrigg Gaol didn't lend itself to the prayers, and the priest had to shout amongst the chaos to be heard. Payments had been made by Fred for four months now: garnish money; favours for Robbie in solitary confinement. That's what they called them, but they were little favours indeed: candles and soap a priority, and the manacles around his ankles to be occasionally removed. And today Robbie's ankles were sore and blistered, hidden beneath his fine suit as he left behind the hellish noise and the clamour; the stench and the abominable stink of corruption for more of the same or the gallows.

Robbie sat with Edwin in the prison van, their journey to Dalton, short but filled with terror. Neither man was allowed to speak, both were handcuffed and manacled; seagulls screeched overhead almost laughing at them for they had their freedom.

Edwin glanced at Robbie sitting across from him; their only contact was a purposeful brushing of shoulders as they passed in corridors; a small intimate token. Edwin, with his cheeks sunken and sallow complexion looked about ninety. He had an overwhelming need to embrace Robbie. Robbie had a cough that all the prison had, it was fortunate that they didn't have the typhus as it was killing more men than the gallows.

Both men had short cropped hair to keep away the ticks and lice.

Today would seal their fate. Frazer Piercy had hired at Robbie's expense a city lawyer, Matthew Thewlis, for both men. Everyone was confident except the accused and Beth.

When Beth saw Robbie enter the courtroom her body stiffened. He stood tall and dignified beside Edwin Wilding and the contrast was phenomenal; this was the first time Beth had ever set eyes on Edwin and their presence together showed how much one man's demeanour could offset another. It was hard for her to grasp this man was Robbie's friend, small, balding, pointy ears, and a crumpled brown suit with his familiar red neck tie. When Robbie spoke his name and pledged the oath on the bible, his voice was fractured, and then straight afterwards, he coughed. The wounds on his head had healed but scarring persisted around his forehead. This couldn't be the man she should have married?

Beth was sitting amongst strangers other than Nora's husband, Albert, and Jackie Bainbridge, Robbie's stockman. The court room was packed, many folks of humble means, and Beth guessed that the woman crying just in front of her was Edwin's wife. The rest were relatives of the Mooks.

Beth wore a dark burgundy suit and a fur hat, with her hair neatly pinned up. Fred, Christie and Nora were all waiting outside for their turn to be witness to these events.

It was only as the courtroom was asked to be seated did Robbie look around, his eyes searching for Beth and as his eyes rested on hers, a glimmer of a smile emerged. This indignity hurt him; his hand cuffs and manacles temporarily removed.

Robbie's heart stirred at seeing her; the dreams he had; those he clung to of Beth, lying beside her in a bed of snowdrops, holding hands, were momentarily cast aside for this one purposeful glance.

The charges were read out and the court commenced. And the first witness to be called was Sally Mook. She looked ridiculous in clothes that didn't fit her that had probably been pilfered for this very purpose. She had clearly been drinking as her nose was redder than the powder on her cheeks and her garish lipstick. Her hat was too small and it cocked precariously to one side and as she spoke it bobbled about.

Sally spoke of the day she met Edwin Wilding at the bridge in Grange and how he had threatened them both. She said she was terrified for she saw he had a gun.

'Were you alone, Miss Mook?' the lawyer for the plaintiff said.

'Yis, and I were tarried. I'm just a young woman ... what match were I fer a man like Wilding.'

Everyone couldn't help but gaze at Edwin and wonder at her honesty as this man was small and weak looking.

'And then when 'e come at our Jimmy wi a shotgun, I screamed but daren't stop 'im. Then the next thing I knows a woman come from nay where and 'ad 'er 'ands around mi throat, like, and another on mi mouth. Then young Robbie

211

come and he wrestled wi' me and I daren't know where't woman went. She left as quick as she come.'

'Are you certain there was a woman?'

'I knows a woman's hands alright and I knows young Robbie's; he's 'ad his 'ands aboot me waist many a neet. An' then when Wilding battered Jimmy and I sees he were dead.... I ran off. Terrified I were.'

Matthew Thewlis started to cross examine her.

'Miss Mook.... Isn't it so that you have an infatuation with Mr Keldas?'

'I daren't know what that means but I loved him once ovver, Sir. We were to wed. He'd asked me to be 'is wife.'

No one noticed Beth recoil.

'Did you see Mr Keldas at any time attack your brother?'

'Nay, it weren't Robbie.... I mean 'im no 'arm. I canna watch you send that man te the gallows, Sir.... He means much te me, we may still wed if yer see fit te release 'im.... It were Edwin Wilding.'

'Why didn't you report the incident? No one would have known about this, if not for a family finding Mr Mook's body in the lake?'

'Well, I were afraid, Sir. You see them Wildings are a savage brood.'

'But I will say to you that you didn't report the incident because a few weeks earlier you and your brother had abused and left Robert Keldas for dead, in a lane near Grasmere. And were afraid more of the law than the Wildings?'

A woman from Stonethwaite was next and she stated she had seen Edwin Wilding banging on cottage doors at an early hour, agitated, and looking for a man called Jimmy Mook and she had spotted Robert Keldas on his grey horse creeping like a man deranged through the Cummacatta Wood.

Then a young doctor from Ambleside was called and he stated that on a January evening he had been rushed to Keld Head to attend to a young man that had been attacked and left for dead. 'The young man that is standing in the dock now,' and he pointed at Robbie.

Nora Given was the next to be called.

'Can you testify the accounts of what happened on the said date in January?'

'Mr Wilding and Mr Richardson called me because they had found Robbie - er Mr Keldas in the lane, half dead. They asked for my help to contact a doctor and my husband to contact Fred Keldas.'

'What condition was Robert Keldas in at that point in time?'

'Close to death, Sir.'

The prosecution spoke up next. 'Wouldn't it be in your interest Mrs Given to lie about these events as Robert Keldas is your employer?'

'He is my employer, but I needn't lie.'

'Did you hear a gunshot that night, Mrs Given?'

'Yes, I did.'

'And did you see who fired the gun?'

'No, Sir ... but later Mr Wilding was upset because he had to protect Mr Keldas, and he said he had fired a gun to scare away the intruders.'

'Were you with the accused when they encountered Mr Mook in Stonethwaite a few weeks later?'

'I was definitely not, Sir.'

'Miss Sally Mook claims a woman was there and restrained her.'

'Well, it wasn't me ... I feel she must be mistaken.'

'And can you prove where you were on that morning?'

'I can, for I was making beds at the Prince of Wales' hotel.'

Christie sat in the corridor beside Fred. The others had come and gone and they had no concept of what the courtroom would be like or what had been said.

He had planned in his head and rehearsed what he would say and hoped no compromising questions were asked as he wouldn't lie. He wrung his hands together, shuffled his black polished shoes on the tiled floor, praying silently that his witness to the events might save Robbie and Edwin's lives. He would be astute and cautious.

213

When his name was called Christie stood and straightened his jacket and his tie, took a deep breath and followed the court usher.

'Please tell us your name, son?'

'Christopher Franklyn Richardson.'

'And what is you occupation?'

'Student and farmer, Sir.'

'Are you the son of the late Sir Franklyn Richardson a Justice of the Peace and layman?'

'Yes, I am.'

'And did your father always ask you to speak the truth, Christopher?'

'He did, Sir.'

'Please tell us, Christopher, how you first met Robert Keldas?'

Robbie was captivated as was the whole court room of this young man's demeanour and presence; the stature of his father was growing inside Christie as it would continue. His youthful skin, his short cropped blonde hair that once looked like it should belong to a woman was today sitting on the shoulders of this handsome young man.

As Christie politely and eloquently answered each question Robbie wondered if this angel of a boy could save his life.

Robbie was shaking. He felt things were going well and relieved Sally Mook had testified his innocence. He had noticed Edwin flinching at her cutting words of his guilt. It was clear to him and he hoped the jury that everyone thus far had spoken the truth.

The Mooks' lawyer licked his lips at cross examining this young man.

'Isn't it true, Christopher, that Mr Keldas is your employer?'

'He was, Sir.'

'And isn't it true that it would be to your best interests if he continued so and you lied on behalf of Mr Robert Keldas.'

'It would benefit no man, Sir, if I did and my best interests lie in the hands of God. But as for my occupation at Keld Head, my time there was to end soon anyway as, alas, my father has just died and I need to assume my role on my family farm.'

'Would it be fair to assume that your young mind may have been corrupted in the time you spent with Robert Keldas and Edwin Wilding. And through ignorance and misguidance wouldn't your God forgive you if you did lie on behalf of the accused. How old are you son?'

'I'm nearly seventeen, Sir, and if Mr Keldas has altered my young mind it has only been for the good and I don't need forgiveness on that account, Sir. I stand before God alone as an adult.'

Robbie felt his throat tighten and he loosened his collar and stretched his neck upwards. He looked across at Beth but she had her head low, she couldn't watch, and when the Mooks lawyer said, 'No further questions,' she looked up again, astonished.

Matthew Thewlis next questioned the boy.

'Christopher, can I take you back to the events of the January evening when Robert Keldas was brutally assaulted and left for dead?'

'Objection ... objection!'

'Objection over ruled.'

'So, Christopher. Did you hear a gunshot the evening Mr Keldas was attacked?'

'Yes, Sir. It was that what alerted me there was trouble.'

'Did you see who fired the gun?'

'No Sir.'

'So what happened when you went to investigate?'

'I saw Mr Keldas, dead as I thought, half naked against a wall and Mr Wilding was holding a shotgun.'

'So you were mortified at seeing your beloved employer in such straits?'

'Yes, Sir.'

'Do you believe Edwin Wilding was bent on taking revenge? For we have heard he had used a shotgun once already.'

'Not really, Sir, for I knew Mr Wilding had no ammunition. Mr Fred Keldas took all the ammunition and locked it away in the saddle room in a glass cabinet where it remains to this day.'

'No further questions, your honour.'

Fred Keldas was the next witness to be called and he corroborated Christie and Nora's claims of Robbie's attack.

'Is it true that you feared that Mr Wilding and your brother would seek revenge on the attack?'

'I did, Sir. I will speak truthfully. But I removed the left over ammunition Mr Wilding had so I knew he couldn't use the gun, Sir. And as for my brother, he was still sick. He has been confused since he was attacked. And I know my brother well, and he is a peaceable man. He would only want this rift to end.'

Frazer Piercy took his tea in a white and gold china cup, chicken sandwiches were cut into triangles; Robbie and Edwin were handed a chipped enamelled mug of tea and some broth made of scraps of chicken skin. For a price they were granted a meeting with Frazer and Matthew Thewlis. Robbie didn't like the man but was powerless. He would be paying heavily for this. With the handcuffs temporarily removed, Robbie looked at the food but he had no appetite.

'Eat it, boy.' Frazer tucked a white napkin into his shirt collar. 'That youth may just have saved your life.'

'It was a good job they didn't ask about him being in Borrowdale; they asked the right questions, because the boy wouldn't have lied.'

'I know, I know.... Freddie was discreet too.'

'They do this to humiliate us.' Robbie pushed the broth away; feeling nauseous.

Frazer Piercy had wondered what it would take to stop this young man from acting recklessly, and Coldrigg Gaol was helping.

Edwin finished his bowl of broth and lifted it to his mouth and sucked the dregs, then scraped the last of the broth out with his finger.

'Mother of thunder, Edwin, how can you eat now?'

'It may be mi last meal, Robbie. Dear Lord, that young Christie's a sparky little tyke, aint he,' then he looked at Robbie's bowl.

'Take it.' Robbie pushed the bowl to him. 'It may be the last gift I give you.'

'Come on boys.' Frazer said. 'Let's be positive.'

Robbie stood and paced the room. 'When the goose is in the dock, Frazer, you'd better make sure the fox isn't on the jury.'

'I can do nought about the jury, Robbie.... They'll have Edwin up next. Just tell the truth. Don't lie and don't try to be clever.'

'Clever ... I leave that te the likes of you, Frazer. Ye would have the skin off a flea's backside, wi what Robbie's paying?' Edwin said.

But it wasn't Robbie that was paying, it was Keld Head.

'That's what we're paying you fer. I've nay cleverness in mi ... mi foolishness may 'ave cost this dear boy 'is life!'

'Stop it, Edwin!' Robbie banged his fist on the table. 'Stop your blathering, for pities sake, man. We must hope.'

'How can I be positive when them nifty pieces of tripe out there will devise owt te see us outta this world and safely escorted te another?'

'Calm down the pair of you.' Mathew Thewlis said as he clinked his china cup back down on a saucer. 'Nobody's going to any underworld as long as I'm in control of these proceedings.'

'Will they let me use the toilet?' Robbie was ashen.

Christie, Fred and Beth dined in a cold room. They were quiet and pensive. Beth was curling her wedding ring round and around on her finger. Christie noticed and put his hand gently on hers to stop her. 'Don't fret, Bethy.... Mr Piercy thinks things are going well.'

'I wish I could believe you, Christie, I do.' She looked across to Fred.

'I can't believe they never asked us about our ride out ... nobody must have seen us.' Fred whispered. 'We were as angels on horseback that day, it seems.'

Christie weakly smiled back at him.

'I've done all I can, Bethy. All my adult life I've had to help him out of trouble. I promised my father I'd continue.' Fred was tearful and the touch of Beth's hand on his removed anxiety and gave him hope.

'Don't blame yourself if it goes wrong. Robbie must answer for his own sins.'

Beth knew Fred was big hearted for his brother. The debts were mounting, feed bills coming in. And the costs of keeping Robbie sane in prison and have some pitiful comforts were extortionately paid and badly used.

'Who was the woman Sally Mook spoke about?' Christie said.

Fred looked at Beth and knew she would understand to keep silent.

The court usher came to them. 'The court is in session.'

The trial lasted several days, with what appeared to be unnecessary adjournments.

The pathologist was called and he stated that the body of James Mook was found with no gunshot wounds only a small bruise on the head, conducive to a blow. He had a large knife in his jacket and his clothes had been weighted down with stones. He hadn't died of drowning but probably a blow to the head.

Edwin started to sob the moment he entered the witness stand and said his oath.

'It's all mi fault your 'onour.' He blew his nose on a red handkerchief. 'Daren't blame that young man ovver there,' he pointed at Robbie.

'I must caution you, Mr Wilding.'

'I'm sorry, Sir....' then he would start again. 'Let me 'ang, Sir.... Save that young man's life ... he's like a son te me.'

'Mr Wilding, you will hang if you continue with this remonstration.'

Edwin composed himself as the prosecutor went through the accounts of that fateful day.

'You had a gun with you, Mr Wilding. And you intended to use it.'

'I did 'ave a gun, Sir, but I had nay ammunition. Freddie - er, Mr Keldas 'ad teken it. I daren't know where 'e put it. I just took the gun te frighten them Mooks. Mr Keldas would nivver 'av a gun int'ouse.'

'But you used it weeks earlier to shoot at someone.'

'Yis, I did, mi lord, but it were self defence. Them Mooks were at Robbie. I only shoot rabbits wi it really, Sir.'

'Witnesses clearly heard a gunshot.'

'They would, Sir. I took a shot in th' dark but I only 'it a tree.'

Robbie wanted to laugh but it really wasn't funny.

'A witness in Grange said you banged on the doors, venomous, with the intention of finding Jimmy Mook and taking vengeance.'

'I daren't know what I was te do, Sir, I didn't think it through, like. But I nivver intended te kill a man.' And the tears came again.

'I say you did intend to do harm and hoped the fog would conceal your evil deeds.'

'I daren't like the fog, nivver 'ave. He came at me wi a knife and I didn't know what te do. I had te protect mi sen. I only 'it Jimmy on th'ead. Just once ovver, that's all.'

'Yes, and it was enough to kill a man, then you hid his body to cover up your crime.'

'I didn't mean te kill 'im, Sir.... I were afraid. So wi put 'im int' river.'

Robbie lowered his head as Edwin's usual rantings gave him away.

'You said "we" and rightly so, and I say that all of this was contrived, Mr Wilding ... with Robert Keldas. You found a man in the fog, confused him, killed him and weighted his body down with stones and threw him in the river.'

'Nay, Sir, I'm an innocent man, like. And so is young Robbie. It were unintentional.'

Robbie was terrified. He had the bearing of a broken man, his cheeks sunken, his shoulders slumped in humiliation. He had been here before, cringing at being labelled a horse thief, afraid of the shame being brought on his family, and this was much worse. He wished it was all over with and he could die for his sins, but the sins he was thinking of were not the ones he was being tried for: keeping bad company; male and female; indiscretion; lack of self control; lack of wisdom; he breathed heavily, then coughed several times; he had to control himself.

Beth dared to watch, she couldn't miss what might be the last time she saw him; hear him speak; have the opportunity to love him and pray for him. She tried to get eye contact, watching him all the time. Robbie saw her and raised his stature.

'Robbie ... Robbie ... Robbie..! Do you mind if I address you by that name?' the prosecutor said. 'That name isn't as formal as Robert, is it, young man?'

'No, Sir.'

'But of course you have changed your surname as well, haven't you?'

'Yes, Sir ... my father did. It was his wish.'

'What was your former name?'

'Kellet, Sir.' He looked at Beth, ashamed.

'Robbie Kellet ... now that name doesn't sound quite as grand does it?'

'No.'

'So why, oh why, would your father want to change your name. A name that has been yours for generations?'

Robbie looked at Matthew Thewlis, and Matthew nodded.

'He thought Keldas was a grander name. It was all done legally.'

'Why would any honest man want to change his family name, legally?'

'I don't know, Sir.'

'I think you do, Robbie Kellet. Wasn't it because he was ashamed of you, because you had discredited your family.'

'Well, yes, that is quite possible, Sir.'

'So, Robbie Kellet ... you don't mind if I address you as such?' But he didn't await his reply. 'I look at your fine clothes and cannot understand why you have any association with a man like Edwin Wilding, unless of course you are as foolish as he is.'

'I have known the family a long time, Sir.'

'Isn't it the case that you use the likes of Edwin Wilding to carry out your own wicked deeds, while undercover of a respectable disguise?'

'No, Sir.'

'It's the opposite!' Edwin shouted from the dock.

'Mr Wilding if you interrupt the court once more you will be ejected.' The judge said.

'Now, Robbie Kellet. I want you to tell me about your affairs with the late Sir Franklyn Richardson?'

'I've had few dealings with him, Sir.'

'We can see his son speaks well of you and your brother is married to his daughter, but what of the father?'

'I don't know, Sir.' Robbie was shaking; this was unexpected.

'Then I will remind you. Didn't you have an altercation with him in Wasdale where you knocked him to the ground and robbed him of his possessions?'

Beth put her hand to her mouth, she felt she would faint as she let out a delicate moan.

'It was not as you stated.... Richardson fell, yes, but it was Sally Mook that pushed him and robbed him, not I. She had already robbed me.'

'And of course you know that your story cannot be corroborated because this gentleman is now deceased. So I say to you, this is why you struck James Mook in the fog because you needed revenge for the way his sister acted? You wanted to end this feud with this family once and for all time; you made a breach of promise to Sally Mook to take her hand in marriage. Killed her brother and used Edwin Wilding as a puppet, then filled the man's pockets with stones and dumped his body in the river, hoping no one would discover your evil deeds?'

'I had no thought of that, Sir. The man was already dead after Edwin hit him on the head. He died instantly. Fell like a stone. And I admit I wrongly disposed of the body and I accept the punishment for that and that alone. I was afraid, Sir. I was still sick and not thinking straight, and as for the promise of marriage to Sally Mook, there was no breach of promise as the statements I made were done in jest. Edwin Wilding is not my stooge, as you say.'

'So are you telling me that in this sickly state you rode a stolen horse to Grange in thick fog, in the depths of winter, over high fell with Edwin Wilding. That you had no intention of killing James Mook?'

'Not exactly, Sir. I rode alone to find Edwin and stop him from whatever ideas he may be contriving.'

Beth left the courthouse alone; she didn't know where she was going. She went to a seat in a small square. A fresh breeze was blowing up the hill. She could smell the sea but it didn't console her. She sat precariously on the seat and stared aimlessly. Someone was pulling at her heart and telling it not to let it deceive her anymore. Robbie hadn't lied; he just hadn't told her the full truth. But wasn't that what they were all doing in this sham of a life of hers; he hadn't deceived her but she wondered if she cared anymore about the outcome of these proceedings. She recalled Robbie's humility on the day he proposed to her; wanting her to see and know what he was really like; he had tried hard, but she hadn't listened. She recalled his repentance before her father, and although he wasn't the man she agreed to marry, he was still touching her soul. She thought of Fred and the burden he had for his brother and admired him the more for his lovely calm disposition.

She heard footsteps running across the lane and it was Christie.

'Hurry, Beth. Hurry. They already have a verdict.'

'I can't do it, Christie. I cannot bear to see him again and hear his fate.' She clung to the seat.

'You must, Bethy. You must do it for him. He cannot bear this alone. You must come for him. He only looks for you.'

Beth started to panic. The word "guilty" streaming through her head. Robbie Kellet ... Robbie Kellet.... Guilty ... guilty ... guilty, words she would dream of. Maybe if she didn't move and stay here it would never happen and she wouldn't have to see him sentenced to death, but how could she bear to lose him; this man, despite everything he had done, that she still loved.

'Bethy ... I must go inside or it'll be too late.' And Christie turned, but she rose and grabbed his arm and followed, sobbing and gasping.

With the defendants standing, Robbie was biting his lips, Edwin was shaking, and all eyes were upon them.

'How do you find Edwin Wilding on the charge of murder?'

'Not guilty.'

'How do you find Edwin Wilding on the charge of manslaughter?'

'Guilty.'

'How do you find Edwin Wilding on the charges of perverting the cause of justice and improper disposal of a body?'

'Guilty.'

Edwin moaned, Robbie clung to the wooden rail as he stood and awaited his fate. Looking for Beth, he could see she was crying, her cheeks reddened, sitting beside Christie and Fred with Jackie Bainbridge and Nora, close by.

'How do you find Robert Keldas on the charge of murder?'

'Not guilty.'

'How do you find Robert Keldas on the charge of man slaughter?'

'Not guilty.'

'How do you find Robert Keldas on the charges of perverting the cause of justice and improper disposal of a body?'

'Guilty.'

Robbie let his head drop and Edwin muttered some indiscernible words of prayer and thanks. He heard jeering in the court room; cries of reproach against his name, people were bustling in the gallery, pushing and knocking, a noisy throng. Christie and Fred stood to protect Beth as they tried to leave as Robbie and Edwin were handcuffed again and dragged away.

Robbie wished he could disappear. He wanted to fall back into the snowdrops in Cummacatta Woods and feel their gentle leaves touch his face. He did start to fall, but the guard's hands held him, and Beth saw him waver.

Clinging to Fred's arm Beth entered a small room, lit only by the late afternoon sunshine, casting a pleasing glow on Robbie's face. He sat in the hard chair and as he saw her, he stood up letting her see his handcuffs.

Fred pulled a chair out but before she could sit down, Robbie let his head drop and his shoulders began to shudder, he held his hand to his forehead but couldn't stop himself from weeping. Beth went to him and bore some of his weight, as she pushed her face close to his. He fell into a chair and sat forward resting his head in his hands so she wouldn't see him.

'I can't go back there, Bethy,' he managed to say. 'Please don't let me go back. Say a prayer to your God and help me, please. I would rather hang.'

Beth's eyes pleaded with Fred for consolation.

Fred leant on his brother's side and muttered. 'You have to, Rob. There's no way out I'm afraid.'

'I cannot endure it, Freddie.'

'It will be better, there will be no isolation.'

'No.... No, that makes it worse. You don't know what you are saying. At least I had safety with the segregation.'

Silence filled the small room. Beth searched for words of comfort; her loathing and anger returning to love. 'Robbie, you will live ... four years will pass quickly. We will see you regularly, all of us.'

'No, woman...! You will never, and I say never, come to Coldrigg.'

Fred took control. 'I'll take care of Keld Head, Rob. I'll do my best.'

'Sell it, Freddie. Sell it. We can't keep it. I want you to take some money out of it so we can keep helping Edwin and Nance and the bairns. Eight years could finish him.' He sniffed then coughed. 'If you don't sell it we'll go bankrupt.'

Beth was torn, how she longed to hold him, she would go anywhere with him; suffer any indignity.

Robbie looked up at her. 'Are you looking after your wife, Freddie, she looks ill?'

But Fred didn't speak.

'Is he being a good husband?'

'He is.' Beth said. 'He's a fine husband. He looks after me well.'

'That's not what I wanted to hear, Bethy.'

'I promised you I'd look after her and I have.' Fred said.

'She has no man's hand, does she?' Robbie's voice fractured again. 'Take her as a proper wife, Freddie. Why should I bind you both with anymore unhappiness?'

Fred stood away from them both. 'Shall I leave you two for awhile to talk?'

'I will only speak to her as a sister, from now on, that's how it must be.'

19

PARASITES

Robbie put his toothbrush and comb under his pillow and picked up a heavy grey serge blanket and shook it. 'McCulloch said this would be clean!'

'It is.' A young man lay on the bottom bunk, blue eyed, blonde hair, much like Christie; he was perhaps two or three years younger than Robbie. He crossed his legs; his heavy boots banging together, the heels and soles were worn. 'You wouldn't have wanted the others.... I saw them.... How much has it cost you?'

Robbie threw the blanket on the floor. 'I'll sleep in the cold and in the raw, rather than sleep under that.'

'You want to sleep with as much on as you can, Robbie ... winter and summer.' The young man's voice was soft; well spoken; educated.

'Thanks for the advice.'

'I'm not just doing it for you. I need to be safe as well.... I paid a good price for you to be my mate.'

'And I you.' Robbie moaned.

'Do you wet the bed?'

'Not usually.'

'Take the top bunk, then ... man alive, you're tall. Will you fit in it?'

Robbie half smiled at the young man, relaxed and peaceful. 'You deal with this well?' glad the young man had a sense of humour.

'No, you're wrong.... I'm just knackered. Today I can sleep, other days I'm as nervous as torment.'

'How did you know my name?' Robbie stood looking at the cell wall and reading some graffiti, but it wasn't funny. He paced the cell floor as if to measure each step, just enough room for a metal locker, two buckets a table and two chairs.

'It was my lucky day; you see everyone knew you were coming.'

'What's your name?'

'Bradley Shafer - Brad. We drew lots in the end for you and I won.'

'I'm popular then?'

'No, not really, it's just that you're not a Sodomite.'

'Dare I ask why you're in here?'

Bradley sat up and swung his legs to the floor. 'I killed a man in self-defence after he embezzled every penny I had.'

'Ah, I guessed you were someone of status.'

'I was a lawyer from Barrow.' Brad sat up, 'and you? What's your crime?'

'I want to say murder, because I wish it was, for it might give me some credibility in here but my true crime is naivety and stupidity.'

'And?'

'And chucking a corpse in the River Derwent ... four years. It should have been more but my lawyer pleaded grounds of diminished responsibility.'

They heard voices outside and as the door unlocked and opened; they both stiffened.

'It's only McCulloch.' Brad said.

Michael McCulloch was a prison guard; a giant of a man, with a crooked nose, heavy build, a face purple, covered with broken veins and scars. 'Are you settling, young Robbie?' a strong Scottish accent that was neither kindly nor fierce; it would depend on who he was talking to and what would be said. 'Don't you like your blanket?' he eyed the grey blanket on the floor.

Robbie shook his head. 'How can you work amongst this filth, McCulloch?' Robbie sat on the chair and leant his back to the cold wall.

McCulloch shut the door. 'Now boys, you know the rules. I do my best for you ... always remember that. Never leave your cell alone. Don't use the lavvies alone, you'll have no secrets and this is the only place we can talk. Brad here knows how the system works. You have to help it work, Robbie.'

Robbie rubbed his forehead. 'How safe are we, McCulloch?'

'The truth is, you're not. There are two hundred plus men in here. Carlisle is full of rioting miners at the moment. Twenty men in here are related to Jimmy Mook, but I guess you know that. You've paid a good price to lodge with young Bradley, but you'll need to pay more if you misbehave. I can't always keep you out of trouble. How much do you value your life?'

'My life is of no value to me, but there are some outside, who think otherwise. You must speak to my brother. Is Edwin safe? Because he can't pay.'

'Edwin is in a different league to you boys. He's poor, and he's old. The typhus could get him or so could a cell mate. There are things I can do for Edwin, get him a few comforts, but in the main he is master of his own destiny.'

McCulloch left and purposely banged the door. They could hear his voice echoing down the corridor; the night terrors would soon begin.

'Do you trust him?' Robbie remained seated and glared through hazy eyes into the darkened room.

'We have to ... what choice do we have. He reckons he's related to the governor. They were both at sea together; prison ships full of Irish convicts and the like. They run this place for his majesty to keep the likes of us interned and earn a pretty penny doing it. They reckon they have a good and orderly prison. I've survived three months since my trial; I have another seven years, plus. My last mate was sent home yesterday; I'll miss him.'

Robbie watched Brad eyeing him but his concerns would be unfounded. Robbie doubted he could be a good cell mate and the next three or more years would be tortuous for them both.

As darkness drew in Robbie lit a candle and sat in the upper bed letting his long legs dangle below. Christie had bought him a farming manual. He didn't really want to read in the candlelight; he thumbed through the book then threw it on the bed.

Brad was silent but the noises outside were becoming sinister as nightfall came. Most of it Robbie knew from past experience was banter; men laughing and joking; some tomfoolery, but other sounds echoing along the corridor were not. Robbie was glad he had Brad's company; glad he was paying; anything to remove himself from these terrors.

The cool night air brought on his coughing again and he heard Brad sigh; agitated, the bed creaked with every cough as Robbie blew out the candle. An hour later Robbie hadn't slept and silence below told him Brad was still awake. No snoring or heavy breathing.

'I thought you were tired.' Robbie's voice fractured with the cough.

'I was.'

'Are you keeping watch in case I jump down and kill you in your bed?'

'I don't know ... I can't trust anyone.'

'Trust me, please,' Robbie said. 'I know they're just words but we both need some peace.'

The day began at five. Emptying buckets, swilling them with cold water, breakfast of cold tea, bread and cold, fatty pork, some days it would just be bread. Robbie was sent to the coast with nine others doing land work. The prison was newly built and a new wing was being added and they had to dig the footings for a wall. It was pouring down and a westerly wind was hitting their backs as they worked with pick axes; their heavy woollen coats, itchy on the skin, became saturated with the wet. There was an armed guard on hand, and as they worked Robbie's cough persisted. He wondered where Edwin was. Brad was working in the cook house and most of the group were young men apart from two, and Robbie knew to keep his head low; work hard and keep out of trouble. But the barracking soon started and no one intervened because no one dared and McCulloch was deep inside the prison counting his money.

'Nay body would know if I chucked you in yonder sea, Kellet; one less mouth te feed.'

Robbie looked up at who was speaking but didn't know the man.

'What's it like te drown with thi clothes cottered up in stones and mire?'

Everyone laughed. Then they were pushed on as another guard arrived and the work resumed.

'Ride a cocked horse to Banbury Cross, te see a fine lady on a stolen 'oss.'

Robbie ignored the jesting and just kept digging. The strength not to retaliate came from past experience. This was going to be a long sentence and the footing was only just started; Robbie wasn't afraid of the work.

'Aye, that's it Kellet. Ye'll be diggin' thy own grave. You'll soon be in it.'

Then someone grabbed him from behind and twisted him towards the sea wall, as waves crashed below. Robbie scrambled free but a knife was thrust on his arm and cut a large gash. He managed to conceal the wound and bind it with a handkerchief yet it stung with each thrust of the spade.

When he returned to the prison that evening he was able to wash with some he trusted and as he queued for his meal, his arm bound in old cloths and bandages, he finally spotted Edwin. Robbie spun around when he heard his squealing voice and his eyes smiled.

'By jings boyo, the work's brought some colour te thi cheeks, at last.'

The queue pushed along and the dinner was served unceremoniously: a dumpling, a piece of cold pork and a spoonful of turnip. Still dressed in grubby work clothes, Robbie didn't speak to Edwin but just managed a smile, watching his food being thrown into his tin bowl. He noticed the kitchen staff bringing more turnip and saw Bradley dressed in grubby navy blue stripes. His face was cut and bruised.

Robbie scowled questionably at the young man, but Bradley just shrugged his shoulders and moved on.

Taking out of his vest tucked under his prison garb, Robbie got his spoon which he would need for the next four years. He headed for the furthest table, two men from his work gang who soon learned to trust him, followed. But it wasn't just for the trust, as they wondered if Robbie's height and demeanour would help them get out of any trouble, too. They also knew he was one of McCulloch's chosen.

Edwin followed and introduced himself, smiling like a child receiving chocolate. 'I've gitten a grand job, Robbie.... Swilling pigs!'

'I'm pleased for you, Edwin ... I hope you'll all be happy together.'

'Nay, daren't scorn, me lad. I'm getten plenty o' that from t'others.'

Robbie dug his spoon into the turnip and glancing up saw young Bradley a second time emerge with another churn of hot dumplings. 'No one has laid a finger on you then, Edwin?'

'Nay, but there's plenty of clarty being said aboot me.'

'You deserve it.'

'You're party to it, young fella me lad, daren't yer forget that.'

But Robbie ignored the truth and started to eat. 'So who's your cell mate, Edwin?'

'Yonder elderly gent on't next table ... he's as deaf as a dead 'oss.'

'It's as well with your snoring. Does he still have a sense of smell?'

The others on the table laughed as they would over the next four years at Robbie's wit and Edwin's gullibility.

'See yonder lad ... yer marra. They beat 'im up this morning.' Edwin had a mouthful of food. Robbie glanced at Bradley again and worried why.

Each empty bowl should have been thrown in a galvanised tub of water that looked like soup, but Robbie licked his spoon dry and clean and also his bowl. He tucked it back in his shirt under his vest; then they played cards for an hour.

Bradley was watching the opened door when Robbie walked in.

'What in heaven's name's happened to you?'

The younger man clambered onto his bed hoping to conceal his wounds. 'Words can't describe those men, Robbie.'

'Who did it?'

'Two of em.... I don't know them but as they were punching the living daylights out of me, they said it would be you next. This was just a starter. I lost two teeth,' and he started to laugh. 'They're in the dumplings.'

231

'Let's hope the scum bags find them. Have you seen McCulloch?' and as he was speaking the man appeared at the door; his large frame blocking out the light. He closed the cell door behind him.

'Poor Bradley, poor Robbie.' And he threw some clean, dry bandages at them, then handed Bradley a bottle of iodine tincture. 'I can't have my boys losing their good looks.'

Robbie stepped forward to help. 'Blast you, McCulloch.... What are we paying you for?'

'Not for this, I can assure you. Brad works with you tomorrow and for the next four years. Can you hack digging trenches young Bradley?'

'I'm a white collar man, McCulloch.' He winced as Robbie knelt at his side and dabbed the wounds on his face with the tincture.

'You were, son, but if you don't change jobs you'll both be in danger. I've gotten rid of the two adjutants from your team, Robbie. You'll have to speak to your brother if you want more favours?'

'Aye, you'll break me, McCulloch ... he'll pay if you can wait a week.'

'Yes, but no longer.'

As he left Robbie stood and leant on the bed frame, easing his back. 'They nearly had me in the sea, today. A guard came just in time.'

'How come, I thought you would be safe?'

'Who knows what we're paying for? They scared the living daylights out of me, I know that, but can we afford not to take the chance?' Robbie lifted his shirt sleeve and carefully peeled off a bandage and showed Bradley his wound. 'I'll have this one for life, now Brad. I'll never forget this wretched place.'

'That needs a doctor.'

'Aye, no doctoring.... May I share the iodine please?'

'My father is struggling to pay as it is. He'll pay up though. I'm the only son, thank goodness. I have no wife. What about you?'

'No ... no wife. The one I loved married another.' Robbie handed the boy the bottle. 'This stings like nothing on earth. Is your mouth okay?'

'It hurts like blazes.'

'Maybe McCulloch will get us some salt?'

Robbie went to the table and took out of his pocket a pack of cards.

'Do you play, Brad?'

'You deal, this might be a long game.'

Fred took the familiar path to Coldrigg in hot sunshine, yesterday's stormy weather had gone. It would be stifling inside the prison and nauseating. The first visit of Robbie in a new wing meant a new routine. McCulloch had been paid to arrange for a private visit. Fred had reluctantly left Beth, anxious back at Spickle Howe. She had been restless since Robbie's internment and Fred feared she would leave him. He had no idea how to console her and he wavered in his pledge. She had made some cakes and tea bread for Robbie all wrapped up neatly in greaseproof paper. Fred hadn't the heart to tell her he may never receive them. They had argued, along with Christie, over Robbie's garnishing money, Beth had pleaded with Fred to pay, but Fred knew the rules and he knew it was all illegal, and they were playing along with it. But Robbie's tearful plea had touched them all.

The first thing Fred noticed was the bandage on Robbie's arm. He demanded to see it and as Robbie wound it open, Fred saw the deep scar, but as they chatted and he watched Robbie's face nervously twitching, he felt great remorse.

'McCulloch can do no more, Freddie, unless we pay.' He didn't move his head but just raised his eyes to look at his brother.

Fred spoke in soft low tones. 'He'll bleed us dry, Rob, you must know that.'

'He said the Mooks in here would finish me. They're already breathing down my neck. They're evil. They beat up Brad to tempt more out of me.'

'Poor devil,' Fred sighed.

'And they'll do the same to me if Brad doesn't pay; this knifing was just a starter.'

'What of Edwin?'

'He's okay ... they know he has nothing. It's the other one hundred and ninety nine men in here that will suffer because of him.' Robbie managed a sardonic smile. 'If you insist we shouldn't sell Keld Head at least I can sell the cattle, Freddie. I can't pay the stockman anymore. Sell the sheep, as well. Bainbridge will have to go.'

'I can't afford to buy the animals.'

'I know, I know, just keep the best for yourself. You've had enough running two farms. Tell Bainbridge and Nora they can stay in the cottages if they'll pay a peppercorn rent, otherwise they will have to move.'

'It's humiliating, Rob. Father would turn in his grave.'

Robbie banged his fist uncharacteristically on the table and shocked Fred. 'I'm in dire straits, Freddie ... do you want my death on your hands, if so, go now, but for pities sake man, haven't you got everything of mine anyway? How do you think that feels? You know nothing, Freddie, nothing.' And he stood and faced the wall, holding his hands flat against it for support, wishing he could push it over and escape. Both men heard voices outside and they listened, giving them time to compose their feelings.

'I'm sorry, Freddie, I shouldn't have said that.'

Fred didn't reply.

'Is Beth well?' Robbie turned and in resignation thrust his hands down deep in his pocket.

'No, she's not well. She's melancholy. She's already sick of me; I can see it in her eyes. I don't think we can do this.'

'It was your idea....Where's the boy?'

'He's with us at the moment. He cheers her. Beth's persuaded him to go to university next year, when he's eighteen. Thank goodness they have their father's income.'

'Law or science?'

'Law, I think.... I'm sorry, Rob.... I'll pay for you.... I'll do what you ask,' his voice fractured.

'I wish I had your sentence, Freddie.'

'Yes, yes, I'm sorry. She made you some bread and cakes. I've given them to McCulloch.'

Robbie just nodded. 'Will you ask Christie to come, please. I think he should see this place, it'll learn him to keep out of trouble.'

Fred saw the lamplight in his cottage glowing in the night. It was later than he expected. He wondered if Beth would already have gone to bed. Exhausted with travelling and overwhelmed with remorse, he gently pushed open the backdoor and took off his cap. Beth was sitting by the fireside and Christie was asleep in the opposite chair. She stood when she saw him and the smile she had he knew was for his brother and not for him.

'How was he?' the look of anguish distorted her beauty.

Fred lowered his head and rubbed his receding forehead, glancing at Christie who was dishevelled from sleep. 'He's putting on a brave face ... he wants to see you next, Christie.'

'Yes,' the boy sat up. 'But will you travel with me, please Freddie?'

'Yes, just the once, then when you know the ropes, you go alone.'

Beth went to the stove and pulled out a plate of roasted beef and vegetables. Her care settled Fred yet he didn't want to eat knowing what Robbie's meagre diet would be.

'You must be hungry?'

Fred went to wash his hands. 'I'm in better fettle than my brother.... He wants us to sell the livestock.'

Beth set the plate on the table and slumped in the wooden chair beside her husband. 'Why, Freddie?' her hand rested on his shoulder to reassure him. But Fred didn't reply; how could he tell her what sort of men Robbie lived with.

With the air in the room sombre, Beth nervously fiddled with the plates, cups and cutlery; she couldn't contain herself anymore and she burst out: 'Please, Freddie, please? I know I'm naive but I want to know how he lives.... I must know of his life. Robbie is my brother too.'

Christie hovered around, shaken with their dis-harmony. 'I want to know aswell, Freddie.'

PARASITES

Fred pushed the plate away and stiffened his back and neck in his chair. 'He's digging footings for a new wall; at least he's outside.... It'll take them a year.'

'He's not afraid of hard work, Freddie.' Christie said trying to reassure his sister.

'Let me finish.' Fred sat forward again and rubbed his face with his hand. 'He was knifed today and they tried to chuck him in the sea ... he's okay but his cell mate was badly beaten up. They play one against the other, McCulloch says.'

'Who's his cell mate?' Beth softened, sobered by the news.

'A young man ... a lawyer. He's doing time for manslaughter.'

Beth shuddered. 'Is Robbie safe with him?'

'Yes, that's why they're together. Neither would stand a chance if the guard, McCulloch, wasn't looking after them.'

'What do you mean?'

'Don't ask any more Beth, please.' Fred now hardened. 'We have to sell his livestock to pay. We will rent out the land and the farm will become dormant until he comes out.'

Beth couldn't tolerate anymore. She was tired of working to keep busy, not letting her mind wander into the mire of Robbie's life at Coldrigg.

'Do you mind if I go to bed?'

'No, please do.... It's late. Thank you for the meal.' He was glad when she left as he would have to tell Christie more.

Beth slowly walked upstairs like the burden she carried was too great, her limbs tired and heavy. She pulled the pins from her hair and let it fall on her shoulders, tousling it loose. As moonlight fell and shone on the brass fittings on her bed, she glanced across to the window. She pulled the curtains and looked out into the night and wondered what tortures Robbie would be suffering. She could hear muffled voices downstairs, droning, mostly Fred's, but she couldn't discern and didn't want to discern what else he might be telling Christie. She let her clothes slip to the floor, splashed her face with cold water and cleaned her teeth. She stepped into her nightdress, then wrapped a turquoise silk night gown over her shoulders and carefully tied the belt.

Kneeling at the side of the bed and praying long and silent she remained, her head resting on the side of the pink Damask eiderdown. It must have been a good hour later when she heard Fred come up the stairs.

Beth raised herself from her knees, aching, and went to the bedroom door. She startled him as she quickly opened the door.

They nervously eyed each other and Beth was the first to speak. 'I'm sorry Freddie. I must apologise for my outburst; I couldn't go to bed on my wrath.'

Fred was captivated by her apology and the softness of her voice which restored her beauty. Yet her eyes still saddened.

'Don't fret, Bethy, please. He'll be fine ... everything will be fine.' And he stopped himself from moving in closer to her.

'Has Christie gone to bed?' she asked.

Fred glanced at Christie's bedroom door. He coughed and surprised himself at what he next said. 'Bethy, if you want to leave.... I won't hold you to this.'

'No ... no.... Don't say it, Freddie, please.'

'Well, I just wanted you to know, that's all.' He lowered his head; her answer was welcome; it would fill the desire, but he would always long for more.

'We're man and wife, in most ways.' They both flushed. 'I want to stay ... I must stay.'

She didn't want to say what she was thinking, and that she needed to be as close to Robbie as she could; she couldn't give him up; her addiction was too strong. 'I'm lonely, Freddie ... I have you and Christie. Some of the women at church are kind, but since Robbie's demise they have cooled somewhat.... They don't want any association with us. I've been wondering,' she stopped and the hesitation in her voice was clear. 'I've been praying,' she said this in a hope it may carry more weight. 'If I could write to Irene, please, and ask if she could stay a few days?' She looked at him, her eyes full of expectation. Two young people held apart by circumstance.

'Bethy, she's a married woman, too. She must be with her husband.'

'I know, I know ... but Tommy often goes on shooting trips, she's often alone.'

Her idea began to have appeal. 'If it would make you happy,' and the resistance in him failed and he moved his hand towards her but she didn't notice. 'I just want to see you happy.'

'Freddie, dear, dear, Freddie.' And she moved closer and took his arm. 'You DO make me happy. You have been kindness itself and more.' Beth released him, realising she was squeezing his arm. 'I'm still grieving for my father ... and the loss of your brother.... I'm sorry Freddie, but I must say this. I think if Irene could come soon, I could talk to her, woman to woman.'

'Then please write ... tell her I will pay her expenses. Please encourage her to come.'

The natural thing to do would be to kiss him right now, but she resisted.

Beth went back to her room and silently closed the door. On the walnut dresser amongst the silver hairbrushes, mirrors and candlesticks and ornaments of red and gold china was a small writing desk. It was her father's. She pulled it out and went and sat on the bed and started to write.

My dear Irene.

I hope this letter finds you and Tommy well. Please do not be overly anxious at what I am to say but I must unburden my thoughts and you being my only trusted female friend I must seek your advice.

I have a pleasant life here at Spickle Howe. Fred is a wonderful husband but he is so young and inexperienced. I can tell he is uneasy with me. Sometimes his youth means lack of thought and knowledge of the female mind. Christie's visits make my life tolerable, he works hard with Freddie when he comes, too hard sometimes, running two farms, but he cannot stay. Father's manager is doing well at Sugar Hills but until Christie turns eighteen he only has a partial say in what happens. Christie is hoping to go to university soon, and I will encourage him to do so.

I was wondering the next time Tommy goes away if you could spare the time to make a trip over and spend a few days with me. Freddie would love for you to come and I will pay your travel costs.

I have confused feelings, Irene. The man I loved is being mutilated and bullied in prison, and I must add, for his own foolish deeds and acquaintances, but I also feel his sentence was harsh. When I saw Robbie's friend Edwin Wilding, I wondered if I had been truly naive as to Robbie's gentlemanly status. And now I find myself married to his brother who is more the gentleman than ever. A man who I feel I could have loved if I had dropped into his arms, but now I fear that can never happen because of our promises. I'm torn Irene. This is no marriage, how can it be, one man I can't love because of law and the other because of a promise.

You will see if you can come to Spickle Howe soon. See what you think of this lovely farm settled here amongst the forest. On all accounts my life should be wonderful, but I feel a dreadful emptiness. I long to speak to someone, and I hope you can console me and help me endure this. I have prayed and prayed for forgiveness in the way I deceived my father, and it was done purely to give him an everlasting hope that his daughter would be settled and happy, but I am neither.

The next four years and beyond will be hard and many letters will pass through our hands. And I just await the time when Robbie is free, but perhaps then greater torments will begin.

Your trusted friend
Elizabeth.

20
SEA VIEW

1908

Christopher Richardson stepped from the train holding a brown leather briefcase. He walked tall and dignified in his brown wool suit amongst the throng of tourists, the day was cold yet he felt warm and clammy. He'd noticed a girl on the train watching him, she would be about eighteen. He hadn't flushed as he wasn't embarrassed; he had seen her before, and he was glowing with self-belief. He would have spoken to her but today he had other things on his mind. Robbie Keldas had taught him many things, some good, some not so good but Christie certainly owed this confidence and his courage to this man, and him alone. Yet others could see in Christie the stature of his father.

Christie was glad that while his father was alive he had made peace and shown a sense of responsibility and Franklyn had died proud of his two children. At the age of twenty-one Christie had grown taller than anyone imagined; handsome wasn't a word you could use to describe his features; attractive, yes. The blonde curls were well shorn and his hair looked darker, but he would remain one of those fortunate people who throughout life would retain a youthful face that would last to old age.

He walked across the road and waited in a queue at the bus stop; some folks were carrying parcels and packages just like him; many of poorer means. Christie clutched his leather case close to his chest; a holder for some precious documents and, as the bus was late, he worried because Robbie would be edgy, thinking he had forsaken him. Yet that was something Robbie had often begged him to do, but Christie had never believed it.

The bus arrived and Christie pushed his way besides some well made ladies with baskets of food to find a seat; they were, in the main, headed for the same place. The bus soon stank of body odour and cooking, it would be nothing compared to the stench that Christie would have to endure for the next hour or so at Coldrigg Gaol.

The trip along the coast road would soon pass; he would let most of the passengers off the bus first and use his long legs and steady stride to pass them all.

He walked up the lane to the prison gate.

'How are you today?' speaking politely to a guard at the door.

'Grand, thanks, Mr Richardson.'

Christie gently smiled.

'Not long now, sir?'

'No....That's good.'

'Four weeks is it?'

'About that, yes.'

The heavy door shut behind him, drowning out the noisy throng of womenfolk outside slowly arriving to meet their husbands and sons. The prison was unusually quiet.

Christie checked in and handed a guard some money in an envelope and hoped this was the last time. He waited.

'We have the sea view today, Mr Richardson, if you want it?'

'Yes, please.... What sort of fettle is he in?'

'You'll see soon enough.'

'Is he well?'

'He'll be pleased to see you.... I'll miss him, by jings.'

'He'll not miss you,' Christie grinned.

'Nay, sir, not until they come back, and then they say they've missed me and everyone wants to be my friend.'

'Robbie won't be back.'

'I hope not.'

Christie was briefly searched and led to a small room at the end of a long corridor. He held his breath as he walked; he couldn't help it. He went straight to the window and opened it and gazed through the metal bars and looked out to sea. Robbie would like this.

Another door banged shut and sharp voices sounded as someone laughed; he was happy today.

Robbie entered the small room and embraced Christie, but neither man spoke as the guard left. The privacy was heavily paid for.

Robbie didn't sit but went straight to the window to peer out through the bars. His eyes squinted in the sunlight. 'It's a glisky day, Christie.' He turned and smiled. 'I long for the sunlight after this bedarkened world.'

'What's happened to your tooth?' Christie stood closer.

Robbie grinned as Christie saw a space at the side of his jaw. There was a small cut above his lip. 'Some people in here are just jealous of my good looks.'

Thank goodness he was laughing, because Robbie had barely laughed in Christie's presence for nigh on four years. He'd spent the first six months of his sentence at death's door. The cough had persisted but then depression set in and weakened him. One consolation was the brief trips to the prison hospital and Brad's nursing care. Brad was a good cell mate and when the cough left Robbie they both found some peace and they bonded.

Brad was good with cards but bad with money; he shared Robbie's sense of humour and his privileges, as did Edwin. The only time they met Edwin was at meal times and Robbie could see he was fading.

He would keep crying, apologising for the mess he'd caused, but Robbie would tire of him. Then they would argue and he would tell Edwin there would be no more treats, but would weaken. Edwin warned Robbie that Brad was a hanger on, but that was just what Edwin was, so nothing different there. Edwin also knew Brad cheated them both at cards, but each put up with the other as Brad's sins were less than the other options.

Robbie saw Christie's brown official bag but he didn't want to talk business today, he knew in a few weeks he would be free and that brought vibrancy to his bones. His hands callused, his face thin, yet still pleasing; the missing tooth would add more character.

'You're not going to bore me with papers are you?' Robbie leant back on the side of the window sill, not looking at Christie, but looking out to sea.

'I'm afraid so. We must do this, Robbie.' And Christie sat at the table and gently removed the documents from his leather bag.

'You just have to sign this, that's all, if you can still remember how to write?' Christie purposely tried to aggravate Robbie into serious mode.

'I'm not so stupid.... So how much has your sister offered for my cottages? What will it buy me?'

Christie bit his lip, not liking the tone to his voice, so he folded the papers and put them back in the bag and called Robbie's bluff. 'Do I really care what happens to you and Keld Head? I can walk away now and leave you to your own devices, at the mercy of the Mooks and their crooked dealings ... yes, I think I will.' And Christie stood.

'Blast you, Christie ... sit down.... I would miss your frankness and your wit if I never set eyes on you again.' Robbie walked across and pulled the chair noisily out from the table. 'I don't want to sell the cottages, but what choice do I have? And I know your sister didn't want to buy them.'

'I know you don't, but you have to, believe you me. It's her money that'll pay for your comforts in freedom and get the farm up and running again. She's spent a lot of her inheritance to help you and Freddie keep solvent and you know that.'

'Aye, and I told you not to let her ... you should have left me to rot!'

'You tell us nothing, Robbie ... nothing. How can we abandon you?' Christie shut his eyes. 'So, shall I go?'

Robbie was woeful. 'No, stay... I'm sorry. You're fighting better today. Where do I sign?' And he held his roughened hand out for the pen.

Christie pulled out the papers. 'This is for the deeds to the three cottages. Beth will keep them for the herdsman, the shepherd, and the Givens. They know nothing of this. The money will pay off some of your debts and there will be some capital when you're released.'

'What do I care for money?'

'You say that, but you know you need it.'

'Better be lucky than rich, eh?'

Christie managed to stop himself from saying that Robbie was neither.

'I'll be on the next boat out there, Christie, across yonder water.'

'What do you mean?'

Robbie took the pen, picked up the document, partially read it, signed it and twisted it back, then threw the pen down.

'What do you mean you're on the next boat out of here?' Christie persisted.

Standing again with his back to Christie, Robbie looked out to sea. 'I want to go to South America.... Or anywhere where I won't feel threatened, and where I can be warm. I'm tired of this, I need to be away.' Robbie knew these words would hurt; he dearly loved Christie, his brother and his sister, but this had to be said. 'I need a new life.'

Christie was stunned.

'That's quietened you down.' Robbie turned back to look at the young man as he nervously put the papers back in a folder.

'Won't you go back to Keld Head for awhile?'

'No.... Keld Head is cursed, I've decided.' Still not looking at Christie he continued. 'I want to sell the wretched place.'

Christie despaired, what else would this man do? They had kept Keld Head alive for close to four years and now to be sold on a whim.

'Do you think that's wise?'

'Wisdom ... wisdom....You speak of wisdom ... since when have I ever been wise?'

'But what about Freddie and your father's wishes?'

'My father won't worry about Keld Head from where he is, and Freddie, well, he already has his prize.... So you see, sometimes, yes sometimes I am wise.' His voice fractured a little. 'We've paid the rent on Edwin's farm for years so Nance and those bairns can still have a home. Where did all that money come from, Christie? I won't be in anyone's debt, least of all my brother.'

Christie didn't reply because he didn't want to argue; they had connived and meddled in things to keep the place afloat, Beth shelving out money along the way as much as Fred, and now Robbie wants to sell Keld Head as easily as this.

'I won't sponge on your sister or Freddie anymore, you hear. But I need to keep helping Nance Wilding.... Keld Head *will* be sold and the cash it makes will give me a new life in Brazil and for Nance a home for the next four years until Edwin's release.'

'Your congeniality is beyond me, Robbie. Are you really in a position to be so generous?'

'My generosity is put to question from a boy...?' Robbie turned to face Christie and held his gaze; his eyes narrowed, void of any softness, in an attempt not to betray his true feelings. 'Isn't it my generosity that helped make a man of you, remember I helped you when you were no but a baby.'

Christie lowered his head. This was Robbie through and through: insistent, unreasoning. He wished Fred were here as he shrank back in his demeanour. 'So what do you want me to do?'

'I want you to see an agent and put Keld Head up for sale, and get me the next ticket on a boat out of here. Brad has given me contacts and business ideas, if I like Brazil I will stay.'

Christie hadn't wept since his father died and now a grown man, he wanted to. It was Robbie's coldness that burdened him; his heartless comments, his survival in Coldrigg Gaol these four years had shown this man's strength. But it was coming with a price.

Christie stood to leave.

'Are you going so soon?' Robbie softened.

'I have nothing else to talk to you about,' Christie muttered in low painful tones.

Robbie walked back to the cell with Michael McCulloch. He didn't speak.

'You've got twenty minutes left.' McCulloch checked the clock.

'I need to go back to my cell, please.'

'Now?' Michael was confused.

245

'Yes, now, for pities sake.'

The door shut behind him and Robbie walked to the wall, he counted his four paces, as he always would from now on whenever he was in dire straits. He gently rested his head against the wall; his shoulders shuddered. He raised his arm and rested his hand flat to the cold and filthy wall to steady himself; he was sorry he had upset Christie but what else could he do to keep well away from Beth.

An hour later Brad arrived to find Robbie flat on his bed. Robbie had heard him swearing and cursing at someone outside and as he entered the small cell, Brad was still cursing.

Robbie swung his legs off the bunk and sat up; glad his friend was back and as always pleased if he was unharmed.

'What's the matter?' Robbie tried to forget his own misery, momentarily.

Brad threw his jacket on the chair back. 'Those pig heads won't let me see a doctor....What am I paying them for?'

'Do you still feel bad?' Robbie watched the young man as he unbuttoned his shirt and he could see in under four years that Brad had lost weight as he knew he had. Robbie saw red blotchy sores on Brad's chest and face, which for a man of twenty five was already lined, thin, and his eyes puffy and sore.

'I've got scurvy or something and those rozzers don't care.' Then Brad suddenly recalled that Robbie was visited today. 'Did you see Christie?'

'Yes, yes, yes....' and he jumped off the bed.

'And?'

'And I told him about Brazil....' Robbie kept watching Brad. 'Darn it man, your eyes look awful. Have you gotten hepatitis? You look like you've been on a bender.'

'I wish I had.'

'Did you not get a visitor?' Robbie was genuinely interested.

'No, father is sick of prison visiting.... When you've gone I'll barely speak to a soul who has any sense.'

'There's always Edwin?'

'I'll get more sense out of that table than with that fool. However did you two meet? How could you have any truck with such a man?'

'It was all about horses, Brad - horses. Edwin had 'em and I wanted 'em. And besides he makes me laugh.... I was a kid when we farmed at Black Combe.... Edwin used to come and visit my father from time to time, to see to his horses ... he knows a good animal.' Robbie wandered about the small room, wanting to punch each wall. 'He passed on to me some of his bad ways, and I hadn't the sense to see it. I used to travel a bit with him ... horse fairs and the like, and I used to play with his kids. Maybe he'll become your cellie?'

'No, I would rather die. And if I don't pay up that might just happen, if I get some murdering tyke. Mother of thunder, I sweat before you came and now I'm going to miss you like blazes.'

'Well I'm not staying, Brad, and I'll not be back, I'll see to that.' Robbie went to the door and looked out onto the landing. 'I'll get McCulloch to come and see to your eye.'

'I can't pay any more this month, Rob.'

'No, but I can.... I'll see to it.' And Robbie wandered the high corridor looking for McCulloch. He heard him on the lower concourse intimidating someone.

Robbie stood by the metal stairs, with one eye on his cell, watching and worrying. His life in four weeks time would give him freedom but not peace, and there would be no Michael McCulloch on the outside to keep an eye on him if Jimmy Mook's relatives decided to get their revenge.

Two men came up the stairs and Robbie ignored them as he stood to one side. As the men came closer than necessary, one of them said: 'How do, gyppo.' Something they often called Robbie because of his association with Edwin. They stopped and Robbie stepped nearer to the stairs and further from safety.

'Daren't gan runnin' te McCulloch, young Kellet.... He'll nay save yer bacon. He has other fish te fry.' And as one man glanced along the corridor to Robbie's room they realised Brad was alone.

247

'One false step and he's done fer,' the man spat and laughed. 'Yer canna watch him when yer out, Kellet. You'll have te watch thi'sen.'

'I'm not afraid of your prattle. I'll have the law on my side out there.' Robbie tried a half smile to conceal the fact that he was terrified and knew he'd let his guard down.

Glancing upwards Robbie saw Brad emerge from the cell, and seeing the dilemma he backed away.

'Can this boy see a doctor, McCulloch?' Robbie shouted.

The two men wandered away, then quickly reversed and ran to Brad and seized him by the collar and pushed him back inside the cell. Robbie ran after them and restrained one of the men. 'No playing silly beggars, boys, come on ...' but as Robbie twisted he felt a sharp stab and warm blood poured from his side and quickly stained his shirt. 'That's just a taster, Kellet ... one more whimper and you and young Bradley will be tomorrow's beef stew.'

Brad came to Robbie's aid as the men ran; McCulloch arrived too late.

At the sight of the blood, Robbie staggered to the wall. Half bent and his face ashen, he held his hand on the wound to stop the bleeding then noticed the look of terror in Brad's eyes. McCulloch shouted and another guard arrived. 'Get the medics ... be quick man?'

Christie was exhausted, but it was the burden of his next assignment that tired him more than the bus, the train, and the long walk up the lane to Spickle Howe. How was he going to break this news to Fred and Beth? He had an appointment with Frazer Piercy first to sort out the deeds to the cottages so he took the bus to Millom.

He clutched his leather bag, holding it tightly like it contained the contents of his heart. His sister's affairs were so close to him; his father's money used in a benevolent way and it seemed right that some of Franklyn's estate would help someone needy and repentant, although, today, Robbie appeared to be neither and he could bleed them dry.

248

Christie himself was holding the major stake with the ownership of Sugar Hills along with much property and capital. He had spent three years at university and now had a degree in law. He had studied hard, to the point of excess, to ease his young mind from what had befallen his family, but was now sick of learning and longed to be working.

He had continued to invest with good advice from his father's manager. He couldn't follow in his father's footsteps as regards public speaking, and neither did he want to; but in helping any lost soul, he would excel, in having being a recipient once himself.

Feeling aggrieved that Robbie could soon become bankrupt with his new scheme, squandering money in South America, appalled Christie. He had to dismiss thoughts of Robbie languishing in hostelries in Brazil with exotic ladies at his pleasure.

And then the thought occurred to him that the loss of Keld Head could affect his sister and Fred's future along with Robbie's. The young man, wise in thought, would try and protect Robbie from his own demise and hope it wouldn't be futile.

Christie knew how much Keld Head was worth as he had been there when the cottages were valued, but could he buy another farm, so far away from Thirsk, to run it and manage it as it should be, he didn't know if that were possible. His manager at Sugar Hills was an honest and reliable man, but could he find the same for Keld Head if he bought it.

He knew Robbie had no love for money; it was life itself that he loved and in a few weeks time he would be handed his freedom back. And it appeared Keld Head wasn't to be granted the right to his ownership.

The bus arrived at Millom and as Christie alighted, he had much thinking to do. He took lodgings for the night in the small town in a house near the river. He woke early, took his breakfast and left for Frazer Piercy's office.

After the cold of yesterday, the January air was deliciously fresh, but his thoughts were with Robbie at Coldrigg.

Having much to think about, nothing as yet resolved; a problem he would have to put to Fred and Beth. Christie even contemplated returning to the prison, but was still angry with Robbie. He didn't understand Robbie's game and he doubted he ever would, yet his love and respect for the man, overcrowded his disdain. He wrongly assumed Robbie would think no more of the spat they had yesterday, whereas Christie had lain awake for hours in the creaky bed, listening to the horses' hooves rattling on the cobbled streets of Millom through the night.

The wound in Robbie's side was a close call. Patched up and sent back to his cell, he had fidgeted and kept Brad awake for most of the night. He wondered how he could work and dig for the next few weeks when this pain was so severe, his wound held together with just a few stitches from the medics and his happiness at his imminent release, marred by this injury; the fears were real. He struggled up for breakfast and hoped when he saw McCulloch they would give him time in the infirmary. He usually looked forward to his breakfast, the porridge and bread was the purest and freshest meal they had, but today he doubted he would eat. As they slopped out, Brad helped him with the metal buckets in the lavatories, swilling them and cleaning them in the malodorous drain.

They met Edwin.

'How's mi boy this mornin'...? Bye the lads, I thought you were a gonner.'

'Thanks Edwin, for the words of confidence.'

'I canna allus be around te help, tha knows.'

'I'm glad of that.'

'I'll worrit mesen te death over thi when tha's gone, young Robbie.'

'You should be "worriting" for Nance and your boys.'

'I allus do, but thank you fer the help thi's given us these past years. I s'pose there'll be nay more?'

'Don't worry your sorry ass over Nance and the boys. I'll see they get the rent.'

Robbie leant gingerly over the drain to pick up his bucket.

'Yer too good te the likes o' me.... I've nivver met another the likes of thee.'

'Aye, well, enough blabbing, Edwin.'

Three more men came in and eyed them. They would have to quickly leave as there was no sign of McCulloch.

Edwin followed Robbie out of the building. 'How were young Christie yesterday?'

'Full of university talk.' Robbie whispered.

'Have yer decided what yer gonna do?'

'None of your business, Edwin, and I think it best you stay in ignorance so nobody can squeeze it out of your soft head.'

'You're nay safe out there, Robbie.'

Robbie stopped dead in his tracks. 'And whose fault is that? I'm not safe in here either. I'll have to take my chance.' He walked swiftly down the corridor.

'Will yer come te visit me?' Edwin purposely choked on his words and ran after him like a puppy following its master.

'I don't care if I never see that turnip face of yours again,' but that was a lie.

Making good use of the pleasant winter's day, Beth was transplanting foxgloves in the garden, a thing she would do every year, as she spread them under the farmhouse window. She heard footsteps on the lane and saw Christie. She smiled, glad he was safe.

And as Beth stood and took in the winter's sunshine, her hands cold, and covered in soil, she breathed in deeply the smell of soil in the air, and the aroma of the pinewood coming from the forest.

She headed for the kitchen door, wiping her hands on her pinafore.

'Where's Freddie?' Christie shouted; the tone of his voice, deep and resolute.

'Er ... I think he's in the barn.' Beth, accustomed to the whims of her brother-in-law sensed there was something wrong.

'Shall I shout for him?' Beth said, as Christie came and kissed her. 'What's the matter now?'

Christie shook his head, 'It's not good.'

'Is he ill?'

'No, no ... he's easier to deal with when he's ill! Go in the house, Bethy,' and he had empathy for his sister, the humble life she led, but he saw contentment in her at last, which he knew was soon to fade.

Beth gathered her tools and she sniffed in the cool air which was making her nose run. 'I'll see there's a hot drink and something to eat.'

Fred emerged from the barn and followed Christie into the kitchen. He kicked off his boots. 'What's wrong?' he pulled straw loose from his socks.

'I think you'd better sit down.' Christie put his brief case on the kitchen table and pulled out a chair.

'Come on, spit it out.'

Christie looked at Beth standing by the grate, waiting for the steaming kettle to boil.

'He wants to sell Keld Head, and this time he means it.'

Fred wasn't a man easily shocked by anything his brother said. 'Nay, surely he's joking?'

'I wish he was....' Christie sat back, relaxing slightly that he had now unburdened the news.

'Why does he want to sell it?'

'He didn't say why exactly, but I know.... He wants to keep paying Edwin's rent.' Then there was hesitation, 'and he wants to go to Brazil. He won't come back to Keld Head.... He's going straight to Southampton for a ship.'

Beth felt the pain more than Fred; she hadn't seen Robbie for over three and a half years since his trial, yet she had counted the days. Despite knowing it was futile her still loving him, she just wanted to see him and know he was safe; she felt cheated again.

'What shall we do, Freddie?'

Fred closed in to her and tenderly laid his hand on her shoulder. Beth let her head drop in his chest. 'It's okay, Betty.... It's okay.'

Beth muttered. 'Does he not care about his father's wishes anymore?'

'Robbie has never cared for Father's wishes. It will have to go then. That's it. I can't bail him out.'

Beth looked across at Christie and understood his silence. She knew what he was contemplating, and guessed there was more to this than money.

21
RED GERANIUMS

The front door stuck fast so Beth pushed it with her shoulder. Snow fell off the weather boarding onto the mat in the kitchen. She tapped her boots on the step, walked in and shut the door. Keld Head didn't offer any heat; it appeared to be colder in the house than outside. She walked over to the window and pulled back the curtains to let in some daylight. She heard a scuffling noise and glancing quickly as her eyes searched the room she saw a mouse running under the sideboard. She momentarily jumped; there would be another twenty-five elsewhere.

Rubbing her fingers along the kitchen table, she noticed very little dust; Nora was keeping this place clean.

As she looked about her at the still life, there was pure silence. Beth hadn't set foot inside Keld Head's doors since the day of Robbie's incarceration. Today Fred had left her in the dry while he walked the land with the agent. He had wanted her to stay at Spickle Howe, but what happened to Keld Head involved her as much as Fred. She recalled the first day she came here in the warm sunshine, happy, nervous and excited. That day the house was filled with the presence of Robert Keldas and the only visible mark left was his shepherd's crook and cane sticks in an earthenware pitcher by the door, along with a pair of riding boots and a whip. The dog bowls were empty and scrubbed clean; their owners happily kennelled at Spickle Howe.

Beth stood thinking of what she shouldn't; of what wasn't good for her. Standing in the place where Robbie had said: "*This union cannot continue.*" She recalled him, tall, elegant and remembered how tortured she had felt. Taking in a deep breath she glanced at the yellow painted stairway door. She had never been any further than the ground floor.

Beth quietly stepped up the steep staircase, glancing through an arched window on the landing where a small minstrel's gallery beckoned her. She looked down into the yard and from this vantage point could see Grasmere in the distance, buried in a snowy blanket.

There were four bedrooms, but all the doors were closed. The landing creaked as Beth wandered and opened the first door. Once again the room was spotless, the bed neatly made. Glancing on the window sill there was a bundle of pine cones, the skull of a sheep and some small fossilized stones. This must have been Christie's bedroom. The next room was mostly empty, a store room for boxes and a trunk, probably still full of objects from under Black Combe. Closing the door, she stopped not wanting to go any further, but temptation led her to the next door. This room was plainer. A bed covered in a blue patchwork counterpane, a marble wash stand with a blue and white jug and bowl. A wardrobe and a tallboy; no pictures, no ornaments, but she recognised one of Fred's winter coats. This would be where he slept when he stayed at Keld Head. One more room.

Beth let her fingers stray onto the latch and momentarily paused, then rested her thumb on the sneck, knowing if she pressed it, it would unlock a secret that her heart was telling her to go to the intimate place of her lover; uninvited. She pressed it; the click so loud it shocked her, thinking they would hear it in Kendal.

The door eased open and Beth walked in, her coat brushing softly as she passed the open door. She saw a large bed; grand and stately. The headboard of curved walnut; large scrolls cut into the wood, the mattress was covered with a heavy deep blue counterpane with branches and leaves of gold swirling handsomely through the weave; it was as if this bed was made for a prince. All the other furniture matched; the wardrobe, the chest of drawers, the wash stand. Walking over to the wardrobe she opened the door and flashed her hand across the suits and coats and shirts hanging there. She opened the top drawer of the chest and found a gold pocket watch in a velvet pouch. She set it on a glass tray.

Then she noticed out of the corner of her eye on the window sill, a large geranium, struggling for life in a china pot. She remembered it. She rubbed the battered stems and the diminished leaves with her thumb and smelt the fragrance of the lemony scent. She felt pity for it and understood it. Beth lifted it from the bowl and leaving Robbie's bedroom, took it downstairs, but as she carefully stepped on each stair she heard the front door open and felt the draught. Ashamed of where she was, she quickly stepped into the kitchen.

Robbie stamped the snow off his boots onto the mat and looked up at her.

They eyed one another as he took off his broad rimmed hat and rubbed his hair straight. His riding coat was soaked in snow. He saw Beth holding the geranium; her face bloomed with cold and the glow of embarrassment. The long curls of her hair falling on her shoulders and onto the fur collar of her coat.

It was an age before anyone spoke.

'It's cold outside, Beth.'

'Yes, yes it is.' She stood motionless.

'It's cold every day for me, now.'

'I'm sorry I didn't think you would be here. You're out early? I thought you were going straight to Southampton.'

He stepped closer. 'Where's my brother?'

'He's on the fell, looking at the land with the agent.'

'They'll see nothing today.'

Speech was painful; words were being pulled out of each one as if they would strangle them. This wasn't meant to happen. Beth shouldn't be here, Robbie thought.

Beth spoke civilly in a gesture of peace. 'Have you seen Christie?'

'Yes, he travelled with me. He's in the village.'

Looking at the man she still loved, Beth saw the sadness in his eyes; his heart being sapped of life. Yet in his mouth and tone of voice there was a sense of hope; a desperate measure to restore some happiness and lose this futility.

'I can't bear this, Robbie.'

'Stop it, Bethy,' he muttered. 'Not now, please.' He held up his hand.

'I must speak ... I must say what I feel.' She stepped closer, pensive.

'You stood there and made your decision,' and as he shook his head Beth noticed flakes of snow still in his hair.

'I'm sorry, Robbie .... I have been a fool.'

'You're no fool, Bethy,' he removed his gloves and dropped them on the table. 'It was like this the day I asked for your hand.'

'I know....' Then Beth moved quickly; he was too alluring to resist and she ran forward and pushed her arms around his waist and let her head fall close to his heart.

'What can I do, Robbie ...? What can I do?'

He let his head drop on hers and felt the soft hair on his face. He thought he would never feel a woman's hair again. He was silent; thoughtful. He rubbed his face slowly, drinking in every emotion that was pouring from her, then his strength and presence of mind took over and the self control he had once been denied came to its strongest, and he put his hand under her chin and lifted her head. 'I told you years ago to have a proper marriage. So you must carry on. My boat leaves in three weeks. I'm going to London with Christie tomorrow, and then I will have a few nights of peace amongst a throng of folk who knows nought about me, then travel to Southampton alone. I only came for some things; I wasn't sure if I wanted to see this old house again.'

'Does Fred know you're here?'

'No, Freddie knows nothing.'

'Robbie, please don't leave me again. Please.'

'I must.' And he held her arms to restrain her. 'You're my sister now.'

'I should be your wife! Can't we do something? When you were in Coldrigg and I couldn't see you, I could cope with that; but now anywhere in the world wouldn't be too far away now as you're free.' She let her eyes do the pleading.

'You don't know what you are saying. I could take you here and now and lead you to another world - a warm one, but I cannot. I never will. You're tied to Freddie. What would your father say? You know you must honour him, and God above, and not bring shame. Think of Freddie ... think of Christie.'

She still clung to him weeping now; his righteousness was greater than hers.

'If I ever come back, we must be friends, only. Cry on my shoulder when you need. Talk to me, please. But this must end. You've seen what my true colours are and I'm not the man you fell in love with.'

'No, you are wrong ... you are that man and more.... I can't do this Robbie.... I can't.'

'You must.... I know I've let you down.... I've let everyone down. Please try and remember me for some good, not for the bad. Live your life. Please love my brother if you can.'

'But I love you, Robbie.'

He took in a deep and meaningful breath. 'Why have you no children?'

'Because we have no marriage.'

Robbie rested his chin on her head, she was warm now in his arms; he had longed for this moment, but it must end; theirs was truly a brief encounter. 'I'll never take you back, Bethy ... you must stop hoping ... this embrace today will be the last. Don't let this foolishness continue any longer. Be a good and proper wife to my brother, please. Think of him.... Don't let me ruin his life any more for I know he loves you.'

The yard gate clicked but he didn't let go of her.

Fred and Christie came into Keld Head's austere walls still chattering. They saw Robbie holding Beth and stopped.

Fred shut the door behind him as Beth stepped away; Robbie moved in to embrace his brother. Fred felt the warmth of his body but smelt the stain of Coldrigg Gaol on Robbie's skin.

'Will you leave us to talk, Beth, Christie, please?' And Robbie and Fred watched them leave as Beth took Christie's arm.

Robbie picked up the geranium off the table and went to the sink and found a jug of water and poured it on the dying plant. 'Are you jealous, Freddie, seeing us together?'

Fred found it hard to speak. 'You're here early.... Have you come to take her away from me?'

'How can I? As much as I want to.'

They were words Fred hoped he'd say.

'No, Freddie, in the Lord's eyes she's yours and she will stay yours.'

Relief was surging through the young Fred Keldas's veins, but what could he say? What temptations and fears would befall them all now? To say thank you was the wrong thing so he just said: 'How did you get out early?'

Robbie rubbed his fingers through his hair. 'McCulloch.... Christie paid him last week. I told him not to tell a soul. This was always my proper release date as we tried to confuse the enemy and give me a bit more time; they think I'm still in the infirmary. I needed to see Keld Head and these beautiful hills just one more time before I left. I'm scared to damnation, Freddie. I felt safer in Coldrigg's filthy walls. McCulloch said some Mooks were conspiring to kill me on my release, so I must go. Christie met me in Millom and I got some money from Frazer.'

'Are you still going abroad?'

'Yes, I sail next month.'

Fred stuffed his hands deep inside his pockets. 'Why are you selling Keld Head, Rob?'

Robbie moved to the door and pulled a walking cane from the stand, rubbing the tarnished silver on the handle which was the shape of a greyhound with his thumb. 'You don't approve?'

'Huh.... What do you think?'

'It's already as good as sold isn't it, to Christie?'

'And you'll let him buy it?' Fred now raised his voice. 'Everything Father did, he did for you Robbie and you've squandered it all.'

'Don't preach at me, Freddie. I never have an excuse. But I know you're making that young woman unhappy if you don't make a proper wife of her.'

Anger welled up in Fred.

'You and I are as Saul and David now,' Robbie said, 'and you have the kingship, not I. Keld Head will at least stay in the family and you will have my wife.'

'Do you not care that every penny we have has been spent on you and your safety? I've nothing left but my farm and my land.

259

Beth has spent most of the capital of her inheritance to buy the cottages and pay McCulloch, and you tell me Christie is to buy Keld Head?'

'You have some fire in you at last.' Robbie grinned. 'I've repented, Freddie ... you know that I didn't ask Christie to buy Keld Head.... That boy does as he wants.... I'll never live here again. I wouldn't be safe as long as there's a Mook alive on this earth. I need warmth ... peace.... I'm thirty now, and some would say that's old. There's some gold mining in Brazil and plantations of coffee. I can invest my capital from the sale of Keld Head and make a decent living amongst the hills of Brazil.'

'How is Christie paying for Keld Head?'

'He says he will sell some property he has in Thirsk.... He's doing this for you and Beth not me. That's what Father should have done ... given Keld Head to you, and not me.'

'Oh why do you do this, Rob...Why do they all worship you? Father ... Christie,' and he hesitated. 'Sally Mook ... Edwin ...' he was about to say, Beth, and stopped himself.

'I don't ask for it - never have. You know that.'

Fred eyed his brother and even after four years of degradation he still looked a king.

He softened. 'So where will you stay tonight?'

'Here.'

'It's too cold here, you can't.'

'I have nowhere else to go. And I won't ever sleep under your roof and hers. No, I'll light a few candles. No one must know I'm here. Christie is staying at the Prince of Wales and we will travel to London tomorrow.'

'When will I see you again?'

'I don't know, I'll write.' And he started to laugh. 'I must be safe, Freddie. I must be warm.'

The snow lay thick and waiting for more. The early morning light kept it cool. Robbie stretched his back in his bed, aching with cold. The morbid prince of Keld Head kept himself awake until the early hours, he was now afraid of the silence as much as he feared the turmoil at Coldrigg. He wished McCulloch was stood outside his door and young Brad under his bed on the bottom bunk; he wished Edwin were here to make him laugh.

He thought of Christie at the Prince of Wales, lazing in a warm bedroom with a hot breakfast to look forward to. Robbie looked out of the arched window and saw more snow steadily falling and he cursed, for he knew Keld Head was now keeping him prisoner. He would have only three days of safety before he left for London. Christie had begged him to let him stay with him but Robbie insisted he left; he would be bad company.

Robbie had no sweet dreams of holding Beth's hand that night. He'd only itched with the parasites in his bed. He didn't need to dress as he hadn't undressed. But he splashed his face and ripping off his shirt washed his body clean in the spring waters of the Grasmere hills. Christie had left some food but ironically he missed the porridge. He listened for the gate clicking all night; sitting now in the minstrel's gallery, watching the lane from this vantage point, he knew the fresh snow in the yard would protect him. When Fred and Beth had left yesterday he couldn't speak, he had hugged his brother and his sister. He was glad he had Christie. He rested his head back on the walls of the window ledge, watching the snowfall. He cursed the snow; he cursed the Mooks; he cursed himself.

It was after nine when he saw a figure walking up the lane; Robbie could tell by the tall and swift pace it was Christie.

He glided down the stairs straight to the door and eased it open.

Christie took one last glance around him and slipped inside.

'It's good to see you, boy.'

'Have you slept well?' Christie removed his hat and shook the snow off.

'Yes, I've slept, but not well.'

Brushing the wet snow off his coat Christie pulled from beneath his jacket a small packet.

It was warm bacon and bread, and was welcome. Robbie ate like he wasn't hungry, not savouring each mouthful.

'Can we get out, Christie?'

'I don't think so.... I sent a telegraph to Windermere. The train isn't running.'

Robbie sighed heavily. 'What can I do? I can't spend another night here.'

'Come to the hotel then, please.'

'Are you a fool, Christie ...? I'll be seen ... every waitress in Grasmere has a liking for me.'

'Then let's go to Spickle Howe. We'll be safe there.'

'In one way but not in another. No, Christie, we'll have to stay put and stick it out.'

Beth pulled back the curtains to see more snow. Some bluetits swinging on a chicken carcass were busy flittering in and out of the garden.

She had knelt at the side of her bed, her head resting on the pink eiderdown and prayed; her long hair falling over her face. She'd prayed Robbie would be safe and she'd prayed for forgiveness; she prayed for fortitude and strength and courage and for her lapse in moral chastity. It wasn't a moment of weakness; it was the end of an ordeal. Knowing while he was in Coldrigg she was safe; he had helped her to keep her integrity and it was he who had strengthened her.

Fred and Beth had had a silent journey back to Spickle Howe in the snow. She had sat huddled next to him on the trap, holding his arm as tears fell silently down her cheeks. They had as usual taken the Elterwater lane, up the hill and close to the fir plantation where Robbie had proposed; she couldn't tell Fred the significance, but every time she would pass this place, for ever more, she would close her eyes.

The dogs were happily barking outside and Beth knew Fred was on his way in for breakfast. He was early. She had heard him leave the house close to five; earlier than usual.

Beth slipped on her dress and wrapped a shawl across her shoulders. It would be warmer downstairs as the fire would be lit.

There was a nervous distance between them, knowing what Robbie wanted for them; for Fred, it was what he'd always hoped for but he doubted it would be for Beth. Fred was relieved at Robbie's decision to leave; he would miss him dreadfully and even the visits to Coldrigg had satisfied his love for his brother, but Fred doubted he could bear it if he never saw Robbie again. Fred considered his trial was the greater, to be so close to a woman like Beth and yet so far away from her.

Robbie had the benefit of his absence; Fred had dreaded this day, yet prayed for it. He'd only once spoken to Beth about their marriage and he had chosen a bad time. It was the day after the trial and she was still upset; he should have waited, but when he told her Robbie's wish to give up their pledge she had snubbed him. He expected she would do the same now; he must know.

'You're early, Freddie. Would you like your breakfast now?' speaking with sympathy in her voice; she knew Fred would be worrying about Robbie's safety.

He looked up and kicked off his boots and smiled. She was a good wife in every way. This same morning's routine for four years. She always cooked breakfast for him and they always embraced each morning. They had lived together through turmoil and drama that bonded them everlastingly and more than they appreciated. They both loved Robbie and that love gave them a purpose and equal interest. If Robbie got safely to Brazil and out of their lives they would have time for each other.

Fred went to wash his hands and as he dried them on a clean towel he leant back on the old stoneware sink and watched her working.

'I hope he's safe, Betty. It's devilishly cold out there.'

She stopped and turned and looked into his brown eyes, the sadness in his face. 'Christie will help him, don't worry.' She poured some cold oatmeal into a pan of hot water.

'Betty, if you want an annulment, we can do it; we have grounds.'

She wiped her hands on her apron. 'Is that what you want?'

He couldn't look at her. 'No, because I would lose the both of you then, but I won't make you stay any more in this arrangement.'

Beth didn't reply but found some salt and sprinkled it in the porridge. 'Do I bring you any happiness, Freddie?'

'You know you do. You must know that.'

Beth had pondered this question all the years of their foolish marriage. If only they had been honest with her father, but at times in frustration she blamed her father and wept in her prayers. If he hadn't have been so dogmatic; if only he could have talked to her properly about love; she condemned him for his pride that had led to her downfall. If he hadn't talked about her attachments to the congregation they could have quietly walked away. Then she would feel remorse and blame herself for falling in love with a man she didn't really know. Franklyn had warned her and told her to be careful and she had been misled.

Beth watched Fred as he looked for the cutlery in the kitchen dresser, then taking the clean plates from the dresser. This home he had made for her was beautiful; his love so apparent; working hard, always pondering, even in adversity. Beth once told him if she had fallen into his arms, it would be he whom she fell in love with and she still believed that, but with Fred's lack of confidence, he didn't believe her; yet he had wisdom that Robbie had once lacked.

In the depth of depression after the trial and Robbie's sentence, Beth had considered returning to Sugar Hills, but then acceptance had to be true and forever. The reluctance to admit it still hung over her like a dark shadow; yet truth is honest, refreshing and helpful.

As she had walked in the pine forest and painted the mountains; walked with Robbie's little spaniels she had thought of him; his dubious friends; his carefree spirit; and the smell of him yesterday lingered in her heart; he couldn't help that; but she could see there was a side to him she hadn't known and in hindsight, she would have been a fool to marry Robbie and maybe Fred had saved her from a bad decision.

'What of you, Freddie? I have been selfish. Do you want to be free, to marry another?'

'There is no other, Betty.'

'But there could be, if I left.'

'I have no attachments in this world other than you and my brother; I would be left heart broken.' He set the plates gently on the table.

The water in the pan began to steam; she stirred the porridge and turned away.

'One broken heart is enough.... What will happen to Robbie?'

'He will have to find his own way in life and somewhere along the lines he'll make more bad decisions but he will always be loved wherever he goes and that will stay with him. Maybe the warmth in Brazil will relax him.' He nearly spoke of the Latin women and stopped himself. 'He may lose all his money or should I say yours and Christie's money from Keld Head, and seem to not care a jot. Then he'll come home laughing and smiling and looking for more. I've worried for him all my life, Betty; even as children, as my poor mother and father did, but now this worrying must stop.'

22

SNOW PRISON

Snowflakes fell through the night; silence became an enemy. Robbie sat in the arched window with his head resting on the cold wall looking out into white oblivion. He wasn't sure if the snow was protecting him or capturing him in its cold comfort as little flakes fell in the darkness like soot, mesmerising his tired eyes. Robbie had begged Christie to stay with him tonight and he had unwillingly complied.

The new day had brought more distress. His meeting Beth had unnerved him. It was finally over; the dreams and delusions had come to nought. Despite her begging and pleading with him, Robbie knew he had made a wise but painful choice. He had nearly weakened and if not for Fred he would have. Christie couldn't console him; he didn't know what love was like and so they'd argued again.

'Stay tonight Christie, please don't leave me again,' and he gave in.

Christie went to lie in his old bed, fully clothed, even wearing his boots in case they needed to run, but this snow would stop everyone; even if the Mooks knew Robbie was out, surely they wouldn't look for him in this foul weather. Christie's pleasant memories for his time at Keld Head were diminishing and the cold and the snow and Robbie's fear would make new memories; poor ones. He would have to change things and get Robbie safely on the train to London.

Christie barely slept as the fear and uncertainty kept him awake more than the cold; he heard Robbie coughing.

Staggering from his room, Christie saw Robbie standing by the window on the landing with a blanket over his shoulders; he twisted around quickly.

Christie struck a match and lit a candle. 'Haven't you been to bed?' he looked on the window ledge and saw a pillow.

'What time is it?'

Christie looked at his pocket watch. 'I can't see. I don't know, but does it matter?'

'I'm sorry.'

Robbie didn't see Christie smile as he sat on the window ledge close to his friend. 'I wonder if it's snowing everywhere tonight. There was nothing in Manchester yesterday, so a chap at the hotel said.'

Robbie leant on the wooden spindles of the gallery. 'Edwin and I were once holed in at Seathwaite ... we didn't leave for a week. We ate dry bread and drank stale beer. Never thought to ask how far the snow lay, until we met some travellers coming from Sty Head and they said there was nothing at Gable and that the fields were green. Edwin had laughed and said he knew all along. I could have choked him.' And the wry smile came. 'He said he'd had a fight with Nance and didn't want to go back and would rather spend the night with me ... I ask you.'

Christie was tempted to wipe some condensation off the glass but stopped himself. 'The snow's late this year.'

'Do you get much in Thirsk?'

'Our fair share. The Pennines are a barrier one side and Sutton Bank the other but the snow often comes off the sea. When the fieldfares are gathering on the land you know it could snow any day.'

'Tell me what Sugar Hills is like?'

Christie was more settled with Robbie's calmness and he too relaxed. 'My father bought it as an old hunting lodge ... it's a bit of a folly really. It's like a small castle and has turrets and ugly looking gargoyles; there's a pretty blue faced clock tower on top. The land's mostly flat but there's a small rising to the front, and the house is south facing. The River Swale is on its west side.'

'Are there many fish?'

'Yes, a few, but I don't like fishing.'

'Ah yes, I remember now..... If I could light a fire we could have had some fish from the beck. We once roasted a pig on that hearth downstairs but we didn't cook it properly and Edwin and Freddie were up all night with the skits.'

'And you?'

'Didn't touch it.... I knew the pig personally and they didn't. What will I eat in Brazil, Christie?'

'They probably eat nothing but pigs and poultry. I'd keep off meat for a while if I were you, until your stomach settles to normal food.'

'I imagine blue skies and pretty girls and that's all; maybe a shack in a coffee plantation, eating pineapples and bananas.'

They heard a noise and both stopped talking. Robbie leant his shoulder back against the wall. 'Keep your head away from the window,' he whispered, his throat tightened.

'It'll be a fox.' Christie said. 'I can hear it scratching.'

'Aye, and it could be a Mook!'

Then a scream shot out as the noise was transported on the snow. It was a fox barking.

'There must be two of 'em ...' They saw two small black shadows stalking across the yard in the virgin snow.

'Nobody knows you are here.... Please relax. You have three days, that's what McCulloch said.'

'Yes and this snow could keep us holed up for three weeks.' Robbie edged closer to the window and peered out. 'What will we do then?' he settled on the window seat beside Christie and pulled the blanket tight across his shoulders.

'Go and sleep in my bed.... It'll still be warm ... I'll keep watching.' Christie spoke with authority and empathy.

Robbie disappeared down the bedarkened corridor and Christie settled to his post exactly the same as Robbie had, and let his eyes be mesmerised by the falling snow. He recalled Beth had a little glass snowscene globe that their father had bought her of Dove Cottage. She had said to shake it and watch the little flakes fall to the ground and settle. Christie wished he could do exactly that under Keld Head's sturdy walls.

Despite Robbie's distaste of the place Christie loved it here; it had given him a life and a hope. When he believed Beth and Robbie were to marry, life eternal was almost possible at Keld Head but that was dashed away unless he could secure ownership. But could it be a happy home? Without Robbie, no.

Then across the corridor he heard the deep sound of Robbie crying and Christie prayed once more he would sleep.

The daylight was slow to arrive because of the freezing fog. Frost hung on the trees sealing each branch and twig like a glass carving. There would be no way they could leave today.

Christie drifted to sleep sitting by the window, covered in the blanket.

'I knew you wouldn't be able to keep awake.'

Christie stirred and smiled as he saw his friend.

'We could both be dead in our beds.' Robbie peered out through tired eyes but could see no further than the stable door. 'No thaw today.' He touched the young man's pale hands. 'You're half starved, Christie, let's eat. It will warm us.'

They wandered down to the kitchen and lit a small stove and over a meagre breakfast the two men talked.

'Will you ever marry, Christie?'

Christie couldn't comprehend how Robbie could remove himself from grief so quickly. This was what he loved about this man; this is why everyone would love Robbie.

'Or have you been disillusioned by my affairs?'

'I'm not interested in women.'

'Aye, not yet, but you will be.' Robbie chewed on a tough crust of bread and swallowed. 'The understanding of women is a science, Christie ... hard to weigh up.... I was never any good at science in my schooling. And I am no good with women, either.'

'That's what you say, but I think differently.'

'Yes, well maybe I have the right chemistry or so it appears, but I'm afraid my biology lets me down.' And Robbie laughed, leaning back on the old kitchen chair. 'Looking good is one thing, but acting good is another ... handsome is as handsome does.'

'Well I doubt I will be either.' Christie chewed on some cold bacon. 'They say better to have loved and lost than to never have loved at all.'

Robbie smirked. 'I don't believe that ... man, it hurts when you lose.'

'Now don't start going all melancholy again.'

'You're just a boy, Christie.'

'How do you do this, go from happiness into mirth, so quickly?'

Robbie looked longingly at the young man. 'One day you will understand, but I hope you never have to. I can see I'll get no compassion today?'

And with his mood changed Robbie couldn't sit still. 'Do you think we could walk to Windermere? Maybe the snow won't be as bad further south,' he said looking through the kitchen window.

'As soon as it's proper light I'll go to Grasmere and ask a few discreet questions. Then we'll see.'

'You can't leave now, you'll leave footprints and we could be spotted.'

'Well, I can't fly!'

'Don't be facetious ... you must stay put; we'll leave this house together.'

Christie leant his elbows on the table. 'The food won't last, Robbie. The snow could hang around for weeks and we'll starve.'

'I thought I'd toughened you up a bit, but you're still like a woman.' He'd said what he shouldn't; unkind, unfeeling, and no longer truthful.

Christie stood up, 'Why do I bother with you ...? Everything I've done is for you. Don't you ever see it? Maybe you're right, I am still like a woman....' he was choking. 'I'm frozen.... I can't think straight.... I just want to be safe.... I'm risking my life, as well as yours.'

Robbie lifted his head and looked at the young man, then spoke without any emotion and without removing his eyes from Christie's face said, 'My life's worth nothing, now. So go.'

Christie took his cap, buttoned up his shirt collar, found his overcoat and went to the door. 'You look after yourself now,' and closed it.

Christie stepped out into the frozen morning, the fog and the cold caused his breath to melt into vapour. He raised the collar of is coat and stuffed his hands deep inside his pocket. He didn't move from the step, letting his boots sink into the deep snow drift on the front door. Whichever way he walked he would leave footprints so he stepped onto the yard and walked boldly through the deep snow; he wouldn't look back. As he reached the hill a cold draught hit his chest and he began to cough. Christie was punishing himself, and he could no longer hold in his remorse. He'd spent most of his adult life running about after Robbie and now to walk away from him because of an unkind word was unforgivable, but pride stopped him from returning; his foot prints would give too much away. Christie started to gasp. He took a handkerchief from his pocket and blew his nose; the difference between grief and anger was so slight, and he covered his mouth to silence himself. If the Mooks were watching and waiting; he didn't care for himself, but what could happen to Robbie was still the overriding fear. A rabbit ran across the lonnin in front of him, as scared and as cold as he was. Christie continued forward as the gaslights in Grasmere peered through the gloom. Stride after stride he walked, desperately trying to compose his thoughts and rid himself of this anger. He had confused feelings running through his head, firing quickly at him and blending together: *I shall tell Frazer Piercy immediately I'll not be buying Keld Head. I shall tell Beth she did the right thing in marrying Fred and not you. I'll save some money for a wife of my own, not waste it on a property that has never been shown or wants to be shown affection.* Looking for his pocket watch, as his cold hands fumbled in his waistcoat, he could see it was only just after eight o' clock so he headed for a small inn on the Keswick road and banged on the door.

An elderly man shouted then opened.

'Do you have provision of a hot breakfast and a warm room, sir?'

The elderly man looked at Christie. 'You look half starved, boy. What in blithering's name are yer doing out in this weather?' Christie didn't answer but stepped inside, stamping the snow off his boots. 'Do you know how far the snow has fallen?'

'It's everywhere lad, as far as t'south. But the glass tells me were in fer a change toneet.... Where'st tha from, lad?'

'Yorkshire.' Christie hesitated. 'I need to leave for London tomorrow.'

The old man smiled. 'It'll gan as quick as it come.'

The breakfast was welcome and warmed Christie, but the guilt rose deeper; yet he couldn't return to Keld Head as he knew it would make it more dangerous for Robbie. And as the day moved on Christie slept in a warm bed, recalling how he had lain under hedges and walls for weeks, hugging trees to keep himself warm when he had run away from Morpeth; eating wild food and stealing from dustbins; Robbie had been his salvation. He recalled when he first set eyes on Keld Head and knew he had found sanctuary. Running away from bullies in Northumberland and a life he didn't want and now he was doing the same. But this was a life he wanted. Robbie was wrong to say he was like a woman, he knew he had courage, intelligence, tenacity. Women were bravely fighting for their rights as he would do; no longer the weaker sex. He knew Robbie's moods well; if he had the freedom he would now be walking the hills instead of being holed up in Keld Head's prison like walls. Christie knew he had made a mistake in leaving and as he lay in bed listening to the outside world of frozen snow, he contemplated his options. Robbie had hinted at marriage for him in the future, yet he had no feelings for it. A pretty girl; no, the right girl only would awaken that feeling.

As Christie's slim frame disappeared into the fog, Robbie had watched him walk away and wanted to run after him. And yet in amongst the frozen trees he thought he could still see the figure of a troubled young man, steeped in worry, with shoulders bent low. Then the image merged into the shapeless trees and laurels that crowded the lane like he had merged into the plantation.

Robbie sat for hours drifting in and out of necessary sleep. Catching up from the labyrinthine night; his hands, his nose, his feet, were frozen. When he could stand it no longer, he re-lit the oil burner, drew the curtains, warmed his hands and boiled water for some tea.

He had dreamt of these days during his four years in prison and the expectations of freedom were dashed. He longed to be on his beloved horse in those wonderful salutary hills. But they now presented danger. The sea was his only route to safety.

Robbie had left Coldrigg, swearing he wouldn't return, with McCulloch well paid and bound to secrecy. Even young Bradley hadn't been told, but Robbie's disappearance was explained as a trip to the infirmary to heal his festered stab wound. McCulloch had said Robbie was to be assessed for his release.

It saddened Robbie to think he couldn't properly say good bye to Brad but safety was paramount. And now this decision to return to Keld Head had been a mistake. Frazer Piercy and Christie had met him at the gates and fed him. Frazer had insisted they go straight on the train to London, but Robbie had demanded he wouldn't leave without seeing Keld Head. For Beth to have been there had unnerved him; her desperate plea was hard to defy. That wasn't meant to happen and the snow and this fear had been a surprise, and Robbie believed that whoever lived in this house in the future would catch hold of his contagious fear that was saturated within the walls like a cancerous disease. How could he stay and bear children, only for them to inherit this torment; always looking over their shoulders, listening for the click of the gate, watching the lane from the arched window; the wounds on Robbie's body, scarred him for life.

He wandered the house to release his stiffened joints and found a few possessions and put them in a small canvas bag; not much to show for his life.

Amongst some clean undergarments he put his father's pocket knife, a small sepia photograph of his family in a fancy silver frame: Fred, young and fresh, his mother thin and tired, his father, proud, resting his hand on Robbie's shoulder; himself, the crooked smile.

Robbie knew another night under these walls would have to be his last, whatever the weather brought. But the night was slow in coming and when it did it brought new terrors. He set his bag by the door; he was dressed in clean clothes, a clean coat and his boots scrubbed meticulously, a clean hat; London would have to learn to like him for his northern manner and style. The food had gone and he cursed himself in coming to Keld Head in the first place. He contemplated going down to the Givens' cottage, but as much as he trusted them, he couldn't let his guard down. The more his stomach burned with hunger the more he cursed Christie for leaving him; the puppy of a man wouldn't return now or he would have been back with food, if he cared anything. So this is how his life was to become: alone.

He took his place by the arched window with hot milkless tea his only comfort. He'd boiled the water late in the evening and put some in an earthenware jar to warm him for the rest of the night.

The loneliness became a new terror and he wondered when this fear began; he never used to care. Was it fighting the Boer? Was it his foolish associates or was it Coldrigg Gaol or the loss of a lover? But there was one thing certain, fear would keep him company for the rest of his life.

His love and the isolation of walking the fells had always been temporary; there was usually an inn or a cottage he could go to when he had had enough, maybe over in Wasdale, Grange or St John's. His brother was back in his pretty farmhouse with his pretty wife, others still banged up in Coldrigg.

Robbie slept more than he imagined, when a new noise awoke him; an incessant noise, close to the house; something persistent, rattling and shaking, or was it someone? He grabbed a rolling pin from close to his side and he edged downstairs. He hadn't lived in this house for years and each new noise confused him. He stopped at the foot of the stairs, the noise louder, rattling on, interminable, persistent. Adrenalin shot through his heart and it beat rapidly, then as he went close to the window he saw in the dim light of dawn, water dripping noisily off the loose guttering onto the floor and missing the downspouts. Gripping his chest to steady his heart he relaxed and leant back on the kitchen wall and saw his bag by the door, glad the thawing snow had woken him, he glanced outside and the tree branches and laurels were exposed, free of their snowy skin, and as he was about to brave the wet and run, he heard the yard gate click. He leant back against the door with the rolling pin when someone tapped the door gently; he shuddered.

'Robbie.... Robbie....' someone whispered.

And recognising the sweet tones, Robbie said, 'Christie.... Man alive, what the blazes are you doing?' He quietly pulled back the three bolts and opened the door with the rolling pin still in his hand.

Christie wisely stood back as Robbie peered around the door, then stepped in and threw his arms around his friend. 'I'm sorry.... I'm so sorry.' And as they embraced the boy moaned as he held his friend close.

Robbie wounded by the young man's apology held on to him for some time and whispered. 'Have we kissed and made up, Christie?' Then pushing the boy away he said, 'You nearly had a rolling pin on you curly head. Have you brought any food?'

Christie pulled from his jacket a soft bundle containing bread and cheeses. 'Hurry. There's a carrier leaving at nine for Windermere, and if we can get to the Keswick road safely he'll take us.'

The news was sobering because although there was relief, Robbie knew he may never set eyes on this place again.

'Are you alright?'

'I've survived haven't I, despite you upping and leaving me.' He unwrapped the food. 'Do we say goodbye here?'

'No, I'm coming to London with you. If you still want my company.'

Well lit with the dawn light before them, they walked at pace up the road, cutting through the woodland path.

'There's the van. Are you sure you want to do this?'

'No, but what choice do I have.' Robbie was gasping, trying not to cough, breathless with the cold. 'Are you sure you want to buy my farm?'

'No, and what choice do I have! But if you still want to sell it, yes.'

Robbie didn't look at Christie. 'Thank you, yes. Maybe one day I'll be able to buy it back.'

*   *   *

The driver said one of them would have to sit in the back. Robbie volunteered and he sat amongst empty boxes with his back to the side of the van, his only view coming from the rear window in the door. He saw nothing but the road and the sky disappearing into the distance, and as the van noisily left Grasmere, Robbie tried to imagine where he was. His belly full, his body warmer, his hands and feet still wet and cold, longing for freedom and hoping this journey in this small van would be his last confinement.

23

SPRING AND THE THAWING SNOW

As they sang the final hymn, Beth clung to Fred's arm. She noticed something about him today; something different. He had politely greeted the few parishioners in the congregation with a gentle handshake and a courteous dip of the head. He had talked briefly of farming to a local man, Jack Cockett, who farmed down the hill from Spickle Howe. Fred's skin was tanned from work, his brown eyes clear and bright. His honey coloured hair, neat and trimmed as was his short beard and moustache and shapely side boards; his teeth, straight and white. Beth didn't know it but Fred was like his father and the few photographs they had confirmed it. Beth had always been amazed at the lack of similarities between the two brothers, but today she noticed something different; something more like Robbie; confidence was oozing out and in some of his conversations Fred had began to show some of the wit of his brother.

Unbeknown to Beth, Fred's confidence had come from hope, and there were signs it was beginning to be realised. Expectation and disappointment had made Fred's heart sick, but Beth's attachment and loyalty to him had raised him up.

He noticed she spoke frequently of Robbie and it didn't cause jealousy; no, that was all in the past; it was her silent thoughts that once wounded him. She was also frank and open about Robbie and started to speak of him as a brother, as if she no longer had anything to hide. And Beth's concern over his own welfare had touched Fred. That she genuinely cared for him meant there must be love hiding somewhere, waiting to emerge. And their physical attraction had grown, too. She leaned on him heavily at times and Fred loved that. He would wrap his arms around her when she wept. She would come and find him if she was worried about things. And as the sale of Keld Head was soon to take place she pampered him and was compassionate knowing his disappointment. She could see Fred develop at the age of twenty five into a fine man, sturdy, well meaning, honest. She noticed people liked him; the men working for him were respectful and obliging, and today he had read the lesson: the apostle Paul's letter to the Corinthians, speaking about love that never fails:

"Though I speak with the tongues of men and of angels, and have not charity, I am become as sounding brass, or a tinkling cymbal. And though I have the gift of prophecy, and understand all mysteries, and all knowledge; and though I have all faith, so that I could remove mountains, and have not charity, I am nothing. And though I bestow all my goods to feed the poor, and though I give my body to be burned, and have not charity, it profiteth me nothing. Charity suffereth long, and is kind; charity envieth not; charity vaunteth not itself, is not puffed up, doth not behave itself unseemly, seeketh not her own, is not easily provoked, thinketh no evil; rejoiceth not in iniquity, but rejoiceth in the truth; beareth all things, believeth all things, hopeth all things, endureth all thing. Charity never faileth."

Beth had listened to his words and admired the man he had become; yes her husband could speak freely and honestly with no hypocrisy; oh how Fred had loved his father, his brother and now her.

They left the small church and walked up the hill, a spring morning made the mountains jump out in splendour. The distant Coniston fells were beguiling and tantalising. As they left the few cottages on the lane, waving goodbye to friends, in Fred's hand was a basket.

He'd promised a picnic if it stayed fine and as the morning warmed and the sun shone, they found a rocky outcrop on the summit of the bank and stretched out a blanket; the picnic was meagre but welcome; home baked bread with cheese and some sweet biscuits.

'Did my reading sound alright?' Fred asked as he eased himself on the red tartan blanket beside Beth, and started to cut the bread with a small knife.

'You were word perfect, Freddie.'

He grinned. 'Would you like some cheese?'

278

She just nodded and thought of her father's readings: bold, colourful, fearsome. She'd often recoiled at what he had said. Fred would never be like that, then looking up at the warm sky, her heart moved to distant places. 'Do you think Robbie will be warm today?'

'I hope so ... I don't like to think of him shivering ... he'll still be sleeping, no doubt.'

Beth smiled, trying to imagine him in a wooden shack, speaking in broken Portuguese to men that didn't understand him but would love working for him.

'He'll never be safe will he?'

'Who knows, Betty ... safe from the Mooks, yes, but still in danger from his own devils.'

She just smiled at Fred's candour and picked up the bread and cheese.

Fred handed her a small bottle of lemonade. 'The blackbirds are getting up early now with the light mornings.' They watched one hopping close, keen for some scraps.

Fred rested back against a small flat rock where they often sat looking across the valley to the mountain ridge of the Old Man of Coniston, and seeing the lane he once travelled with his father when they moved house from Millom, he recalled his father crying, and now here he sat with his wife, a new start; unbelievable. He wished he could tell his father he was happy and that Robbie was safe; and Keld Head was, in effect, still in the family. That would be all he wanted to know.

Beth leant her head on Fred's shoulder and shut her eyes, the warm spring sunshine touching her face.

'We'll climb yonder Old Man one day, Betty. There are some lovely rocks and crags beside a tarn, so Robbie once said.'

She took off her straw bonnet and didn't reply.

'The mine leaves a nasty scar on the landscape, doesn't it? I wonder if our Robbie's found any gold in Brazil?' he glanced down and noticed her eyes shut. He looked at the lemonade bottle out of his reach; and despite his thirst he wouldn't disturb her. He continued to talk: 'We must invite Jack Cockett for dinner one evening, he's lonely.' The meaningless conversation continued. 'I think Topper might be lame. He struggled yesterday ploughing. I'll get Bainbridge to have a look at him next time he's over. That young heifer, Ruby, she's giving plenty of milk now.'

Beth stirred. 'I love it that you give them all names. Father never named any of our cattle.'

'My father said: give a cow a name and it will give you more milk.'

She just smiled, her eyes still shut.

'I think Christie should get the deeds to Keld Head this week. I've offered to send him some of Robbie's animals; a gesture, you know.'

But Beth heard none of it, just his gentle and comforting voice.

She slept for twenty minutes, but Fred didn't mind, although he wanted to move his arm and his back ached a little, resting against the stone.

When she awoke he was still talking. 'I'll have to meet Christie tomorrow. We need to sort out some of Robbie's stuff. Bring any valuables here, if you don't mind?'

Beth stretched a little. Putting her hand on his knee and turned and was unable to stop herself from kissing him on the lips.

Fred responded by holding the back of her head to support her. And as she pulled away he noticed she gently and purposefully sucked her bottom lip as if to taste the sweetness of his kiss.

'Will we be happy, Freddie?'

'I think so... I hope so, from now on.'

'Yes, from now on.'

'Do you want to sit a little longer?' He said looking at the clouds building on the horizon above Dow Crag.

'Right now, I want to sit here forever; if nothing ever changed from this I would die happy. I've been a fool, Freddie, I know it.'

'No, Betty, you haven't, none of us have. We just tried to do the right thing. I am as much to blame for that. It's worked out in the end.'

'I'm looking forward to seeing Christie. Do you think he will have any news?'

'I don't know, love. Don't expect too much will you.' Fred sat forward and wrapped up the few provisions and put them neatly back in the basket. Beth stood and straightened the long folds on her tweed skirt; she put her bonnet back on and waited.

'When I was a little girl, I dreamt of being married. I suppose all girls do. I used to sit by the River Swale and sketch garlands of flowers and flowing lacy wedding gowns. I'm sorry our wedding day was a sham. And I've prayed and prayed for forgiveness.' Her voice fractured. 'Do you think we could go away somewhere; somewhere special, just the two of us?'

'I don't know, Betty... I have little money and I can't leave the farm for long.'

'It doesn't really matter where we go, or for how long,' she took his hand as they walked, 'anywhere would be special.'

Spickle Howe wasn't a grand farm by any stretch of the imagination. The farmhouse was much smaller than that at Keld Head and also indistinguishable from the outbuildings. The latched door went straight into the yard; the kitchen small, but enough room for a good dining table. It was a warm house, sheltered by the forest on one side, nesting in a hollow, and well hidden.

The lane met the village road and people walked by regularly; callers were always welcome. Fred's main income came from sheep and the sale of a few beef cattle and a small dairy. He was a tidy farmer because his father was; he was a good worker because his brother was.

Spickle Howe became an open house and Beth loved it that way. She welcomed most and visitors soon began to realise there would always be a piece of cake and tea. The postman got his breakfast regularly, usually with Fred. Beth learned to utilize their income well, it wasn't difficult, and although it wasn't what she was accustomed to at Sugar Hills, she became happy. Christie had promised once he took over Keld Head he would help provide her with some income from the cottages she bought off Robbie which were still housing Robbie's redundant farm workers.

Fred and Beth pooled their income and shared all. They trusted each other but at times Beth felt that Robbie had been close to draining them dry, but her charity in giving did bring her some happiness as she considered him to be safe in Brazil. She used to watch Fred give the village children coppers for treats, as she had seen Robbie do. They couldn't afford it really but Fred would give away his last penny if he felt someone needed it more than him.

On Monday morning the black and white feathered cockerel was awake before Fred. That was unusual. Fred lay still in bed, warm and content. He had the animals to feed then a ride to Keld Head to meet Christie. He would take the trap as he had some of Robbie's belongings to bring back.

The cockerel persisted but Fred lazily ignored it, he turned over and the bed creaked. If he wasn't meeting Christie he would have lingered.

Sitting up on the edge of the bed he rubbed his beard then tried to straighten his honey coloured hair. He saw his work clothes folded neatly on a chair, waiting. He softly crept to the wash basin and poured in some cold water and splashed his face and his bare chest, looked at himself in the mirror over the fireplace as he checked he was tidy. He stepped into trousers and fastened the fly buttons as he reached for his vest and his shirt. Looking back on the bed, he paused as Beth was still sleeping, her long dark hair falling across the pillow just as it had fallen onto his shoulders last night. He hesitated momentarily, then moved away. The cockerel screamed louder as Fred shut Beth's bedroom door and whistled as he wandered downstairs.

When Fred left for Keld Head, Beth stood at the door and waved. He had promised to be home that night; he would help Christie sort through Robbie's stuff.

She made herself busy baking, thinking Christie may return with Fred. The stove was lit and the oven warm; the early morning sunshine, welcoming, as it peeped through the window and thawing the early frost. Beth pondered over Robbie's possessions, feeling uneasy. Everything she had in this little farmhouse came from Sugar Hills or from under Black Combe and a few wedding presents they'd brought, but to have Robbie's things unnerved her and feared that the reminders would be troublesome.

She knew Fred would be discreet, but he too would be sobered by the job he had to do. Christie's buying Keld Head seemed the only solution at the time but it was a decision they had made sitting around the kitchen table, the three of them conspiring again.

Fred had told her at one time he was letting his father's property slip away like dry sand through his fingers and he could do nothing to stop it, but his greatest possession, his wife, truthfully belonged to him, with no more pretence or deception and was firmly in his grasp.

Beth took some apples they'd stored from autumn, peeled them and put them on the stove. She pulled out a large earthenware jar of flour and carefully weighed some flour, then put it in the bowl along with the fat. The apples soon simmered and the kitchen started to smell welcoming. She heard Robbie's spaniels yapping, so she stopped and wiped her hands, rubbing them dry on her flowery apron. She leant on the window sill and watched the kennels as the dogs frantically barked at what was clearly a stranger.

Beth had never felt afraid at Spickle Howe but with Fred being away she was edgy. She walked quickly to the kitchen door and pulled the bolt, tight shut, then went back to the window. The dogs continued to bark as Beth checked the clock; it was too early for the postman. As she heard soft footsteps tapping on the gravel as someone walked stealthily and at pace, Beth waited from her vantage point close to the curtains. She saw a small woman approach with ragged clothes; a stranger; maybe a gypsy. She wondered at the woman's interest and guessing she was begging, quickly decided she could feed the woman and no more. She didn't want to be pestered by lucky heather or trinkets and fortune telling.

A loud knock came to the door and Beth unbolted it and, as she opened it partially, she saw a small, dark haired, tanned skinned woman. She peered into the woman's tired and bloodshot eyes but didn't speak.

'Missus Keldas?' The woman said.

'Hello, yes, good morning.'

'It's me, missus. Nance ... Nance Wilding.'

Beth peered at the woman, much aged from the last time she saw her sitting in the gallery for Edwin and Robbie's trial, much diminished and in grubby clothes.

'Heavens above Nance, come in, come in.' Beth pulled the door open wide. 'How are you?'

'I'm nay too well, missus ... but I've walked all this way te find Robbie. Is 'e 'ere?'

'I'm afraid he isn't, Nance. But come in and sit down, let me get you some refreshments.'

'Thanks ... yer 'ospitality is gratefully received.'

As she passed Beth could smell her body odour; sour and unwashed, and her hair was matted at the back and her skin, grubby. Nance looked like she'd just come down the chimney.

'Is Freddie 'ere, then?' Nance didn't go to the chair but straight to the stove to warm her hands.

'Freddie has gone to Keld Head, Nance. He won't be back till late.'

'Curses, I must a missed 'im.... I walked through t'woods. I've been te Keld Head looking fer Robbie, but the place is still boarded up, like.'

'I know.'

'Well, I must speak te Robbie soon, Missus Keldas, do yer know where 'e is?'

At that moment in time Beth wished beyond reason she knew where he was. 'I'm sorry Nance, but Robbie has gone abroad to a warmer climate. He sailed straight after leaving Coldrigg. Let me get you some tea. You're starved.'

'I've getten the influenza, Missus Keldas.'

'You shouldn't have come out. How long have you been walking?'

'Two days, missus. I'm not as strang as I used te be.'

'How's Edwin?'

'Well, that's partly why I've come. He's pining fer Robbie. He canna do wi'owt him ... nivver could.'

Beth knew what that felt like and she flushed at the thought.

'He says 'e can't abide any more at Coldrigg, if Robbie daren't come and see 'im, 'e'll perish.'

'But Robbie needed to be away, Nance; you must understand it was dangerous for him to stay.'

'I knows that ... and that's another reason why I come.'

Beth was fast in a situation she didn't want to be in; caught in a trap with no helper. How she wished Fred was here. How she wished Robbie was here. She eyed Nance Wilding as she came across to the kitchen table, her clothes shabby; the only means of warmth was from a lacy purple shawl that was probably passed on from Fred's mother. She had no rings on her fingers, and her brown hands looked calloused and arthritic with filthy finger nails. She probably wasn't much older than Beth.

'Well I must thank yer fer 'elping me family, Missus Keldas. I knows Freddie's been good te us, 'elping with the rent, an' all.'

'Robbie insisted, Nance. How are the children?'

'Me eldest as gone te Lanarkshire, mining ... he's only fourteen. Me second is looking after t'youngest.'

'Are they alone?'

'Aye, they're safe in Wasdel.... Naybody goes there. I've left 'em food.'

Beth knew that the middle boy would only be about ten years old and was looking after a six year old.

'Well, when Robbie returns, will yer tell him 'e's safe now, and te come an' see our Edwin.'

'What do you mean, safe?'

Nance leant on the table as if she was about to fall asleep. As Beth was so absorbed in the conversation she forgot about making the tea. Nance looked closely at the empty tea pot on the table.

Beth saw her eyes move and quickly roused herself.

'Well, I 'ardly dare tell yer, Missus Keldas ... oh, I wish Robbie were 'ere.' Nance pulled a crumpled and grubby handkerchief from her pocket and blew her nose. 'It's Sally Mook.... She's dead.'

'Dead!'

'Aye, she is a gonner, alreet.... They found her by't railway lines at White'aven, butchered up from'th train.'

'Dear Lord.' Beth put her hand to her mouth.

'It were an accident ... folks said she'd been at the bevy when'th train 'it her, full pelt it was. So she won't be moidering Robbie again.'

'Nance, please, you must understand, it's not just Sally Mook that was troubling Robbie, you must know he never feared that woman ... it was her family.'

'Nay, Missus Keldas, you're wrang. Robbie's been done ... 'ad ... good and proper. Edwin sent me te tell 'im.' Nance should have been choking on her words but the strength of the news she was telling gave her vitality. 'It were McCulloch.... He's twisted 'em all.... Robbie, Bradley and young Christie.... He made it all up aboot them coming after Robbie.... It were nobbut lies just te get money out on 'em.... No blasted Mook cared aboot Jimmy or Sally.... If the truth be known they's all 'appy they's gone.'

'Are you sure all this is true, Nance?'

'As sure as am sitting 'ere wi' you. McCulloch planned it all.... It were a scam!'

Beth looked to the steam rising from the kettle on the stove.

'My Edwin were told when Robbie left an' no more money were coming in fer McCulloch.'

Beth felt a pain grip her heart and she held the table. Endeared to this poor woman as she was telling this tale, she who had been abused by so much, grateful she had put Robbie's well being before her own, despairing at the consequences.

'Nance, will you stay with us tonight...Wait till Freddie gets back and tell him what you told me... Have a hot meal and sleep in a warm bed. Freddie will take you back to Wasdale tomorrow.'

'Well, thank yer, Missus Keldas, I'm grateful. Yer will tell Robbie tho' won't yer, not te fear anymore on account o' them

Mooks.... It's good news really, missus. But beg 'im please te come and see my Edwin ... it'll break 'is 'eart if he doesn't.'

Beth wondered where all this would end, maybe it was now. She loved her husband and she realised with this news that she still loved his brother. Everything they had done, houses they had sold; ways and means of concocting plans for Robbie's safety was futile, and Fred was soon to be handing over the keys of Keld Head and would be rifling through Robbie's belongings to break up the home he'd tried to make. Christie had painstakingly journeyed back and forth from Thirsk to Millom to Grasmere to help Robbie; selling some of his property, bartering with agents, holed up in Keld Head for three days all to no avail.

The only blessing was that Christie had bought Keld Head and no other. Beth felt abused, cheated, sick that they all had been deceived, dreading telling Fred the news. She recalled Fred's anger at Robbie selling Keld Head in the first place. How he said Robbie had pleaded with him to keep him safe in prison and keep him secure out of it.

The thawing snow had brought Robbie freedom at a heavy price; it had given Beth a marriage and a future; but what that future would be, she was uncertain. In the years that she first came to Westmorland she had gone through months of turmoil then hope; and she wondered that as long as Robbie was alive if she would experience more pain. She doubted she could live with it; she had heard her lovely Fred leave that morning, a man at last, happy in this marriage, only to return and be struck down by disturbing news. She believed she had sinned in her deception to her father and she believed she may be reaping the consequences and feared they may last forever.

Nance eyed Beth and understood with her tired and maltreated mind, that Beth was struggling with the news. She stretched her pathetic hand across the table and took Beth's.

'Daren't fret, Missus Keldas, what's done is done ... 'e'll be safe now.'

Beth couldn't speak.

'I knows you were meant fer him and not Freddie, Edwin told me.'

Beth blushed.

'Ye'll be alreet wi' Freddie, believe me, 'e's the best un te have. It's best te 'ave a 'usband as 'im. Robbie and my Edwin, well. they'll nay make anyone 'appy but themselves. I knows it... Rob were a fine man, I know, and I couldn't blame anyone fer falling fer him, but yer did right, I guess.'

'Do you think so, Nance?' Beth, weary eyed, looked at this pitiful woman for courage.

'I knows so, Missus ... look at me.'

Fred arrived at Keld Head long before Christie and he did exactly the same as Beth had done weeks earlier and wandered through the house, looking at the memories and items of his father's and his brother's. Some made him smile.

He had no idea what to bring back and what to leave. He wandered each room and found in the minstrel's gallery a pillow and a blanket and an empty plate. He folded the blanket gently, and laid it on Robbie's bed and took the plate downstairs.

He opened the wardrobe and pulled out Robbie's wedding suit; pristine. He gently began to fold things and put them flat in a large chest that was his father's; there were shoes and boots, clean shirts. He saw under the window a travel trunk; brand new. It was stained in pale green and had embossed on the side in gold letters and ivy leaves, R and E. He opened the lid but it was empty. It would have to stay at Keld Head.

Fred heard a motor vehicle outside, he glanced through the window and seeing Christie step from the cab, went downstairs to meet him.

'Have you had a good trip?'

They embraced.

Christie stepped close to Fred as he paid the driver. 'Is Bethy well?' he asked, hopefully.

'Very... have you heard from Rob?'

'Yes, just a telegram. No details, just his new banking information.'

'He must be there then.'

'Yes, safe at last....' Christie looked youthful still. 'Is everything alright here?'

'Oh yes.' Fred wandered back to the house. 'No danger ... just as you left it. I've spoken to Jackie Bainbridge. He says he hasn't seen a soul.'

'Good.'

'I don't know what to take or to leave. What do you want?'

Christie looked around the kitchen where he had sat in happier times with Robbie and Edwin, recalling Beth. 'Robbie doesn't want anything that's left. Just take his personal stuff. You could leave some furniture if you've no use for it. I may need it for a tenant, if that's alright.'

'Of course it is. I have no room at Spickle Howe any way.'

Christie stopped. 'If Robbie ever comes back then it's all here for him.'

'Don't waste any more time thinking he'll come back ... you know that he's not that predictable and even if he did, how could he stay. He's terrified here.'

'I know, I know.... I just wanted to do it for him.'

'Don't you feel you've done enough?' to be counselled on his charity struck Christie, as he had once counselled Robbie.

'Freddie, I'm only twenty two.... I don't know what to do with a place like this. I have enough to worry over with Sugar Hills.... I'm glad I have a good manager.'

'I'm sorry, I'm sorry.'

They worked all day folding clothes, emptying drawers and cupboards of personal possessions, just a few photographs and valuable silver items; antiques from under Black Combe, everything was packed in boxes and trunks and put on the cart.

'Where will you stay tonight?' Fred heaved the last of the boxes onto the cart.

'I don't want to sleep here, that's for sure. I think I can get a room at the inn on the Keswick road. I can't afford, or should I say, I don't want to stay at the Prince of Wales.'

Fred smiled because he understood. They were all just getting by on what they had to keep Robbie safe, who at this moment in time was probably bartering on diamonds and gold with no clues as to how they all lived.

'You're welcome to come back to Spickle Howe?'

'No thank you, Freddie. I'd love to see Beth, but tell her I will come soon, I'm tired and I must get back to Yorkshire tomorrow.'

Christie rubbed his hands of the dust as they loaded the last of the things onto the carriage, it was a simple gesture, hoping that he was clean from the sin of this man he had so loved and helped.

'Is Beth coping?'

'Yes, yes she is.'

'You look well and happy?' that was a question.

'I am.... We are both fine. Everything will be okay. We don't have much, but Betty's well looked after.'

The journey for Fred was slow back to Spickle Howe as Topper struggled, pulling the laden cart; the horse knew exactly where he was going, Fred could have shut his eyes and the bay gelding would walk all the way home. They took the steep path up to Deerbolt's Wood then on to Loughrigg Tarn. On the road a few motorists slowly clambered by them as Topper's ears flicked back at the unaccustomed noise. It was still light as Fred turned into the yard and Beth was waiting at the door.

Her first instinct was to come out to meet him but he detected straight away something was wrong. The look of worry had returned; had he been deluding himself all along that she loved him?

He tethered the horse and slackened the straps on the harness, letting the traces on the carriage drop. He pulled Topper loose. 'What's wrong, Betty,' his voice a little cold from fatigue and disappointment.

She hung around him as he led the horse to water.

'We have a visitor.'

'Who...? Good lad, Topper, come on.'

Beth followed them. 'It's Nance Wilding.'

'Nance?'

'I know, she's ill, Freddie.... She's walked from Wasdale and left the bairns alone.... I've helped her rest and get cleaned up. I've given her some new clothes. She's sleeping now.'

'What does she want? Is Edwin alright?'

'No he's not, Freddie. He's pining for Robbie.' Beth looked at the boxes and possessions and felt a morbid fear of them and bit her lip. This was going to be harder than they imagined.

'I'll put them in the granary till morning, they'll be dry there.'

'She's brought news. She was looking for Robbie; they didn't know he was abroad.'

'What's happened, honey?' and he stopped and dared to look her in the eye.

'We've been conned....'

'What do you mean?'

'Sally Mook is dead.... And Robbie was never - never in any danger from the minute he went into Coldrigg.'

'I'm sorry, Betty, I don't understand.'

She went close to him and he tingled as she let her head drop on his broad shoulders. 'He needn't have gone, Freddie. He needn't have sold Keld Head.... McCulloch conned him. No Mooks care about Jimmy or Sally. It was all just a scam to get money out of Robbie.... Out of us!'

That night as Beth lay in Fred's arms she knew he wasn't asleep; she was comforted by his sturdy body. She thought he was mulling over in his mind the loss of his brother and Keld Head and was grieving. She was uneasy that Nance was still here, yet glad she could help her, knowing that tomorrow her lovely husband would have to make another long journey on the account of his wayward brother.

24

RIVERS OF WATER AND IRON

The train was late. Christie checked his pocket watch and fidgeted. The station platform was draughty as he faced the wind, listening and looking for far-away signs of an oncoming train. He heard the chuff - chuff in the distance, the metal wheels grinding against iron. He saw the puffs of smoke rising across the distant fields with stone walls criss-crossing up low gradients. He picked up a leather bag which was his father's; embossed on the side was F.C.R

Christie knew the train and he knew the ticket officer, the porter, and the guard. He would try and sit at the rear so he could watch the little engine streaming through the beautiful landscape like an artery to the world and a way home.

'We'll see you again soon, Mr Richardson?' the porter said pulling a trolley alongside Christie at the end of the platform.

'No, not too soon.' He had to shout over the rumble of the metal wheels on the trolley. 'My business is nearly finished here.' And Christie knew he had in his possession the details of a transaction for a farm he had bought, but didn't want. 'I need to be home awhile,' he said as he stepped onto the train. And smiling, with a pleasant disposition, Christie walked the corridor glancing in each compartment for an empty and private seat.

The train was full of visitors heading back to Lancashire, Yorkshire, and beyond. He settled for a carriage with just an elderly smartly dressed gentleman reading a newspaper and the man lifted the paper higher as Christie entered; despite the snub, Christie said good day. There was no reply.

A whistle sounded and the train slowly pulled out, driven by bursts of steam; black smoke drifted by the windows, crazily passing him in the breeze as he watched Westmorland disappear. He was tired of travelling; tired of talking money; he wanted to enjoy his summer at Sugar Hills. Keld Head was in his possession and he had no clues to other news that awaited him of the massive deception of Michael McCulloch. The ones he was fond of had become a burden; but he would bear them always. He was also tired of Frazer Piercy and his alcohol induced mistakes; of travelling back and forth to Millom to orchestrate and rectify legal exchanges. Christie didn't like to hear Frazer bemoan Robbie's personality; heavens, he'd benefited much by Robbie's behaviour. Christie had seen a land agent in Kendal about finding a tenant for Keld Head until he had the time to restore it as a working farm. He had insisted no women or children should stay at the house; it had to be purely a male occupancy. Christie hoped soon to restock the farm and Bainbridge would be re-employed along with the Givens. Some income would come from the tenancy and the farm would yield enough for him to pay Beth some capital from the cottages she had bought.

The train stopped at Oxenholme and a young woman slid open the carriage door and seeing the empty seats across from Christie, hesitated, as she saw the elderly man purposely shake his newspaper. She was attracted to Christie and his smile as he shrugged his shoulders. Then he partly stood and pointed to the empty seat; he recognised the girl.

'This seat is vacant, miss.' He politely lowered his head. 'If you prefer to travel facing the oncoming scenery I will relinquish my seat for you.'

'Thank you for your kindness,' she said recognising him. 'I have no aversion to travelling backwards.'

'May I lift your baggage on the shelf for you?'

'Thank you, that will be most kind.'

Christie cautiously eyed the girl as he was aware she coyishly glanced away when he looked across. The last time he had seen her he was on his way to Coldrigg.

Words were slow to come forth, but his heart was begging his brain to think of some. 'I've seen you on the train several times recently, miss.'

'Yes, sir,' the girl said. 'I think you left the train at Coldrigg,' she spoke dispassionately, but the girl knew very well where she had seen him leave the train, for she had watched him on the platform, then run up the steps to the road.

Christie was surprised his departure had been noted; what would she think?

'I had business to pursue at the prison. My name is Christopher Richardson.' Christie sat forward, encouraged that the young woman seemed to want to talk and he held out his hand.

'How do you do,' she nodded and gently grasped his hand. 'My name is Emily Laird.'

Christie didn't hear; spell bound at the girl's blonde curls and rosy complexion. She had slim hands; delicate, with a few freckles partially hidden under powder. 'Are you travelling far?'

'To York ... and you?'

'Thirsk,' delighted that hours of conversation were left. 'Have you friends and family in York?'

'Oh yes, York is home.... I've been visiting my sister in Bootle.' 'And you?'

'I'm travelling home to Thirsk. I've had friends to see to and business to deal with.'

Emily contemplated her next question but didn't want to appear intrusive. And an uneasy silence ensued as the elderly man rustled his newspaper to remind them they weren't alone.

Christie continued. 'I know York well ... it's a pleasant place. Do you live in the city?'

'My father has a butcher's shop and a coffee house close by the minster.'

'Ah....' Christie was running short of questions and was helped when the guard arrived to take their tickets.

'It's a good day, Mr Richardson?'

'Yes, it is.' Christie hoped it would get better.

'Could I reserve you a table in the dining car today?'

'Yes, please.'

'For one is it, sir?'

'Perhaps you would like to join me, Miss ... Laird?'

Emily blushed. There was nothing better that she wanted to do. 'Thank you Mr Richardson. I would love to.'

Delighted with her acceptance, Christie realised he had put himself in an awkward situation. If he didn't like the girl he was stuck for the next hour or so, and if he did like her he would be disappointed when they finally parted.

'Would you like the venison soup, sir?' the waiter asked.

Christie contemplated this question carefully as he always had soup, but felt it an impossible task to eat carefully on this train. 'No, I will have the salmon pate, please.' He paused until the waiter left. 'You say your father has a coffee house, Miss Laird. I have a friend in Brazil who's interested in importing coffee.'

'We do have a good supplier.'

'Oh no, please, sorry. I wasn't touting for business.'

She straightened the cutlery on the table. 'No, I was merely stating a fact,' and she smiled.

'What line of business are you in?'

'I farm.'

Emily, very surprised said, 'You don't look like a farmer. I thought you may be a legal representative of some kind.'

'Ah, you are correct.... I do have attachments to law, but I'm afraid farming was my father's choice for me and at this moment in time it is my main occupation.'

'Do you farm near Thirsk?'

The waiter arrived with the food and more condiments, so they paused.

'Yes, I do and in Westmorland.'

'Westmorland? Please tell me whereabouts?'

'In Grasmere, close to Mr Wordsworth's house. Keld Head is a small hill farm.'

'How enthralling. I imagine it is a beautiful place?'

'Yes, it has a tower ... a Pele tower, built to protect the farm from the border invaders. I wouldn't call it beautiful though - imposing, yes.'

'I think I may have seen it. The place looked empty last time I was there.'

Christie hesitated. 'Yes, I only secured ownership of it yesterday.'

The meal was meagre but to their liking. The waiter removed the plates.

'Do you require anything further, sir ... madam?'

'No thank you, we have had an elegant sufficiency.' Christie recalled this was an expression Robbie often used as he joked about prison food; what other winsome words had this man taught him?

'Will someone meet you from the train, Emily?'

'Oh yes, my brother.... We only have a short walk from the station.'

'I've enjoyed your company today.'

'Yes, and I too, likewise. If you ever come to York, you must locate our coffee house and I will return your kindness.'

'Yes, that would be grand, thank you, yes, thank you.'

The River Swale was bordered by four fields and as the river cut through the land it calmly twisted and meandered its way. Willow trees were planted densely along the river bank. Christie had planted some of the trees years ago with Tommy Bright on one of his holidays.

He rode Tilly the length of the river; as far as it stretched out on his land, watching the sand martins swooping down and disappearing on exposed areas of the sandy banking, making small holes.

Tilly trotted playfully today as she always did with Christie, loving his sweet voice and his kindness. He was well used to her now and she him. He understood why Robbie loved this horse, but despite her character she wasn't worth the heartbreak that surrounded her.

The saddle and the reins still belonged to Robbie, and Tilly was the only living thing that Robbie possessed in England.

Christie was thoughtful today. He was also angry and his ride on Tilly was a means of escape. He knew he was doing exactly the same as Robbie would, and he could understand why and, in that, he and his troubled friend were the same.

It was the letter from Beth that had done it. It arrived three days after his return from Westmorland; three days after his purchase of Keld Head. It read in part:

"Everything has been futile, Christie. We've almost bankrupted Freddie for no cause. What can I say?

Nance Wilding arrived before Freddie came home with Robbie's things. She's a poorly woman. She told us Edwin was pining for Robbie, as we all are. That Sally Mook is dead; killed in a drunken stupor by a train. We've been fooled by Michael McCulloch and that Robbie's life was never -. never in any danger.

What will become of us all? I'm overwhelmed with great remorse that I'm reaping as we sowed. Fred asks if you could please cable Robbie and tell him the news. Maybe it's not too late for him to return and re-purchase Keld Head from you."

Tilly danced as Christie pulled her to a halt. He sat tight and deep in the saddle as his slim legs clung to her side. He looked heavenward for wisdom, staring then to the eastern skyline, watching the early sun rising over the Whitestone Cliff in the distance. He had been out all night and had to return home.

A long train journey to comfort Beth was considered, but he reasoned Fred should be the one. This marriage must continue and be nurtured. It was a bad idea to see if Robbie would come home straight away, he knew his return wouldn't help Beth but hinder her progress and as for re-purchasing Keld Head, Fred guessed that much of Robbie's capital may already be diminished in buying shares and he would already be living the good life in Brazil.

Tilly fidgeted and Christie became equally impatient with her. 'Keep still ... be still, Tilly!' he snapped at her; words driven from fatigue and sorrow. He reined her in tighter and made her wait a few moments, then released her head and turned her back towards Sugar Hills. He would have to cable Robbie and give him the facts. What Robbie did with them would be his decision.

Christie recalled their last day together in London; dining at the Ritz, then some musical theatre later. Robbie looked stunning in his new clothes, his hair cut, his beard removed, his teeth now clean and white; all indulgent treats and any odour of Coldrigg Gaol was well and truly washed down the drain with the bath water. Robbie had laughed as they parted as he stepped onto the train for Southampton, but behind the laugh Christie had seen fear. When people touched him or shook his hand; the busy throng at the theatre that brushed past him; Robbie would always flinch and hate to be hemmed in; uneasy with any close contact; glancing over his shoulder when he heard men's voices as he had in the plush dining room at the Ritz.

Christie had spent the rest of the day wandering London; he'd promised to look up an old Oxford friend but lost the desire as he had lost Robbie; his true friend was gone and Christie feared he may never set eyes on his handsome face again. Loneliness had remained with him all the day. But now Beth's letter, despite its grim and sickening news gave him hope and a means to look forward to a peaceful future.

He had considered returning to Keld Head; at least he could be near Fred and Beth, but the agent had worked quickly and a tenant was already signed up; the income from the tenancy would be welcome.

For three weeks Christie brooded; the only pro-active thing he could do was to wire Robbie and await a hopeful reply; but as Fred had predicted none arrived. In a moment of frustration and in need of greater companionship than a white horse, Christie bought a train ticket to York.

The city of York kept the summer heat within its sturdy walls. Christie wandered the city walls looking down the ramparts, eyeing the gardens and the minster.

The bells were ringing and the noise carried clearly in the blue sky. He browsed through the little shops and bought a pair of brass candle sticks for Beth and Fred. Every shop he passed he glanced in at the produce and looked up at the name on the boarding.

He easily found Laird's butcher's shop and purveyor of fine meats, and the coffee house was sitting beside it, nestled in a cobbled snickleway. He walked through a courtyard, decked with potted palms and as he cautiously opened the door, a bell rang out loudly, but no one in the busy shop noticed the tall young man as he removed his hat.

Nervous in the crowd, he weaved through the tables and quickly found an empty seat in the corner to his liking; the

298

cloths on his table were heavily starched white, with shiny silver cutlery and condiments.

He picked up the menu to read and the selection of coffee impressed him.

'Would you prefer a better seat, Mr Richardson?' someone said from behind.

Christie spun around in his chair, half standing in politeness to see Emily.

'How lovely to see you,' and he dipped his head. 'This table will be fine.'

'No, Christopher. I insist you come to the window.'

Embarrassed, he reluctantly stood and followed her, his eyes watching the shift of her long skirt and the slimness of her waist, as the curls of her fair hair, neatly pinned back, tumbled onto her neck. She stopped at the window and grinned. Emily Laird was just as attractive as he remembered; perhaps even more so through his tired and worried eyes.

'I'll see that a waitress comes quickly for your order. I was just on my way out.'

'Don't let me keep you any longer.'

'Oh, it is no pressing matter. I needed to get some vegetables from the market. Have you travelled to York today?'

'Yes, I came on the train.' Christie felt awkward him sitting while she was standing.

'You must have business in the town?'

'No, it's purely a pleasure trip, it's some time since I last visited York. I wondered if it had changed.' He cleared his throat. 'Would you have time to join me for coffee later?'

She glanced at the large fingers on a grandfather clock in the corner. 'I can spare sometime now, yes. But only if you would let me re-pay you for your kindness in buying my lunch on the train. You must have some of our best coffee and perhaps some lunch on the house. My father would want it.'

Christie nodded, uncertain at his impulsive decision to come here, made from frustration. But Emily Laird had made his decision a good one.

Once ordered she sat across from him looking out of the window, long shadows cast down as pleasing sunrays fell on the lawns around the minster, blossom on the trees, resplendent as petals fell in soft summer breezes.

'I like to sit in this window and watch the world go by.' Emily took her gaze from him and looked outside. 'People dress so differently these days and I like to admire or criticise their fashion. I try to guess who is married and who isn't? Who are the happy ones and those who are sad?'

Christie wanted to check his appearance, but was confident. 'And what would you assume of me, Emily?'

'You dress well for a farmer.' She teased. 'I would imagine you have a young wife and child, and are longing to see them. But there is sadness in your face.'

'Is there?' He raised his back straighter in the chair.

'Yes, deeply so.' She paused and thought he may respond but he didn't.

Sensing Emily's empathy he longed to divulge the truth, just as he often unburdened himself on Beth in his youth.

'I'm afraid you read faces well, Emily. But there is no wife or child. And my countenance has given away too much already; I won't burden you with my worry or details of my life, but suffice to say, I have friends in dire straits and I long for them to be happy.'

'Your care and charity for your friends is commendable, Christopher.'

'It is also non-negotiable and unavoidable; done with love and duty, but longing to have freedom for my own selfish pursuits.'

The waitress brought coffee cups and saucers and Christie straightened the crockery as Emily poured.

'I'm sorry, Christopher. I didn't mean to pry. It is only out of kindness. I didn't ask for any personal gratification.'

'Please, don't apologise if my countenance speaks quicker than my mouth.... It has long been a traitor to my thoughts. I'm afraid my burdens are many and I wouldn't wish to impose them on you.' These were more words of charm he had heard Robbie say, the use of adding gender and personality to his qualities.

'I would find it no burden, only a means of relief for you.'

'Yes, and it would be.'

Christie looked deeply into her pretty face. 'When you saw me on the train close to Coldrigg, I was there because of a friend, a dear friend. You thought I was a lawyer, but I was purely a messenger and deliverer of comfort and hope.' He looked down at the crowds walking the path to the minster. 'My friend was interned in Coldrigg Gaol.' And he lifted his hand momentarily as if to stifle his speech. 'A great deal of injustice has been done on his part and my good friend has suffered since.'

'Is he still there?'

'No, Emily. Thankfully, no.... He is now a free man. He is the gentleman who has interests in the coffee plantation in Brazil. The one I spoke to you about, and if he was to walk by this window and you saw his persona and his bearing, you would see no facade, but a very honest and just man, and no greater could grace these doors.'

'He sounds a good friend.'

'He is and more so.'

Emily offered no more questions; she saw Christie's passionate declaration and it told her a great deal of his personality. She left him to enjoy his coffee and went back to the kitchen and closed the door behind her. She put her hand to her mouth, so none of the other girls could see she had the radiance of a young woman who was in love.

Emily Laird appeared in no hurry as she sipped coffee and poured Christie more. They spoke freely and easily, happily. Christie was quick to realise his trip was to be a success and a good decision.

'Do you have far to walk to the market?'

'No, it's just five minutes away.'

'I haven't seen the market, could I walk with you, please.'

'Have you ventured far already?'

'No, not really. In fact my train had only recently arrived.' He raised one eyebrow and his lips twisted with the simper of his smile, for he wanted her to know what he was feeling; he had seen Robbie do this.

'Then that would be wonderful, once we have bought the vegetables maybe I could take you a brief walk around our lovely city.'

The narrow streets were warm with summer heat. A street musician played a melancholy dirge on a violin as the tune echoed eerily down the cobbled streets. Some people addressed Emily as she walked and Christie could see she was well known and well liked.

"The love of a woman is a science," Robbie had said, and Christie knew science wasn't easily learned, it took study, patience, sense of mind and clarity of thought. He would do this with Emily and not be overly quick as his sister had been in romance.

He found by examining Emily's personality her to be, by nature, kind and caring, and she had a beguiling humour. When she spoke, she spoke well, but earthy. She neither gossiped nor nagged. The pauses after each exchange of sentence were polite; Christie didn't know her age, but he assumed she was younger than he. Listening to the minster bells chiming and the summer breezes caressing the trees around the minster gardens, he checked his pocket watch as time was passing far too quickly. He only had an hour to decide on his future.

'If you don't mind, Emily, I have some personal shopping to do while I'm here. Could I walk you back to the coffee house?'

'No, Christopher, I'll be fine thank you. I wouldn't want to impose on you anymore.'

'It has been no imposition.'

She waited as he gently took her hand. 'Perhaps next time I'm in York I could call and see you again?'

'I would like that.'

She waited as she could tell he wanted to say more.

'My friends call me Christie.'

25

KELD HEAD

Black Combe was finally conquered by way of a shattered rocky path buried between two folding fells. Christie didn't know which farm below had belonged to Robbie and Fred's father, Samuel.

From the summit the view out to sea reminded him of Robbie. On the edge of the land he could see Coldrigg Gaol and hoped he never had to visit again; the new south wing and Robbie's wall, as he called it, was visible.

Christie would make a penultimate trip to Millom today and hoped this space here on Black Combe would strengthen him and help him be firm in his resolve, not for just himself but for Keld Head. He must ask Fred someday how Samuel Kellet had acquired their farm and property with enough to share for two boys. A cool breeze touched Christie's face and he moved on along the western ridge to the beacon; his brain wracked with tension and work. He was pleased his father had met Samuel Kellet and had bought the shorthorn bull, which had now fathered many a fine beast and part of the herd at Sugar Hills; that gave him added reason in what he was about to do.

The walk back to Millom was done with a nervous pit in his stomach; he disliked Frazer Piercy and his ways, and as soon as he was in his grubby office the barracking began.

'Is he keeping out of trouble?'

No need to ask who.

'Yes sir.' Christie stood tall, determined. 'He's safe and lodging with Brad Shafer's brother.'

'Is that a good thing?'

Christie didn't reply because he had wondered the same.

'So you want to make a will and it concerns Keld Head?'

'Yes.'

'I recall Samuel making his will. He would have abandoned Robbie that day and he would do now if he were still alive.'

303

'Maybe so.... I never met Robbie's father.'

'He was my longest standing client.'

That didn't surprise Christie as he suspected most of Frazer's clients soon abandoned him once they knew of his drinking.

'The day he bought Keld Head that philandering boy went missing; Freddie should have got the lot.'

'Freddie had enough with Spickle Howe to manage back then.'

'He'll gamble it all away, Christie. The capital you gave him will soon be gone.'

'He doesn't gamble anymore.'

'Aye, that's what he tells you.'

'Look, can we discuss this will please,' tired of the reproach to his friend.

'So what are you going to do with it ... Keld Head?' Frazer wandered around his desk and picked up a note pad; there was reluctance and apathy. It would help Christie.

Frazer pushed several papers in front of the younger man as he sat at the desk opposite. Then he slipped off his chair and went to an old dusty cabinet and pulled out two glasses and chose a decanter of whisky. 'Shall we drink on this?'

'No sir. I don't drink and besides, there's nothing to celebrate.'

'No, I can see you're not a drinking man, you're healthy looking ... clean eyes and clean skin.'

'I don't forbid it anyone else, Frazer. I'm just not partial to it nor the ridicule and abuse it causes,' he kept eye contact.

'Robbie said you were outspoken, and that you are. For a young man you speak with authority when you know little of life and the reasons why fine men cripple themselves by taking to the bottle.'

'That's maybe so. And I'm sorry if I've spoken out of order, but I only say what I see.'

'I guess Robbie taught you that, you would see plenty with him.'

'You would like to think that wouldn't you ... but you're wrong, Robbie has taught me plenty of good things.'

And at this statement Frazer threw down his pen. 'So what of Keld Head?'

Frazer sat and leant back as the old leather chair creaked. Then he took his glass, swilling the whisky around and around.

'I have found a tenant and the land is to be farmed. And if Robbie comes back he may want to buy it back and I will sanction that.'

'Don't bank on that, boy ... his money will be gone and he'll be left with nothing. And he'll come back with that grin on his face and beg for more ... pleading like a spoilt child.'

'Frazer!' Christie stood. 'I think under these circumstances after you have drawn up this will that I take any future business elsewhere. I want these wishes orchestrated.' He handed the solicitor a piece of paper.

'Aye, we've maybe had enough of each other young man, but remember it's always me who's helped Robbie Kellet get out of trouble.'

Christie resumed. 'Keld Head and Sugar Hills will go to Freddie and Beth, should I die, but if I have a wife and children they shall have Sugar Hills, but Keld Head remains with Beth and Freddie.... Is that clear? This is my last piece of business with you Frazer and I hope you have the sense of mind to orchestrate this will accurately, good day.'

The nervous feelings had been replaced by those of anger; yes, he had been short tempered but he had had enough. Pleased he had made the right decision and pleased he would soon cut ties with this man, Christie headed for the train as he was to meet Beth; he had much to tell her.

Beth had spent the morning with Aunt Charlotte Webb. Fred had left her at the ferry. She knew the route well; the short sail across Windermere, a cab up the hill to the station; and then the train to Kendal. It would be a route she would take for most of her life.

Christie had written and said he had news, and by the feel of the words it was to be good. News of Robbie's continued safety would be welcome; she knew Fred had concerns as she had.

Charlotte Webb had been troubled for Beth alone at Spickle Howe; visiting was hard with difficult access. She had worried about the early years of her marriage and although she admired and respected Fred, she could see he was very young. When Robbie was imprisoned and the newspapers awash with the story; the understanding and relief of why Beth had married Fred and not Robbie were clear. Today Charlotte thought Beth looked radiant, and for the first time completely and truly happy, and not some facade she was showing.

A small poodle yapped when a knock came at the front door and they knew it would be Christie; he too appeared happy. They all embraced and the little sunny parlour decked in Victorian artefacts and china was filled with happiness.

Christie took off his jacket and sat in his tweed waistcoat and shirt sleeves.

Charlotte fussed over the young people, feeling the responsibility of being their only adult relative and mentor.

She was proud of her nephew; perhaps more so as he had become a fine man, grown much in stature and appearance and confidence. She watched him talking to Beth, calmly, freely, sipping tea as the sun shone on his gold watch chain hanging from his pocket which Charlotte knew was her late brother's.

'So I believe you have secured Keld Head, Christie?' Charlotte asked.

'Yes, I have. How was Freddie today, Beth?' He said.

'Well, very well.' And Beth handed him a plate of buttered spiced fruit loaf.

'Did Frazer Piercy do the right job?'

'Of a fashion. He was drunk as usual. I'm changing solicitor and have hired a relative of his in Kendal, solely to care for affairs here in Westmorland; he is as professional as Frazer was lax.'

'Be wise in your choice, Christie; be careful with the deeds. The buying and selling of property and land can be tiresome.'

'It will be more convenient to lodge some of my affairs in Kendal.'

The front doorbell rang again and the small poodle yapped. Charlotte straightened her long skirt and left. As soon as she was out of the room, Beth looked over her shoulder and said: 'I'm going to have a child, Christie... shhh.' And she reddened and beamed. Christie, overwhelmed with the news was about to stand but before they could embrace they heard Charlotte say goodbye and bang the front door.

Beth put her finger to her mouth. 'We'll talk alone, later.'

'Yes, because there is something I have to tell you,' he whispered.

Charlotte returned and the two young people continued to eye each other and smile like naughty children with a secret. Charlotte resumed her conversation about nothing of any consequence while Beth and Christie were silently devising schemes of how they could be alone to discuss their plans. It was Beth that succeeded.

'Aunt Charlotte, the afternoon is drawing on and I have some shopping to do in the town before I leave. I don't want to be late back for Freddie.'

'No dear, it's a complicated journey for you.'

'I must go to the post office too,' Christie said.

They left Charlotte Webb's house arm in arm, bound in their mutual happiness. They walked down the steep hill to the little town of Kendal, as cool afternoon sunshine left dark shadows from the sycamore trees in full leaf.

'I need to speak to you earnestly, Beth. How wonderful your news is, but what I need to tell you cannot be done in the street.'

Beth glanced around. 'There's a small walkway by the river. There are some private corners and benches. We can talk there.'

They walked at pace, both excited and bursting to speak. They stepped down cobbled paths and Beth clung to Christie's arm for support, protecting her unborn child. They passed the edge of the river and walked to an isolated seat in the distance.

Beth chatted as they walked. 'Are you happy for me, Christie?'

He squeezed her arm. 'It's wonderful news. You must look after yourself, Beth. Don't work too hard or chase any cattle and sheep around.'

'No, doctor.' She beamed.

'How has Freddie taken the news?'

'He's beside himself. He's so happy,' she moved in closer to him as they approached the seat. 'So what is your news?'

'I've much to tell you, Bethy ... and ask your advice.' He sounded sober rather than happy.

'Is all well with Robbie?' She had to ask.

'Oh yes, very, he's working hard. He's safe anyway. He says very little in his cables, he just makes requests. I help him with his banking and some shares he has. But what I have to tell you concerns Keld Head and your news today has made my decision firmer.'

She looked across as some swans and ducks headed across the river towards them.

'I want Keld Head to stay with the Keldas family ... your family. I intend if anything happens to me that Keld Head should be left to you and Freddie or your children.'

'But Christie, what if you ever have a family?'

'Yes well, that is my next news. I have met a young lady.' He hesitated, embarrassed. 'She's from York. We met on the train. I've been to visit her several times and if you approve I think I will ask her to become my wife.' He coughed to clear his throat. 'That's what I wanted to tell you ... to ask your advice about.'

'Christie, this is wonderful news.'

'Well, I don't want to rush things.... I'm still young and I feel I must wait; do you think I am right?'

'If you love this young lady, Christie, you have nothing to fear, but to be sure, don't rush.' She hesitated.

'Yes, but things have worked out haven't they.' And without meaning to be indiscreet he looked at her abdomen, at the small lump that would be her unborn child.

'So what is her name?' Beth asked.

'Emily ... Emily Laird.'

The swans and the ducks arrived noisily, milling around in the water. A pair of ducks flew up across the river and gabbled around their feet looking for crumbs, but finding none.

'So what about this will, Bethy? What do you think? Now as you are with child it makes more sense.'

She lowered her head and lifted her hand on to his knee. 'Christie ...' Beth waited, and the pause would be a thing she would always do; cautious for the rest of her life. 'You and I have become interlaced in this family, more than I ever imagined. I think it was because, in effect, we are orphans and the Keldas family have embraced us. I love Fred and I love Robbie. Does that sound awful? One day you will have a family of your own.'

'Aye, and they will have Sugar Hills.' He was passionate in his speech. 'No, Beth. I feel Keld Head should go to you and Freddie and your family. If Robbie ever returns and wants to buy it back, he is to be given first refusal. I want to give him that opportunity. Despite him once saving me from a life of drudgery, I cannot bequest him Keld Head. He volunteered to sell it easily; he is as Esau, selling his birthright for a pot of stew. But I will not surrender it the same. The stone walls, imposing as they are, have a hold on him, Bethy. I don't know what it is, but I could not and will not see the place abandoned; this is perhaps a punishment for Robbie. Frazer Piercy said in a drink induced meeting some home truths which I will not burden you with.'

'Does Robbie know of this will?'

'No, but I may tell him someday. Heavens, I don't expect to be leaving this earth just yet,' he smiled. 'It's Father's money that has bought Keld Head, Bethy. I don't know how my own children will turn out, if I am blessed with any, but to do things this way, you and Freddie would inherit some of what Father and Robbie had.'

'This is a heavy weight, Christie.'

'Well, let's put it this way, Keld Head deserves to belong to someone who will look after it and love it. Whoever that man or woman may be, they have to be fervent. At this moment that's you and Freddie, in the future, who knows who they may be. But it must be someone who you love and who will love Keld Head.'

'Let's not talk anymore about morbid subjects, Christie. How are things back in Yorkshire?'

'Well, on that I also have news for I'm to follow in Father's footsteps and become a Justice of the Peace. I want to further my studies in law, and maybe in a few years, provided I'm elected, I can sit on the bench.'

The burden on Christie's mind was unloaded and he slept better that night in Aunt Charlotte's guest room. Today he would find Frazer Piercy's brother, Angus. He was unravelling and enacting a scheme he had been planning for weeks. It would be gratifying to have things safely down in writing. Beth's news was an answer to a prayer, that his design was a just one. He hoped Robbie would see it that way. He knew Robbie well, and as he had easily given up Keld Head, out of fear, so could Christie bequeath it to his brother and sister out of justice.

Angus Piercy was found to be a true gentleman and business like. He knew of Christie and he knew of the Keldas brothers. And as Christie sat in his cold and austere office he noticed how precise and clean everything was; the blotting paper, the ink wells. Angus was a tall man, bespectacled; his offspring would be the same. Angus had seen Christie at a young age in court defending Robbie's life and now he was holding his property in his hands.

He didn't want to go back to Aunt Charlotte's straight away and so he took a stroll along the river bank, his mind clearer than it had been in weeks. And that gave him the luxury to think of Emily and his future. And as he wandered he decided on their next meeting to propose to her and hoped she would accept. He had a tenant lined up and waiting to move into Keld Head, and could relax awhile and enjoy the income.

The happiness he had the few months he lived with Robbie was returning; his friend was safe abroad and safe if he came home, wherever that would be; but Christie still missed him; Robbie had become embedded into his heart as much as he had with Beth. He hoped one day they could be together again; time would have to pass and Christie, Beth and Fred would have to live their own lives, always knowing one day Robbie could return and be secure, no matter how long that took.

26
ARABESQUE

1912

I don't want a blasted horse, Edwin, least of all from you.' Robbie slipped his woollen vest over his back, shivering, then pulled on his shirt and with cold hands tried to fasten the buttons.

Edwin Wilding watched his friend dressing, seeing Robbie's tanned skin contrasted against the white lines where his undergarments had been.

'That water's nithering today, colder than I remember.'

'Well, what did yer want te do a blasted fool thing like that fer any'ow, swimming in't lake?' Edwin was sitting on a rock beside Robbie, grimacing as his brown teeth chewed on his old pipe; he then spat and looked out across Wast Water.

'You should get washed Edwin, you filthy devil ... you still smell of Coldrigg.'

'I 'ad a wash, week afore last when I come out.'

'When I was in Brazil I yearned for the cold water here.... You can't sleep because you're too hot and you can't work... I pity those poor devils back there.'

'Aye, and I recall when thi were in Coldrigg thi were longing te be warm.'

Robbie stopped dressing and despite the cold looked at the beautiful fells; the drama as Kirkfell, Gable and Lingmell like massive garlands surrounded the lake.

'Every day I thought about this water, Edwin – every day.'

'And ivery day I thought o' you Robbie, but ye nivver come. Nay, not once.'

'I'm here now aren't I?' Robbie raised his head, unashamed.

'Aye, and fer 'ow long?'

'As long as I like.... I'm a free man, in body and in soul ... I'll go and do what I likes.' He bent low and picked up his socks pulling them awkwardly over his damp feet.

'That's nay good, Robbie, nay good at all. You're like a ship without an anchor, dangerous, yer can drift anywhere. Nay woman, nay home, nay...'

Robbie spun around and slapped him. 'Shut up Edwin, shut up.'

'What's te do? You're as grumpy as an awd hog without a sow. Weren't lasses in Brazil te yer liking?'

'The young women in Sao Paulo were beautiful,' he reached for his boots, and in broken tones continued, 'but they wrinkle in the sun prematurely, not like our English lasses. They talk too fast, they nag. They liked me, I knew they did, but I would have no truck with them. I want fair skin and blue eyes.'

'So what about this 'oss then, Robbie?' Edwin jumped up and jingled a few coins in his pocket. 'I need some cash. I've nowt left.' And he pulled some coppers from his pocket and held them flat in his hand. 'That's all I's getten.'

'You've been out two weeks, Edwin ... two weeks. If I keep paying your rent you'd never work again ... and Nance and those boys would starve.'

'I'm an old man, Robbie.... Daren't be 'eartless; I'm nigh on fifty.'

'Heartless! I've fed you for close to eight years while you were in prison. I've little left myself. Trade in Brazil has kept some of my money safe, but it's not grown.'

'Well ye'll need te get aboot so come an av a look at this 'oss. She's a beauty... an arab cross.'

'No horse ... no blasted horse, Edwin.'

'Well come back te farm and see Nance an mi boys, and we'll feed *you* today.'

Robbie pulled on his coat and his hat, his body glowing with the cold. Edwin stumbled behind him.

'What have you got to eat? I'm starving, I could eat a scabby donkey.'

'Nance has some good 'am ... and a puddin'. We were saving them fer Sunday but when she sees you she'll be over t'moon. Bye the lads, she will.'

'Ham sounds good. I've had nothing but bully beef and chicken, canned potatoes and limes.'

'Will yer stay with us toneet?' Edwin was hopeful.

'I won't sleep in your lice infested house; I'd sooner sleep at Coldrigg.' That was a lie.

'Where will you gan? Yer'll not leave us now.' Edwin caught him up, gasping.

'I'm going to walk to Sty Head, and then who knows where.'

'If you buy this 'oss you'll getten there sooner.'

His plea was ignored.

'There'll be nowt at Keld Head fer thi, Rob.'

'Don't I know that!'

'Well are yer gannin te see Freddie and Beth?'

'Aye, maybe, then I'm off to Yorkshire to see Christie and meet his wife. Surprise them.'

'Shock 'em you mean. She'll nay want you under 'er roof if she's as delicate as 'im.'

'Maybe, maybe not, but she'll know all about my prison life. But remember, Christie's not delicate anymore. A man of law and justice, so I hear.'

Robbie walked on kicking stones with his boots, looking up at Gable; black clouds hung over Sty Head. A westerly breeze behind him pushed him on as they walked. Robbie knew it would be wet in Borrowdale.

'I've more news on Bradley and McCulloch.' Edwin gasped.

'I don't want to know, Edwin.' Robbie quickened his pace to remove himself from a conversation he didn't want.

'Well it's bad news ... bad, aye it is .... I 'ardly dare tell thi. McCulloch'll do time fer sure. He's murdered young Brad, he 'as.... He killed him 'cos he couldn't pay up... he said it were an accident but it were no accident. He'll go down fer this.'

Robbie didn't stop but inwardly groaned. 'There's nothing I can do for a dead man ... that's grim news, indeed. It's in the hands of the Lord now, not me.'

'Should we tell? Stand up fer young Bradley's soul.... We knows what McCulloch's like. If you and young Christie come forward, he'll get more time and you can get some revenge. '

'I'll not say a word....' Robbie spoke quietly, studying the mountains to see if they had changed; whispering as if someone could hear despite the fact that there wasn't another human soul for a mile. 'He'll answer one day ... good and proper for what he's done to us and Bradley. Let God be his judge, Edwin.'

'You're too passive, young Robbie ... always 'ave been.'

'Oh yes, and where did your violence get us? That was one of the few good things my father would say of me.' He picked up the pace.

'McCulloch needs punishin'... I canna say owt, can I...? He did nowt te me, 'cept boxed me lugs a couple o' times.'

'Well, leave it that way.... Forget it. It'll not bring Brad back and we'll never get a penny.'

'You nivver sees McCulloch laughing after yer left. Swanking and bragging he were. He told em all you were scared.... He said you were weak ... a coward.'

'Sweet mother, Edwin! No more, no more,' and Robbie choked on his words.

Silence walked with them back to Raike's Farm. Edwin bordering on tears, whimpering like a scolded whippet and Robbie, grieving over Brad Shafer. As they approached the farm Robbie noticed in the stable a grey horse, its head bobbing up and down as it spotted the men. It whinnied as Edwin looked up.

'Her name's Arabesque ... Robbie look, she's a crying fer you. I calls 'er, Harry, fer short.'

Into the yard Nance arrived with a pail full of potato peelings to feed the pigs. She dropped the pail when she saw Robbie. 'Bless me, bless us all. Robbie, dear boy... is it really you?' she peered through heavy brown eyes, her dark skin creasing in wrinkles around her bony face.

Robbie moved quickly towards her, and like a child he hugged her tiny fragile body. He enveloped her in his arms, knowing it was the only affection she ever received. There was a strong smell of dirt on her hair and body but he didn't mind as it reminded him of her.

'Thank you, Robbie, thank you... fer what thy's done fer us.'

He pulled away and held her arm. 'Edwin tells me you have some ham, Nance.'

315

'It's good sweet meat. Edwin killed a pig last week and we 'ave plenty of it. Come and see Robbie.... Mickey... Eddie ... come an' see who's here?'

A young boy came through the back door; he had no shoes and wore short scruffy trousers. His feet and legs filthy, blotchy and red. He stood and eyed Robbie, expressionless.

'Come here, Mickey... don't say you've forgotten me?' a smile emerged on the boy's face and disregarding the cold and the stones on the yard he ran forward and Robbie picked him up and spun him around, playfully dropping him and catching him.

'You're a grand boy, Mickey... see as you daren't take after your father.'

The boy still didn't speak but stood, hands in pockets. Robbie took a few coppers from his pocket. 'Get yourself something ... a pair of shoes. Don't give any money to your father.' Mickey spied the coin and finally said, 'Ta Robbie, ta very much.'

Robbie took another coin and gave it to Nance. 'Buy some new shoes for young Eddie as well, Nance.

Nance worked in the small kitchen producing weak tea in cracked cups. She drank hers from a jam jar. She kicked a cockerel out of the kitchen that had been walking on the table; there was a dead mouse underneath. Robbie sat in an old wooden chair by a meagre fire.

They ate cold ham with onion pickle. Robbie never felt discomfort at Raike's Farm and he always felt safe.

'It's a shame Missus Keldas lost her babby.'

To hear Beth spoken of as Mrs Keldas brought forth the reality Robbie had tried to forget, and the image of her that he had every day of his life, swam through him, tantalising him as it always did. 'Grim news you have for me today.'

'Well, I could see she weren't fit fer carrying no bairn, 'er eyes looked muddy... she needed some nettle tea ... I told 'er so. She'll nay 'ave another; it'll kill 'er so Freddie says.'

Robbie sat forward in the chair, uncomfortable.

'Nay daren't fret, Rob. That lassie would 'ave been nay use te thee.'

316

Wisdom acquired over years of toil and heat won the battle and he didn't speak but stood to leave.

'If you've 'ad yer fill, come and see this 'oss then?'

'You don't give up do you, Edwin.' Robbie walked into the yard, glad to get some fresh air. 'I thought I might buy myself one of those motorised vehicles.'

'Nay, Robbie, nay... they gan too fast and folks are killing 'emselves on 'em.'

The horse was still looking over the stable door as Edwin walked across the yard towards her and he pulled a lump of sugar from his pocket and put it behind his ear. 'Watch this ... watch it.' He leant towards the horse and she nuzzled her soft mouth behind his ear and pulled out the sugar, crunching it. 'By jings, she's a fine animal.' And he pulled back the bolt and walked in and taking the horse by the halter, led her out.

Arabesque was steel grey; dark mane and tail; dark grey body. She pranced a little as Edwin held her. 'Yer thowt Tilly were a good 'oss, well this un's better.'

'Yes, Edwin, and remember, I still own Tilly,' yet he still eyed the horse.

'Yer canna tek 'er owt a Yorkshire, away from Christie. She's been with 'im nigh on eight years now, she'll pine fer 'im.'

'So you'll have me buy a new horse to stop the old one a fretting? Since when have you been kind to a horse, Edwin?' Robbie walked around Arabesque and rubbed his hand slowly along her spine and down her back legs, then the front, lifting the hooves, looked in the eyes, her mouth, looking hard at her teeth to check her age. Edwin stood back and let him; he was hopeful. 'She's sound as a bell ... and steady as yonder mountain.'

'She'll have to be sound, but I don't want steady. I like something with a bit of spirit, you know that. I like my horses like my women.'

'Mickey... gan and get the saddle ... tack her up fer Robbie.'

'Whoa ... whoa ... it's no good. I'll not take her. The last horse I bought from you got us both into bother.'

'Nay, she's mine alreet ... through and through.'

'Then how did you get her?'

'She were insurance money, Rob ... insurance? When I getten banged up, I let me brother 'ave most of me livestock and 'e kept me capital and bought me this 'oss when I came out. So nay body could tek owt from me.'

Robbie, reminded of Edwin's tenacity, grinned. 'How much is she then?'

'Nay... I'll not talk money in front of the 'oss.... It 'umiliates 'em. Come back in t'ouse and we'll settle it ovver a glass.'

Robbie knew what that meant, as sly as Edwin was he would get him drunk and then charge the earth. 'I've touched no liquor in eight years; it would go to my head.... I had to keep myself chaste. We'll talk now, or there's no deal.'

Robbie left Raike's Farm in the saddle of a new horse. He didn't look back at Edwin as he guessed he was gloating over the price that he had promised if the horse was sound. But what Robbie didn't know was that he would never pay for that horse; it was a gift.

Edwin wept as he left; glad of his deception; his charitable gift was small compensation for what Robbie had done in keeping the rent paid on the farm for him and his family.

Arabesque was spooked as she walked an unfamiliar passage, but soothed by Robbie's kindly voice. She didn't look at the direction she was headed; her ears flat back and twitching watching the horizon, sniffing the air, she walked slowly and awkwardly.

'Come on, Harry, come on lass....' Robbie clicked and gently stuck his heels into her side. Then she walked on and responded and as they reached the chapel she rebelled again and would go no further. 'Come on, Harry, come on,' he said, but she wheeled around. Frustrated, he slid off her back and held the reins close to the bit. 'I know, I know, it's hard.... You'll be better off with me.' He slid his hand down her neck and pulled the reins over her head and raised the stirrups. 'I'll walk with you this time,' and he clicked again and she walked beside him.

Man and horse walked slowly to the small chapel; Robbie recalled his first meeting with Christie's father on this lane. If he didn't have the horse he may have gone inside and prayed for forgiveness, yet he had done that over and over in the four years in Coldrigg. He recalled Franklyn's gesture of reconciliation and felt humbled.

They struggled up the track with Gable beside them on the left. Arabesque was still flighty, spooked at some falling stones, then some sheep passed and scattered playfully down the fellside and he had to constantly encourage her.

'You're all I have, lady,' he whispered. 'You'll do me fine.'

The horse responded to his voice and quickened the pace, her head bobbing as she walked; her long steely grey mane blowing wildly in the winter's breeze.

Robbie gasped as he walked; the years of hard labour and confinement, then those of scorching heat had sapped his energy. He knew he had aged, yet at thirty four, he was still slim and attractive, but the fear and the cold had lined his face as much as the heat and the loneliness.

The jaws of Piers Ghyll before them terrified Arabesque, as Robbie continued to walk beside her, just as he had done with Tilly years earlier; continually talking sweet words of comfort to the horse. The drizzle soon met them and he pulled the collar up on his coat. He shivered as drifts of rain fell across them, the path ahead only just clear.

They stopped under a crag and Robbie rested back against the rock to shelter from the prevailing wind and rain; the young horse struggling and twisting in the cold.

Then the thought of returning to Keld Head, the farm he had lost, set him into a black and morose mood. Water fell down his hat onto his face and merged with tears; Edwin was right; he was adrift with no anchor.

He considered crouching behind a stone to let himself be taken by the cruel cold that had always been hunting him. He did so, feeling the back of his legs wetting as he sat back against a rock. But Arabesque became more distressed, so he let go of her reins. She turned and looked down at the path they had just walked, clouded in fog, then she reared up and spun back to Robbie, standing closer beside him; it was her turn to console him now and protect him. He wept as he had never wept before; tears ripped out of him; recalling his meeting with Fred up here with the news that his father had died.

He longed to see Fred and hold him and tell him all was well; but to see Beth would open wounds that were healing; this was the end. It had to finish here and now in this mountain pass; no more anxiety for any one; the thought of letting his life be taken was over powering and he couldn't resist it; he would relent and become death's willing subject. He couldn't escape its grip; the feeling was master over him; the sentence would be long; peaceful; eternal.

It was Edwin's news about Brad Shafer's murder that had first weakened him and then Nance's news of Beth losing a child. Christie had telegraphed several times a year and told him some things; Keld Head was let out to a man from London; the land being partially farmed by Jackie Bainbridge.

Robbie recalled his father, and how he knew he loved him, but had done nothing in eight years to recoup any honour. He had lost his good name and his home.

Arabesque stood for an hour shielding his sodden body. Robbie slept and woke, dreaming of Brazil and the women folk nagging him; the bustle of the city; hating the crowds, longing to be in Cumberland. His chin began to quiver with each waking moment, as his whole body shivered so much as the wet and the cold poisoned him. His teeth chattered together and as he opened his eyes and saw the horse, breathing heavily and still protecting him, Robbie raised himself up; still sobbing; kindness – kindness – kindness, were his father's words.

Then great pity for the innocent animal came over him. With shaking hands he lowered the stirrups and pulled himself up into the saddle, raising his legs clumsily and wearily, flopping down and resting heavy on Arabesque's neck; he couldn't leave her here to die with him, so, trembling still, he gripped the reins and turned her head into the oncoming rain and headed for Seathwaite, he dug his heels in and she responded. Robbie sat deep in the saddle clinging to her; she had saved him from an irrational and impulsive course; one he had never considered until that moment and one he would live to recall with remorse.

He slept in a warm bed in a cottage in Grange for two days. Nothing had changed there. Fully restored and master again of his own destiny, he washed and walked into the breakfast room winking at the waitress.

Robbie was surprised and embarrassed at his mood in Sty Head. Never in his life had he wanted death. Then he recalled the fear of his capture and the hangman and he considered death then to be a friend; one to remove him from torment. Yet today brought new life and hope; he would cherish it.

Arabesque was saddled and she nodded and ambled to him; the bond was now irremovable. He headed for the bridge and stopped as he saw the clearing into the woodland to the Cummacatta Wood where he had hidden from Sally and Jimmy Mook. The snowdrops he had lain in were still waiting, resplendent as the bright winter's day. They had been a comfort then and now. He had thought once over he would die there but now he was still alive; his heartbeat strong, but his spirit weakened; his horse changed. He would go to Keld Head today.

Arabesque struggled on the rocky plateau above High White Stones, as Robbie let the wind slap his face; he must waken from this stupor. He had been dormant for eight years and accomplished nought. Arabesque was young and her inexperience showed. He had shown mercy towards her as he had Tilly. He slipped off her back as they followed the narrow path down Easdale, over the pass, jarring his knees as they descended slowly into the valley.

With each step the wind eased, he didn't re-mount until they found the flatter land and the last walk to Grasmere.

The day was cool and hazy light teased them. January mist had cleared and made the visibility better. But in the distance he saw the tower at Keld Head, still there and more alive than he was and waiting for him.

Despite knowing he should be safe, Robbie felt a sense of unease.

Christie had said in a letter of McCulloch's deception. But the time in Brazil and the lack of strength and desire to seek a new life in England had passed slowly; his capital still good, but diminishing, his hair slowly greying. Christie had offered to let Robbie re-purchase Keld Head, but the offer was declined and the letter torn up but not forgotten; never would that be the case; Keld Head was slotted in a part of Robbie's heart, in a secret compartment along with the love of his brother's wife; never wanting to be re-opened. That was until today.

A young bearded man was on the lawn at the back of the farmhouse painting. Robbie had seen him from a distance, but with the haze and poor eyesight was unable to discern his features. He was sitting on a stool beside an easel and the unusual setting conjured up all kinds of images in his mind, none of them pleasant. But with Arabesque's vitality and Robbie's surrender, they approached.

The man looked up when he heard the horse's hooves on the shaley lane.

'Good day,' he said.

Robbie didn't speak at first but focused on the young man's face as he rested forward on the pommel of the saddle. The relief that the man was a stranger, made Robbie speak up. 'It's windy on the top of the fell.'

'Have you come a long way?' The young man stood and came over to Robbie, still holding the paintbrush, captivated by the handsome man on the handsome horse.

'Brazil,' was the reply, and he smiled.

This was pure fantasy in the creative eyes of the young artist. 'On the horse?'

'Well, with the help of the angels.'

'Then can I offer you refreshments, you must be famished.'

Robbie slid off Arabesque and lifted the reins over her head. 'Thank you, yes that would be welcome. Might I tether my horse in yonder yard; I believe there is a water trough.'

'Yes, please do. The buildings are out of my jurisdiction.'

'Yes, I know they belong to my friend, a relative.'

'Are you familiar with these parts?'

Robbie smiled the crooked smile and removed his hat and said no more than, 'Robert Keldas,' and held out his hand.

The kitchen was just the same, yet it held a different aroma than what he remembered for there was the clinical smell of paint and turpentine.

'How long have you been here?' Robbie wandered around his own kitchen remembering his own furniture.

'Four years in spring... It was April when I arrived.'

'Is the house to your liking?'

'There are no ghosts, unless you've come today to prove me wrong?'

Robbie shrugged his shoulders because that might just be the truth.

The boiling kettle was lifted off the stove. 'This is a cold house, but I came for the drama and the atmosphere. I won't stay another winter.'

'Have you painted much?' he picked up a sketch pad on the table and sat down.

'The fells, the hills, the tower.'

'Do you live here alone?'

'Mostly, I have no wife but my cousin comes most weeks.'

'I have some friends close by in yonder cottages I would like to see?'

'Oh yes, they are about, they look after the place.... Nora and Albert Given and Jackie Bainbridge.'

Robbie just nodded.

'Would you like a room to stay over?'

'That's most kind, but this house and I had an altercation and neither of us are ready for me to sleep peacefully under its roof. I'll press on and see my brother. I need to see Bainbridge first about my horse.'

27
SWEET SUGAR HILLS

Beth looked at the snowdrops on the windowsill. She nervously teased them into place in the little glass vase. She went to the stove to check the oven; the beef was cooking. It would soon be time; time was always her friend or her enemy.

Fred was whistling as he came across the yard, he kicked off his boots as he entered the farmhouse kitchen.

'Hurry, Freddie, get washed, he'll be here soon.'

'He won't come early, Betty. I know him better than you.' Fred straightened his honey coloured hair from under his corduroy cap then came across and held her. 'Are you still alright with this?'

Beth let her head drop onto his shoulders. 'I love you more than ever, Freddie, you know that. But to be truthful, I'm nervous. I don't know how I will feel.'

'It has to be done, he couldn't stay away forever, he is my brother.'

'I know, I know. Look, hurry and get washed, we'll get through this together.'

Fred ran upstairs and left her to rearrange the cutlery on the kitchen table for the fifth time. Sunday dinner was a usual habit; visitors and friends often invited, but Beth had never worried about the cooking like she did today.

She checked herself in the mirror and straightened her shining raven black hair, neatly cut into a stylish bob. She hoped Robbie would like it; he hadn't seen it cut shorter. Beth knew she was pale and that the colour on her cheeks was false.

Fred was now upstairs banging the wardrobe doors and shutting drawers looking for clean clothes; she knew he was equally nervous. When Beth heard the dogs bark she quickly glanced at the clock; it was too early. Then she heard horses' hooves clattering on the cobbles; men were laughing. She dared to look out and saw a scruffy man riding a small fell pony, then Robbie on a dark grey horse; a bitter sweet feeling as her inquisitiveness got the better of her. Peering through the window she kept her eyes away from Robbie, lest she gave away those feelings; she eyed the man on the fell pony and by the colour of the neck scarf she knew it was Edwin.

Anger was her first thought.

She hurried upstairs and Fred was still dressing. 'He's brought Edwin Wilding with him. I can't believe it!'

Fred looked at Beth's demeanour and, despite her anxious fear, he laughed. 'That's how it is with him. You'll have to get used to that. If you'd have wed our Robbie you would have had Edwin Wilding at your door each week. He would never let his foot be rare.'

'It's not something I find amusing. How am I supposed to feel; he's so insensitive.'

Fred approached her as she peered out of the bedroom window and he saw Robbie and Edwin on horseback talking to a man on the lane. He put his hand on her shoulder. 'He'll have done it on purpose, to break the ice.... Edwin will be here to help him. He's not insensitive; in fact it's his sentimentality that has done all this. All will be well.'

The horses were tethered and with a fake charade Robbie banged heavily on the farmhouse door at Spickle Howe.

'You go, Freddie, you see to him first.' Beth lingered in the bedroom, fidgeting with the buttons on her blouse.

Fred didn't rush but ambled to the door and opened it. 'You're early!'

'I can't get anything right, can I?' Robbie couldn't help but look over Fred's shoulder for Beth.

'Hello, Edwin. Good to see you safe and well, come in the both of you.'

Edwin pushed forward into the kitchen. 'That beef smells grand.' And he went to the stove and started to lift the pan lids.

'You look well, Freddie.' Robbie held his hand out for his brother. Fred took it and as they closed in together, they embraced.

'Dinner smells good.' Robbie grinned and Fred saw the smile he had longed to see, and seeing the missing tooth, he was reminded of why they paid every penny to see his brother safe. 'Where's Beth?' Robbie dared to ask, his heart thumping.

The stairway creaked and Beth stepped quietly and serenely down the stairs. She stood at the door, unsure of what to do, but Robbie had thought this out long and hard, this would have to be how things were from now on. He stepped forward and went to hold her shoulders and kissed her on the cheek. 'Are you well, Elizabeth?'

'We've missed you.' She spoke softly.

'You'll soon be sick to death of me.' And it was done.

Edwin was sleeping and snoring in the chair in front of the fire. He and Fred had talked non stop through dinner. Beth noticed Robbie was quiet and his appetite, poor. She cautiously watched him eat, just with fork in hand, pushing food around on his plate. She worried it wasn't to his liking, but that wasn't the case; his stomach was still adjusting to years of poor food in Coldrigg and San Paolo.

Beth stood to side the plates and knowing Robbie was watching, fumbled and almost dropped them. Sensing her discomfort he said. 'Can we go for a walk, Freddie?'

'Well, if Betty doesn't need any help?'

'No, you go, I will be fine. I want to see to the poultry any way.' Beth said.

Robbie stood and took his coat from the back door and left the house waiting for his brother.

'I'll just get the dogs.' Fred said.

They walked the lane to the forest with Robbie head down and hands in pockets, Fred humming by his side, astonished at his brother's pace. 'Thank you for coming,' Fred chatted in his carefree way, with Robbie not replying. 'She was anxious to see you.' More scuffing of boots on the gravel.

Robbie bent down to pick up a stick for the dogs to chase. 'She'll keep an eye on Edwin.... See he doesn't die in his sleep.'

And they watched the dogs chase the stick.

'Are you staying, Rob?'

'No, I'll not stay here. But thank you.... I think it best if I go to Sugar Hills tomorrow. Christie doesn't know that I'm back in

England, yet. I'll stay at the inn tonight.' Robbie raised his head, he loved the smell of the pine forest and the wood from the trees, protecting them from the winter's chill. They saw red squirrels, blackbirds, a group of goldcrests, and as the footpath inclined up a small ridge it appeared that the forest was alive.

Fred continued to chatter and Robbie had forgotten how much his brother could talk and he only replied when necessary.

'What about Keld Head. Are you going to buy it back?'

'I won't. Christie offered it to me but I can't give him the right price and I won't swindle him.... He offered me a loan but I don't want to burden myself, it's best he owns it or I'd lose it again any way.'

'What will you do then?'

'I don't know. I may stay in Yorkshire awhile. Then I might ask him if I can rent Keld Head.... It was a hard decision.'

'Will you feel safe there now?'

'I still feel uneasy, if the truth be known.'

'Dad would be pleased. That's what he would have wanted. You being there and all.'

'He should have given it to you in the first place.'

'No, it would have been a burden.'

'It already is a burden.... At least I can try and make something of it.... I've considered buying a small dairy herd. Go into milk production again, if Christie agrees. Start afresh.' Robbie stopped walking and faced his brother. 'At least Keld Head will stay in the family; he tells me if aught happens to him, you and Beth are to get it back. That's my punishment ... a tenant in a house that doesn't want me, for as long as I live. Just a keeper of the house, that's what I'll be.'

'And does that suit you?' Fred headed for a small gate, opened it, then walked through to a narrow path into a dark wooded area.

Robbie turned as he walked. 'You've given her a nick name, Freddie; a term of endearment?'

Fred was shocked at his sudden change in tack. 'Er, I suppose so ... everyone calls her Betty.' He slowed the pace. 'Wait, Robbie, stop,' and Fred grabbed Robbie's arm and they turned

327

into the gloom of the forest away from listening ears. 'What if she falls in love with you again?'

Robbie looked into his brother's eyes and saw the terror. He lingered in this and wanted to capture Fred's fear and remember it, as it would help him. 'You needn't fret, she won't do that.'

'But how do you know?' Fred turned and rested his back against a tree looking into nothingness.

'For pities sake! Don't you think I haven't thought of that? Her feelings and yours...? It doesn't matter about my feelings anymore.'

'We did a stupid wicked thing, Robbie.'

'How can you say that when all is now well? Does she not love you?' Robbie dare not move; he must resolve this.

'She says so.... She said it this morning. But she also said she didn't know how it would feel when she saw you again. Will you not marry? Are there no women in your life?'

'Is that a question or a plea? Blast it, Freddie, women were in short supply in Coldrigg - at least those by nature, and the women in Brazil were not to my liking.'

Embarrassed at his declaration Fred shrunk back.

'It hurts like hell doesn't it?' Robbie looked into Fred's eyes again. 'Trust in your own love for her, and forget me. I've had eight years to practise that. She won't fall in love with me again ... I'll see to that.'

Emily Richardson was mending a pair of Christie's work trousers when she heard a heavy knock at the front door. She put down the garment and pushed the needle into the soft lamb's wool fibres in the pincushion. She heard Annie Dowson speaking to someone but she couldn't discern who.

Annie's footsteps echoed across the black and white tiled hallway floor as she hurried to find Emily. 'There's a gentleman to see Christie.'

'Who is it, Annie?' Emily stood, not certain of what to do. 'Could you ask him in please?'

'The gentleman just said he was a relative.'

'A relative?' Emily wandered across to the window to look into the yard, then brushed her skirt smooth. 'What does he look like?'

'Tall ... very tall.... Tanned, possibly of foreign descent; a true gentleman, handsome with dark hair.'

Emily left in a hurry as a rush of blood surged through her veins when she guessed who the visitor was; a man she had been longing to meet. 'Annie, oh Annie.... Where's Christie? Please find him quickly... he'll be so happy.'

'Shall I invite the gentleman to the parlour first?' realising Robbie was still standing in the front hall.

Emily covered her cheeks to hide the blotchy rash that appeared on her skin when she was anxious. 'No, please bring him here to me. Do I look respectable?'

Robbie was ushered into a large sitting room and seeing Emily's pretty face, came forward and held out his hand. 'My name is Robert Keldas. I'm related to your husband.'

Emily approached enthusiastically and took his hand. 'Are you Robbie?' blushing as she spoke.

'Yes, yes I am,' and he smiled.

'Please sit down. Annie has gone to find Christie. I hope she won't be long. We're not too sure where he is.'

Annie Dowson threw a shawl over her shoulders and hurried to John Dowson in the dairy. 'Where is Christie, John?'

'Try the office.'

On hearing his name and Annie's quick footsteps, Christie emerged from the office and rolled up his shirt sleeves. 'What's the matter?'

'There's a gentleman to see you ... a relative, he says.'

'What is he like?'

'Tall, yes very tall.'

Christie didn't wait to reply, but left for the house, burst into the kitchen, looked into the empty hallway, then pushed open the parlour door as he heard voices.

Neither man spoke as they embraced. Emily stood back, her heart bursting with happiness for Christie. She followed Annie to the kitchen.

329

'Annie, please. Can we have some tea and refreshments? Oh Annie.... This is Robbie ... he's come back ... he's come back. Christie will be so happy.'

'You've grown taller. You're as tall as me. You're broader too.' Robbie looked Christie in the eye, admiring his physique as a father would a son. 'You have a pretty wife and an elegant house. Does she look after you well?' Emily had returned and Robbie addressed the question at her, and winked.

'Yes, she does.' Christie smiled at Emily. 'Have you come from Westmorland today?'

'Yes ... just today.'

'Have you seen Freddie and Beth?'

Robbie lowered his head. 'I did.'

Christie's wisdom told him not to pry.

A tea tray was set before them and Robbie was invited to sit down.

'How long have you been back in England?'

'I came back only last week. I travelled to Millom first to sort out some affairs with Frazer Piercy. Then I went to see the Wildings.'

'How are they?'

'Well, yes, well. Edwin's release was a relief on Nance and the boys. I bought another horse from him which, incidentally, I have left at Keld Head for Bainbridge to mind. I hope that was in order.'

'Of course.' Christie nodded. 'Will you take Tilly back?'

'Take Tilly where?' Robbie scowled. 'I've no plans for Tilly. You must keep her, Christie. The horse is yours - a gift from me, if you still want her.'

'I love the horse; thank you ... thank you. Would you like to see her?' Christie looked at Emily, quietly listening, smiling; sitting on the edge of the sofa raising her eyebrows as if to gesture something to her husband.

He coughed. 'Yes, we too have news, Emily and I.'

Robbie glanced across at the young woman.

'We are expecting our first child.'

'I'm pleased for you both, you appear happy.'

330

'We are happy,' Emily spoke up. 'And I think from today, Christie will be happier.'

'You think so.' Robbie gave a wry smile. 'You won't stay that way if I live under your roof for a month!'

'It depends which roof you sleep under, Robbie.' Emily joked.

'I like your humour, dear girl.'

They wandered the farm together. Every animal inspected and every pasture appeared to be in good order. The house, from the walk up the drive, commanded respect. It was three stories high and its turrets gave it the stature that Franklyn Richardson had intended. Robbie wandered the house, saw oil paintings on the landing; one of a woman who Robbie assumed was Christie's mother. There were portraits and photographs of Beth, ones he didn't linger to look at; even a wedding photo of Beth with Fred.

The house was grand and Robbie felt humbled by it; to think once over he had courted Beth who he now considered far above him. Realising how much she must have loved him and Keld Head to want to leave all this for marriage, and now to be with Fred at the even more unassuming Spickle Howe. For Christie to have runaway from here from his father's grasp and live in the cold at Keld Head, surprised him.

He could see nothing but goodness in this farm and its buildings; even in its lovely mistress, Emily. He took pride in Christie as he had often done. The only thing lacking here was the scenery. The flat plain leading to Sugar Hills looked wet and unappealing with the Great North Road, near its doors; the flooded River Swale was speedily flowing. There were no hills on this land and Robbie guessed it was wishful thinking on someone's part to name it as such. In the near distance were the Hambleton Hills and the Whitestone Cliff, with the North Riding's great moorland beyond that.

Robbie leant back against the tree trunk, his eyes closed, his panama hat falling down purposely on his forehead; he could hear Tilly beside him pulling enthusiastically at the lush grassland. Christie approached on foot and muttered her name.

'Move away Tilly... mind Robbie's legs.' He pushed the horse and slid down beside Robbie on the grass. 'I thought I might find you here.'

'You're not going to give me any peace and quiet then?' he didn't look up.

'I would if it was good for you, but you've been alone too long.'

Robbie didn't reply; the young man was probably right.

'What do you think of my farm then? Did you not sleep, you're up early?'

'Yes, good, to the first question; perfect for you, Christie ... a wife and a child on the way; a lovely home.'

'Yes, all's well here.... What about you? What are your plans? I didn't like to ask in front of Emily last night.' Christie pushed Tilly's nose away as she was standing far too close.

'Are you tired of me already?'

'What do you think?'

Robbie smile was hidden under his hat because he knew Christie loved him.

'I'm not in good fettle, you must know it.'

'I can see you are disheartened. What's on your mind?'

'I had bad news on my return that I must tell you.... I'm sorry to spoil your utopia.' Robbie sat up a little and pushed his hat back. 'It's a shame that Freddie and Beth have no children.'

'Yes, it's a bitter blow for her.... She is happy for us though. She bears no envy.'

'Aye, that's what she tells you. But there's more. There's no easy way to say this but McCulloch has murdered Brad Shafer.... He said it was an accident.'

'The man's evil, Rob.'

'Edwin wants us to talk to the police and get him hanging on a noose.'

'And what do you want to do?'

'I want to forget the evil gowk.'

'Maybe let others do the job, Robbie. I think you're wise.'

'Well I don't know if Edwin can keep his mouth shut.... But I'm done with police and prisons.... I just want a life and some peace.'

Christie didn't reply.

'Did your father give many sermons on hope?' Robbie shuffled a bit to straighten his aching back.

'Hope?'

'The Brazilians have a saying. "*A esperanca e a ultima que morre,*" it means hope is the last thing that dies. They're a kind people, open hearted; religious through and through. I only had one true friend, a man called Miguel. He was the manager at the plantation. He was much like me, quiet, and had a beautiful wife and family but he used to be up and about early checking the estate on horseback. I used to ride with him, often. He will miss me and I him.'

'I'm pleased there was someone.'

'He was a devout Roman Catholic, as most of them. There are a few Jews and Muslims too, but they are all superstitious as a race; they dabble in stuff like astrology; it's important to them; black magic, even. It gave me the shivers sometimes. Miguel used to say things were in the lap of the gods but I know that things lie in our own hands. I used to tell him not to be burdened by mumbo jumbo. He laughed because I believed he knew I was right, but didn't want to jib against their tradition.'

The two men idled; it didn't matter what the time was; Christie was at ease with his friend, and he knew his warm interest was healing the tired soul.

'My father preached about everything, Robbie ... hope and love and other stuff.' Christie looked up at the clear blue February sky.

'Promise me you'll never tell a soul... I'm only telling you now because of your trust. When I came home and wandered over Sty Head, I thought of ending it all and if it wasn't for hope and that grey horse Edwin sold me I may have just done it.'

Christie shuddered. 'I'm glad you resisted.' The younger man didn't move a muscle and although he felt jittery inside, he wanted to keep Robbie calm.

'And then you get a day like this, the sunshine, friends, family and everything seems fine. Edwin, as filthy as he is, has his little family. Freddie and Beth have each other; you have Emily and a child on the way, but I have nothing but a blasted horse. Don't you think that's kind of cheerless?'

'Stop feeling sorry for yourself.'

'I'm not really; I'm just telling you the truth. I wanted you to know - only you. The world is in a mess, Christie. There's poverty and unrest everywhere you go. I've seen it. And that's partly why I came back, before I wasn't free to travel. Europe, Ireland, the Middle East is in turmoil. Men are striking all over England, women striving to be equal. They may ask us to fight if there's war, but I'm done with fighting. I did my time in South Africa and I won't do it again. What would your father say about that?'

Christie relaxed and stretched his legs out in front of him and put his arms behind his head. 'He hated it ... war ... conflict.... He refused to preach it in the pulpit; in that he was a dissenter as in many other things - he wasn't always popular for that.'

'So would you go and fight?' Robbie rubbed his forehead and replaced his hat.

'If I had the choice, no.'

'And what if you didn't have the choice?'

'I don't know about that.... What about you?'

'I'm too old now, anyway, but if I were your age, I wouldn't go again. I'll die for God but not politicians. I'm no coward, Christie, and it takes a brave man to stand up for their conscience.'

Christie was listening, agreeing with every word, because that was just as his father had spoken.

'And you are to be a Justice of the Peace, I believe.'

'I hope to be soon, yes.'

'Doesn't that put you in a predicament?'

'In what way?'

'You'd be in the limelight, boy. If you judge, others will judge you. You will have to be spotless and live spotlessly, or they will come down on you heavy. For me it suits to be a bit wayward because my status can only improve, but for you there could be a decline.'

'But I feel I can make a difference - see justice is done.' Christie saw Robbie grin, but inside he knew he was giving him a strong warning. He folded his arms. 'I've been thinking.... I have a small cottage in the village. It's empty at the moment. It's a woodman's cottage but I can't afford the luxury of such things. You can stay if you want to, or you could go back to Keld Head in spring when the artist moves out. He's already given notice.' There was silence. 'Or there's still the option to buy Keld Head. I will sell it for just the same price as I paid.'

'You're kind to think of my welfare, but ...'

'No, you saved my life once over.'

'And I think I've had more than enough compensation ... no, my answer remains the same. It will be safer in your hands.'

'Well, there's a home there if you want it. Maybe rent it from me or we could share farm it. But I must tell you what I have written in my will, that should I die it will go to Beth and Freddie.'

'Yes, Fred told me. Is that my punishment?'

'That's justice, I think.'

Christie stood up, his buttocks felt damp through the cold. 'Don't sit there too long.... You'll get a bad back.'

28

BLUEBELLS AND FOXGLOVES

Bluebells carpeted the woodland lining the road; swathes of deep blue; pleasing to the eye and soul. It was good to be back in Westmorland; good to be farming again and good to be on horseback, riding the high open ground. Robbie had loved his time in Thirsk but was itching to be away. He had Arabesque as his companion, but had mixed feelings about being back at Keld Head, alone. As they trod the road from Keswick via St John's in the Vale, the few motor cars on the road spooked the novice horse; Robbie cursed each car. He had spent two days under Helvellyn and Fairfield sleeping in a shepherd's bothy. He considered wandering the Dodds to Threlkeld but his back was aching and his knees were sore. He had left Keld Head with Bainbridge in charge, happy to see his incorrigible master back home. The new herd would soon be grazing the meadows, slowly being restored; there was a new shippon and dairy. Robbie was working hard, nonstop, and when he came crashing to a halt, it would only be the mountains that could restore him and give him peace, strength, and time to reflect.

He'd been given a young and scruffy lurcher from Edwin and, along with Arabesque, was a gift; Robbie had tried to push money into Edwin's hand but he refused. The lurcher was a mangy dog, it growled persistently, it was smelly and pitiful, but it had a deep bark when needed, it was young and obedient, and would be a good watchman.

The dog had been bathed as soon as he left Wasdale. He had thrown it in Sty Head Tarn, the river under Stockley Bridge, the River Derwent and Easdale Tarn and it still stank. Robbie called it Maggot.

His first night at Keld Head was spent sitting at the kitchen table, with Edwin sleeping in the chair, unafraid and unconcerned as usual. Robbie threw books at him to stop him snoring and resorted to tipping him out of the chair onto the floor. 'Mother of thunder, Edwin, how do you sleep when this is all your doing? You don't care a jot.' He'd said.

'Relax, Rob ... yer safe now.'

'I don't feel it.'

Edwin had fallen against the hearth and banged his head. 'Have mercy on me.... I'm an old man.... I might die any day.'

'You'll not die that easily, Edwin ... you'll always be around to moider me ... it's your role in life, sent by the devil, I believe.'

The second night was spent without Edwin, with just the dog and a rolling pin. Edwin had left in a mood telling Robbie he hadn't been right since Sally Mook gave him that bang on the head. 'You've getten yer sen deranged ... frightened of thi own shadow.'

'And whose fault is that?' Robbie would tell him.

The third night he made it to the bedroom with just the rolling pin, with Maggot in the kitchen and the doors heavily barred, and that would be how it would remain.

Arabesque danced her way through Keswick as Robbie headed to Bassenthwaite; Maggot loped after them. He passed through the bluebell wood and the soft colours eased his mind, the days in the mountains had worked their magic, so in better spirits and with hope, he approached a farm he knew with the intention of buying some more dairy shorthorns. Then he stayed the night at an inn and decided to ride to the back of Skiddaw for he knew the road would be quieter. The peace and safety was softening Robbie and by the time he reached Caldbeck, and Mungrisdale was passed, he was whistling and singing. Under Blencathra he stopped and viewed the lonely ride home through St John's; he had had enough isolation.

He knew he could travel easy and be home before nightfall, but in the balmy day he lingered in the sunshine as it slowly dropped behind Grizedale fells. The last time he had been to St John's he was worrying about Beth and the possibility that he had fallen in love with Sir Franklyn Richardson's daughter.

Arabesque wandered nervously; all new territory for her; but she learned to trust Robbie and his kindness had been noted. They weaved through a narrow track under High Pike, passing woodland and pine forest; small birds twittering high in the trees above. More bluebells lined the track as a comely friend with the foxgloves starting to grow, waiting for their turn to shine. Glancing across the valley he recalled the guest house where he once stayed; where he had seduced the young sixteen year old Clarissa Hutchinson. She would now be twenty four or five. The crooked smile broke out and he turned the horse off the walled lane, across some wet pasture land towards the village, across the bridge and over the beck. Arabesque jibbed a little, but like all the women in Robbie's life he managed to persuade her onwards. They trotted purposely in the lane and when he approached the guest house he slid off the horse's back and walked up to the door. A woman opened.

'Do you have a room, Missus, and a stable or pasture for my horse,' he asked with a sparkle of expectation in his eyes, removing his wide brimmed hat.

'Have you stayed before?' the woman smiled, looking hard into his eyes.

'Yes, indeed.... Maybe, eight or nine years ago.'

'Different horse?' she asked.

'Yes,' Robbie held out his hand. 'Robert Keldas.'

'I remember you clearly, you befriended my daughter.'

'Ah,' he stepped back, purposely reticent; would this be a rejection? 'Are you Mrs Hutchinson?' and he awaited her reply as a small, defensive and apologetic smile emerged.

'And you are Robbie...? Come in, please. Tether your horse at the back of the house. I can fulfil your wishes.'

The house was immaculate; just as he remembered, and the proprietor, Ruth Hutchinson, as accommodating. Robbie followed her to a small lounge with a view across the valley, looking out to the rocky table on Bleaberry Fell.

'You can let your horse graze in yonder paddock. Your dog can't sleep in your room I'm afraid; it will have to sleep in the wash house.'

'Suffice to say, that will suit ... but I cannot speak for the dog; I think it shall pine for me.'

She liked his humour. 'Shall I get you some tea? I have no beer.'

'Tea will be fine.... Beer is an instrument of ridicule and I don't wish to humiliate myself any more than I already have done.'

'Are you hungry, Mr Keldas?'

'Do you know, I am?' And that surprised him because for the first time since leaving Brazil he had an appetite. 'How is your daughter?' Robbie did recall her name but didn't wish to use it in case he was seen to be romantically interested.

'She's well.... You'll see. She will be back soon.'

Ruth Hutchinson took him to a large guest room at the front of the house, overlooking the paddock. It was just right for keeping an eye on the horse. The dog would have to look after itself.

Robbie led Arabesque to the paddock and unfastening the girth, unsaddled her, and rubbed her back with his hand. He lifted a small pouch of corn to feed her and removed the bridle, but she wouldn't budge. Robbie pushed her neck and she reluctantly wandered to the paddock, knelt on the floor and rolled on her back rubbing her spine, stretching and arching her back.

A noise behind made Robbie nervously wheel around as he eyed a young woman, almost unrecognisable; shorter hair than he recalled; slim, clean; prettier as she had turned into a woman. She was wearing a rough grey dress as if she had been working; her skin pallid, her lips thin and pale, her hair, dark, her eyes, blue.

'Hello, Robbie.'

'Clarissa?' he stepped forward to take her hand. 'You have altered.'

'Yes ... but you are the same.' But on closer inspection of his features she saw the missing tooth and a few strands of greying hair; tired eyes and tanned skin. She knew why he had aged.

'Mother tells me you are staying over. Are you travelling home?' she came and stroked the dog's head and leant back on the gate watching Arabesque grazing.

'Yes, I am. I've travelled a few days and I needed some sustenance and hospitality. I've been on business.'

'How far have you come?'

'Not far.... But I'm tired and the last few miles could finish me and the horse.'

'You look as if you have been abroad.'

'Brazil.'

'And where is home, Robbie?'

The question lingered in his mind: Where was his home? What he had told her before, he couldn't recall. That was often a thing he purposely lied about, yet he said, 'Keld Head.... Do you know it?'

'The hamlet with the tower?'

'Yes, I farm there.'

'I didn't realise you lived so close to here.' She smiled for she knew well where he lived and who he was, and she wanted to test his integrity all the more. 'And what have you been doing with yourself these past few years? Have you been in Brazil long?'

'No, not too long ... four years was enough.'

'Did you not like it?'

'The village I lived in was good in only one sense, and that it was easy to leave.'

'Ah.'

'Anyway, what of you?' And Robbie looked down at her elegant fingers on her folded arm and noticed she wore a wedding ring.

Clarissa saw his eyes rove about her so she held her hand out flat. 'Married ... and widowed.'

'Oh, forgive me. I'm sorry.'

'Kenny died last year, he had a chest complaint and I've barely left St John's since. I haven't the heart. I get anxious when I'm away from home ... overly much.' She watched as Arabesque came to the gate and Robbie rubbed the horse's nose, not looking at Clarissa.

'And you ... are you married?'

'Nay... I doubt I ever will be, though some would wish it.'

'Why's that?' She turned, brazenly looking at him.

'It appears I'm a temptation that needs to be put out of reach.'

'Ah yes, it appears you are a rogue, Robbie Keldas.'

'You speak correctly, a rogue, I am.... But I must add, in my defence, you will never meet a kinder and genial rogue in your life.' Then came the crooked smile; he liked her humour.

'I know what I've read in the news sheets, about you perverting the course of justice.'

'Ah, my reputation supersedes me. I'm afraid me and him will always follow one another around, but I must confess I am the greater of the two of us; he is far uglier than I. It's as well you know.

'I did four years choky for that crime, and if it worries you, I will catch my horse and leave you and your good mother here and now in peace.'

She twisted her body a little. 'When I was sixteen, Robbie, and you kissed me, I wanted to believe you would come back for me when I was older. You know how young girls are? You were my first true love. When I heard the news of your demise, I wanted to deny it, but to hear you were in Coldrigg sobered me from my foolish yearning.'

'Yearning ... but not foolish,' he winked at her. 'So how do you feel now?'

'I don't know ... but I do know my heart is pleased to see you and my eyes can't leave you.' Her smile was one she hadn't shown for years.

Robbie woke up at four as the dawn chorus began, as birds chattered on the roof and gutters of the house. He slipped from the bed, bleary eyed, and went to the window, pulling back the curtains. He leant on the window sill and peered out.

Arabesque was grazing near the gate; she had been long awake. Then listening for awhile and realising he'd let his guard down, he remembered Maggot. He sat on the edge of the bed and rubbed his knees. All was quiet. He found the chamber pot, and listened to the birds as he made himself more comfortable then fell back on the bed. The next noise he heard was much later and it was a woman talking outside.

He leant on the window ledge and saw Ruth Hutchinson giving Maggot some water. He smiled, rubbed his stubbled chin, and picked up his watch; it was seven thirty.

There was no sign of Clarissa at breakfast time; he watched each door open and close, listening for voices as Ruth fed him and two or three other guests.

Robbie chatted across the small dining room to them as he chewed on the toast and marmalade and drank coffee. 'Well good day to you. I must see to my animals.' And he left for the yard, with his coat and hat.

Arabesque saw him come to the gate and she trotted towards him; he rubbed her forehead and neck. 'Have you had a good night, Harry?' he spoke softly; then he heard Maggot squealing from the washhouse in response to his voice. He went to let him out and picked up his saddle and bridle.

'You weren't going to leave without saying goodbye, were you?' Clarissa appeared at the gate on a bicycle.

Robbie waited as she approached; rubbing Maggot's head as it leapt up trying to lick his face. 'Get down you brute.' And he pushed the dog away and stepped forward towards Clarissa. 'If I didn't see you, I would have been disappointed,' he spoke truthfully. 'I thought you didn't leave the valley?'

'Correct. I've been delivering milk and newspapers in the village. Did you have a good night?'

'I did, thank you.... Did you feel safe in your bed having a villain in the house?'

'We're probably safer having a man like you as a friend, rather than an enemy. Are you going back to Keld Head today?' she leant the bicycle against the wall and modestly straightened her skirt.

'Yes, but I'm in no hurry. Dare you walk some way with me? There's something I want to show you.'

'Robbie, I haven't left the security of this valley since I lost Kenny.'

'There's no secure place anywhere in this world, I'll tell you that Clarissa, but you would be safe in my arms.'

Clarissa looked at the back door of the house and pondered. 'Why not. My mother will be talking to the visitors; she won't need my help.... Can you untie me from these chains I'm in, Robbie?'

'I'm well aware you have fears, Clarissa. The whole world has fears, me included ... but if we walk these paths together we can rid ourselves of the torment.'

He led Arabesque as she ambled close to his side; Maggot always at the rear, but not wanting to be left.

Clarissa clung to his arm and as she sweat beads of fear, Robbie steered her gently as he did his animals: kindness - kindness - kindness.

He spoke compassionately, purposefully; she was helping him to be of use; needed and wanted; could his life be richer with her? Thinking of her needs and not his own.

'How long is it since you last went on the Keswick Road?'

'Nigh on three years.'

'Good.'

The talking was smooth; their spirits high. They had no delusions or aspirations just hope. 'I never asked you if you had any children?' Robbie spoke softly to calm her.

'No ... I don't. I would have liked some but Kenny didn't live long enough.'

'And you?' she laughed.

'Not any that I know of, but I would have liked some.' They approached the stream and walked close to a group of trees, oak saplings, ash, and silver birch. 'Close your eyes, Clarissa.' And she obeyed. 'Let me cover them with my hand.' He tied the reins up and let go of Arabesque.

Clarissa felt his hands; soft, healing hands. She was aware his eyes were resting on her. Then the intimacy of the feel of his fingers on her eyes was gentle and soothing, yet it felt right; she was no longer afraid.

'Not far ... trust me.'

They stopped, 'Open them now.'

A carpet of bluebells, lush and green, appeared before them.

'They're beautiful... I once came here as a child ... I had forgotten this woodland existed.'

The kiss was spontaneous. The day was deliciously mild. Robbie held her hand and led her to a grassy island close to a

343

tree. She didn't resist him and gladly followed and as they relaxed together on the grass, the animals rested.

'I feel like I'm in blue heaven.'

'If you close your eyes and open them again and again, it's the same every time, beautiful blue.' He kissed her again. 'Your lips are healing me.' Robbie admitted.

'And yours too,' she leant back on her elbows.

'I haven't much money, Clarissa. I'm a poor tenant farmer. Last night for the first time in eight long years I thought of you instead of another. Could I call back and see you soon.'

'Robbie, Robbie, I'm a widow... I'm alone, apart from my mother. I must have hope of friendship, I'm still young.'

'And I'm thirty-four.... Some would say too old to be of use, but I'm a healthy man, Clarissa ... I've had to be... so may I call again?'

They parted at the gate by the main highway. He kissed her again, mounted Arabesque and shouted Maggot. He said no more but looked back and grinned; she watched him well into the distance, as he held his arm aloft at the few motorists startling his horse; Maggot skulking behind with a death wish to be run over. Robbie found himself whistling; Arabesque's ears flicking back and forth, her tail swishing, shaking her mane from side to side; she was restless and wanted to be safely back at Keld Head, but she sensed her master was happy. He could look over the pleasing water at Thirlmere and think of Clarissa. If he was to please his brother and keep his body out of harm's way, he had begun this task, and a happier one than he anticipated. He would tell Clarissa about his character; warn her of his moods, his lonely wandering and his friendships in Wasdale; his fears; his life. She would have to deal with that.

He liked Clarissa, and the physical attraction was there. She was a beauty; she was gentle.

Robbie wouldn't rush this; hope was within him and he would relish it and let it grow properly, not just for his sake, but for Clarissa's.

The journey back passed quickly, his pocket and heart lighter. The few dairy shorthorns he had bought in Bassenthwaite would soon arrive, each in calf ready for the autumn, ready for the new dairy.

He understood both he and Clarissa would often have their real loves haunt them; she would still pine for her dead husband and Robbie, from time to time, would ache to have dear Bethy in his arms, they both knew that whatever attachment they made would be in compensation, but each had enough desire for the other to show passion and friendship.

Keld Head lay on the horizon, dormant for years, but about to spring to life like the bluebells under his feet; a harbinger of life to come.

Every Friday Fred went to Keld Head; sometimes Beth came with him sometimes she just couldn't. The day was wet; the air warm; spring had led to a wet summer. The bluebells were gone and they made way for the foxgloves; they straddled the lanes with their tall stems with buds and seeds climbing like ladders in the grass. Beth wanted to see the foxgloves and she also wanted to look at the work Robbie had done on the shippon and farm buildings. She hadn't left Spickle Howe in weeks and was beginning to feel edgy.

'It's a gloomy day... I wished you'd have stayed at home. He'll be in poor spirits.' Fred said.

Beth knew well what spirit Robbie would be in; she had seen it often since his return. 'I've made him a lamb stew.' She was nursing a basket on her lap as Topper trotted gently the rise of the lane to Grasmere. 'He's eating much better now.'

The carriage approached the yard; there was the glow of candles and lamps burning in the house because of the gloom of the day. Maggot sprang from the barn and greeted them. Beth pushed the dog away as it got a hint of the home baking in her basket; then Robbie came from the house laughing.

'Get down, dog!'

His sharp outburst didn't help Beth as she held the basket higher, taking a step backwards.

'Down Maggot, get down.'

'I'm sorry, Beth.' Robbie laughed, and reached for the basket and kicked the dog away.

Beth looked at Fred releasing the tack on the horse's harness; he didn't speak but raised his eyebrows as Robbie walked back to the house, taking the meal out of Maggot's way.

'He's in better fettle than I thought.' Fred spoke softly to his wife.

Beth waited; she wouldn't go in the house alone. 'Why is he dressed up!' she too whispered.

'Is he... I didn't notice.'

'Of course he is, Freddie.... He has his suit on. Why is he happy? It's worrying, unnerving.'

'Stop it, Betty.' Fred rested his hand on her shoulder. 'Come on, don't spoil his day.'

Fred walked to the house and tapped on the open door. Robbie appeared, beaming. 'Come in, Freddie ... come in, Beth. There's someone I want you to meet.'

A young woman stood by the window; she appeared edgy and was watching Robbie expectantly.

'This is Clarissa Hutchinson,' he gestured. 'Clara ... this is my little brother Freddie and his wife Betty.' Clarissa stood forward but Fred was quicker. 'So pleased to make your acquaintance ... very pleased, indeed.'

Clarissa eyed Beth, waiting for a greeting but it was slow in coming.

'Dash it, Betty, come and say hello....' Robbie muttered.

Beth looked at Clarissa from head to foot, and cleared her throat. 'I'm very sorry, Clarissa. I am pleased to meet you. Have you come far?'

Clarissa noticed the tremor in Beth's voice. 'St John's, just this morning. Robert came for me.'

'In the rain!' Fred questioned.

'We came by motor.'

Robbie excitedly wandered around the parlour. 'Come through please. All of you sit down. We have news.'

'What news, Betty...?' Fred dared to speak, sitting in the trap far enough away from Keld Head not to be heard. 'He's kept this quiet. All along us thinking he's been grafting over the dairy. Hope she knows what she's taking on ... fine girl ... a widow? Fancy that ... attractive girl wasn't she? Just like Robbie, eh.... What news Betty, what news? A wedding this back end.'

Yes, what news, she agreed, but her heart was reading a situation and deceiving her; Robbie's arrogance; his happiness, what carefree spirit he was showing. How could he? Beth bit her lip, and his indifference towards her destroyed her.

Fred didn't notice her silence, as he continued to chatter. 'She'll make him happy at last. Thank God ... yes, thank God, Betty. Father would like it ... maybe children at Keld Head. Dash it all.' He didn't see Beth turning around and around on her finger her gold wedding band. It was Robbie's last way of inflicting pain on her.

29

HORSE THIEVES

1914 -1918

The children came thick and fast; all girls. Three for Christie, but he did have a head start, and two for Robbie and Clarissa. Edith was their first. When she was born she didn't cry; she rarely did. She was a sour little girl and nothing like her father. Robbie struggled to sweeten her, he would pick her up and spin her around in the air, tickle her, whistle for her, but one thing that did make her smile was his smile. It gave her a feeling of happiness; she would put her hands to his mouth and pull his lips if he was gloomy; but Robbie's smile borne under duress often covered his real feelings. Edith loved him dearly. Robbie said she would grow broad and flat chested and he would be right.

Hetty was the opposite, a slight baby, dark hair, blue eyes like Robbie, with beautiful fine features like her mother. After Hetty's birth, barely nine months after Edith, Clarissa became weakened and the feelings of agoraphobia returned, it probably happened when her mother passed away. She rarely left Keld Head, there was no need. She would refuse to go to Fred and Beth's place or a take a trip to Keswick or Ambleside. Robbie wondered at the pair they made; one who couldn't stay at home and the other who couldn't leave.

Clarissa was glad of the isolation at times but she could see her husband was nervous of strangers; the yard gate clicking, or Maggot barking would always send him into an unreasonable fear.

Beth too loved Hetty and Edith, and as Clarissa weakened she helped all she could. But each time an announcement was made that either Emily or Clarissa were pregnant, Beth felt the pain yet showed happiness; what else could she do.

The two women talked as they worked with the children, walking only the lane and the garden with the girls in a pram and they became close. How could Clarissa not love Beth? The secrets they had, had become open as Robbie had told Clarissa about Beth, not wishing to hide anything. But there were times when Clarissa thought she could see his eyes watching Beth, and then look away; she couldn't scold him as she often thought of Kenny and compared him to Robbie. She often noticed Beth deliberately avoid asking after him if he was away and there was often edginess to her voice if he was troubled.

And one afternoon as the two women sat in the garden at Keld Head, worlds away from the war raging in Europe, they heard news and it was Robbie who brought it. 'Clara ... good day, Betty.... It's not good news this crazy war. The country's going bankrupt.' Robbie went to Hetty in the pram then looking for Edith, picked up the girl, 'Have you missed me you little shrew?'

'Don't call her that, Robbie. She'll remember.' Clarissa punished him.

'Nay... she'll love it, Clara.'

Beth was more sober. 'What's happened?' She looked at this little family and thought of Christie at the other side of England.

'War divides us all. They say the first casualty of this war is common sense ... things have been bubbling a long time ... Christie told me Tommy Bright, Irene's husband, has already signed up and gone.

'Lloyd George has given stern warnings; but British society will struggle without railway men, transport workers, and strikes wrecking the economy, but he says this war will bind everyone together ... a united purpose gripping the nation.... It will for a while, maybe ... but the world will change ... mark my words. Things'll never be the same again. Kitchener is touting for soldiers, even old beggars like me might be drafted up eventually, but they will need someone to keep the land farmed.'

'What about Christie,' Beth worried.

'He once told me he would never go.... Man alive, he hates killing anything ... he could never kill a man. But that boy's got courage alright. It will take a greater strength to resist. We're supposed to encourage our men to go and fight. Dash it all. They'll get more money fighting than what I can pay 'em.'

A small cry murmured from the baby in the pram; Beth was first to react.

'No Betty, stay put ...' and Robbie went to the child and picked her gently out of the pram and rocked her. 'Have you missed me little Hetty? Have you?'

'Where have you been, Robbie?' Clara asked.

Beth cringed she dare ask, but he didn't reply.

'They're bringing in more changes; a new act, I heard today. The Defence of the Realm.... The army already has twenty five thousand horses, but they've diminished and they need more. They'll train a good horse in three to twelve weeks and send it to the western front and they'll put kids on their backs from the cities who know nought about a horse. They'll use 'em for pulling artillery and goodness knows what else.'

'What about Arabesque?'

'I don't know for sure. I don't want to lose her bloodied in some battle field, but mobilization will mean they can just take her. They'll take all Edwin's stock and leave him with little else.'

'What about Topper?'

'I don't know. He's a working animal, the only one Freddie has.'

Every time Christie saw Kitchener pointing his finger he looked away. His men had told him he would be an officer yet he had no interest in war, despite any status it would bring him. He knew his views were radical and, unlike his father, he would keep them safe. The only persons he knew who would back him up were Robbie and Beth. Only single men were being conscripted at the start; he didn't speak of it to anyone.

Some of his men had already gone and as Christie watched them marching and smiling in their uniforms as they left, bravely hoisting their weapons on their shoulders, then dying quickly within weeks of getting to France, now they weren't so keen to go. But Christie's main concern was for Tilly. He could legally stay and manage his farm without being conscripted but Tilly couldn't. Robbie had warned him this would soon come to pass, that horses would be mobilized and it soon happened.

He went to the stable and leant on the door. Tilly was resting, her back relaxed, her heel bent, and her head low. He had ridden her out that morning looking at the land, hoping he was sowing the right crops that his manager had suggested, hoping he was being a good farmer and husband. But the cash was slow coming in and the war was crippling them all. Emily had just given birth to the third girl. This was a surprise, not a disappointment, but not a good time. He had felt uneasy she was pregnant again during these unsettled times.

"Oh bonny brid... why did thee come just when thee did?" But Emily wanted the baby as much as Christie.

He had heard there had been many in the town crying coward at some boys for not going to war. But once conscription started and several men were incarcerated in Richmond for their beliefs, Christie's silence aroused suspicion amongst some in the town, especially those who knew of his father's views on neutrality.

Christie recalled Robbie warning him of becoming a Justice of the Peace. He had said others would judge him, and he feared that might soon happen.

John Dowson saw Christie at the stable door and slowly approached, throwing his cigarette butt away to one side. 'Thy'll not be able te stop 'em taking 'er, lad.'

Christie lowered his head and turned. 'No, I expect not.'

'She'll be gun fodder like all 'em young uns, dead in the mire in Flanders.'

At that thought Christie's heart shrunk back and he wanted to stop John's talking but respect for the older man prevented him.

'I knows yer feel as thi father did, lad, I dare say yer own opinions are stronger, if silent.'

'I won't speak of my opinions in this climate, John.'

'Nay, it wouldn't be wise ... but time will come when ye'll have te decide not just aboot Tilly but aboot thi sen.'

Courage seized Christie's spirit and enlivened it. 'I don't care what others say, John, but I may as well suffer for a principle than the lack of one.'

'Aye, it's all reet Robbie Keldas given thi wild ideas aboot pacifism. When he's a man who knows what it's like te be incarcerated. I know doubt he'll lose that bonny Arab mare of his.'

'My ideas are my own, John, borne from my father, not Robbie. Robbie fought in the Boer War and he knows injustice first hand.'

'I've heard some talk, Christie. I have te be honest with thi. Thirsk is a small town.... Your father was loved by some and despised by others, those who were liberal or pious, yet he was neither.'

'And what are your views, John?' and Christie's frank question made the older man blush. 'I'm too old fer war, Christie.'

'And if you weren't?'

'I daren't know.... I had respect fer thi father but I didn't allus like what he said.'

'No, sometimes truth is hard to take.'

'When you where nobbut a lad, I thowt they'd ne'er make owt of thi... and look at thi now... fine wife, fine childer, good farmer, good maister.'

Christie, embarrassed at the confession unbolted the stable door and went in to Tilly and he rubbed the soft velvety grey fur on her nose with the flat of his hand. 'This animal means a lot to me, John.'

'Aye, that's as mebee ... but they'll tek her. She'll become a war horse.' John spat on the floor and turned back to the dairy leaving Christie alone with the horse.

Christie contemplated as he gently stroked Tilly's nose, remembering sleeping in her stable the night he found Keld Head. How Robbie scrubbed the green paint off his body as he stood naked in a tub on the kitchen floor when he had first fled from Northumberland. He recalled time after time seeing Robbie return safely home on her back and happy as he always was that his tutor had returned. This horse had unwittingly put

Robbie in prison twice; could she do the same to him? Christie let his head fall on her neck, and took in a sharp breath. He wanted to pray for the animal but folks were praying up and down the land for their young men in war. If Tilly went to France or Belgium she would keep some young man safe at the risk of her own life as she had often done with Robbie. Christie wouldn't lie for her life but he would do his best to preserve it.

Robbie left Keld Head in the rain. He'd packed food for himself and some for Arabesque; Edwin was with him.

Edwin had been deprived of most of his useful horses and deprived of much of his livelihood at the requisition of three of his best animals. The rest; the poor; the old; the lame were abandoned. The military had come up from Lancashire and swept the west coast for good horses; they were to go to the border and back down into the lake country. Edwin had done all he could and he was known as a horse breeder and so his best horses were hard to conceal. He had spent the next two weeks at Keld Head crying.

Clarissa would have no more to do with him; and after initially consoling him he had become a nuisance and she begged Robbie to send him away, but Robbie had misguided compassion and let him stay another week; Edwin would be useful for what he had in mind. Then the news came that the military were approaching Keswick; it was time they left with Arabesque.

The familiar walk to Borrowdale was done slowly, at night; with Edwin and Robbie sharing the ride. Wasdale's isolation beckoned as they hoped the military wouldn't return there to that far away place. Arabesque knew nothing of her fate but she knew where she was headed and was slow and in poor spirits; the rain didn't help.

Robbie sent Edwin down into Stonethwaite to ask after the militia, but they had not returned. They had swept the Borrowdale Valley and found many good horses and now were headed for Keswick and would then journey south through to Grasmere.

Robbie slept the first night below Greenup in the old shepherd's hut, sheltered under some crags. In the early morning hours he heard footsteps and heavy breathing and knew it was Edwin returning.

'I'd stay another night, Rob. They've only gone just yesterday. At least that grey 'oss waren't stand out ovver much.'

Robbie leant on the old door frame and stooped under the lintel to get some fresh air. 'I'll lose her, Edwin, I know it!'

'Nay, daren't be down 'earted. We'll do us best, but I canna keep wandering up and down yonder fell side, it'll kill me. I'm an old man tha knows.'

'I know.... You remind me often.... You've been an old man since you were twelve.' Robbie pulled some bread from his bag and gave it to Edwin; tearing it in half and watching him eat.

'I'll tek it thanks, Rob, although I did have some porridge int village afore I come up.'

Robbie grabbed the crust of bread back, as Edwin stuffed it in his mouth. 'Sweet mother, Edwin. I'm starving, if that bread hadn't have been in your filthy hands I'd have eaten it,' and he gave the crust to the horse.

'It's not legal, son, te give dry bread te 'osses or poultry. Folks is starvin'.'

'Aye well, I'll take the risk. You won't tell a soul and my horse aint talking.'

'Yes, well yer can live off of nowt can't yer, son. I've seen it in Coldrigg and all.'

Robbie looked at the Borrowdale road below and apart from a few sheep blaring there was silence.

'I don't know how long I should stay up here.... I don't know if I can escape the law.... I don't want to go down a third time. But no man is going to take my horse. Besides, she's never been paid for, so in theory she's still yours.'

'Well I nivver registered 'em, but they still come. I resisted but I were given nay choice -nay choice at all. And I couldn't hide 'em all. I'll be penniless without them 'osses. I'll be int work 'ouse.'

Robbie went back inside the hut and leant against the wall. 'Come in before someone sees you. We'll stay here till dark and then move on.'

'I'm nay staying up 'ere in this nithering place.... I'll see thi in Seathwaite tonight.' And he left.

Robbie wanted to swear, and loudly, but just shook his head and removed his wide brimmed hat. He thought of Clarissa and the children; he thought of Christie over the banks of the river Swale and wondered if Tilly would be safe.

Emily was at the window with a baby, suckling; a soft cream blanket was swaddled about it. She saw Christie come across the yard, head down, walking slowly; thinking.

She heard him come in the house and bang the back kitchen door. She heard Annie Dowson speak then his footsteps slowly coming up the stairs.

'Emily... Emily...'

'I'm in the nursery.' She spoke softly.

The door pushed open, slowly, respectfully. 'May I come in?'

'Yes, but I'm feeding Suzy.' She spoke with soft tones as the baby suckled and cooed in her arms.

Christie walked across; the sunlight from the window put a halo like glow about his wife and child. He bent his head low to gently rub Suzy's downy head with his hand. He watched his wife's countenance, peaceful, serene, and knew what he was going to do would disturb her.

'What is the matter, Christie?' Emily was in front of him.

Astonished she could read his face as Beth could, he just said, 'Why?'

'Christie ... Christie... I know you well.'

He went across to the window, his eyes squinting in the sunlight and looked at all he had around him: his land; his livestock; his property; his wife and children; his spirit.

'I'm going away for a few days ... maybe weeks.'

She sat up from her languid position in the nursing chair and held the baby tighter, pushing its little head closer to her breast. 'Where are you going?'

'I will not tell you ... it's best you do not know.'

'Christie, this is uncharacteristic of you ... whatever's wrong?'

'Oh, it is like me ... you don't as yet know all my traits.... I'm sorry.' And he walked to the door.

'I do know you well.' She knew what Annie Dowson has said of him running away from his father; Christie's stubborn streak. How he had first met Robbie Keldas.

'When are you going?'

'I have to leave today. Will you manage?'

'Of course we will manage ... Annie will help.'

He walked back to his wife and kissed her full on the lips.

'Are you going to sign up?'

He didn't answer, but said, 'I love you, Emily.'

'Christie, please; what's wrong? Nothing should come between man and wife.'

'I know, I know.... But these are troubled times we're living in and I must act.' He didn't turn as he left; he couldn't look at the peace he was leaving behind. 'I'll try not to be away too long ... I promise.' And he softly closed the door.

Emily let her head fall close to the baby. 'Oh Suzy, Suzy ...what will we do you with your daddy?'

Christie left Sugar Hills on Tilly, laden with food and warm clothing. He'd instructed John Dowson to see to things and never gave a hint of why or where he was going.

He rode eastwards and headed along the narrow lanes and bridleways, avoiding Thirsk, avoiding the villages towards the Hambleton Hills. By nightfall he was at the Whitestone Cliff and he pulled Tilly into a woodland to rest. He thought of Robbie in Westmorland and wished he were with him. "*A coward dies many times,*" were the words that sprung to mind. He'd slept in a hedge bottom before but he still felt uneasy. He thought of his father and wondered what he would have done. Face up to things possibly; if it was just his own reputation, maybe he could; he could stand up to the persecution, the name calling; it was the women folk that were the worst, he'd seen them, he'd heard them, he wore no armband of allegiance. White feathers had been pushed into young men's top pockets, and some he knew had buckled under pressure and gone to France and now lay in a muddied grave. That's where the white feather got them. But the persecutors showed no remorse to those with a decision of conscience, and despite Christie's position being a reserved occupation, his integrity was at stake. He loved his family and he would protect them, but he believed it wasn't in his hands to kill a man, one who should be his brother, whether Christian, Muslim, black or white, east or west, and he feared God greater than man.

He loved Tilly and she was the first one who could be mobilized. If he could hide out and keep away from the militia he may succeed. She wasn't technically his horse as she too had never been paid for.

Night fell; cold and damp spread in as Christie lay in a burrow of dead leaves and covered himself in a thick blanket. He used Tilly's saddle as a pillow as she stood as a sentinel by his side. He would rest until midnight then try and find his way in the seclusion of the dark to the old drover's road and Black Hambleton. It was some time since he had been this far east. He'd been as a youth with his father and Tommy Bright on shooting trips. The grouse were good on the moors, the heather was lush and deep, but Christie never shot a thing; it was intended; and neither did he eat what his father shot; he hadn't the stomach.

They climbed into the woodland close to the lake and up high onto the bank top. Their eyes accustomed to the dark. Tilly was led slowly and carefully, twisting along the paths and finally reaching a wall. They walked for miles until day break and higher onto the moor, away from all human life. Christie found the old shooting hut his father often used and went inside and waited. The view eastward as the morning's sun rose above the North Sea now spread before them, the mass of land of Ryedale and the North Riding moorland beyond, Whitby and Scarborough. He could see the lofty spires of York Minster and then Downton Abbey on the horizon. He would move no further but watch from this cold vantage point the movement of militia and horses.

Edwin never did return to Robbie that evening; it would be as well. He could get on better and quieter alone. He took the path above Langstrath Valley; deeper into the chasms of the Scafells. The rain continued, thick drifts softening his face, his wide brimmed hat acting as a flimsy barrier, water dripping from the rim onto the shoulders of his riding coat. He knew what he was doing was reckless and dangerous, not just for him but for Arabesque; he walked on the narrow path not knowing if he was leading her to safety or danger. He knew these mountains intimately; he knew their moods and hoped he could keep in their favour. The incline steepened and, clouded by fog and persistent mist, he relentlessly moved on, guided by the path close to the beck and the occasional shepherd's cairn, resting occasionally to check his path. He was more familiar with the path to Sty Head but he knew it could be a busy place as it was a packhorse road; at least this route should be unused by the military. He wouldn't stop until he reached Sprinkling Tarn.

Robbie worried of his plight, yet often he was more comfortable in the mountains than at Keld Head. He thought of little Edith and her future happiness depending on him and yet he recklessly put his life and freedom at risk for a horse. His dear little Amazonian girl; how he hoped he would bring no further disgrace to his family name.

Water poured onto the path off the gullies as they climbed higher and higher, cursing the rain, cursing the war. He considered it ironic that the first time he walked this high fell with this horse it was she that protected him from death at his own hand. And now he was hoping and praying he could shield her.

The night was long, and Robbie's tired limbs ached with the wet and the nithering cold. Saturated, he persisted until he felt a gusty head wind slapping his face; Arabesque threw her ears back and resisted him.

'Damn it, Harry.... Walk on, walk on.' He clicked and pulled, she was as stubborn now as she was back then. Reluctantly he stopped and with cold trembling soaking wet hands he pulled from his saddle bag one of the loaves he had brought. He pulled a chunk from it and held it flat on his hand as she nuzzled the morsel. He bit into it and ate a piece then put the rest back in his bag, knowing it would have to last.

'We're nearly there. Feel the wind, Harry...? It's changed, this must be coming from Esk Hause. We must be near the top of the pass ... walk on, walk on. Dear God, help us now please?'

They trudged onwards into wild oblivion until the sole of his riding boots felt the land flatten beneath his feet and the wind dropped. And Sprinkling Tarn, like a treacle lake, was in front of him.

The wind came straight off the North Sea and sped at pace across the moorland, Christie could smell in the air the dampened heather and the soil of peaty earth. He ate some of his ration and sipped some water from a bottle in his bag. He thought of his wife and his girls; his new baby; this act was reckless.

Tilly was outside the shooting hut grazing, how safe this was Christie didn't know. He looked across to the coast, miles and miles of open moorland. When he was a child his father told him stories of the sea beyond the Whitestone Cliff. Christie recalled his first trip here and wondered why he couldn't see it from the top of the moor. Back then he'd thought his father had lied and he felt cheated. It wasn't till years later when they first went to Scarborough had he first set eyes on the dark grey blue waves on the east coast; he should have known his father never lied, but Christie didn't know if he could do the same. He had no plan or strategy as Robbie had; he wasn't used to deceit. He had no close friends he could call on to help to conceal Tilly.

Five days and five nights he spent in the shooting hut; his rations lower, his nerves stretched; talking to his horse, talking to himself, talking to God. His worry for Emily should he be caught concealing the horse; what would she be thinking if she knew what he was doing.

He left Tilly by the hut to walk alone but she followed him. 'No girl, stay put. Shoo - shoo. I'll be back in an hour or so.' But it was useless, so he removed the bridle from her head and then her saddle. He pulled a halter from his bag and tethered her to the door of the hut, so she could come in and out. He would come back at night fall and he set off at pace down the valley below, still walking eastwards. He couldn't stop looking back, he looked a weary traveller, a worried man; his face aged with fear. The track was good and steady and he finally dropped out of the wind. One last look at Tilly but she was in the hut sheltering; it was better this way.

The small village of Hawnby sheltered honey coloured stone houses with orange pantile rooves, tucked below the Hambleton Fell. People were leaving for work; a milkman, a postman. Christie walked up to the post office and a man looked suspiciously at him; these were dangerous times; ones of mistrust and judgemental attitudes. He knew he would look unsightly with his stubbled beard, his hair dishevelled beneath his hat, his face grubby.

The bell on the post office door rang loudly as he entered. A surly woman arrived. 'Good morning sir. 'ow can I 'elp?' she looked him up and down, his clothes a little unkempt but a coat of a fine weave and strong tailor made boots.

'Do you have any sustenance, Mam?'

'I canna give thi any bread, sir, but I 'ave eggs.'

'Will there be anywhere I can get a meal? I can pay.'

'Nay, sir ... there's nay but tied workers cottages and th'undertaker 'ere.'

'Would you be able to cook me the eggs, Mam, please?'

'Thi 'as an honest face.... Where are thi from?'

'Thirsk way.'

'Ay'll cook thi eggs and maybe a little oatmeal if that'll suit. And a hot drink.'

'You are most kind.'

Christie looked around the shelves in the small shop and they were empty.

'I can let yer 'ave beans an all, sir.... I've canned beans.'

'Yes, yes, please.' Christie took his wallet from his pocket and the woman noticed his wealth.

'Have yer nivver signed up, young man?'

'I'm a married man, with children. I have a small farm; the government needs the farmers to work hard.'

'Aye, aye, mebbe so. Are yer travelling far?'

'Yes, on foot. I need to help a friend in dire straits.'

'I have oat cakes and potato cakes if yer want te tek some.'
Yes, please.'
'Sit thi down and I'll get thi some hot food.'
'Have many of your young men gone to war, Mam?'
'All of em sir ... there's just the old uns left.'
'And horses.... Have all your horses gone?'
'Aye sir. That were a sad day, bye it were ... last of em went a few days gone. Military come and getten the last uns.'
'Which way did they go?'
'Gone south now, over Malton way.'
'Let's hope this war will soon be over, eh?'
'Aye sir, tis a waste o' young life.'
'Yes, it is.'

Christie sat in the small parlour on a hard chair eating a welcome yet meagre meal, it was slow in arriving but Christie didn't mind, he had all day. The woman continued to ply him with questions and Christie was cautious with his answers. As he ate his stomach churned, he felt sick with worry. 'Do you have a local newspaper?'

Robbie was holed up in Stake Pass for a week, the weather had been kind but his tired mind tricked him. Hunger overwhelmed him and he doubted he could hold out any longer. Surely it would be safe to go to Wasdale now. Arabesque was fractious at the start, but then her appetite for something more sustainable than mountain grass overwhelmed her and she too became passive and weakened.

Robbie slept most nights in a bothy and as the evening's sun broke down he lay outside on his stomach on a flat rock, watching for any life below; his beard grown, his body still clean from bathing in the tarn. He slept on the watch and all the time thinking of Beth, Clarissa and Edith. He couldn't let his little girl suffer the indignity of her daddy dying up on this fellside; he couldn't let Beth suffer the torment of his end being as this; he couldn't let Clarissa become a widow a second time for the sake of a horse. His mind drifted into corners it shouldn't, longing for Beth, dreaming he would take her away to Brazil, but his notions were wrong and maladjusted, thoughts of a troubled mind; how he wished he could remove the clothes of his skin: his personality; to slough off the old and reveal a beautiful new one.

He was awakened by a scratching noise and he thought it was the mice back in the roof at Keld Head. As he lay on his stomach, his cheek flat to the rock and only one ear listening, he raised his head a little, his body stiff, he opened his eyes and saw the blue sky above him. How long had he lain there, he didn't know. He must leave before he slipped away into oblivion. The scratching came nearer; again and again persistent, the sound made clearer now as Robbie closed his eyes.

Edwin walked softly, slowly, scanning the mountain pass. The dark grey horse was camouflaged, but he couldn't shout; he daren't, but he whistled; Robbie's whistle. He waited for a response but with poor hearing carried on. He spotted Arabesque first by the tarn grazing; she lifted her head when she saw him. She had just a halter on, no saddle or bridle. His eyes scanned the perimeter of the tarn and he wandered slowly around to the horse, scratching his feet step by step on the rocky path.

He saw a man on the rock, dead to the world and he quickened his pace, constantly checking he wasn't being followed.

'Robbie, dear boy,' Edwin croaked and whimpered and hastened to his side. He touched Robbie's face and it was cold. He tried to raise him and he slowly stirred. 'Waken up Rob, come down, it's safe ... it's safe. They've all gan te Cheshire.'

Robbie opened his sticky eyes, sealed by pus and sleep. He smiled and managed to sit upright. 'What day is it?'

'Ne'er mind the blasted day,' Edwin pulled from his pocket a small brown tea cake and broke it with his hand. 'I've only got this Rob, I've nowt fer t'oss.'

'Why did you leave me, Edwin? Why?'

'I had te, they were all over the spot. They doubled backed to do another sweep o' Borrowdale. Can yer stand? Where's the tack. They've gone now and warn't come back te Wasdel.'

Edwin grabbed Arabesque. He found her saddle in the hut and tacked her up.

'Give me a leg up, please.' And the older man lifted Robbie's bended knee and dead weight and he flopped down heavy into the saddle and led them to safety.

'We'll 'ave te get 'er indoors. She waint go out. We'll wait till after dark. The night's closing in by the time were down, she'll be safe. We'll walk the field across the river.'

Robbie clung to the horse, dreaming and waking, as they struggled down the steep slope, Edwin watching all the while for pack horses or other riders and walkers under Great Gable. There was relief when they reach Raike's Farm in the dark of night.

'Thank you, Edwin, thank you. God have mercy on us.' Robbie removed his sodden hat and breathed deeply to remove the numbness from his brain. From his pocket he pulled a knife. 'Get me thread; catgut and a needle. What do you stitch the horses up with?' he found an armful of hay and threw it on the floor for Arabesque. 'Fetch your strongest boy; I need him to hold the horse.'

'For pities sake, Rob, you're not thinking straight... you're all wrong int 'head.'

'No, I must do this. It's one last thing, she must be hamstrung ... It could save her if those horse thieves come back.'

Edwin grabbed Robbie's wrist and held his arm taut. 'You'll never touch that 'oss, boy.'

'I must.... Christie said the kings in bible times used to have the horses hamstrung so they would be no use in war.... So they would rely on God rather than horsepower.'

Edwin's healthy spirit fought against Robbie's weak one and the knife dropped in the straw.

'Then you rely on your God now, Robbie, for I tell yer, no man comes back te Raike's Farm a second time, unless he 'as te.'

Christie arrived back at Sugar Hills on foot with Tilly walking slowly beside him, her spine slumped, her head tired and low. A dog barked in the yard. 'Shush animal, shush.'

He tethered Tilly in the stable and with weak limbs fed her; it would soon be day break.

Christie closed the loose box door and went in beside the horse and fell in the straw. He sat back against the wall, his knees bent up under his chest, his head dropped onto his knees. He could hear the cattle in the dairy, lowing. It would soon be milking time, A light was on in the house and he wondered if Emily was up feeding the baby. He fell asleep.

The noise of men's voices roused him as sunlight shot through small cracks in the pantile roof. Stirring quickly he pulled a small razor blade from his pocket wrapped in paper. He stood slowly as Tilly was sleeping, lying in the straw, exhausted from hunger. Christie fell to his knees beside her and let his head fall on her neck and muttering incoherent words, he held onto her shoulder; how could he hurt her? He wanted to weep as he lay with the blade still in his hand, but slowly put it back in the paper.

30
A DECISION OF CONSCIENCE

This was the first time in twelve years that Tommy Bright had been to Sugar Hills since his wedding. He wished Irene and his family were with him instead of what he had to do today.

The hedges, the paths, looked just the same, maybe not as tidy.

'We should have done this farm last week, Sir.'

'Aye, we missed it on the edge of the Great North Road, so we could trawl this area and pick up the stragglers then get on to Wetherby and York.'

'There's no hosses at Sugar Hills, Sir.' Tommy turned to his superior in his riding seat. 'They're all dairy... they 'ave no work animals 'ere anymore.'

The officer ignored his suggestion.

'I thought we were going to Pickering, Sir?' Tommy persisted and this time received a reply.

'We have to go direct south from here ... orders is orders.'

'Still we could save time if we left Sugar Hills, the farm's nigh on a mile down the lane, close to the river.'

'Shut up, Bright.'

The small group of soldiers dressed in khaki rode the long lane to Sugar Hills; Tommy hated this job, yet relieved his posting wasn't, as yet, the battlefield. He'd wrenched hundreds of good horses from their homes and each time with regret; they had to, there was no choice, but he hoped to mobilize them into good hands and take most of them all the way to France.

The incoming infantry caused a stir at Sugar Hills. John Dowson shouted Christie.

'They're coming lad, and there's nought thi can do te stop 'em now.' Christie was sickened and disappointed he'd failed. His time on Black Hambleton was futile.

He took in a deep breath and marched tall across the cobbled yard. He saw Tommy dismount and a glimmer of hope fell like the sunlight that flashed on the clock tower on Sugar Hills' roof.

Both men nodded in recognition but no more. Christie went straight to the officer.

'Good day, Sir. Can I offer you and your men refreshments?'

'No, sir. May I ask if you have any horses that would be useful to King and country. You haven't registered any. '

'I have no horse of my own to register.'

'Could my men search your buildings? They tell me in the town you *do* have a horse. '

Young men at the speed of a flick from a horse's whip spilled into the yard and pushed open every closed door. They soon found Tilly and shouted the officer.

'We have a horse here, sir.'

'It doesn't belong to me. It's sick. It belongs to another gentleman.'

The officer pointed his riding stick. Christie found eye contact with Tommy Bright and screwed his face questionably at him. Tommy shrugged his shoulders.

'Please let us examine the horse. It would have been better if you'd registered the animal.'

Animal, yes, that was what Tilly was, just an animal, and this statement shrunk this noble horse to lower levels, but the man was right. Christie inwardly moaned. This animal as they put it was a queen amongst their kind.

'The horse may have been registered back in Westmorland.' Christie said these words knowing it was probably a false notion; trembling now.

'Then the boys in Westmorland would be glad if we see to it.'

'Bright..... Bright.... Get the horse.'

A soldier pushed forward to restrain Christie disregarding his plea.

'Is she sound, bring her over? Check her out, Bright.'

Tommy led Tilly by the halter; he clicked and led her to a trot around the yard. 'I think the gentleman is correct, Sir. This horse is sick.' And Tommy ran his hand down Tilly's spine and checked her legs, looked into her eyes, checked her teeth and nose. He saw her eyes were muddied. 'There's some disease in this horse. Could be kidney or liver trouble.'

'What's the matter with the horse, sir?' The officer asked.

'She's been ridden hard, on poor rations.... I think she has a kidney problem.'

The officer slid off his horse and wandered around Tilly, weighing up the situation. 'Was she sick before she was ridden hard?'

'No Sir,' he had to be honest. 'But she'll fail you. She's lost her spirit.'

'I'll take that chance.'

Christie stepped closer, but John Dowson gripped his arm and pulled him back. 'Let her go, Christie,' he muttered.

'No John, I won't just let her go. This isn't my horse ... she's in my care. I cannot sanction this.'

'It would be better if we do this job quietly.... I'm a reasonable man and I wouldn't want you to contravene the Defence of The Realm Act. That would be a criminal offence.'

Christie's throat constricted as he was still restrained by John Dowson's strong hand.

'To blazes with this war.' Christie pulled away. 'You don't take this horse.'

Things happened quickly. Two foot soldiers ran forward, their boots scuffling loud on the cobbled yard; they cocked their rifles and pointed them at Christie.

'Stop ... halt. Release your arms.... You are a gentleman of some importance in this town. I will ignore this remonstration and my men will retreat, but I ask you to make no more of this or you will be arrested. No matter who you are.'

Christie shrank back. He couldn't look at Tilly; he couldn't look at Tommy Bright. He knew many eyes were watching him; maybe his dear wife and daughters from the windows of Sugar Hills. He felt he had failed Robbie and that burned in his gut. He walked to the house and could do no more.

'I beg you sir, please don't take any action against this young gentleman.' Tommy spoke mercifully. 'I had some attachment to the man's father. It was he who taught me all my horse skills.'

'Fear not, Bright. This young man's one of many - one of many.'

There was no banging of doors, or shouting or swearing at Sugar Hills. Christie's anger was usually silent to all but himself; it would be his body that would face it; the stomach cramps, the chest pains, the headache; they would all arrive and vent their qualities upon him. His veins were toxic; a grown man moved to tears for this beloved horse. If he had no small children or wife he would have wept openly.

Emily was waiting in the hallway; a remote figure standing on the black and white marble floor; as still as the saline statue of the wife of Lot. She knew what Tilly meant to Christie; his senseless mission to the hills and on his return, them both half starved. She feared deeply for Christie's conscience that was long tested; but she loved this man for his integrity and would back him to the hilt. The salt melted and she moved quickly to him.

Christie ignored her embrace and moved away, only because he knew if he fell into her arms he would be weakened to tears.

Emily understood; she watched him walk; his broad shoulders slumped as he climbed the red and gold carpeted stairway, his hands clinging to the polished banister rail; walking like a man sentenced; she would leave him be, awhile, but knew in time he would seek her reassurance.

When she found him later he was sitting in the nursery with Suzy in his arms.

'Let go of your feelings, Christie ... there's no shame in front of me.'

He held his arm out to her and she closed in. He didn't speak but let his head rest on her shoulder. Suzy nestled in closer.

'How can I tell him that Tilly's gone? I can't do that to him, Emily.'

'Robbie knew all along this could happen. He warned you; you tried and hard. He won't blame you. Who knows by now Arabesque may have been seized.'

'Tilly's exhausted already. If I hadn't have taken her to Hambleton, she would have been fitter.'

'She'll recover. She was tired and that's all. She's a healthy horse. They won't send them straight away, surely.'

Suzanne whimpered and Christie responded by gently rocking her in his arms. He kissed the soft down on her head; smelling her skin.

News of Tilly arrived three weeks later by way of a letter.

Dear Christie

I felt it my duty to write and let you know of Tilly. There is some good news that she is recovering and that vitality is returning. Thank the lord she was put in my care.

She has twelve weeks training before she is sent to the western front, and I will go with her.

Our commander, a kindly man, has allowed me to choose Tilly as my mount. We will look after each other. It will give me comfort to know what attachment you had to her.

I miss my Irene and I miss my bairns. I wanted to go while I had the choice for now as conscription has started there will be none. I'm afraid of the battle field and I wish I was walking the river banks and fishing with your father. May your God preserve us alive, Christie. And forgive anything on my part if my actions in going to war were wrong. We are different you and I. I know your faith is stronger; stick to what you believe in.

Your faithful friend
Tom Bright.

Melancholy set in and persisted, it was cold comfort that Tilly was with Tommy Bright; it was little relief that Christie's reserved occupation gave him protection because many were disregarding and signing up any way. He would sit in his study alone most evenings; reading, studying, praying. He punished himself and his little family and as many months passed, Emily wrote to Beth and asked her to visit.

Beth finally arrived in the summer of 1916; she too with a heavy heart. To be back at Sugar Hills gave her morbid feelings of her father and her deception; and to leave Fred for any length of time was a wrench; she couldn't speak as she kissed him goodbye at the station; it always reminded her of the early days in Westmorland when she came to visit Robbie, but it was always Fred waiting for her. They hadn't suffered as much isolated in Spickle Howe. The country needed food and Fred's sheep were a valuable asset to the nation, his horse was spared because it was a valuable asset to the farm, as was Fred. No one challenged that. But this war was suppressing them and Christie's mood wasn't unusual, if the circumstances that brought it were.

Beth managed to remove Christie from Sugar Hills one afternoon. She wanted to see Thirsk again, buy the children some gifts, so they took a bus ride into town and had a stroll in the market. Christie knew of a small coffee house that Emily recommended and he took Beth for lunch. She unpinned her hat and set it on the chair beside them looking around for a waitress. Christie was as dignified as ever in his tweed suit and clean white shirt and collar; his short beard neatly clipped, his hair, smooth and tidy. They sat for some time easily talking, unburdening their minds; he couldn't help but ask after Robbie and she couldn't help but speak with a torn heart.

'We were saddened about Tilly but equally saddened at your worry. Robbie struggled to save Arabesque and her future is now in Edwin's hands, hiding in Wasdale.'

'Will she be safe?'

'The military won't go back to Wasdale. Robbie jokes and says he's the only fool who goes back to Edwin's for a second time.'

'Edwin won't be able to feed her much; maybe Tilly's fate will be better, at least she will have rations.'

'That's not what I heard; at least Arabesque will have peace.'

Christie glanced around the small room and noticed everyone was eating but them. He looked over his shoulder for a waitress, but none were apparent. 'They give them poor rations, they have very little.'

'Yes, Irene writes regularly, Tommy tells his usual happy story but Irene reads between the lines.'

'How's everyone in Westmorland?'

Beth fiddled with her silver hat pin in the colour and shape of a purple thistle. Glancing up and checking her wrislet, but still no waitress, as her eyes danced around the small room. 'They're working hard, as I know you are. Freddie just has a lad to help but swears that as soon as he reaches sixteen he'll sign up.... They're training girls over in Carnforth to come and help. Freddie thinks it won't work. He has no confidence in the scheme.'

'And Robbie?'

'Robbie hasn't left Keld Head since the day he left with Arabesque.' She lowered her voice. 'I can see in his eyes,' yes she dared to look in them, 'he's itching to be away.... Is no one going to serve us?'

They both looked around, Beth continued. 'You know Jackie Bainbridge is dead, don't you.'

'Nora's husband will be next. Although he swears he'll never leave Keld Head; if they raise the age of conscription he may have to.'

Christie twisted in his chair as a waitress, head held high, came to clear the next table, clattering the cutlery, nervously.

'Could we order please, miss.' Christie was soft and polite.

'We're not serving any more lunches today, sir.'

'But it's only two o'clock.' Beth said.

'You may get tea elsewhere, Miss Richardson.'

'Pardon! You've only just served those ladies and we were here first.'

Christie took Beth's hand and squeezed it. 'Come on, Beth. Get your hat.' Christie lifted his black trilby and pulled his coat from a stand.

'What sort of establishment is this?' Beth couldn't restrain herself.

'The sort that doesn't entertain cowards...! I knows what your father spoke of, Mr Richardson.' The waitress eyed him, defiant, cold hearted.

Beth flushed as she stood. 'My father spoke of....'

'No more, Beth, we must leave.' And he took his hat and coat. 'Good day, Mam.'

'You should be in Richmond with those other cowards, Mr Richardson.'

He took Beth's elbow and gently ushered her away from a controversy.

As they left the shop, Beth challenged him. 'What's this all about? Why won't they serve us? How dare they speak like that to us?'

They stood in the little cobbled market place of the old town of Thirsk, buttoning up their jackets. 'That was nothing Bethy....'

'What do you mean, nothing...? Is that how they treat you?'

'Look, let's walk back ... do you have everything you need?'

She clung to Christie's arm and for the first time in her life felt uncomfortable in her home town.

'What did she mean about Richmond?'

'Look, I don't want to talk about it.'

'I think you should ... if this is what's mithering you and making you unhappy.'

'What are things really like in Westmorland, Beth?'

'Not like this, that's for sure. Everyone respects Robbie and Freddie for the food they provide for the village, they're working the skin off their hands.'

'I know, I know, so am I.... Okay, I will tell you what I've heard from the courtroom.' Christie walked sharply out of the town and Beth followed. 'There were sixteen of them incarcerated in Richmond Castle; men who wouldn't fight because of their conscience. Some went as stretcher bearers but others said they wouldn't go. Kitchener and Hague wanted to strengthen their hand and make an example of them. I know three of them ... so did Father. They are honourable men, Bethy, Christians ... bible students. And although they never signed up they were viewed as conscripts and kept in pitiful conditions. They were eventually sent to France, bound and wired and forced to watch traitors shot before a firing squad; it should have been their fate. They were sentenced to death and illegally marched before three thousand troops, but when Kitchener suddenly died it saved them and the Prime Minister intervened and they were given ten years in Dartmoor instead, terrified and half starved.'

'Oh my Lord, this war is horrible – horrible. I can't bear this. Can you do anything for such men?'

Christie didn't reply.

They walked silently; Beth gripped his arm tighter. Once they were out of town and crossed the Great North Road close to Sugar Hills they spoke more freely as the afternoon sun glowed down on them. Tired and faint with walking, they rested on the grass verge. 'Thank goodness yours is a reserved occupation, Christie. Do they always treat you like this?'

'Mostly.... I keep away from the town as much as I can.... I've had to relinquish my role as a J.P... I prefer to go to York where I'm not as well known.'

'Then you should have said. How do they treat Emily?'

'She knows none of this ... I hope you never tell her ... please. Let's hope this all ends soon.'

Their footsteps gently tapped on the road, both grave in heart. Beth found it hard to understand Christie's view, yet she knew what her father had spoken of and it went against much of what many were preaching in the pulpits, but their father would have resisted and more strongly than Christie. He would have spoken against preaching about war and blessing young men to go and kill. Nationalism was sweeping the country and that was good for the politicians but not for those with a conscience; those who feared God more than man.

Beth reflected and she thought Robbie would have similar views as he had often spoken of his time in South Africa. He believed he had to answer to a higher source.

'If Father were alive, he would back you up.'

'I think so, but I'm afraid mine is a silent protest.... I wear no armbands of allegiance and that's the best I can do.'

'You were very composed back there ... how you tolerated the woman's abuse, you showed great courage and self control.' She looked at the ground as they walked on, arm in arm.

'I haven't always been like that, at first I did retaliate, verbally, I might add. I don't like them to think I'm a coward.'

'No ... no, I can understand.... Robbie speaks of your courage. He admires you for your tenacity. But maybe it's pride that hurts you more than the persecution.'

'How do you mean?' he stopped walking and gently challenged her.

Beth looked him in the eye and she paused; a thing she would always do when she spoke to find some wisdom. 'They called you a coward and you have no way of proving it otherwise. But surely it's your integrity here that's called into question and not just by the women in Thirsk, but by a mightier force than we can see. And you have spoken little of that.'

Christie's heart stabbed, because he knew she was right. 'Then I am a sinner, more so than those women I condemned in the town.'

They walked beside the inn where a gibbet stood, where many a local man had been hanged. Christie shuddered. Then Beth smiled and reassured him of her sisterly love. 'And I know your motives, deep inside are pure. Robbie once spoke of purity; he said that Tilly was a white horse, yet in the snow she looked yellowy - grey compared. There is naught whiter than snow. He once said he wished somebody could whiten him. But if Father's future dreams come true maybe one day we will all attain to that, but don't expect it of yourself now, or guilt will cripple you and stifle you and bury the love and bravery and happiness you have here to give.'

The last evening of her visit Beth purposely wandered Sugar Hills alone. She'd spent her last day with her brother and it was a sad one. Emily was bathing the children and Christie was with John Dowson working out the feed rations for the cattle.

Beth sat in her father's old office and recalled telling Christie as a youth how one day he would sit here and hand out the wages to the men, and how they would all love and respect him; that dream had come true. She recalled her father advising her on marriage. Had she listened, she believed she would still have married Fred, because good sense at the time would have dictated that. Oh how her father would have loved him had he the opportunity to get to know him. He had become the loyal son-in-law that Franklyn had hoped for. Robbie would have done no more than diminish their good name.

Tomorrow she would leave and take her memories with her. Sugar Hills no longer felt her home, and she realised how much she loved Lakeland.

She would be sorry to leave Christie's darling girls, the eldest, Jane, the middle girl, Elizabeth, and little Suzy. They loved Aunt Betty, as they called her. They asked frequently of Uncle Freddie and Robbie, who they adored. She was missing Fred and desperate to be back home, back in Westmorland. The time away had given her the realisation of how much she had settled at Spickle Howe and how much she loved her husband.

Robbie was waiting; leaning on the farmhouse door at Spickle Howe, chewing a piece of straw, his hat cocked to one side, his teeth white, his smile; well, you know what that was like.

Beth was surprised, shocked even, to see him there; he hadn't been to Spickle Howe in months. The next thing she noticed was how handsome he still looked.

Fred helped her from the trap and lifted her suitcase from the back. She straightened her skirt; she couldn't stop herself, and she tidied the locks of her hair.

When Robbie smiled at her everything became unravelled again.

'You've had a good trip, I trust?' Robbie shouted but didn't move from the doorway.

Beth's response was a weak smile.

'Go and get freshened up and I will make some tea.' Fred gently coaxed her from the yard. He lifted her small Gladstone bag and followed.

As she approached Robbie stepped forward and gave her an involuntary kiss on the cheek. 'How was Christie and his brood?' he followed her into the kitchen.

'He's having a tough time over the conscription.' She let her jacket slip from her shoulders, relieved to be home.

'In what way?'

'People are talking about him. He's not as isolated as we are. People in the town call him all sorts of names.'

Robbie grinned. 'Nay, Christie can take it.... I've called him plenty.'

She smiled at his impudence. Nothing had changed.

'I've set the clipping shed up, Freddie.' Robbie went over to the door and picked up his stick. 'See to your wifey and I'll get the sheep up.'

Beth stepped upstairs into her room and saw the old walnut dresser, the oak fireplace with a jug of freshly picked pink roses on the hearth. She was touched as to how much Fred thought about her. The sun was casting pleasing shadows on the white painted walls of her bedroom. Everything looked lovely. The bad memories of returning to Sugar Hills were now surpassed by her arrival back at Spickle Howe, even Robbie's presence.

How she loved this place. On her dressing table was a small silver plate sat next to her writing box; she noticed two letters. She picked them up, checking the hand writing. One was from Aunt Charlotte Webb and the other from Irene.

She would wash first and open them later.

Beth could hear Robbie outside laughing and it pleased her. He had come to help with the clipping. Fred's voice was as always, soft and monotonous. She hoped Robbie wouldn't leave too early and she hurried to wash and change and made more effort than she needed to. She picked up the mail and sat on her bed to read. The banter between the two brothers continued, drowned by the noise of the sheep and lambs.

The yard outside was filled with the smell of sheep. Ewes bundled into a small holding pen, lambs were bleating at being separated from their mothers, and put into a walled paddock. Beth wandered under the barn; Fred was pushing a ewe at Robbie as he did the clipping.

She'd watched them do this often each year; he was quicker and stronger than Fred. There was more banter between the two men, Robbie still laughing; he looked up and caught her gaze. He finished clipping the ewe and threw it to its feet and watched it run away. He rubbed his hands together, blackened by the wool and the grease; the sheep had a spring in its step and it leapt away with the dark roan on its coat apparent.

'Robbie ...?' he was startled that she had addressed him. Both men looked at her face, now saddened. She'd been crying. She held a letter in her hand.

Robbie rubbed the sweat from his face with his clean forearm and stepped forward, glancing at Fred who didn't seem to notice his wife looked concerned.

'What's the matter, Beth?' Robbie straightened his back and moved closer, putting his hand shears down on the floor amongst the sheep wool.

Fred just held onto the next ewe and waited. Then realising the lack of concern for his wife, threw the ewe loose.

'It's Tommy, he's been killed.' She had Irene's letter in her hand.

Robbie took the letter from her and tried to read through weak and misty eyes.

'Tilly went down with him ... she's gone.'

He rolled his eyes and threw back his head, turning his face away from her so she wouldn't look at his sadness.

'They died together in France. Poor Irene, those poor children.' Beth wanted to touch him and comfort him, but a greater sense of mind stopped her.

'Blasted war ... blasted war,' he growled and went back and picked up the shears. 'It's better she's gone now, so flaming quickly, at least she'll not suffer and starve to death like the rest of 'em.' He grabbed at the ewe and tipped it sideways and started to clip her belly. 'It'll be all over soon ... the war to end all wars....' gasping as he clipped, in oblivion. 'When it's over Beth, Freddie, we will have a picnic in the garden at Keld Head. Christie can come with his tribe ... and my girls ... my darling girls. Yes, that's what we will do. All together one family, one family.'

31

WAR IS OVER – WAR BEGINS

1925

'Did you find him?' Beth looked up at Fred as he sat beside her on the tartan blanket laid on the lawn.

'No.... But I know where he is.... I'm tired now; he'll have to walk home alone.' Fred lay back on the blanket and picked up a small baby that was crawling away from him. 'Come on Georgie ... come to Uncle Freddie.' Fred held the boy away from him and playfully shook him. 'You're a handsome little tyke, just like your daddy. But don't be wandering off all the time.... Uncle Freddie's getting too old to keep chasing after wayward kinfolk.'

Beth twisted around. 'I'll go and fetch you something to eat.... So where is he?'

'Edwin's on his way, I've just passed him up at Thirlmere. He's left Rob at Cockermouth cattle market. He reckons he's buying a bull.'

At the thought of Edwin arriving at Keld Head Beth moaned as she stood. 'I'll send the girls to Nora's. I don't like them being around Edwin.... Hetty...! Edith...!' she shouted over the garden wall as two girls played in the paddock with old Maggot.

'How's Clara?' Fred struggled to hold the young boy which was now itching to walk.

'She's a bit better this morning. I still don't think we can leave her. The sickness is still there, and she's very weak.'

'If Nora would help out with the girls, we could take George back to Spickle Howe with us?'

'If Robbie's not back tonight ... maybe yes.'

'What time is Christie due?'

'Any hour.'

'It will be so grand to see them all.... I was hoping we could still have the picnic if Robbie gets back. That's if it doesn't rain.'

'We'll have the picnic without him, Betty. He shouldn't have left Clara any way. He knew she was weak.'

'He doesn't abide sickness does he?'

'Never has, it's because he's hardly ever sick. He was just the same when Father died.' And Fred recalled the rain soaked meeting up at Sty Head to tell Robbie of their father's death and was surprised that it still made him waver.

Beth looked across the paddock as two girls arrived, running and startling Arabesque. The horse jumped a few yards and continued grazing.

Robbie's two girls were as different as he and Fred. Edith was sober; she had sandy brown hair and was plain for a girl; she had little beauty and was more masculine, she loved her daddy, but didn't spare him any rebuke when he left her mother for days at a time; sometimes weeks. She was now eleven years old and Robbie wondered where she had come from. Edith didn't like dresses and Clarissa couldn't feminise her; Robbie wagered she would never marry and he would be right. Hetty was the opposite; ten years old and a beauty, as Robbie watched the young girl grow, he could see himself in her. Dark hair, blue eyes, restless. She was a happy girl, rarely moody, she wouldn't be left a spinster, but she wasn't as healthy as her father and much like her mother, lack of fortitude would kill her. Clarissa had been told to have no more children; the two girls were enough, but Robbie had wanted a son. He didn't push Clarissa, he did the opposite, but she feared if she didn't give him a son he would find one elsewhere, and the insecurity of that dogged her for years. George had been born out of sacrifice on her part and a hope and a chance to pacify Robbie, but it didn't. George was a short-tempered child, fractious, complaining; constantly crying and he irritated his father.

Beth went upstairs to Clarissa and Robbie's bedroom, she tapped the door and gently opened it; her conscience always gave strong reminders every time she entered this room of the day she secretly slipped inside and found the dying geranium.

Clarissa was sitting by the window with a patchwork blanket over her legs; the summer's heat bearing down on her. She was still wearing her nightdress. Her attractive features pale, her eyes had a glassy look about them; she smiled as she saw Beth.

'Has Freddie found him?' Clarissa spoke with a thin voice.

'He's in Cockermouth, it seems. Gone to buy a bull.'

'Oh yes, that's right. He complained a lot about our little shorthorn. He said he's lazy.'

'How do you feel now?' Beth approached and looked out of the window, watching the lane for the same man.

'I'm alright really, Betty ... don't fuss over much for me. I'll dress I think ... be nice for when he gets back. If he comes back for the picnic it will please him to see me up and about.' But as Clarissa stood she wavered and Beth caught her by the arm.

'You're not at all well, Clara ... don't pretend.'

'I have to, Betty... I must be strong.'

Beth paused. 'I think we'll take George back with us to Spickle Howe, if it's alright with you, whether Robbie comes home or not. Fred can handle him.'

Clarissa's eyes smiled. 'I wish George were yours, Betty. This should be you.'

'Now don't start up, Clara. This is the way things are. We have to accept that.'

Not looking at Beth, Clarissa continued. 'It's a bitter blow you not having any bairns.'

'Yes, well, I wouldn't have done Robbie any good in the end would I?'

'He still loves you, you know.'

'Don't Clara ... stop it.' Beth straightened the curtains.

'No, it must be said. It's the truth, but he's been a good man to me. I know I don't always make him happy. Robbie brought me out of widowhood, out of St John's and gave me a life. I'm grateful for that. He says he's been faithful, although I fear he's not. He's been a good provider in one sense.'

'Have a rest and try to sleep and I'll come and get you when Christie arrives; Freddie says it may rain.'

Beth moved away, heavy in heart.

*   *   *

Robbie came in from the rain, head down, but someone spotted him; he tried to avoid conversation with the man and pressed on. 'You're looking well, Mr Keldas.' The man said, and Robbie did look well for a man of forty-eight.

Robbie just grunted and pushed his way through the crowd of farmers gathering at the auction ring. He didn't like to push by but he had spotted a quiet place above the ring on the stone gallery; he could sit and wait for his lot to come up.

His heart was beating rapidly and he still felt edgy in crowds, never liking to be in close proximity to any man, let alone this throng of countrymen, their hats and coats dampened with the rain, many smoking; some stinking.

Climbing the stairs he relaxed away from the hoard, sat on a wooden bench and pulled out a small catalogue from the pocket of his raincoat. He glanced at the lot numbers for the bull, then listened to the auctioneer; twenty lots to go; not too long.

Robbie rolled the booklet around in his hand and tapped it nervously on his bended knee. He stared aimlessly down at the crowd, he guessed he would know many and many would know him, but the feelings of claustrophobia misted his vision and gave him temporary blindness. When he could finally focus he looked hazily and listened. The auctioneer's quick sharp voice rattled out the numbers. The cattle were ushered in and out of the show ring by a scruffy youth with a cane, and he constantly tap - tapped it on the rear of each beast in the small arena to keep it moving. Robbie checked his watch and then glanced up again at the arena. Smoke and steam were rising in the stagnant air; he hated the smell of cigarette smoke and longed to be out and walking back to Keld Head. He noticed one man in a navy blue coat; a tall man in a sailor's cap, standing in amongst the farmers, prominent by his height, the man appeared to be looking his way; the features were indiscernible to Robbie's hazy eyesight. But the sailor appeared grubby and dark; an older man. Then the thought struck Robbie that the man was looking right at him. It took strength on his part not to look behind; maybe there was a clock on the wall that the man was staring at, yes there was, he remembered a clock somewhere. Lowering his head he unfurled and re-checked the catalogue; the bull was next.

Two young men led the red roaned shorthorn bull into the arena. One pulled it by a stick and ring in its nose and the other tapped heavily on its rump. The young bull tossed its head and didn't want to capitulate; it struggled for freedom but couldn't find it.

The bidding started and Robbie waited for the price to lower, then he waited until others had shown their intent; he still waited. He eyed the hands and listened to the auctioneer to search for other bidders as he briefly raised his catalogue and was spotted by the auctioneer. The bids went higher and faster, the auctioneer frantic now, then down came the gavel; bang! 'Sold, to Mr Robert Keldas ... next lot.'

Robbie glanced back at the crowd to find the easiest way to leave and noticed the man in the sailor's cap had gone. Robbie sat awhile, unnerved by it, then took in a deep breath, felt for his wallet on the inside pocket of his jacket and slipped through the crowd and headed for the office.

The payment was made and Robbie was two hundred guineas lighter, he wandered across to the holding pens and looked for a haulier who he could trust to get his new bull back to Keld Head. He leant on the cold damp rail, more than happy with his purchase, as the red coated bull wandered the pen. Robbie spoke to him. 'Don't worry, son; we'll soon have you out of here,' and he patted its woolly neck and playfully pulled its ear. Then he was aware of a shadow behind him; the air seemed darker and, the bull, seeing the closeness of another person raised its head. Robbie spun around.

Because of his height Robbie didn't often look a man directly in the eye, but this one he did. He peered into the man's face and took a step backwards, his back against the bull pen.

The man stepped forward, closer, Robbie could see him now; smell him. He stepped to one side and looked for an exit.

'You still stand out in a crowd, Kellet.'

'McCulloch ...?' Robbie muttered, unsure if this was really him, and not wanting the man to see the fear in his eyes. 'Coldrigg has done you no favours ... you look a hundred.'

'And you still jest, but I'm not laughing.'

'Have you finished your time, or did you buy your way out with a dead man's money?'

McCulloch stepped closer and grabbed the collar on Robbie's coat. 'You'll pay for your blabbing, Kellet!'

'You should have been hanged, McCulloch.'

And McCulloch pushed Robbie, crushing him against the bull pen. 'Couldn't keep your mouth shut, could you?'

Robbie turned his head away from McCulloch's breath. 'Your demise is none of my doing. It wasn't needed ... you had plenty of enemies in Coldrigg without me getting involved.'

'Don't lie, you're a coward, aren't you...? Too scared to live in a man's world.'

'Coldrigg Gaol is no man's world. It's a world of the ungodly.' Robbie found strength within him that he didn't own. 'Whatever your sentence was, McCulloch, it wasn't due to me.' And Robbie grabbed McCulloch's hand and pulled it from his collar and turned away.

Out of the corner of his eye he was aware of men keeping their distance, other farmers and stewards, and the bull was his only ally.

'I'll make you pay, Kellet, you and your poxy friend.'

'Huh ... I have nothing left.' And Robbie moved away but McCulloch took a revolver from his pocket.

'I'll use this, I'm not afraid to pull the trigger.'

'Then you'll have to, because I have nothing. I'm a dead man anyway.' In Robbie's brain images flashed up of Clarissa, Beth, Edith, Freddie, all running like a Sunday parade in his mind; what would they think? How would they manage if he died here? Clarissa, poor Clarissa; he hadn't even kissed her when he left.

'If my gun doesn't make you pay up, maybe this will. I'll torment you and your genteel friends for the rest of your lives.' And McCulloch waved the revolver sideways and the men standing behind moved further back. 'Your scabby friend, Wilding, canna keep his mouth shut. Telling stories about young Christie. That he was the so called woman that was with you when Wilding killed Jimmy Mook in the fog up at

Stonethwaite. How Christie had his hands on Sally Mook's neck to restrain her. These stories could be told and his reputation smeared amongst the Yorkshire Society and true justice could be done to a young man who tried to pervert it by deception. No matter how many pretty daughters he has; the man's as weak as you are and a coward and a conchy.'

Robbie grabbed McCulloch's wrist and strength borne from fear raised the arm aloft. 'That man has no fear of what men speak of, his reputation matters only in the sight of God.... Besides, your assertions were false in Coldrigg, maybe they're false now.'

The gun went off and the bullet hit the roof, as glass and grey slate fragments shattered and fell. McCulloch ran, but Robbie squatted low, putting his hands over his head to protect himself from the debris.

There seemed an age of silence; Robbie remained in a squatting position covering his head with his hands like a naughty child pushed into a corner. But as the debris stopped falling he felt a sharp cut on his face. His coat was covered in dust, grime, shards of glass and broken fragments. It seemed no one would be brave enough to come and help, so looking at the ground in front of him, his knees aching with bending low, he finally realised he was alone, apart from the shorthorn bull. Embarrassed, he slowly stood, aware of many distant eyes watching him. He grabbed the rail of the bull pen to steady himself and with gentle hand strokes, brushed the fractured masonry from his clothing.

'Shall we get the police, sir? Are you okay?' A young man approached looking behind him all the while; it was the boy who had been leading the bull.

'No, lad ... I'm not alright.'

'Do you need a doctor?' The young steward said as he peered at Robbie's bloodied face.

'It's just a graze ... my nerves are hurt more than my flesh, I'm afraid.' And he pulled a handkerchief from his pocket and started to lightly dab his face. 'Did they catch the sailor?'

'No sir.... No one here could tackle him; big feller, he was. He were loose wi a gun an' all.'

'Yes, you're right, son, but I'm afraid I instigated it. It was my fault. I antagonised the man.' Robbie held out the palms of his hands and rubbed the dust from them. 'I'll settle it, don't worry. Let me know if you require payment for the roof.'

Edwin's mangy jacket, his pipe and tobacco were on the kitchen table. He was sitting there eating a pork pie that Nora had made. Beth, Fred, Christie and Emily were with him. The children were playing in the garden as it had finally stopped raining.

Robbie saw Christie's eldest girl first as he unlatched the yard gate; she was much like Beth. He avoided her gaze and burst into the kitchen.

The surprise of the sudden intrusion and the manner of his appearance shocked them all; the feelings of happiness at being together for what was supposed to be a family picnic, shattered liked the roof of Cockermouth Auction.

Robbie went straight to Edwin, grabbed his shirt and pulled him up from the table. 'Man alive, Edwin ... you babbling, babbling idiot...! Heaven help you now with what I'm about to do to you!' He stretched his other arm across the table pushing Edwin's coat and smoking paraphernalia along with Clarissa's best china to the floor. Cups, plates, coloured with yellow and mauve pansies crashed to the floor along with sandwiches and cakes; tea spilled and milk from the jug spattered to the floor.

'Get your filthy stuff off my table ... get your cruddy body out of this house! Go, blast you, go ... and never ever return.'

Beth couldn't help but shriek; she had never seen him like this, this was something new and abhorrent; she noticed the wounds on his face.

Edwin grabbed his coat and his stuff from the floor as Robbie thrust him aside like an old rag. 'What's thi matter Robbie, I aint done nowt wrang! Why's thi all blathered aboot somatt?'

'Just get your filthy stuff out of this house. Don't you know there's a sick woman upstairs?' Robbie kicked Edwin's backside as he scuttled to be free. 'You're a mindless fool, Edwin.... You've ruined me and my family.'

Almost spitting with fear Edwin said, 'I am a fool, Robbie, that is correct. But I daren't know which foolish thing yer alludin' to, as I's done many. Ye come across as a gentleman and yet yer 'ave truck wi the likes o' me ... who's the fool now, eh ... who?' Edwin banged the door closed.

Resting his hands flat on the kitchen table, letting his pounding heart move inside his chest, Robbie looked across to Beth as she attempted to clear some of the broken china and cutlery off the floor. He shook his head and with his voice broken said, 'I'm sorry, Beth ... leave them. I'm sorry, forgive me for the outburst ... leave it and I'll sort it out later.'

'What the blazes has happened?' Fred said, stupefied.

But Robbie addressed Christie, looking intently at his adult face. 'Christie, please leave us. Take Beth and your wife. I need to speak to Freddie alone. I'll greet you properly later.'

'Can I help in any way?' Christie held a sturdy hand out to his friend, one that Robbie longed to grasp and steady himself with.

'No, Christie ... no help ... not any more. You've done enough,' and he surged forward and embraced the younger man. 'I need to speak to you privately, later.'

Fred watched them leave; Emily was clinging to Christie's side. Robbie prowled around the kitchen like a man possessed of a great terror. They closed the door.

'I'm done for, Freddie.' He was trembling.

'What ... what the dickens has happened? What's wrong?' And Fred finally unstuck his feet from the concrete they were set in and moved to his brother; he spoke with compassion; kindness –kindness - kindness.

'I've just met McCulloch at Cockermouth. He took a shot at me with a pistol. Darn fool missed but he threatened me. He knows Christie was with us when Edwin killed Mook. He's threatening to tell if I don't pay up. Edwin told someone, I don't know who ... stupid, stupid Edwin. I would have killed the man with my bare hands if Beth and Christie hadn't have been here. But for two pins, he'll never set foot in this house again.'

'We must tell Christie, Rob ... we should warn him.'

'I know, I know.... But I've thought things through on my race back from Cockermouth. How can I burden him with this? I don't know if I should tell him or not, because I've decided to do nothing. McCulloch made threats last time and most of them were lies. We won't bend any more for him. We will accept the threats. If I end up a dead man because if this, then so be it. Maybe some will be happier.' Robbie went to the window and saw Christie on the lawn with his young family. 'All girls ... all girls. Where's Georgie?'

'He's upstairs with Clara.'

Robbie straightened his shirt. 'Clara, poor Clara ... how is she?'

Clarissa lay on the large kingly bed with a small child by her side, both were sleeping.

Robbie slipped into the bedroom, took off his jacket, unbuttoned his shirt collar and let it fall to the floor. He unbuttoned the top of his vest and lay gently on the bed beside his wife and child. Clarissa opened her eyes.

'What's happened, Robert? What were you shouting for?'

'Nothing, Clara, nothing.... I'm just tired of Edwin. You won't be seeing him again.' He picked up the young boy and held it tightly, smiling at the baby's handsome face and chubby legs and arms. Then he put his other arm around Clarissa's shoulder and she nestled closely in to him and rested her head on his chest.

Christie was alone by the tower, leaning against the doorpost. He reflected on the day he first came here and hid in Tilly's stable; the day this man who he loved saved his life.

Swallows dipped their little bodies onto the cobbled yard, searching for mud in the puddles. Some cattle across the paddock were lowing.

The children had gone walking with Beth and Emily up to the tarn. They would play by the waterfalls and pester him when they got back; they wouldn't want to leave.

Robbie approached, still only half dressed, his hair and body in complete disarray. Yet he smiled; he would always smile.

He couldn't stop himself from touching Christie's arm as he came closer. 'The rain won't come back now, son. The girls will have a good walk.'

Christie couldn't reply; he was worried.

'Are you taking stock of all your empire?' Robbie glanced around at the land and the farm.

'It's not really mine and you know that.' Christie said.

'What kind of a business man are you?'

He just lowered his head.

'I hope you live a long time then, son, because my brother will soon have me pay my dues. I'll be merely a pretty chatelaine.'

'Well, I hope I live long enough to torment you with my preaching, but you don't really think that do you.' Christie's warm blue eyes smouldered.

'I need you Christie as much as you need me, I think .... It's a shame they had no children.... Fred and Bethy.... What will become of this place when we're all gone?'

'I'll leave that to them, but I'm sure they will choose wisely. They are close ... thick as thieves.'

'So how are things in Yorkshire?'

'Okay, I think. The land and the farm are yielding well.' Christie hesitated and looked skyward. 'I'm afraid I haven't the same social standing since the war. You were correct in one thing, Robbie.... My demise was painful. But I haven't let my neutral stand become wasted for I have started a small Peace Society in the town.'

Robbie looked into Christie's eyes and saw the love and he paused. How could he burden this young man with more woe? His secret would remain. He couldn't let another man live with this fear.

'What did you want to talk to me about?' Christie breathed heavily.

'Oh, just to tell you I've finished with Wilding.'

'About time.'

'Yes, maybe so.... Look, Christie, I don't know how often I'll get across to Sugar Hills, but maybe one day.'

Christie rested compassionate eyes on Robbie's troubled yet kindly face and knew he was acting. 'So what was the row with Edwin about?'

'Huh ... it's just something I should have done years ago, that's all.'

32

THE BIRTH OF OBSESSION

They didn't expect McCulloch would come straight away to Keld Head. That was the way he usually worked; allow time to build the fear.

Robbie knew he had days, maybe weeks to think. There were some things that puzzled him that needed answering and some things he must do to pacify his conscience. Arabesque stood motionless, and Robbie rested his knuckles on her mane; it had been a long damp ride to the coast. Old Maggot skulked behind as a lookout, sniffing and urinating for what appeared to be a hundred times on the tufts of long grass. The sea was tinted blue from the sky; the green headland of Scotland was visible off the cliff. Robbie turned to look northwards to Coldrigg along the coastline. He could just see the south wall he had helped to build; it was now known as the Wall of Hunger. The gates of Coldrigg were hazy in the distance and behind him was Black Combe.

He'd thought a lot about his father today on this journey. He wished he could go into their old kitchen and see him sitting at the table counting his worthless money. Robbie had considered bringing little Edith with him; she had pestered; she had scolded him for leaving Clarissa. It hurt him but it didn't stop him. These things needed to be done in private; he'd bring her another day. He knew George and the girls were now at Spickle Howe with Beth and Clarissa; her health much improved.

He pulled on the reins and turned hard and clicked. Arabesque walked and the lurcher followed, creeping behind. They took the Wasdale road and Robbie waved his riding whip high for passing motorists. He whistled for Maggot.

Robbie had never found it easy to apologise and you think he would have by now with all the needs. But it was more than apologies that he needed to make today. He recalled how easily

Franklyn Richardson had forgiven him for his tricks up in Wasdale; heaven knows what he would have done if he had married his daughter and broken her heart. Could anyone be so righteous?

The lane to Raike's Farm always pleased Robbie, the lake and the mountains draped together tantalising him, but he had no desire to walk or swim today, despite the water looking as silk and the hills as a green mossy stairway to paradise. He recalled the people in Brazil and their prospects for hope; it was the last thing that dies, they had said; he had to cling to that. He hoped Edwin would forgive him, but more so he hoped his family and Christie's would be safe. He hoped Beth wouldn't think badly of him; it still mattered.

The horse's breath was muffled in the stony lane between the blue stone walls. In the near distance a group of sheep and ponies grazed the small walled paddocks that surrounded Raike's Farm. He hoped Edwin was home; this was the first place to start and look for the man. He sorrowed that Nance wouldn't be there. She had died three years earlier of tuberculosis. The house would be no cleaner or happier without her.

Robbie saw Mickey, Edwin's middle boy, in the yard, leaning on the gate watching him.

'Bless us all.' The young man said. 'Have yer come te cheer us or finish us off?'

Robbie leant forward in the saddle. 'Neither,' he held out a gloved hand to the lad.

Mickey grabbed it.

'Dad'll be well made up te see thi ... I think so, any road ... as long as there's nay more aggravation. Is the mare in good fettle?'

Yes, she's grand.' Robbie relaxed.

'He's in t'house.'

Smoke was rising from the chimney stack and forced down by a draughty cool breeze around them.

'I thought he would have been out already with a gun.' Robbie said.

'He'll ne'er set foot a gin out o' t'house ... nay he wai'nt.'

391

Unsure of what Mickey was implying, Robbie scowled. The boy discerned and said, 'Gan and see fer thi sen.'

Robbie wearily slid off Arabesque, letting his boots land heavily on the cobbled yard. He slipped the stirrups up and relaxed the girth on the saddle. 'Could you give her a drink please, Mickey?'

A deep breath was the normal way to enter Edwin's farmhouse; the last chance for clean air until this visit was resolved. Banging purposely on the door as it slowly opened he heard Edwin swear. 'Go away ... whoever ye are ... be off.... Can ye nay leave an old beggar te die?'

Robbie lowered his head as he dipped under the lintel. 'Edwin ... where the blazes are you?'

'I'm 'ere ... botheration! Who ist tha?'

The small sitting room bedecked with grubby furniture was just the same. Edwin was sitting in a high backed chair in his underclothes; a tatty and dirty blanket was draped half across his body, most of it on the floor.

'What's befallen you?'

'Is it my boy? Is it Robbie?' Edwin had the look of a child.

'You know well it's me, Edwin. What in heaven's name has happened?' he leant forward and pulled up the blanket to cover the older man.

'I've had a seizure, Rob ... a stroke, tha knows. All doon one side 'as gan useless.... I'll ne'er be any use te a woman agin.'

Robbie couldn't help but inwardly laugh. He composed himself. 'When did this happen?'

'Last Tuesday I thinks, although one day is the same as the next ... after I left yer spot I took te drink and fell int kitchen. I were on mi tod. Mickey were in Millom. I lay fer three days and nights on that blasted cold floor. By jings.... I dragged yonder stobby mat and slept on that ... I thowt someone had cut me arm off, like.'

The enthusiasm in his voice began to grow from sorrow to glee as Edwin spilled out his sorry tale. 'Then I chucked yonder poker threw't window te shout on somebody... fiddlesticks ... stupid fool thing te do as nay body ever passes that window and a spent three nights frozen to death. It were't porridge I had that mornin' that kept me alive until Mickey found us.'

The lowest sink of humanity sat before Robbie and the mercy of his own prompted him to act. 'Have you eaten?' and he went across to the fire and threw on a couple of small logs, pressing them safely in the grate. 'Is Mickey looking after you?'

'Nay.... I'm finished ... but blind me ... it 'eartens me te see thi at my door. What's changed thi mind? What did I do te yer?'

Taking off his hat and with raised eyebrows Robbie apologised. 'I shouldn't have done what I did to you ... that's the truth ... but when –when will you keep your blabbering mouth shut?'

'I'll nay get chance te blab te many folks now, will I?'

'No, I don't suppose you will.' Robbie stood over by the window and looked up to the hills, watching them rise high above Raike's Farm.

'What did I say wrang?' Edwin spat slithers of spit onto his crumpled handkerchief. His hand and arm were swollen and red.

'You must have told McCulloch about Christie being with us the day you killed Mook. Holding Sally's neck, he said.'

'As God is mi judge, Robbie, I nivver said a word aboot that young gentleman. Sweet mother, mebbe I did, now as I come te think on it ... but I wouldn't a told McCulloch, he's a slimy turnkey.... I getten kaylied the night I come out and I daren't remember much, it's all a fog now.'

'Stop wittering, Edwin ... what's done is done. McCulloch's after my cash or my life. One or the other.'

'Have yer seen 'im then?'

'Aye, last week at Cockermouth.... He threatened me with a pistol, and when I rejected him he pulled the trigger.... Man, I could be dead.... He threatened to tell about Christie. By the lads, why do you think I was angry with you? Why?'

'He's teken his time then ... he's been owt a Coldrigg months.... Had he followed you?'

'I doubt it.... I met him at the auction ... he was just there.'

'Well, blind me, if that man meant te find you he'd a done it a lot quicker than that ... he'd a come straight te Keld Head. He's bluffin' agin.'

'Aye, but he knew things about Christie's status that tells me he's been to Yorkshire, snooping about.' Robbie left him and went to the kitchen. He could speak no more of this, it was killing him. Opening and closing cupboard doors he checked the pantry and saw two dead rabbits hanging ready to be skinned. He shouted back. 'Have you eaten today? You have no food in this house.'

'I'll starve te death, I knows it, son. What a way te end.... I'm close te a hundred now, boy.'

Returning with a wet cloth, Robbie pushed it into Edwin's good hand. 'You never could count Edwin.... Here, wash your face, man. At least you can be clean when you meet your maker.'

'It's nay my fault, Robbie.... It's our Mickey ... he drinks all he earns.'

'What are the animals eating ... the horses?'

'Nay, I cannna be bothered worriting over animal kind, when I'm starving.'

'No.... No,' with reluctance. 'I'll get some ham and bread from the village,' and he turned to go, frustrated, then stopped. 'For pities sake, Edwin, why do you always do this to me?' and he slapped his head with his hand. 'I'll have to take you back to Keld Head ... I can't let you stay here.... Stay with us ... and I'll pay for Nora to see to you.'

'Nay, Robbie.... No woman's gannin te manhandle me.'

'Well you must stay here and rot. I can offer you no more.' He went upstairs and found some clothes; the cleanest there were. Then he threw the bundle on Edwin's lap. 'I'm no nurse, Edwin, I can't cook and I can't knit ... you'll have to help me wash and dress you.'

They struggled together; the bathing was done in lukewarm water in a small tub. Robbie boiled kettles and found carbolic soap; he lifted Edwin like a child into the galvanised tub and let him wash himself. Robbie struggled pulling on Edwin's clothes on his damp body; the sleeves, the cuffs, standing him up for the trousers; kneeling at Edwin's feet for the socks. The care from this man was heart-warming, done with reluctance and yet love. He tied the bootlaces and cleaned and polished the boots. Taking a comb from his waistcoat pocket he handed it to Edwin's useful arm, and he struggled to comb the greasy strands that were left.

Edwin handed Robbie the comb back. 'No, keep it.' Robbie set it on the table. 'I'll get Mickey.'

'Mickey?' Robbie shouted at the door and wandered into the small farmyard. 'Come and help me with your father. Have mercy on him boy, you must help him.'

'I daren't knows what te do.' The boy looked truly bemused.

'You feed him for a start. Skin and cook those rabbits you shot. Wash him each day. Dress him and take him outside. Come and help me lift him, then you go and get your brother from Egremont.'

The two men lifted Edwin's limp body into the fresh air and sat him on a small seat by the back door. 'You bring him out here for an hour every day, rain or shine. If it's wet set him under yonder fold yard roof. If it's hot you put him in the shade.'

Time was passing too quickly for Robbie, his nursing, his shopping trip to Gosforth took up precious time. He doubted he could be back at Keld Head for night fall.

When he felt he could safely leave Edwin, cleaner and tidier in front of the fire. Robbie held out his hand.

'Yer a good man, Robbie Kellet ... nay matter what others say.'

'That's as maybe.' And he grabbed Edwin's strong hand and shook it.

'Before ye go, Rob. I've been thinking, yer should take mi gun. Mickey 'as 'is own but I 'as no need for one.'

Robbie stood at the door, half stooping. 'No, Edwin. No gun at Keld Head. I'll have no weapon in that house.'

'Well, I were only offering, like.'

'I know, I know.' Robbie softened.

'There's another thing. In yonder stony paddock there's a skewbald gelding. Barak ... tek 'im fer little Edi. She'd manage 'im. Just 'er size. I daren't want money. Just tek it.'

Robbie glanced at the group of hungry ponies and wished he could take them all.

'There's tack te go with it. Mickey knows where't stuff is.'

'Thank you, Edwin ... thank you. I won't leave you lonely. I'll be back. I'll take the pony thank you....It'll be happier with me.'

'I dare say it will.' And Edwin yawned.

Robbie struggled up the narrow stony path to Sty Head with two horses. He would have to press on quickly before nightfall; the place was dangerous in mist. He led the pony and let Arabesque trail behind tethered to his belt; egging her on, clicking and gently coaching, The sight of Sty Head Tarn relaxed him and as he settled for a while on a familiar stone he let the two horses graze, pulling hard at the coarse grass on the mountain pass. He recalled the dreadful day when he first came here with Arabesque; the only day in which he had ever thought of taking his own life; but the horse had looked after him then and she was still looking after him, and paying him back for protecting her from the ravages of the battlefield. He recalled that back then all he possessed was a horse and a mangy dog but now he had a wife and three lovely children; and the use of a good working farm; a better reputation, and freedom from guilt, but McCulloch still niggled him.

Taking Edwin's advice and reassurance he would do nothing.

He had thought, as Edwin had said, that the meeting at the auction was just an opportune chance; an accidental meeting. He knew if McCulloch did talk to the police, there was no one alive who would speak against Christie to corroborate - no one. It would be futile. His greatest fear was the smearing of Christie's good name and he knew what that felt like. He knew Christie would never lie and they were fortunate at the trial that no one had thought to ask the right questions; Christie's cautious and astute replies had sufficed. Robbie would do everything he could to protect his family, but he couldn't - wouldn't, allow McCulloch to destroy his hope. He had his own fears and there would be times when he would hear the gate click, that he would be nervous at Keld Head; he mustn't let this contagion pass on to his dear children. Edith could take

McCulloch on single handed. He threw his head back and grinned as he chewed a dry crust he had rescued from Edwin. His darling girls; how they would love Barak. He was pleased he had made amends with Edwin. It had been easily done and Edwin made it so. The nursing and future care, well that would have to be done with sacrifice. Edwin never blamed Robbie for his stroke; in fact the doctor had told him it was his own foolish lifestyle that had done it. Robbie considered buying some kind of chair for him, so Mickey could wheel him around the yard and down the lane under the mighty mountains of Wasdale. At least Edwin was spirited still, and wouldn't give in. He was safe in Wasdale, providing his family would help; surely they would.

It was close to dark when they descended into Seathwaite. It was too late to get a room and few would have provision for two horses and a dog. There was the isolated barn on Stonethwaite fell where he had often slept rough with Edwin, heading for some covert adventure; where he had once found Christie asleep at his prayers; it would have to do, but he didn't relish a cold night sleeping on rough straw; he was getting too old for that.

The night hours passed slowly and sleep didn't come until well after three. Worrying over Edwin; worrying for Christie; his family; McCulloch; then he fell into a deep sleep. It was Maggot that woke him, hungry.

The ride over Greenup was slow with Barak; they were all famished for none had barely eaten any sustenance in twenty four hours. As they entered the vale and saw Keld Head's tower, Robbie thought he could discern Fred's truck in the yard. He should have quickened his pace but Barak was struggling on the stone on the Easdale path. By the time they reached Keld Head the sun was bursting through the mist and the day becoming warmer. Closer now, he approached Keld Head; through the silver birch plantation, across the beck and the bridge, and in the garden sitting on the lawn he spotted Beth.

She was with George on a red tartan blanket, sitting by the beck.

*   *   *

The small stream that ran through Keld Head had nourished its occupants for years and was like a noisy friend; always talking and laughing; refreshing. Beth sat with George on her lap and reflected. She always felt at ease with this house that should have been her home, which one day might still belong to her. She sat with a child that should have been hers; one she would never tame; she thought about the man who she once loved, who she knew she could never own.

Beth knew Fred was anxious over Robbie again, but she had no idea why; she wouldn't let that spoil what was a pleasant morning. She had tried to teach George to speak and did her little alphabet game for him, picking up flowers and objects. A is for apple; B is for bread; C is for cow and D is for Daddy.

Beth saw Robbie in the distance, and despite the years still felt a tinge of gladness he was safe. She smiled when she saw the brown and white pony with him and knew he must have found Edwin. George heard the horses' hooves and momentarily glanced up from playing, then continued to push a small red wagon made of wood that his father had crafted.

'Where's Freddie,' Robbie shouted, worried that Fred had left them alone. He dismounted and led the horses to the water trough, glancing nervously around him.

'He's gone to the village ... some errand or other.' Beth showed no signs of anguish.

Robbie ambled across to the lawn, weary yet smiling, the young child unconcerned his father was back.

'I thought you would have been home last night?' It was no criticism or objection, just a statement; there was no discipline in her voice.

He looked at her and still found himself captivated by her bright eyes; still so in middle age, her hair cut shorter, in a bob; greying slightly; her complexion, milky white, with rose tints on her cheeks. He leant forward and picked up the boy. 'What are you doing you little gammerstang?' and he playfully shook him in the air.

The child giggled, his deep blue eyes widened; then that was enough and he wrestled his father to be free.

Robbie settled with George on the blanket beside Beth and let the boy go.

'I got way-layed at Edwin's ... he's had a stroke; I couldn't leave him. Can you believe it?'

Then he leant back, putting his hands beside him for support to his aching back; letting the morning's glorious sunshine touch his unshaven face.

'How bad is it?' Beth questioned.

'All down one side. He can't walk ... never will.' Robbie wasn't looking at her; he was watching George playing with his wooden toy, spinning its wheels.

'How will they manage?'

'I offered to bring him here.... One more sick person in the house wouldn't make much difference, but he wouldn't come ... he's better off in Wasdale. His family will have to see to him.'

'We must help in some way.'

'I can't offer much in the way of capital, his boys are old enough to pay.... Young Mickey can run the farm; he'll have to learn ... too much charity won't help them.'

Robbie turned to her as he fidgeted. 'I slept in a hay barn last night....' He laughed. 'I'm getting too old for that.'

Beth dared to peer closely into his eyes, she knew every speckle and mark on the deep blue iris; she could read them like a hieroglyph. She understood the sparkle and the glaze like a coloured leaded window in a church and could read their story. She saw his dishevelled hair and clothes. There was still a tiny part of her that was always undecided to which of the Keldas brothers her true allegiance lay. Robbie hadn't changed in twenty one years. He was set in time; outdated.

He noticed her gaze.

Embarrassed, she said: 'Whose is the pony?'

'It's from Edwin ... it's for Edith.... Barak, he's called, he's a real gem ... bomb proof.'

Maggot wandered onto the lawn following George as he toddled with his truck with a baked biscuit in his other hand. The dog had soon learned that where a child was, there was often food. Maggot licked the trail of crumbs from the grass. Robbie leant across and tapped the dog gently on its nose.

'Leave him be, Maggot,' and the dog tried to dodge its master's hand.

'I'll get a bath chair I think for Edwin ... that's all I can do for now. Visit when I can. I've worked hard here, but there's not enough to feed two families. My father once said that hard work never killed anyone, it just makes you a funny shape.'

Beth had to laugh. Then there was a long silence, with both smiling.

The ease of character in her voice relaxed the troubled soul in Robbie, as it would always do. And he noticed her hand on the blanket, close to his, fractions away. The urge to move his fingers closer was strong, but Robbie had learned how to control it and restrained himself. Beth noticed and blushed and quickened back into conversation, edging her hand discreetly away, then reached to get George back on the blanket.

'You know Christie says he doesn't want Keld Head,' she said.

'I know, but it's safer in his hands, I'd only lose it again.' Robbie was looking at the grass, ashamed. 'Well you and Freddie will benefit if aught befalls him. His girls won't want a northern hill farm that has no spirit. And I don't know how my children will turn out. George is unpredictable like his daddy. He may be a rascal.'

'He will be,' she dared to say. 'Christie says that blood isn't always thicker than water. He loved you more than our father. He said Keld Head should belong to someone who would appreciate it and love it.'

'Whoever that man may be, it is not I.' Robbie's voice was dispassionate.

The small boy fell playfully onto Beth's knee.

'Did your father ever preach about better times, Beth; Christie speaks of it, but not by man's hands?'

'He did, Robbie, always. I hope you will see it.'

'I have hope, Beth ... but my faith maybe isn't as strong as yours.' He looked at her, pleading with his eyes. 'Would a man like me find a place in such a world?'

She laughed softly. 'I'm no judge, Robbie ... I don't decide these things. But I do know you are a humble man and an honest one.'

'And my honesty is telling you right at this moment, I can hardly resist not to take hold of you and to kiss you. This should have been how things were, Bethy: us three here.'

'I know, Clara says that.'

'She's always saying it. I do my best for her you know.'

Then from somewhere a strange gurgling noise came; inhuman. They all looked for its source; it was Maggot, standing close to them, his legs astride, his back arched, ready to pounce. Hackles raised, bubbles of foam seething through clenched teeth. His brown eyes searching and seeing something they hadn't.

Lifting his head high, Robbie knew what he would see; a tall man in a navy blue coat and sailor's cap, confronting them on the edge of the garden, with a pistol.

Beth held George tight to her bosom and tried to turn his head away so he wouldn't see, but he resisted her; the child had to watch the man in navy blue. Then George looked at his father's face and saw the fear; a thing he would remember all his life. A shot rang out; smoking; terrifying, and Maggot fell to the ground. Then the silence stupefied them as George's little blue eyes widened as he struggled to be free. Robbie leant across and enveloped them all in his arms as a shield. Then he looked at McCulloch and spoke slowly, calmly, bravely. 'You could finish me off McCulloch, but you will be straight back in Coldrigg to hang.'

'Nay, I don't want to finish you, Robbie; I just want to have some fun.'

'Then not at my expense. This ends today.'

McCulloch stepped closer. 'I will talk about you, Robbie Kellet. I will talk about your young friend and his secrets.'

'You will tell who you like, McCulloch, because no one will listen. You've put your money on the wrong horse this time. This one's not running.'

Fred was walking back to Keld Head with Albert Given when he saw the man in the sailor's hat from a distance. He knew who he was.

Albert turned at pace to run to the village for help. Fred pressed on forward; his heart almost collapsing within him.

He slipped over the wall at the side of the house, out of eyeshot, and crept painfully, slowly, towards McCulloch. It was almost Fred Keldas's destiny to do what he next did. No one knew he was there; but an act of courage that wouldn't go unnoticed. A responsibility he would shoulder always; the care for his brother and his wife and the young child.

He stepped in front of his family as a guard, holding his hands in the air. This wasn't difficult for he loved his wife and he loved his brother and the young boy.

'The police are fifteen minutes away, McCulloch. If you leave now you may escape but they will still catch you. If you kill me now you'll hang. This is easy for me as my life would be nothing without my wife and family.'

McCulloch eyed Fred and saw the belief in his eyes. He turned and left as slyly as he arrived.

Then everything froze, a scene trapped in icy glass, like the little snowscene globe.

Beth was the first to move and she stood and walked up to Fred's side and held him, and she knew where her true allegiance lay. She would often recall this day, not because of the fear, but because it taught her how much she loved her husband and how great a sacrifice he was willing to make for them all.

With A Northern Spirit

Robbie knelt on the stone floor in the front porch of the farmhouse. He was chopping kindling sticks with a small axe ready for the fire. Wood splintered and shattered around him as he tirelessly worked: Chop- chop-chop. The folks down in Grasmere would hear him. He was grinning today as contentment and happiness were lodging with him as they often would.

Occasionally he looked up to the magnificent hills as they tempted him; his feet itching to be away. Arabesque was grazing close to the wall, her constant companion, Barak, was with her. She looked up at Robbie and nodded; a real temptress, but he resisted.

Three children played around a small picnic table in the garden singing nursery rhymes; girls screaming; laughter.

They say it takes a brave man to rear a family singlehanded, but here was such a man.

Clarissa had died two years earlier, leaving the children without a mother.

The yard gate clicked and only Robbie and the young boy looked up. It was just Nora.

The girls ran to her for they knew she would have treats. George ran close to his father and stood beside him. His face was grubby but his clothes were spotless. 'Dad, tell Hetty to shut up. She keeps singing stupid rhymes about me.'

'What's she singing, George?'

The boy said, 'Georgey porgy pudding and pie, kissed the girls and made them cry.'

'And did you kiss the girls, George?'

'No Dad.'

'Then you have nothing to worry about have you.' Robbie rubbed his sleeve over his brow. 'And why *is* she teasing you?'

'Cos I hit her.' George fidgeted with his hands in his pockets then started to pick some flowers from a trough in the wall beside his father. He pulled at the stem of a red geranium and started to break the petals.

Robbie could smell the lemony scent; a reminder of something he once owned. Then he gently removed the flower from the child's hand. 'No George, no, be careful.' And he pulled the boy close to his heart and enveloped his arm around him. 'You see these small flowers ... they are so delicate, soft. Always pick them gently. This is how you treat people, George, with kindness always, especially girls.'

THE END

*   *   *

Other books by Lindsey J Carden

Northern Spirit

Last Boat to Nowhere

To Paint a White Horse (digital version only)

See Amazon.co.uk

Cover artwork, illustrations and logos by Paul Middleditch at www.tenfathoms